The Best British Mysteries 2005

The Best British Mysteries 2005

Edited by

MAXIM JAKUBOWSKI

This edition first published
in Great Britain in 2005 by
Allison & Busby Limited
Bon Marche Centre
241-251 Ferndale Road
London SW9 8BJ
http://www.allisonandbusby.com

A catalogue record for this book is available from
the British Library.

ISBN 0 7490 8200 3

Typeset in Plantin by The Old Tin Dog Design Co.
Brighton

Printed and bound in Great Britain by
Bookmarque Ltd, Croydon, Surrey

Contents

Introduction

The opening salvo in our series of annual anthologies celebrating the best of British crime and mystery writing enjoyed a great success, confirming our belief that we can hold our own against all brands of American crime, be it noir or cosy or psychological, let alone the recent afflux of much welcome translated material that is finally seeing the light of day in our criminal pages.

So, once again, I set off on a hardy exploration to discover what gems our homegrown writers have been committing and published in 2003 and, once more, the results have proven particularly fruitful. Worthy stories appeared not just in magazines, but were spread around a variety of anthologies and diverse sources such as BBC Radio 4 broadcasts in two cases, as well as the catalogue for a literary festival. Perseverance was needed, but the rewards were delightfully stimulating.

We present with much pleasure and satisfaction the winner of last year's CWA Short Story Dagger (Jerry Sykes' story) for the second time, together with some of the other shortlisted stories; new tales of crime and treachery by established mainstream authors like Christopher Fowler, Francis King, Muriel Gray and screenwriter Stephen Volk; many of the more popular and prizewinning British practitioners of the British art of deceit and intrigue with original stories by Robert Barnard, Lindsey Davis, Edward Marston and Peter Lovesey; and, joy of deathly joys, new cases for some of today's most memorable sleuths: Ian Rankin's Inspector Rebus, John Mortimer's Rumpole, Reginald Hill's Dalziel and Pascoe, Bill James' Harpur and Iles and Amy Myers' Auguste Didier. And so many other stories guaranteed to scare, intrigue, fascinate and dazzle the unsuspecting reader.

So, yet again, a splendid and vintage year for crime and a book it has been a pleasure compiling. Our initial volume of *The Best British Mysteries* is still available in paperback format if you missed it, and I hope this year's instalment will prove as popular so that Allison & Busby and I can keep on bringing you this annual feast for many years to come.

Savour this cornucopia of sins.

Maxim Jakubowski

Saturday afternoon, John Rebus left the Oxford Bar after the football results and decided that he would try walking home. The day was
clear, the sun just above the horizon, casting ridiculously long shadows. It would grow chilly later, maybe even frost overnight, but for
now it was crisp and bright – perfect for a walk. He had limited himself to three pints of IPA, a corned beef roll and a pie. He carried a
large bag with him – shopping for clothes his excuse for a trip into
the city centre, a trip he'd known would end at the Ox. Edinburgh
on a Saturday meant day-trippers, weekend warriors, but they tended to stick to Princes Street. George Street had been quieter, Rebus's
tally finally comprising two shirts and a pair of trousers. He'd gone
up a waist size in the previous six months, which was reason enough
to cut back on the beer, and for opting to walk home.

He knew his only real problem would be The Mound. The steep
slope connected Princes Street to the Lawnmarket, having been cre-
ated from the digging out of the New Town's foundations. It posed
a serious climb. He'd known a fellow cop – a uniformed sergeant –
who'd cycled up The Mound every day on his way to work, right up
until the day he'd retired. For Rebus, it had often proved problemat-
ical, even on foot. But he would give it a go, and if he failed, well,
there was a bus-stop he could beat a retreat to, or taxis he could flag
down. Plenty of cabs about at this time of day, ferrying spent shoppers home to the suburbs, or bringing revellers into town at the start
of another raucous evening. Rebus avoided the city centre on
Saturday nights, unless duty called. The place took on an aggressive
edge, violence spilling on to the streets from the clubs on Lothian
Road and the bars in the Grassmarket. Better to stay at home with a
carry-out and pretend your world wasn't changing for the worse.

A crowd had gathered at the foot of Castle Street. Rebus noticed
that an ambulance, blue lights blinking, was parked in front of a sta-
tionary double-decker bus. Walking into the middle of the scene,
Rebus overheard muttered exchanges of information.

'Just walked out…'

'…right into its path…'

'Wasn't looking…'

'Not the first time I've seen…'

'These bus drivers think they own the roads, though...'

The victim was being carried into the ambulance. It didn't look good for him. One look at the paramedics' faces told Rebus as much. There was blood on the roadway. The bus driver was sitting in the open doorway of his vehicle, head in his hands. There were still passengers on the bus, reluctant to admit that they would need to transfer, loaded down with shopping and unable to think beyond their own concerns. Two uniformed officers were taking statements, the witnesses only too happy to fulfil their roles in the drama. One of the uniforms looked at Rebus and gave a nod of recognition.

'Afternoon, DI Rebus.'

Rebus just nodded back. There was nothing for him to do here, no part he could usefully play. He made to cross the road, but noticed something lying there, untouched by the slow crawl of curious traffic. He stooped and picked it up. It was a mobile phone. The injured pedestrian must have been holding it, maybe even using it. Which would explain why he hadn't been paying attention. Rebus turned his head towards the ambulance, but it was already moving away, not bothering to add a siren to its flashing lights: another bad sign, a sign that the medics in the back either didn't want or didn't feel the need of it. There was either severe trauma, or else the victim was already dead. Rebus glanced down at the phone. It was unscathed, looked almost brand new. Strange to think such a thing could survive where its owner might not. He pressed it to his ear, but the line wasn't open. Then he looked at it again, noting that there were words on its display screen. Looked like a text message.

TELL ME WHO TO KILL

Rebus blinked, narrowed his eyes. He was back on the pavement.

TELL ME WHO TO KILL

He scrolled up and down the message, but there wasn't any more to it than those five words. Along the top ran the number of the caller; looked like another mobile phone. Plus time of call: 16.31. Rebus walked over to the uniformed officer, the one who'd spoken to him.

'Larry,' he said, 'where was the ambulance headed?'

'Western General,' the uniform said. 'Guy's skull's split open, be lucky to make it.'

'Do we know what happened?'

'He walked straight out into the road, by the look of it. Can't really blame the driver…'

Rebus nodded slowly and walked over to the bus driver, crouched down in front of him. The man was in his fifties, head shaved but with a thick silvery beard. His hands shook as he lifted them away from his eyes.

'Couldn't stop in time,' he explained, voice quavering. 'He was right there…' His eyes widened as he played the scene again in his head. Shaking his head slowly. 'No way I could've stopped …'

'He wasn't looking where he was going,' Rebus said softly.

'That's right.'

'Busy on his phone maybe?'

The driver nodded. 'Staring at it, aye…Some people haven't got the sense they were born with. Not that I'm… I mean, I don't want to speak ill or anything.'

'Wasn't your fault,' Rebus agreed, patting the man's shoulder.

'Colleague of mine, same thing happened not six months past. Hasn't worked since.' He held up his hands to examine them.

'He was too busy looking at his phone,' Rebus said. 'That's the whole story. Reading a message maybe?'

'Maybe,' the driver agreed. 'Doing something anyway, something more important than looking where he was bloody well going…'

'Not your fault,' Rebus repeated, rising to his feet. He walked to the back of the bus, stepped out into the road, and waved down the first taxi he saw.

Rebus sat in the waiting area of the Western General Hospital. When a dazed-looking woman was led in by a nurse, and asked if she wanted a cup of tea, he got to his feet. The woman sat herself down, twisting the handles of her shoulder-bag in both hands, as if wringing the life out of them. She'd shaken her head, mumbled something to the nurse, who was now retreating.

'As soon as we know anything,' were the nurse's parting words.

Rebus sat down next to the woman. She was in her early thirties, blonde hair cut in a pageboy style. What make-up she had applied to her eyes that morning had been smudged by tears, giving her a haunted look. Rebus cleared his throat, but she still seemed unaware of his close presence.

'Excuse me,' he said.   'I'm Detective Inspector Rebus.' He opened his ID, and she looked at it, then stared down at the floor again. 'Has your husband just been in an accident?'

'He's in surgery,' she said.

Rebus had been told as much at the front desk. 'I'm sorry,' he said. 'I don't even know his name.'

'Carl,' she said. 'Carl Guthrie.'

'And you're his wife?'

She nodded. 'Frances.'

'Must be quite a shock, Frances.'

'Yes.'

'Sure you don't want that tea?'

She shook her head, looked up into his face for the first time. 'Do you know what happened?'

'Seems he was starting to cross Princes Street and didn't see the bus coming.'

She squeezed shut her eyes, tears glinting in her lashes. 'How is that possible?'

Rebus shrugged. 'Maybe he had something on his mind,' he said quietly. 'When was the last time you spoke to him?'

'Breakfast this morning. I was planning to go shopping.'

'What about Carl?'

'I thought he was working. He's a physiotherapist, sports injuries mostly. He has his own practice in Corstorphine. He gets some work from the BUPA hospital at Murrayfield.'

'And a few rugby players too, I'd guess.'

Frances Guthrie was dabbing at her eyes with a paper tissue. 'How could he get hit by a bus?' She looked up at the ceiling, blinking back tears.

'Do you know what he was doing in town?'

She shook her head.

'This was found lying in the road,' Rebus said, holding up the phone for her to see. 'There's a text message displayed. You see what it says?'

She peered at the screen, then frowned. 'What does it mean?'

'I don't know,' Rebus admitted. 'Do you recognise the caller's number?'

She shook her head, then reached out a hand and took the phone from Rebus, turning it in her palm. 'This isn't Carl's.'

'What?'

'This isn't Carl's phone. Someone else must have dropped it.'

Rebus stared at her. 'You're sure?'

She handed the phone back, nodding. 'Carl's is a silver flip-top sort of thing.' Rebus stared at the black, one-piece Samsung.

'Then whose is it?' he asked, more to himself than to her. She answered anyway.

'What does it matter?'

'It matters.'

'But it's a joke surely.' She nodded at the screen. 'Someone's idea of a practical joke.'

'Maybe,' Rebus said. The same nurse was walking towards them, accompanied by a surgeon in green scrubs. Neither of them had to say anything. Frances Guthrie was already keening as the surgeon began his speech.

'I'm so sorry, Mrs Guthrie...we did everything we could.'

Frances Guthrie leaned in towards Rebus, her face against his shoulder. He put his arm around her, feeling it was the least he could do.

Carl Guthrie's effects had been placed in a large cardboard box. His blood-soaked clothes were protected by a clear polythene bag. Rebus lifted them out. The pockets had been emptied. Watch, wallet, small change, keys. And a silver flip-top mobile phone. Rebus checked its screen. The battery was low, and there were no messages. Rebus told the nurse that he wanted to take it with him. She shrugged and made him sign a docket to that effect. He flipped through the wallet, finding bank-notes, credit cards, and a few of Carl Guthrie's own business cards, giving an address in Corstorphine, plus office and mobile numbers. Rebus took out his own phone and punched in the latter. The silver telephone trilled as it rang. Rebus cancelled the call. He nodded to the nurse to let her know he was finished. The docket was placed in the box, along with the polythene bag. Rebus pocketed all three phones.

The police lab at Howdenhall wasn't officially open at weekends, but Rebus knew that someone was usually there, trying to clear a backlog, or just because they'd nothing better to do. Rebus got lucky. Ray Duff was one of the better technicians. He sighed when Rebus walked in.

'I'm up to my eyes,' he complained, turning away to walk back down the corridor.

'Yes, but you'll like this,' Rebus said, holding out the mobile.

Duff stopped and turned, stared at it, then ran his fingers through an unruly mop of hair.

'I really am up to my eyes…'

Rebus shrugged, arm still stretched out. Duff sighed again and took the phone from him.

'Discovered at the scene of an accident,' Rebus explained. Duff had found a pair of spectacles in one of the pockets of his white lab-coat and was putting them on. 'My guess is that the victim had just received the text message, and was transfixed by it.'

'And walked out in front of a car?'

'Bus actually. Thing is, the phone doesn't belong to the victim.' Rebus produced the silver flip-top. 'This is his.'

'So whose is this?' Duff peered at Rebus over the top of his glasses. 'That's what you're wondering.' He was walking again, heading for his own cubicle, Rebus following.

'Right.'

'And also who the caller was.'

'Right again.'

'We could just phone them.'

'We could.' They'd reached Duff's work-station. Each surface was a clutter of wires, machines and paperwork. Duff rubbed his bottom lip against his teeth. 'Battery's getting low,' he said, as the phone uttered a brief chirrup.

'Any chance you can recharge it?'

'I can if you like, but we don't really need it.'

'We don't?'

The technician shook his head. 'The important stuff's on the chip.' He tapped the back of the phone. 'We can transfer it…' He grew thoughtful again. 'Of course, that would mean accessing the code number, so we're probably better off hanging on to it as it is.' He reached down into a cupboard and produced half a dozen mains adaptors. 'One of these should do the trick.'

Soon, the phone was plugged in and charging. Meantime, Duff had worked his magic on the keypad, producing the phone number. Rebus punched it into his own phone, and the black mobile trilled.

'Bingo,' Duff said with a smile. 'Now all we do is call the service provider…' He left the cubicle and returned a couple of minutes later with a sheet of numbers. 'I hope you didn't touch anything,' he said, waving a hand around his domain.

'I wouldn't dare.' Rebus leaned against a workbench as Duff made the call, identified himself, and reeled off the mobile phone number. Then he placed his hand over the mouthpiece.

'It'll take a minute,' he told Rebus.

'Can anyone get this sort of information?' Rebus asked. 'I mean, what's to stop Joe Public calling up and saying they're a cop?'

Duff smiled. 'Caller recognition. They've got a screen their end. IDs the caller number as Lothian and Borders Police Forensic Branch.'

'Clever,' Rebus admitted. Duff just shrugged. 'So how about the other number? The one belonging to whoever sent that message.'

Duff held up a finger, indicating that he was listening to the person at the other end of the line. He looked around him, finding a scrap of paper. Rebus provided the pen, and he started writing.

'That's great, thanks,' he said finally. Then: 'Mind if I try you with something else? It's a mobile number...' He proceeded to reel off the number on the message screen, then, with his hand again muffling the mouthpiece, he handed the scrap of paper to Rebus.

'Name and address of the phone's owner.'

Rebus looked. The owner's name was William Smith, the address a street in the New Town. 'What about the text sender?' he asked.

'She's checking.' Duff removed his hand from the mouthpiece, listening intently. Then he started shaking his head. 'Not one of yours, eh? Don't suppose you can tell from the number just who is the service provider?' He listened again. 'Well, thanks anyway.' He put down the receiver.

'No luck?' Rebus guessed. Duff shrugged.

'Just means we have to do it the hard way.' He picked up the sheet of telephone numbers. 'Maybe nine or ten calls at the most.'

'Can I leave it with you, Ray?'

Duff stretched his arms wide. 'What else was I going to be doing at half past six on a Saturday?'

Rebus smiled. 'You and me both, Ray.'

'What do you reckon we're dealing with? A hit man?'

'I don't know.'

'But if it is...then Mr Smith would be his employer, making him someone you might not want to mess about with.'

'I'm touched by your concern. Ray.'

Duff smiled. 'Can I take it you're headed over to that address anyway?'

'Not too many gangsters living in the New Town, Ray.'

'Not that we know of,' Duff corrected him. 'Maybe after this, we'll know better...'

The streets were full of maroon-scarved Hearts fans, celebrating a rare victory. Bouncers had appeared at the doors of most of the city-centre watering-holes: an unnecessary expense in daylight, but indispensable by night. There were queues outside the fast-food restaurants, diners tossing their empty cartons on to the pavement.

Rebus kept eyes front as he drove. He was in his own car now, having stopped home long enough for a mug of coffee and two paracetamol. He guessed that a breath test might just about catch him, but felt OK to drive nonetheless.

The New Town, when he reached it, was quiet. Few bars here, and the area was a dead end of sorts, unlikely to be soiled by the city-centre drinkers. As usual, parking was a problem. Rebus did one circuit, then left his car on a double-yellow line, right next to a set of traffic lights. Doubled back on himself until he reached the tenement. There was an entryphone, a list of residents printed beside it. But no mention of anyone called Smith. Rebus ran a finger down the column of names. One space was blank. It belonged to Flat 3. He pushed the button and waited. Nothing. Pushed it again, then started pressing various bells, waiting for someone to respond. Eventually, the tiny loudspeaker grille crackled into life.

'Hello?'

'I'm a police officer. Any chance of speaking to you for a minute?'

'What's the problem?'

'No problem. It's just a couple of questions concerning one of your neighbours...'

There was silence, then a buzzing sound as the door unlocked itself. Rebus pushed it open and stepped into the stairwell. A door on the ground floor was open, a man standing there. Rebus had his ID open. The man was in his twenties, with cropped hair and Buddy Holly spectacles. A dishtowel was draped over one shoulder.

'Do you know anyone called William Smith?' Rebus asked.

'Smith?' The man narrowed his eyes, shook his head slowly.

'I think he lives here.'

'What does he look like?'

'I'm not sure.'

The man stared at him, then shrugged. 'People come and go. Sometimes they move on before you get to know their names.'

'But you've been here a while?'

'Almost a year. Some of the neighbours I know to say hello to, but I don't always know their names.' He smiled apologetically. Yes, that was Edinburgh for you: people kept themselves to themselves, didn't want anyone getting too close. A mixture of shyness and mistrust.

'Flat 3 doesn't seem to have a name beside it,' Rebus said, nodding back towards the main door.

The man shrugged again.

'I'm just going to go up and take a look,' Rebus said.

'Be my guest. You know where I am if you need me.'

'Thanks for your help.' Rebus started climbing the stairs. The shared space was well maintained, the steps clean, smelling of disinfectant mixed with something else, a perfume of sorts. There were ornate tiles on the walls. Flats 2 and 3 were on the first floor. There was a buzzer to the right of Flat 3, a typed label attached to it. Rebus bent down for a closer look. The words had faded, but were readable: LT Lettings. While he was down there, Rebus decided he might as well take a look through the letter-box. All he could see was an unlit hallway. He straightened up and pressed the bell for Flat 2. Nobody was home. Rebus took out one of his business cards and a ballpoint pen, scribbled the words 'Please call me' on the back, and pushed the card through the door of Flat 2. He thought for a moment, but decided against doing the same for Flat 3.

Back downstairs again, he knocked on the door of the young man with the dishtowel. Smiled as it was opened.

'Sorry to bother you again, but do you think I could take a look at your phone book...?'

Rebus went back to his car and made the call from there. An answering machine played its message, informing him that LT Lettings was closed until ten o'clock on Monday morning, but that any tenant with an emergency should call another number. Rebus jotted it down and called. The person who answered sounded like he was stuck in traffic. Rebus explained who he was.

'I need to ask about one of your properties.'

'I'm not the person you need to speak to. I just mend things.'

'What sorts of things?'

'Some tenants aren't too fussy, know what I mean? Place isn't their own, they treat it like shit.'

'Until you turn up and sort them out?'

The man laughed. 'I put things right, if that's what you mean.'

'And that's all you do?'

'Look, I'm not sure where you're going with this... It's my boss you need to speak to. Lennox Tripp.'

'Okay, give me his number.'

'Office is shut till Monday.'

'His home number, I meant.'

'I'm not sure he'd thank me for that.'

'This is a police matter. And it's urgent.'

Rebus waited for the man to speak, then jotted down the eventual reply. 'And your name is...?'

'Frank Empson.'

Rebus jotted this down, too. 'Well, thanks for your help, Mr Empson. You heading for a night out?'

'Absolutely, Inspector. Just as soon as I've fixed the heating in one flat and unblocked the toilet in another.'

Rebus thought for a moment. 'Ever had cause to visit Gilby Street?'

'In the New Town?'

'Number 26, Flat 3?'

'I moved some furniture in, but that was months back.'

'Never seen the person who lives there?'

'Nope.'

'Well, thanks again...' Rebus cut the call, punched in the number for Lennox Tripp. The phone was answered on the fifth ring. Rebus asked if he was speaking to Lennox Tripp.

'Yes.' The voice hesitant.

'My name's John Rebus. I'm a detective inspector with Lothian and Borders Police.'

'What seems to be the problem?' The voice more confident now, an educated drawl.

'One of your tenants, Mr Tripp, 26 Gilby Street.'

'Yes?'

'I need to know what you know...'

Rebus was smoking his second cigarette when Tripp arrived, driving a silver Mercedes. He double-parked outside number 26, using a remote to set the locks and alarm.

'Won't be long, will we?' he asked, turning to glance at his car as he shook Rebus's hand. Rebus flicked the half-smoked cigarette on to the road.

'Wouldn't imagine so,' he said. Lennox Tripp was about Rebus's age – mid-fifties – but had worn considerably better. His face was tanned, hair groomed, clothes casual but classy. He stepped up to the door and let them in with a key. As they climbed the stairs, he said his piece.

'Only reason William Smith sticks in my head is that he pays cash for the let. A wad of twenties in an envelope, delivered to the office on time each month. This is his seventh month.'

'You must have met him, though.'

Tripp nodded. 'Showed him the place myself.'

'Can you describe him?'

Tripp shrugged. 'White, tallish...nothing much to distinguish him.'

'Hair?'

Tripp smiled. 'Almost certainly.' Then, as if to apologise for the glib comeback: 'It was six months ago, Inspector.'

'And that's the only time you've seen him?'

Tripp nodded. 'I'd have called him the model tenant...'

'A model tenant who pays cash? You don't find that a mite suspicious?'

Tripp shrugged again. 'I try not to pry, Inspector.' They were at the door to Flat 3. Tripp unlocked it and motioned for Rebus to precede him inside.

'Was it rented furnished?' Rebus asked, walking into the living room.

'Yes.' Tripp took a look around. 'Doesn't look like he's added much.'

'Not even a TV,' Rebus commented, walking into the kitchen. He opened the fridge. There was a bottle of white wine inside, open and with the cork pushed back into its neck. Nothing else: no butter, milk…nothing. Two tumblers drying on the draining-board, the only signs that anyone had been here in recent memory.

There was just the one bedroom. The bedclothes were mostly on the floor. Tripp bent to pick them up, draping them over the mattress. Rebus opened the wardrobe, exposing a single dark-blue suit hanging there. Nothing in any of the pockets. In one drawer: underpants, socks, a single black T-shirt. The other drawers were empty.

'Looks like he's moved on,' Tripp commented.

'Or has something against possessions,' Rebus added. He looked around. 'No phone?'

Tripp shook his head. 'There's a wall-socket. If a tenant wants to sign up with BT or whoever, they're welcome to.'

'Too much trouble for Mr Smith, apparently.'

'Well, a lot of people use mobiles these days, don't they?'

'They do indeed, Mr Tripp.' Rebus rubbed a thumb and forefinger over his temples. 'I'm assuming Smith provided you with some references?'

'I'd assume he did.'

'You don't remember?'

'Not off-hand.'

'Would you have any records?'

'Yes, but it's by no means certain…'

Rebus stared at the man. 'You'd rent one of your flats to someone who couldn't prove who they were?'

Tripp raised an eyebrow by way of apology.

'Cash upfront, I'm guessing,' Rebus hissed.

'Cash does have its merits.'

'I hope your tax returns are in good order.'

Tripp was brought up short. 'Is that some kind of threat, Inspector?'

Rebus feigned a look that was between surprise and disappointment. 'Why would I do a thing like that, Mr Tripp?'

'I wasn't meaning to suggest…'

'I would hope not. But I'll tell you what…' Rebus laid a hand on the man's shoulder. 'We'll call it quits, once we've been to your office and checked those files…'

But there was precious little in the file relating to Flat 3, 26 Gilby Street – just a signed copy of the lease agreement. No references of any kind. Smith had put his occupation down as 'market analyst' and his date of birth as 13 January 1970.

'Did you ask him what a market analyst does?'

Tripp nodded. 'I think he said he worked for one of the insurance companies, something to do with making sure their portfolios didn't lose money.'

'You don't recall which company?'

Tripp said he didn't.

In the end, Rebus managed a grudged 'thank you', headed out to his car, and drove home. Ray Duff hadn't called, which meant he hadn't made any progress, and Rebus doubted he would be working Sunday. He poured himself a whisky, stuck John Martyn on the hi-fi, and slumped into his chair. A couple of tracks passed without him really hearing them. He slid his hand into his pocket and came out with both phones, the silver and the black. For the first time, he checked the silver flip-top, finding messages from Frances Guthrie to her husband. There was an address book, probably listing clients and friends. Rebus laid this phone aside and concentrated on the black one. There was nothing in its memory: no phone numbers stored, no messages. Just that one text: TELL ME WHO TO KILL. And the number of the caller.

Rebus got up and poured himself another drink, then took a deep breath and pushed the buttons, calling the sender of the text message. The ringing tone sounded tremulous. Rebus was still holding his breath, but after twenty rings he gave up. No one was about to answer. He decided to send a text instead, but couldn't think what words to use.

Hello, are you a hired killer?

Who do you think I want you to kill?

Please hand yourself in to your nearest police station...

He smiled to himself, decided it could wait. Only half past nine, the night stretching ahead of him. He surfed all five TV channels, went into the kitchen to make some coffee, and found that he'd run out of milk. Decided on a walk to the corner shop. There was a video store almost next door to it. Maybe he'd rent a film, something to take his mind off the message. Decided, he grabbed his keys, slipped his jacket back on.

The grocer was about to close, but knew Rebus's face, and asked him to be quick. Rebus settled for a packet of sausages, a box of eggs, and a carton of milk. Then added a four-pack of lager. Settled up with the grocer and carried his purchases to the video store. He was inside before he remembered that he'd forgotten to bring his membership card; thought the assistant would probably let him rent something anyway. After all, if William Smith could rent a flat in the New Town, surely Rebus could rent a three-quid video.

He was even prepared to pay cash.

But as he stared at the rack of new releases, he found himself blinking and shaking his head. Then he reached out a hand and lifted down the empty video box. He approached the desk with it.

'When did this come out?' he asked.

'Last week.' The assistant was in his teens, but a good judge of Hollywood's gold dust and dross. His eyes had gone heavy-lidded, letting Rebus know this film was the latter. 'Rich guy's having an affair, hires an assassin. Only the assassin falls for the wife and tops the mistress instead. Rich guy takes the fall, breaks out of jail with revenge in mind.'

'So I don't need to watch it now?'

The assistant shrugged. 'That's all in the first fifteen minutes. I'm not telling you anything they don't give away on the back of the box.'

Rebus turned the box over and saw that this was largely true. 'I should never have doubted you,' he said.

'It got terrible reviews, which is why they end up quoting from an obscure radio station on the front.'

Rebus nodded, turning the box over in his hands. Then he held it out towards the assistant. 'I'll take it.'

'Don't say I didn't warn you.' The assistant turned and found a copy of the film in a plain box. 'Got your card?'

'Left it in the flat.'

'Surname's Rebus, right? Address in Arden Street.' Rebus nodded. 'Then I suppose it's OK, this one time.'

'Thanks.'

The assistant shrugged. 'It's not like I'm doing you a favour, letting you walk out with that film.'

'Even so…you have to admit, it's got a pretty good title.'

'Maybe.' The assistant studied the box for *Tell Me Who to Kill*, but seemed far from convinced.

Rebus had finished all four cans of lager by the time the closing credits rolled. He reckoned he must have dozed off for a few minutes in the middle, but didn't think this had affected his viewing pleasure. There were a couple of big names in the main roles, but they, too, tended towards drowsiness. It was as if cast, crew and writers had needed a decent night's sleep.

Rebus rewound the tape, ejected it, and held it in his hand. So it was a film title. That was all the text message had meant. Maybe someone had been choosing a film for Saturday night. Maybe Carl Guthrie had found the phone lying on the pavement. William Smith had dropped it, and Guthrie had found it. Then someone, maybe Smith's girlfriend, had texted the title of the film they'd be watching later on, and Guthrie had opened the message, hoping to find some clue to the identity of the phone's owner.

And he'd walked out under a bus.

TELL ME WHO TO KILL.

Which meant Rebus had wasted half a day. Half a day that could have been better spent…well, spent differently anyway. And the film had been preposterous: the assistant's summary had only just scratched the surface. Starting off with a surfeit of twists, there'd been nowhere for the film to go but layer on more twists, deceits, mixed identities, and conspiracies. Rebus could not have been more insulted if the guy had woken up at the end and it had all been a dream.

He went into the kitchen to make some coffee. The place still held the aroma of the fry-up he'd amassed before sitting down to watch the video. Over the sound of the boiling kettle, he heard his phone ringing. Went back through to the living room and picked it up.

'Got a name for you, sorry it took so long.'

'Ray? Is that you?' Rebus checked his watch: not far short of midnight. 'Tell me you're not still at work.'

'Called a halt hours ago, but I just got a text message from my friend who was doing some cross-checking for me.'

'He works odder hours than even we do.'

'He's an insomniac, works a lot from his house.'

'So I shouldn't ask where he got this information?'

'You can ask, but I couldn't possibly tell you.'

'And what is it I'm getting?'

'The text message came from a phone registered to Alexis Ojiwa. I've got an address in Haddington.'

'Might as well give it to me.' Rebus picked up a pen, but something in his voice had alerted Ray Duff.

'Do I get the feeling you no longer need any of this?'

'Maybe not, Ray.' Rebus explained about the film.

'Well, I can't say I've ever heard of it.'

'It was news to me, too,' Rebus didn't mind admitting.

'But for the record, I do know Alexis Ojiwa.'

'You do?'

'I take it you don't follow football.'

'I watch the results.'

'Then you'll know that Hearts put four past Aberdeen this afternoon.'

'Four-one, final score.'

'And two of them were scored by Alexis Ojiwa...'

Rebus's mobile woke him an hour earlier than he'd have liked. He blinked at the sunshine streaming through his uncurtained windows and grabbed at the phone, dropping it once before getting it to his ear.

'Yes?' he rasped.

'I'm sorry, is this too early? I thought maybe it was urgent.'

'Who is this?'

'Am I speaking to DI Rebus?'

'Yes.'

'My name's Richard Hawkins. You put your card through my door.'

'Did I?'

Rebus heard a soft chuckle. 'Maybe I should call back later...'

'No, wait a sec. You live at Gilby Street?'

'Flat 2, yes.'

'Right, right.' Rebus sat down on his bed, ran his free hand through his hair. 'Thanks for getting back to me.'

'Not at all.'

'It was about your neighbour, actually.'

'Will Smith?'

'What?'

Another chuckle. 'When he introduced himself, we had a laugh about that coincidence. Really, it was down to me. He called himself "William", and it just clicked: Will Smith, same as the actor.'

'Right,' Rebus was trying to gather himself. 'So you've met Mr Smith, talked to him?'

'Just a couple of times. Passing on the stairs… He's never around much.'

'Not much sign of his flat being lived in either.'

'I wouldn't know, never been inside. Must have something going for him though.'

'Why do you say that?'

'Absolute cracker of a girlfriend.'

'Really?'

'Just saw her the once, but you always know when she's around.'

'Why's that?'

'Her perfume. It fills the stairwell. Smelled it last night actually…'

Yes, Rebus had smelt it, too. He moistened his lips, feeling sourness at the corners of his mouth. 'Mr Hawkins, can you describe William Smith to me?'

Hawkins could, and did.

Rebus turned up unannounced at Alexis Ojiwa's, reckoning the player would be resting after the rigours of the previous day. The house was an unassuming detached bungalow with a red Mazda sports car parked in the driveway. It was on a modern estate, a couple of neighbours washing their cars, watching Rebus with the intensity of men for whom his arrival was an event of sorts, something they could dissect with their wives over the carving of the afternoon sirloin. Rebus rang the doorbell and waited. A woman answered. She seemed surprised to see him.

He showed his ID as he introduced himself. 'Mind if I come in for a minute?'

'What's happened?'

'Nothing. I just have a question for Mr Ojiwa.'

She left the door standing open and walked back through the hall and into an L-shaped living area, calling out: 'Cops are here to put the cuffs on you, baby.' Rebus closed the door and followed her. She stepped out through french windows into the back garden, where a tiny, bare-chested man stood, nursing a drink that looked like puréed fruit. Alexis Ojiwa was wiry, with thick-veined arms and a tight chest. Rebus tried not to think about what the neighbours thought. Scotland was still some way short of being a beacon of multiculturalism, and Ojiwa, like his partner, was black. Not just coffee-coloured, but as black as ebony. Still, probably the only question that would count in most local minds was whether he was Protestant black or Catholic black.

Rebus held out a hand to shake, and introduced himself again.

'What's the problem, officer?'

'I didn't catch your wife's name.'

'It's Cecily.'

Rebus nodded. 'This is going to sound strange, but it's about your mobile phone.'

'My phone?' Ojiwa's face creased in puzzlement. Then he looked to Cecily, and back again at Rebus. 'What about my phone?'

'You do have a mobile phone, sir?'

'I do, yes.'

'But I'm guessing you wouldn't have used it yesterday afternoon? Specifically not at 16.31. I think you were still on the pitch at that time, am I right?'

'That's right.'

'Then someone else used your phone to send this message.' Rebus held up William Smith's mobile so Ojiwa could read the text. Cecily came forward so she could read it, too. Her husband stared at her.

'What's this all about?'

'I don't know, baby.'

'You sent this?' His eyes had widened. She shook her head.

'Am I to assume that you had your husband's phone with you yesterday, Mrs Ojiwa?' Rebus asked.

'I was shopping in town all day... I didn't make any calls.'

'What the hell is this?' It appeared that the footballer had a short fuse, and Rebus had touched a match to it.

'I'm sure there's a reasonable explanation, sir,' Rebus said, raising his hands to try to calm Ojiwa.

'You go spending all my money, and now this!' Ojiwa shook the phone at his wife.

'I didn't do it!' She was yelling too now, loud enough to be heard by the car-polishers. Then she dived inside, producing a silver mobile phone from her bag. 'Here it is,' she said, brandishing the phone. 'Check it, check and see if I sent any messages. I was shopping all day!'

'Maybe someone could have borrowed it?' Rebus suggested.

'I don't see how,' she said, shaking her head. 'Why would anyone want to do that, send a message like that?'

Ojiwa had slumped on to a garden bench, head in hands. Rebus got the feeling that theirs was a relationship stoked by melodrama. He seated himself on the bench next to the footballer.

'Can I ask you something, Mr Ojiwa?'

'What now?'

'I was just wondering if you'd ever needed physio?'

Ojiwa looked up. 'Course I need physio! You think I'm Captain Superman or something?' He slapped his hands against his thighs.

If anything, Rebus's voice grew quieter as he began his next question. 'Then does the name Carl Guthrie mean anything to you...?'

'You've not committed any crime.'

These were Rebus's first words to Frances Guthrie when she opened her door to him. The interior of her house was dark, the curtains closed. The house itself was large and detached and sited in half an acre of grounds in the city's Ravelston area. Physios either earned more than Rebus had counted on, or else there was family money involved.

Frances Guthrie was wearing black slacks and a loose, low-cut black top. Mourning casual, Rebus might have termed it. Her eyes were red-rimmed, and the area around her nose looked raw.

'Mind if I come in?' Rebus asked. It wasn't really a question. He was already making to pass the widow. Hands in pockets, he walked down the hallway and into the sitting room. Stood there and waited for her to join him. She did so slowly, perching on the arm of the red leather sofa. He repeated his opening words, expecting that she would say something, but all she did was stare at him, wide-eyed, maybe a little scared.

He made a tour of the room. The windows were large, and even when curtained there was enough light to see by. Rebus stopped by the fireplace and folded his arms.

'Here's the way I see it. You were out shopping with your friend Cecily. You got to know her when Carl was treating her husband. The pair of you were in Harvey Nichols. Cecily was in the changing room, leaving her bag with you. That's when you got hold of her phone and sent the message.' He paused to watch the effect his words were having. Frances Guthrie had lowered her head, staring down at her hands.

'It was a video you'd watched recently. I'm guessing Carl watched it, too. A film about a man who cheats on his wife. And Carl had been cheating on you, hadn't he? You wanted to let him know you knew, so you sent a text to his other phone, the one registered to his fake name – William Smith.' Smith's neighbour had given Rebus a good description of the man, chiming with accident victim Carl Guthrie. 'You'd done some detective work of your own, found out about the phone, the flat in town...the other woman.' The one whose perfume had lingered in the stairwell. Saturday afternoon: Carl Guthrie heading home after an assignation, leaving behind only two glasses and an unfinished bottle of wine.

Frances Guthrie's head jerked up. She took a deep breath, almost a gulp.

'Why use Cecily's phone?' Rebus asked quietly.

She shook her head, not blinking. Then: 'I never wanted this... Not this...'

'You weren't to know what would happen.'

'I just wanted to do something.' She looked up at him, wanting him to understand. He nodded slowly. 'What...what do I do now?'

Rebus slipped his hands back into his pockets. 'Learn to live with yourself, I suppose.'

That afternoon, he was back at the Oxford Bar, nursing a drink and thinking about love, about how it could make you do things you couldn't explain. All the passions – love and hate and everything in between – they all made us act in ways that would seem inexplicable to a visitor from another planet. The barman asked him if he was ready for another, but Rebus shook his head.

'How's the weekend been treating you?' the barman asked.

'Same as always,' Rebus replied. It was one of those little lies that went some way towards making life appear that bit less complicated.

'Seen any good films lately?'

Rebus smiled, stared down into his glass. 'Watched one last night,' he said. 'Let me tell you about it...'

When his brother-in-law arrived, Harry Tolman was watching afternoon racing. From behind the curtains he studied Cliff locking the doors to his motor and then remembering his fags and having to open up again. Motor. Harry shrugged. Walk like that, talk like that: it was bred in the bone. Only the elderly said motor or fags these days. As if to prove his point an incautious movement of his arm produced that sudden jolt a junior doctor at the hospital had described to him as a deterioration of the brachial nerve. Or somesuch. He winced as he walked to let Cliffie in. The two men embraced without warmth.

'Let me say, straight off and before everything else, how choked everybody still is about Jean,' Cliff said. 'Even now, even after all this time.'

'Yeah, well.'

'I tried to put into words how we all felt at the funeral, Harry, but you were out with the fairies that day and no mistake.'

'If you say so,' Harry said. He walked into the kitchen to make a pot of tea.

Jean, through her brother Cliff, had been his last connection to that wise-guy London thing and after she died he all too willingly let it drop. He had not been up the Smoke for a six-month and then only to drink at pubs where he knew he could not be recognised. Came home on the early evening train.

The seaside bungalow they stood in now was Jean's choice of a nice place to live, just as the perennials in the flower borders were hers. Harry ate from plates she had chosen, slept under the duvet she had selected from the catalogue. Her clothes were still in the wardrobe. That was the story. She was his woman, he was her man.

That was the story and what the neighbours had not seen with their own eyes they invented. Harry Tolman was that nice man at 32 whose wife had died so suddenly. Kept himself to himself, had an unexpectedly flat belly and strong forearms, looked sixty, could be younger, could be older. A former soldier, perhaps. Politely spoken, but with that characteristic cockney croak. A one-time market trader, maybe.

Cliffie drummed his fingernails on the kitchen worktop. 'Don't you want to know why I'm here?' he asked.

'Let me guess. You're in trouble.'

'Big time. But I mean big time.'

Harry smiled to himself. 'Now don't get me all excited, Cliff.'

'My hand to God,' his brother-in-law muttered.

'So? What do you want, money?'

'Be realistic,' Cliffie snapped, with enough sudden bitterness in his voice to make Harry glance up from the kettle and take notice. 'Would I ask you for money? Am I stupid?'

'Then it's business.'

'I am asking a favour of you.'

His nervousness was beginning to annoy Harry. When he saw that, Cliff ducked his head in acknowledgement. Licked his lips. 'This, then. You put your motor through the Tunnel, buzz off to France, drive to a meet with some lads we have business with there, deliver a certain package, money changes hands. And that's it.'

'What's in the package?' Harry asked.

But his brother-in-law had exhausted his small stock of guile for the moment and took his tea out on to the lawn, the set of his back and shoulders indicating a sour response to sea-breezes and distant gulls.

Harry joined him. 'So, what's in the package?' he repeated.

'I told you, it's a business thing,' his brother-in-law said far, far too lightly.

They walked down to the sea together, hands plunged in pockets. It was one of those calm spring days when the grey of the water stretched all the way to the horizon and then seemed to curl upwards into sky. There was nothing to look at and no trick of the imagination could invent France, less than thirty miles away.

'Come on. Harry, give me a break,' Cliffie mumbled after another few minutes of uncomfortable silence. 'I more or less told them you're the man for the job. I mean you wasn't named, I never named you, blah-blah-blah, but it's all down to me to see it right, see it goes off.'

'Is it drugs?'

Cliffie burst out laughing from pure nervous release.

'Drugs?' he cackled incredulously.

Harry threw his ice-cream cone into a wire bin and wiped his lips with the back of his hand. A total of eighteen years in prison, the last six in Parkhurst, had much altered his views on the life of crime. The sheer boredom of being banged up with other dreamers was worse than actual death: nowadays he lived on his pension and a little occasional delivery driving. In the old days he had a certain quiet class; as, for example, tooling Fat Tony up to Birmingham along the M1 in a stolen Aston Martin, establishing what turned out to be an unshakeable alibi and, as Tony said admiringly, a land speed record.

'What do you drive now?' Cliffie asked, punting him a double voddie in the Carpenter's.

'Nothing fancy.'

'Good. That's good. Look, I don't want to put no pressure on you, Harry, but it's my arse if I cock this up.'

'How much is in it for me?'

'A grand,' Cliffie suggested, looking doubtful.

'And what's your end?'

'Jesus, Harry, you don't need to know all that. These guys I'm talking about – the geezers who want the job done – would have your balls off just for coughing in the wrong place. What can I tell you? Just that I'm bearing the heavy end of the load here, know what I'm saying?'

He glanced round the perfectly empty pub and then mouthed a single word: 'Russians.'

If he had said his principals were the Band of the Irish Guards Harry could not have been more surprised. He stared at his brother-in-law, his thinning hair and faintly blue lips, the over-expensive suit hanging from sagging shoulders.

'Who has the package now?'

'Not relevant. I bring it to you. Then you drive it over. You know, just dead casual. It'll be in the boot. A bit of cathedral bashing if you're asked where you're off to. Just a little spring break.'

'How big is this thing?'

Cliffie hesitated. He brushed his lapel distractedly. 'I need you to say yes before I go back to town. Then the final arrangements are made and then it goes down.'

'When?'

'When I tell you.'

Walking back up the road, Harry pointed out several plants he'd thought of growing in his own garden.

But Cliffie was jumpy. 'Nice, I'm sure, but I'm seeing Bungalow City here, Harry. And that's all I'm seeing.'

'Where d'you drink these days?' Harry asked him, far too casually.
'Some things don't change,' his brother-in-law said.

But then again, some things change very nicely. Where before
there had been a timber yard opposite the Bear and Staff in
Stockwell, there was now a supermarket and its generous car park.
Harry sat munching a salt-beef, watching the pub door through
binoculars. Cliffie was presently with a heavy-looking blonde in her
forties. Two nights running they parked up round the comer and
then walked in single file into the green painted pub Harry remembered very well from the days of his pomp.

On the third night they were inside, presumably boring the arse
off their chosen cronies, a black Lexus pulled up and a huge guy got
out to fetch Cliffie. The poor chump actually came to the kerb to
talk to the passenger in the Lexus with a V and T in his hand, a reck-
less piece of bravado. The conversation was short and Cliffie was still
making his points when the car pulled away into traffic. He stood
there looking lost. Harry felt sorry for him.

Cliffie followed the Lexus and Harry followed after, tooling
along listening to the BBC World Service, a bit of a thing with him
in recent years. The meet took place in a furniture repository, very
Russian in its forlorn dilapidations. Harry watched through glasses
from the perimeter fence of a skip hire company.

The Lexus people carried out a white parcel wrapped in gaffer tape
and stood it on end. One of them lifted the hem and showed Cliffie
the nature of the goods. A peachy white bum flared for the moment
in the beams from passing cars. There was some jolly laughter.

'Where was you last night?' Cliffie shouted. 'I told you to stay by the
phone.'

'Got the maps?'

'I said to stay by the phone. You can't mess with these Russian
geezers. Now listen. The goods are in the back of my motor and I'm
going to put them in yours. And then you're going to drive to the
spot marked X. Tomorrow. Have you got that? Not the day after,
not some time over the weekend. Tomorrow.'

'Are the goods perishable?' Harry asked, just for the pleasure of
seeing his brother-in-law sweat. Then he relented and put on his
unlaced shoes. 'I'll give you a hand.'

'You stay right where you are. Here's the map. Read the map.'

There really was a spot marked X. It lay less than a hundred kilometres from the coast, close to the Rouen-Paris motorway. Cliffie went over the plan, such as it was, again and again, passed across two hundred in notes and (a thoughtful touch) fifty in Euros for the petrol and a cup of tea and that.

'You make the switch, right, and they'll give you a grocery bag of dosh. Bank wrappers, all that.'

'Do I count it?'

'Don't worry,' Cliffie said bitterly. 'It'll all be kosher, believe me. They are messing with people who could start a third world war. They know that. You're just the bloody messenger. They ain't going to cross nobody.'

'Well, give me a clue. How much dosh?'

'One hundred thousand in US dollars,' Cliffie said. 'Which is like chump change to these geezers. Soon as you got it, you bell me, I'll meet you back here at the ranch.'

After he'd left, Harry walked into his garage via the door in the kitchen, opened the boot to his car and studied the package. He tore off some yards of tape, rolled back the fabric and touched a bare foot. It was warm. Just behind the ankle was an artery and he held his thumb to it. Whoever was inside the wrapping was drugged to the eyeballs, doubtless, but comfortable. In the circumstances. He went back to the kitchen, lit a small cigar and sat listening to the fridge.

Along that part of the French coast are dunes and marshes. Next to a rainswept golf course there is a lopsided clapboard property painted black, the kind of place only an Englishman would consider taking on as a commercial proposition. It is labelled MOT L. Derek Jukes greeted Harry like an old mate, which, after all, he had once been.

'How's Ricky?' Harry asked, out of courtesy.

'That little fairy! It was too quiet for him here. What it is, Harry, I've put you round the back, there's like a row of three but two is boarded up. It's the salt. Do you need to put the car under cover?'

'No, mate. I'll be out of here by three. Four at the latest.'

He passed across Cliffie's two hundred inside an Oxfam envelope.

'Good boy,' Derek said absently. 'I've had the old paraffin heater on all night. You'll find it warm enough.'

It was, in fact, stifling. Harry laid the package on the bed and cut it open with a Stanley knife. Inside was a girl in her early twenties. As he had imagined, she was naked and none too clean – the smell of her was overpowering enough to make him open the window. He checked her pulse. It was slow but regular.

Derek knocked at the door with a little tin box of works. He took in the situation at a glance, nodded, raised one of the girl's eyelids. 'She's only a kid,' he murmured.

'Safe to risk it?' Harry asked.

'Run the shower. She's going to be spewing her ring for an hour or so. Don't worry, mate. I am a former medical orderly of Her Majesty's Royal Air Force. You can't get better, this time of the morning. I take it what we have here is battlefield conditions.'

'You're a straight-up bloke, Derek,' Harry said.

'Not exactly, not as such.'

He took out the syringe and shooed Harry into the bathroom. She was called Marika. Passing through international frontiers as a comatose parcel was a bit of a thing with her – she had been abducted by Cliffie's set of geezers three months earlier as part payment of a gambling debt incurred in Düsseldorf, where she had been unhappy, but not desperate, so to speak. This bold stroke had got up the nose of the Düsseldorf Russian, whose girl she had been, and so far three people had been killed in the ensuing business negotiations.

'Well, now it's all back to square one,' Harry suggested.

'You are crazy,' Marika observed with Slavic despair.

'You get to go home – Düsseldorf anyway – and the London geezers get their debt paid in cash. Where's the prob?'

'For something so simple they have to do me up like a turkey? Why not I fly to Düsseldorf? Why they need you?'

Harry considered. 'Because when they get you back, they're going to kill you.'

'For sure.'

All this while she sat on the bed naked, accepting little spoonfuls of a lightly boiled egg. She seemed to sense that Harry and naked women had not been strangers in the past: her movements and gestures were entirely unselfconscious. 'You don't want to know why they kill me?'

'I probably wouldn't be able to follow it in detail. A hundred thousand dollars has been mentioned, though.'

'Ha! And pigs might fly,' Marika said with a rare stab at idiom.

'Yes,' Harry said.

Derek poured them both a Stella. 'Look at it this way,' he said.

'Say the dosh exists. For a hundred grand I could lose you both in this country, no probs.'

'For a few months, maybe.'

'All right then, say it doesn't exist. You still get their car, whatever gear they have on them, their watches, wallets and all that – you're still coming out ahead on the day. And, put it this way, the more mess you make, the more it turns into a war-type situation where you and the kid become idle bystanders, mere nothings.'

'Making good sense now, Derek.'

'Or,' the former medical orderly and Brighton drag queen concluded, 'you could just knock her out again, deliver the goods and sod the lot of them.'

'What have you got in the way of weaponry?'

'Me?' Derek protested.

'Bloody hell,' Harry said.

They were going to have to do this work with a pistol that hadn't been fired since 1987 and five rounds of ammunition, arms that until last night had been under a floorboard in Harry's bungalow. He sighed.

'You know what this is all about? Honour. These geezers have seen too many films. The girl goes home in the most insulting way possible, done up like a turkey. It's a power thing, like I spit on your shoe, Düsseldorf. Yeah, Düsseldorf says, and I spit in your eye because there is no hundred thousand dollars. That is the bones of the plot, Derek.'

'You got five shots. You miss with two, that's three shots to off the boys who turn up. Which requires a cool head.'

In that instant they heard a distant and unmistakable report out in the marshes. M. Dieumegard, a retired lawyer from Soissons, was playing at duck-hunting with his Japanese pump-action. It was all very illegal, what he was doing, and he turned to greet the car with French plates with the faintly queasy feeling that he had been rumbled. Which he had. He surrendered the gun and nineteen cartridges, accepted a receipt for them scribbled on a pink slip, gave a false address and counted himself lucky. As the jovial plain-clothes policeman pointed out, the gun was in any case pretty useless. A duck would have to be sitting at the next barstool to be sure of being slaughtered.

'It was an impulse buy from a catalogue,' M. Dieumegard admitted gloomily.

Back to Marika, wearing some jeans and a white T-shirt Harry had purchased at a supermarket the moment they got off the ferry. No bra or knickers but a pair of what looked like red bowling shoes, two sizes too big.

'Now listen,' Harry said. 'I'm going to have a go at these people we've been talking about.'

'Impossible!' Marika cried.

'No, it's just ordinary common sense. But none of it need involve you. If you stay here, you should be safe for a week or so. So long as you don't go outside. And if there are any dollars, then I'll see you right.'

'They will kill you,' the girl said.

'Maybe.'

'I know. Because, if they were going to do business, then they wouldn't send old man like you. You and me both pffft. That is the plan.' She put her forefinger to her head and pulled the trigger.

Harry glanced at his watch. 'I'm taking Derek with me for company,' he said.

The meet had been arranged an hour after sunset, a time when the last tractor had grumbled away into the gloom. The spot was well chosen, for it lay upon a crossroads at least two kilometres from the nearest farmhouse. Harry's car was parked up on a little rectangle of ground where the local council kept their pile of gravel. There was also a very handy bottle bank on short stilts.

The Audi with German plates drove up at normal speed, turned left and disappeared into the night. Harry stared at the pistol in his lap, opened the car door and then drew it gently to without engaging the latch. The seat was pushed back as far as it would go, leaving his arms free of the steering wheel: other than these precautions he did not have the faintest idea what to do. Except smoke. He lit a rollie he'd made earlier.

When the boys came back it was from the direction they'd taken earlier. The lights were on main beam and raked the interior of Harry's car. The Audi slewed to a halt a hundred metres away.

'Yes. Get out of the car please,' a guy yelled from the driver's side.

'Let's get out together,' Harry yelled back.

The Mexican stand-off. A long-eared owl, a European rarity, flew through the Audi's beam and then veered indignantly away. After an uncomfortable pause three doors of the German car opened and the same number of men got out, each carrying an Uzi. Harry opened his own door and stood behind it, the pistol dangling in his right hand. The only good thing so far was that these guys were young.

'Where is your passenger?' one of them cried.

'I have a parcel in the boot,' Harry countered.

Every second that passed, he felt heartened. They were cocky wee sods, toting their own shooters at arm's length, chewing gum, acting up. Tarantino. They sauntered towards the car.

'Stay very still, old man,' one advised.

'No probs,' he said, trying to match the international tone.

'Stand away from the car.'

'I'm scared, boys.'

It got a laugh. They ambled a little closer.

'You are a dead man,' the smallest of the three suddenly decided.

Harry missed with the first shot, hit with the second as Derek let loose with the shotgun from underneath the commune's bottle bank. All three Russians fell, cursing. Harry fired twice more and jumped back into his car, reversing away in a shower of gravel and the smaller roadside weeds. Four more agonising minutes passed, punctuated by a final blast from the shotgun and then he saw the Audi speed away, Derek driving. The headlights blipped in a victory signal.

Bloody hell, he thought. This is too easy. It was only then that he realised that all along the Russians had been firing at him. He was sitting in a pool of blood. The old motor was handling a bit funny but he drove the back roads to the coast with what he liked to think of as professional calm, passing through village after village of shuttered houses and empty streets.

'They were after your tackle,' Derek murmured in the scorching heat of Cabin 7. The wound that had caused all the mess was inside his right thigh, high up. It had passed through the car door before hitting him, which accounted for what the ex-medical orderly called a rare bit of good luck but a nasty jag all the same.

'There was no money, of course.'

'Nah. We got the Audi, one of the guns, a laptop and a few hundred Euros.'

'You are brave men,' Marika said, holding Harry's leg down while the wound was sutured.

'Was anyone killed?' he asked.

Derek tutted. 'And you a hardened criminal! These were kids sent on a man's errand, Harry. It's terrible, the things that happen nowadays. And d'you want to know what I think?'

They did.

It happened that the European Cup Final was held that year in Dortmund. The two Russian rivals who had started all these shenanigans met in a hospitality suite high up in the stands where they were photographed sharing a joke. One was toting a recent Miss Austria and the other one had girl-band superstar and Essex bimbo Robyn Nevill on his arm. The mood was cordial, fuelled by cocaine.

'So, how's your big boat?' one of them said in rapid Russian, referring to a monstrous white mini-liner presently moored in Monaco.

'It's good. How is your island?'

'Yeh, yeh, the island. It's good. But I tell you frankly, the Sicilians can be a pain in the arse about such matters. With them everything's a history thing.'

'History!' his rival repeated jovially, and they both laughed long and loud at the absurdity of the concept.

'These pumped-up clowns had very little sense of yesterday. They are villains with no need of the healing balm that memory provides the rest of us,' said Derek, trying to teach Harry how to play golf. 'That, and the simple fact that they'd rather be pop stars or footballers than decent honest criminals. They are shoppers, is what they are. It's a bloody disgrace, Harry boy.'

'Grateful to you as ever, Derek.'

At that moment, Derek was fiddling about, moving Harry's fingers this way and that on the golf club. It was, apparently, all in the grip. 'Heard from the girl?' he asked.

'What a romantic old queen you are, Dekker.'

Even Cliffie survived the adventure, though minus the toes on both feet, which he explained was just a bit of fun, just their way of marking his card. He walked a bit strange and his shoes cost a bloody fortune these days but all in all he counted himself a lucky man. He looked around the Carpenter's, where the whole scheme was first hatched.

'Don't you ever get tired of living down here?' he asked.

'No,' Harry said. 'It suits me. Jean liked it.'

'What a stroke you pulled, son,' Cliffie muttered. 'That kid owes you her life.'

Harry threw him a very sharp glance. 'Nice of you to say so,' he said with elaborate irony.

It passed clean over Cliffie's head. As Jean always said about her brother, he wasn't thick exactly but he never really got out of the playground. Mind, Harry thought, if he asks one more question about Operation Crossroads, I'm going to tear his lungs out. He watched indulgently as Cliffie reviewed all the possible things he might say next.

'I always loved her, you know. Jean, I mean.'

Harry touched him on the sleeve of his jacket and called for two more doubles. As happened once every three days or so, the fruit machine down at the far end of the bar paid a jackpot. Neither man looked up. Now there really was an activity designed for losers.

"The Scales of Justice have tipped in the wrong direction. That's all I'm saying, Jenny. Now it's all in favour of the defence, and that makes our job so terribly hard. I mean, we catch the villains and, ten to one, they walk away from Court laughing."

Bob Durden, resplendent in his Commander's uniform, appeared in the living room of Froxbury Mansions in Gloucester Road. He was in conversation with Jenny Turnbull, the hard-hitting and astute interviewer on the *Up to the Minute* programme.

"You've got to admit he's right, Rumpole." She Who Must Be Obeyed could be as hard-hitting and astute as Jenny. "Things have gone too far. It's all in favour of the defence."

"Why don't you – and the Commander, of course – try defending some unfortunate innocent before the Mad Bull down the Old Bailey? You'd have a Judge who's longing to pot your client and is prepared to use every trick in the book to get the Jury on his side, a prosecutor who can afford to make all the enquiries and is probably keeping quiet about evidence that's slightly favourable to the defence, and a Jury out for revenge because someone stole their car radios. Then you'd find out how much things are slanted in favour of the defence."

"Oh, do be quiet." She Who Must didn't have time for a legal argument. "I'm trying to listen to the Commander."

Bob Durden ruled the forces of law and order in an area half crowded countryside, half sprawling suburbs, to the north of London. When the old East End died, and its streets and squares became inhabited by upwardly mobile media persons, ethnic restaurants, and the studios of conceptual artists, it was to Commander Durden's patch that the forces of lawlessness moved. He was a large, broad-shouldered, loose-lipped man who spoke as though he were enjoying some secret joke.

"But aren't there cases where the police haven't been exactly on the side of the law?" said Jenny Turnbull.

Well done, Jenny, I thought. It's about time someone asked that question.

Hilda, however, took a different view. "That girl," she said, "should learn to show respect to the people she's interviewing. After all, the man is a Commander. She could at least be polite."

"She's far too polite in my opinion. If I were cross-examining I'd be a good deal less respectful." I addressed the television set directly. "When are your officers going to stop bribing witnesses by putting them up in luxurious all-expenses-paid hotels, and improving on confession statements?"

"Do be quiet, Rumpole! You're worse than that Turnbull woman, interrupting that poor man."

"You know who I blame, Jenny? I blame the lawyers. The 'learned friends' in wigs. Are they part of the justice system? Part of the injustice system, if you want my honest opinion." The Commander spoke from the television set in a tone of amused contempt to which I took the greatest exception. "It's all a game to them, isn't it? Get your guilty client off and collect a nice fat-cat fee from the Legal Aid for your trouble."

"Have you got any particular barrister in mind?" Jenny Turnbull clearly scented a story.

"Well, Jenny, I'm not naming names. But there are regular defenders down at the Old Bailey and they'll know who I mean. There was a case some time ago. Theft in the Underground. The villain, with a string of previous convictions, had the stolen wallet in his backpack. Bang to rights, you might say. This old brief pulled a few defence tricks and the culprit walked free. We get to know them, 'Counsel for the Devious Defence,' and quite frankly there's very little we can do about them."

"Absolute rubbish!" I shouted fruitlessly at the flickering image of the Commander. "Trevor Timson got off because he was entirely innocent. Are you saying that everyone with previous convictions should be found guilty regardless of the facts? Is *that* what you're saying?"

"It's no good at all you shouting at him, Rumpole." Hilda was painfully patient. "He can't hear a word you're saying." As usual, She Who Must Be Obeyed was maddeningly correct.

A considerable amount of time passed, a great quantity of Château Thames Embankment flowed down parched legal throats in Pommeroy's Wine Bar, a large number of custodial sentences were handed out to customers down the Bailey, and relatively few of those detained went off laughing. Gradually, as small shoots of promise appear when spring follows winter, my practice began to show signs of an eventual re-bloom. I progressed from petty thievery (in the

Case of the New Year's Resolutions) to more complicated fraud, from actual to grievous bodily harm, and from an affray outside a bingo hall to a hard-fought manslaughter in a sauna. It was in the months before I managed to play my part in the richly rewarding case – in satisfaction rather than money – that I am about to record. I was sitting in my Chambers room enjoying an illicit small cigar (Soapy Sam Ballard was still in the business of banning minor pleasures) and leafing through the *Oxford Book of English Verse* in search of a suitable quotation to use in my final speech in a case of alleged gross indecency in Snaresbrook, when a brisk knock at the door was followed by the entrance of none other than Dame Phillida Erskine-Brown – once the much-admired Portia of our Chambers, now the appealing occupant of Judicial Benches from the Strand and Ludgate Circus to Manchester and Exeter Crown Court.

"You'll never guess what I've seen, Rumpole! Never in a million years!" Her Ladyship was in what can only be described as a state of outrage, and whatever she had seen had clearly not been a pretty sight. "I just dropped in to tell Claude he'll have to look after the children tonight because I've got a dinner booked with the Lord Chancellor and the babysitter's got evening classes."

"All part of the wear and tear of married life?"

"It's not that. It's what I saw in the clerk's room. In front of Henry and Denise. Claude, flagrantly in the arms of another woman!"

"When you say in the arms of," I merely asked for clarification, "what were they doing exactly? I take it they weren't kissing each other?"

"Not that. No. They were hugging."

"Well, that's all right then." I breathed a sigh of relief. "If they were only hugging."

"What do you mean, 'That's all right then?' I said, 'Am I disturbing something?' and walked straight out of the clerk's room and came to see you, Rumpole. I must say I rather expected you to take this extraordinary conduct of Claude's rather more seriously."

I couldn't help remembering the time when Dame Phillida, once the nervous pupil whom I'd found in my room in tears, now a judge of the Queen's Bench, had herself tugged a little at the strict bonds of matrimony and conceived an inexplicable passion for a Doctor Tom Gurnley, a savagely punitive right wing Tory MP who believed in mandatory prison sentences for the first whiff of cannabis, and whom I had had to defend in the Case of the Camberwell Carrot. I suppose it wasn't an exact parallel – the Learned Judge had not been discovered embracing the old hanger and flogger in our clerk's room.

Now that the Erskine-Browns' marriage seemed to have sailed into calmer waters, I was unwilling to rock the boat. I offered an acceptable solution.

"Exactly whom was your husband hugging?"

"I couldn't see much of her. She seemed to have blonde hair. Not entirely convincing, I thought."

"A black trouser suit? Shiny boots?"

" I think so, now you mention it."

"Then that would be our new Director of Marketing and Administration."

"I believe Claude told me you have one of those. So that makes it perfectly all right does it?" I could see that the Judge was not entirely satisfied. "Is part of her job description snogging my husband?"

"Not snogging. Hugging."

"All right then, hugging. Is that her job – is that what you're saying?"

"Provided it's Thursday."

"Rumpole! Are you feeling quite well?"

"Her name is Luci. She spells it with an 'i'."

"Does she do that to irritate people?"

"That might well be part of it. She had the idea we should all hug each other at work on Thursday. She said it would improve our corporate spirit and lead to greater harmony in the workplace."

"You mean you *all* hug each other?"

"If you look on the noticeboard, you'll see that Soapy Sam Ballard has commended the idea to 'Everyone at Number 4 Equity Court'. He's very pro-Luci because I told him she fancied him."

"Rumpole, has the whole world gone mad?"

"Only on Thursdays. That's when we're meant to hug each other. On Fridays Luci has decided that we dress down."

"What does that mean, exactly?"

"It means that Ballard comes in wearing jeans and a red sweater with diamonds on it. Oh, and white gym shoes, of course."

"You mean trainers?"

"Probably."

"Do you dress down, Rumpole?"

"Certainly not. I can't afford the wardrobe. I stick to my working clothes – black jacket and striped trousers."

"I thought I saw Claude sneak out of the house in jeans. He hasn't told me."

"Your Claude has a nervous disposition. I expect he was afraid you'd laugh at him."

"I certainly would. And about the hugging. Do you hug, Rumpole?"

"Embrace our clerk Henry? Snuggle up to Ballard? Certainly not! I told them hugging always brings me out in a rash. I have a special dispensation not to do it for health reasons. It's like taking the vegetarian dish."

"What did Ballard say when you told him you wouldn't hug?"

"He said I could just say 'Good morning' in an extra cheerful manner. Does that set your mind at rest?"

"I suppose so." Phillida seemed reluctant to abandon a genuine cause for complaint against the unfortunate Claude. "Provided he doesn't embrace that woman too enthusiastically. She's far too old for that haircut."

"It was pure coincidence that you came in at that moment," I told her. "If you'd come in ten minutes later you'd have found him wrapped around Hoskins, a balding middle-aged man with numerous daughters."

"You're always counsel for the defence, aren't you, Rumpole?"

"I can only say that, in any situation which looks guilty, I can sometimes offer an innocent alternative to the Jury."

"Bob Durden would call that another trick of the defender's trade. Did you see him on television the other night?"

"I certainly did. And I just wish I had the chance to wake the Commander up to the reality of life when you're on trial at the Old Bailey."

At this the learned and beautiful Judge looked at me with some amusement – but my chance came sooner than either of us would have expected.

The earthshaking news was read out by Hilda from her tabloid newspaper one morning in Froxbury Mansions. She looked seriously upset.

"Feet of clay, Rumpole! That sensible policeman we saw on *Up to the Minute* turns out to have feet of clay!"

I had been trying to catch up with some last minute instructions in a fairly complicated long firm fraud when She Who Must handed me the paper, from which the face of Bob Durden loomed solemn and severe from beneath his cap. The headline, however, suggested that not only were his feet clay but that the rest of him was by no means perfect senior-police-officer material. The Commander had been arrested on no less a charge than taking part in a conspiracy to murder. It took a good half-minute before I was able to suppress an unworthy tendency to gloat.

Of course I read every detail of the extraordinary case. It was suggested that the scourge of defence lawyers had been prepared to pay a contract killer to do away with a local doctor, but I was sure that the last member of the Bar he would call upon to defend him was that devious Rumpole who spent his life helping guilty villains walk free from courtrooms, laughing triumphantly at the police. So the Commander took his place at the back of my mind, but I was on the lookout for developments in the newspapers.

One memorable day Ballard appeared in my room with a look of sublime satisfaction and the air of a born commander about to issue battle orders. I have to say that he had smartened up a good deal since I let him know that our Director of Marketing and Administration nursed tender feelings for him. He had invested in a new suit, his hair was more dashingly trimmed by a unisex stylist, and he arrived in a chemical haze of aftershave which happily evaporated during the course of the day.

"This, Rumpole," he told me, "will probably be the most famous case of my career. The story, you'll have to admit, is quite sensational."

"What's happened, Ballard?" I had no wish to fuel Soapy Sam's glowing self-satisfaction. "What have you landed now? Another seven days waiting before the rating tribunal?"

"I have been offered, Rumpole," the man was blissfully unaware of any note of sarcasm; he was genuinely proud of his eventful days in court with rateable values, "the leading brief for the defence in *R. v. Durden*. It is, of course, tragic that a fine police officer should fall so low."

Of course, I realised that the case called for a QC – (Queer Customer is what I called them) and, as I have said, that the defendant policeman would never turn to Rumpole in a time of trouble. I couldn't help, however, feeling a momentary stab of jealousy at the thought of Ballard landing such a sensational front-page *cause célébre*.

"He hasn't fallen low yet." I thought it right to remind our head of chambers of the elementary rules of our trade. "And he won't until the Jury come back to Court and pronounces him guilty. It's your job to make sure they never do that."

"I know, Rumpole." Soapy Sam looked enormously brave. "I realise that I have taken on an almost superhuman task and a tremendous responsibility. But I've been able to do you a good turn."

"What sort of good turn, exactly?" I was doubtful about Ballard's gifts.

Then he told me, "You see, the Commander went to a local solicitor, Henry Crozier (we were at university together), and Henry knew that Durden wouldn't want any sort of flashy clever dick defence QC – the sort he's spoken out against so effectively on television."

"You mean he picked you because you're not a clever dick?"

"Dependable, Rumpole. And, I flatter myself, trusted by the Courts. And as I believe your practice has slowed a bit since..."

"You mean since I died?"

"Since you came back to us. I persuaded Henry Crozier to give you the Junior brief. Naturally, in a case of this importance, I shall do most of it myself. If the chance arises you might be able to call some formal undisputed evidence. And of course you'll take a note of my cross-examination. You'll be capable of that won't you?"

"My near-death experience has left me more than capable of conducting even the most difficult trial."

"Don't worry, old fellow." Soapy Sam was smiling at me in a way I found quite unendurable. "You won't be called on to do anything like that."

As I have said, Commander Durden's patch was an area not far from London, and certain important villains had moved in when London's East End was no longer the crime capital. They ran chains of minicab firms, clubs and wine bars. They were shadowy figures behind Thai restaurants and garden centres. They dealt in hard drugs and protection rackets in what may have seemed, to a casual observer, to be the heart of Middle England. And no one could have been more Middle English than Doctor Petrus Wakefield, who carried on his practice in Chivering. This had once been a small market town with a broad main street, and had now had its heart ripped out to make way for a pedestrian precinct with a multi-storey car park, identical shops, and strict regulations against public meetings or yobbish behaviour.

Doctor Wakefield, as I was to discover, was a pillar of this community, tall, good-looking, in his fifties. He was a leading light in the Amateur Dramatics Society, chairman of various charities, and the doting husband of Judy – pretty, blonde, and twenty years his junior. Their two children, Simon and Sarah, were high achievers at a local private school. Nothing could have been more quietly successful, some might say even boring, than the Wakefields' lives up to the moment when, so it was alleged, Commander Bob Durden took out a contract on the doctor's life.

The local police force, as local forces did, relied on a body of informers, many of whom came with long strings of previous convictions attached to them, to keep them abreast of the crimes and misdemeanours which took place in this apparently prosperous and law-abiding community. According to my instructions, the use of police informers hadn't been entirely satisfactory. There was a suspicion that some officers had been using them to form relationships with local villains – warning them of likely searches and arrests and arranging, in the worst cases, for a share of the spoils.

Commander Bob Durden was commended in the local paper "for the firm line he was taking on the investigation he was carrying out into the rumours of police corruption". One of the informers involved was a certain Len "The Silencer" Luxford – so called because of his old connection with quietened firearms – who had, it seemed, retired from serious crime and started a window-cleaning business in Chivering. He was still able occasionally to pass on information, heard in pubs and clubs from his old associates, to the police.

According to Detective Inspector Mynot, Bob Durden met with Len the Silencer in connection with his enquiry into police informers. Unusually, he saw Len alone and without any other officer being present. According to Len's statement, the Commander then offered him five thousand pounds to "silence" Doctor Wakefield, half down and half on completion of the task, the choice of weapons being left to The Silencer. Instead of carrying out these fatal instructions, Len – who owed, he said, a debt of gratitude to the doctor for the way he'd treated Len's mother – warned his prospective victim, who reported the whole matter to Detective Inspector Mynot. The case might have been thought slender if Doctor Wakefield had not been able to produce a letter he'd found in his wife's possession, telling Judy how blissfully happy they might be together if Petrus Wakefield vanished from the face of the earth.

Such were the facts which led to Bob Durden – who thought all Old Bailey defence hacks nothing but spanners in the smooth works of justice – employed me, as Ballard made painfully clear, as his *junior* counsel.

"I'm afraid I have to ask you this. Did you write this letter to Doctor Wakefield's wife?"

"I wrote the letter, yes. She must have left it lying about somewhere."

"You said you'd both be happy if Doctor Wakefield vanished from the face of the earth. Why did you want that?"

We were assembled in Ballard's room for a conference. The Commander, on bail and suspended from his duties on full pay, wearing a business suit, was looking smaller than in his full-dress appearance on the television screen. His solicitor, Mr. Crozier, a local man and apparently Ballard's old university friend, had a vaguely religious appearance to go with his name; that is to say he had a warm smile, a crumpled grey suit, and an expression of sadness at the sins of the world. His client's answer to my leader's question did absolutely nothing to cheer him up.

"You see, Mr. Ballard, we were in love. You write silly things when you're in love, don't you?" The bark of authority we had heard on television was gone. The Commander's frown had been smoothed away. He spoke quietly, almost gently.

"And send silly e-mails to people who fancy you," I hoped Soapy Sam might say, but of course he didn't. Instead he said, in his best Lawyers as Christians tone of deep solemnity, "You, a married man, wrote like that to a married woman?"

"I'm afraid things like that do happen, Mr. Ballard. Judy Wakefield's an extremely attractive woman."

There had been a picture of her in the paper – small, smiling mother of two who had, apparently, fallen in love with a policeman.

"And you, a police commander, wrote in that way to a Doctor's wife?"

"I'm not particularly proud of how we behaved. But as I told you, we were crazy about each other. We just wanted to be together, that was all."

Ballard apparently remained deeply shocked, so I ventured to ask a question.

"When you wrote that you'd both be much happier if he vanished from the face of the earth, you weren't suggesting the doctor would die. You simply meant that he'd get out of her life and leave you to each other. Wasn't that it?"

"Yes, of course." The Commander looked grateful. "You're putting it absolutely correctly."

"That's all right. It's just a defence barrister's way of putting it," I was glad to be able to say.

Soapy Sam, however, still looked displeased. "You can be assured," he told our client, "that I shall be asking you the questions, Mr. Durden. Mr. Rumpole will be with me to take note of the evidence. I'm quite sure the Jury won't want to hear the sordid details of your matrimonial infidelity. It won't do our case any good at all if we dwell on that aspect of the matter."

Ballard was turning over his papers, preparing to venture on another subject.

"If you don't mind me saying so," I interrupted, I hoped not too rudely, "I think the Commander's affair with the doctor's wife the most important factor in the case, whichever way you look at it. I think we need to know all we can about it."

At this Ballard gave a thin watery smile and once again bleated, "As I said, I shall be asking the questions in Court. Now, we can obviously attack the witness Luxford on the basis of his previous convictions, which include two charges of dishonesty. If you could just take us through your meeting with this man…"

"Did you use him much as an informer?" I interrupted, much to Ballard's annoyance.

But the Commander answered me. "Hardly at all. In fact, I think it had been a year or two since he had given us anything. I thought he'd more or less retired. That was why I was surprised he came to me with all that information about one of my officers."

Durden then went through his conversation with The Silencer, which contained no reference to any proposed assassination. This had been made quite clear in our instructions, so I excused myself. I slipped out of the door, counted up to two hundred in my head, then re-entered to tell Soapy Sam that our Director of Marketing and Administration wished to see him without delay on a matter of extreme urgency. Our leader excused himself, straightened his tie, patted down his hair and made for the door.

"Now then," I gave our instructing solicitor some quick instructions as I settled myself in Ballard's chair, "have a look at our client's bank statements, Mr. Crozier. Make sure that an inexplicable two and a half thousand didn't get drawn out in cash. If the account's clean, tell the prosecution you'll disclose it providing they give us the good Doctor's."

"Very well, Mr. Rumpole, but why...?"

"Never mind about why for the moment. You might help me a bit more about Doctor Wakefield. I suppose he is pretty well known in the town. Has he practised there for years?"

"A good many years. I think he started off in London – a practice in the East End. Bethnal Green, that's what he told us. Apparently a pretty rough area. Then he came out to Chivering."

"To get away from the East End?"

"I don't know. He always said he enjoyed working there."

"I'm sure he did. One other thing. He is a pillar of the Dramatic Society, isn't he? What sort of parts does he play?"

"Oh, leads." The solicitor seemed to brighten up considerably as he told me about it. "The Chivering Mummers are rather ambitious you know. We did a quite creditable *Othello* when it was the A-level play."

"And the Doctor took the lead? You're not suggesting he blacked up? That's not allowed nowadays."

"Oh, no. The *other* great part."

"Of course." I made a mental note. "That's most interesting."

A minute later a flustered Ballard returned to the room and I moved politely out of his chair. He hadn't been able to find Luci with an 'I' anywhere in the Chambers, a fact which came as no surprise to me at all.

When I got home to Froxbury Mansions, I happened to mention over shepherd's pie and cabbage, that Commander Bob Durden had admitted to an affair with the Doctor's attractive and much younger wife.

"That comes as no surprise to me at all," Hilda told me. "As soon as he appeared on the television I was sure there was something fishy about that man."

I was glad to discover that, when it came to telling lies, Hilda could do it as brazenly as any of my clients.

In the weeks before the trial, I thought a good deal about Doctor Petrus Wakefield. Petrus was, as you will have to admit, a most unusual Christian name, perhaps bestowed by a pedantic Latin master and his classically educated wife on a child they didn't want to call anything as commonplace as Peter. What bothered me, when I first read the papers in the *R. v. Durden*, was where and when I had heard it before. And then I remembered old cases, forgotten crimes, and gang rivalry in a part of London to the east of Ludgate Circus in the days when I was making something of a name for myself as a defender at the Criminal Bar. These thoughts led me to remember Bill "Knuckles" Huckersley, a heavyweight part-time boxer, full-time bouncer, and general factotum of a minicab organisation in Bethnal Green. I had done him some service, such as getting his father off of a charge of attempting to smuggle breaking out instruments into Pentonville while Bill was detained there. This unlooked for success moved him to send me a Christmas card every year and, as I kept his latest among my trophies, I had his address.

I thought he would be more likely to confide in me than some professional investigator such as the admirable Fig Newton. Accordingly, I forsook Pommeroy's one evening after Court and made instead for the Black Spot Pub in Bethnal Green Road. There I sat staring moodily into a pint of Guinness as a bank of slot machines whirred and flashed and loud music filled the room, encrusted with faded gilt, which had become known, since a famous shooting had occurred there in its historic past, as the Luger and Lime Bar.

Knuckles arrived dead on time – a large broad-shouldered man who seemed to move as lightly as an inflated balloon across the bar to where I sat. He pulled up a stool beside me and said, "Mr. Rumpole! This is an honour, sir. I told Dad you'd rung up for a meeting and he was over the moon about it. Eighty-nine now and still going. He sends his good wishes, of course."

"Send him mine." I bought Knuckles the Diet Coke and packet of curry-flavoured crisps he'd asked for and as he crunched his way through them, the conversation turned to Doctor Petrus Wakefield. "Petrus," I reminded him, "not a name you'd forget. It seemed to turn up in a number of cases I did in my earlier years."

"He treated a friend of mine." Knuckles lifted a fistful of crisps to his mouth and a sound emerged like an army marching through a field of dead bracken. "They did get a few injuries in their line of business."

"What do you mean by that, exactly?"

"Knife wounds, bullet holes. Some of them I went round with used to attract those sorts of complaints. You needed a doctor who wasn't going to get inquisitive."

"And that was Doctor Petrus Wakefield?"

"He always gave you the first name, didn't he? Like he was proud of it. You got any further questions Mr. Rumpole? Don't they say that in Court?"

"Sometimes. Yes, I have. About Len Luxford. He used to come in here, didn't he?"

"The old Silencer? He certainly did. He's long gone, though. Got a window-cleaning business somewhere outside London."

"Do you see him occasionally?"

"We keep in touch. Quite regular."

"And he was a patient of Doctor Petrus?"

"We all were."

"Anything else you can tell me about the Doctor?"

"Nothing much. Except that he was always on about acting. He wanted to get the boys in the nick into acting in plays. I had it when I was in the Scrubs. He'd visit the place and start drama groups. I used to steer clear of them. Lot of dodgy blokes dressing up like females."

"Did he ever try to teach Len Luxford acting?"

My source grinned, coughed, covered his mouth with a huge hand, gulped Diet Coke, and said with a meaningful grin, "Not till recently, I reckon."

"You mean since they both lived at Chivering?"

"Something like that, yes. Last time I had a drink with Len he told me a bit about it."

"What sort of acting are you talking about?" I tried not to show my feeling that my visit to the deafening Luger and Lime Bar was about to become a huge success, but Knuckles had a sudden attack of shyness.

"I can't tell you that, Mr. Rumpole. I honestly can't remember."

"Might you remember if I called you as a witness down the Old Bailey?"

My source was smiling as he answered, but for the first time since

I'd known him his smile was seriously alarming. "You try and get me down the Old Bailey as a witness and you'll never live to see me again. Not in this world you won't."

After that I bought him another Diet Coke and then I left him. I'd gotten something out of Knuckles. Not very much, but something.

"This is one of those unhappy cases, Members of the Jury. One of those very rare cases when a member of the police force, in this case a very senior member of the police force, seems to have lost all his respect for the law and set about to plot and plan an inexcusable and indeed a cruel crime."

This was Marston Dawlish QC, a large beefy man much given to false smiles and unconvincing bonhomie, opening the case for the prosecution to an attentive Jury. On the bench we had drawn the short straw in the person of the aptly named Mr. Justice Graves. A pale, unsmiling figure with hollow cheeks and bony fingers, he sat with his eyes closed as though to shut out the painful vision of a dishonest senior copper.

"As I say, it is, happily, rare indeed to see a high ranking police officer occupying that particular seat in an Old Bailey courtroom." Here Marston Dawlish raised one of his ham-like hands and waved it in the general direction of the dock.

"A rotten apple." The words came in a solemn, doom-laden voice from the Gravestone on the Bench.

"Indeed, your Lordship." Marston Dawlish was only too ready to agree.

"We used to say that of police officers who might be less than honest, Members of the Jury." The Judge started to explain his doom-laden pronouncement. "We used to call them 'rotten apples' who might infect the whole barrel if they weren't rooted out."

"Ballard!" This came out as a stentorian whisper at my leader's back. "Aren't you going to point out that that was an appalling thing for the Judge to say?"

"Quiet, Rumpole!" The Soapy Sam whisper was more controlled. "I want to listen to the evidence."

"We haven't gotten to the evidence yet. We haven't heard a word of evidence, but some sort of judicial decision seems to have come from the Bench. Get up on your hind legs and make a fuss about it!"

"Let me remind you, Rumpole, that I'm leading counsel in this case. I make the decisions—"

"Mr. Ballard!" Proceedings had been suspended while Soapy Sam and I discussed tactics. Now the old Gravestone interrupted us. "Does your Junior wish to say something?"

"No, my Lord." Ballard rose with a somewhat sickly smile. "My Junior doesn't wish to say anything. If an objection needs to be made, your Lordship can rely on me to make it."

"I'm glad of that." Graves let loose a small sigh of relief. "I thought I saw Mr. Rumpole growing restive."

"I am restive, my Lord." As Ballard sat down I rose up like a black cloud after sunshine. "Your Lordship seemed to be inviting the Jury to think of my client as a rotten apple, as your Lordship so delicately phrased it, before we have heard a word of evidence against him."

"Rumpole, sit down." Ballard seemed to be in a state of panic.

"I wasn't referring to your client in particular, Mr. Rumpole. I was merely describing unsatisfactory police officers in general."

It was, I thought, a remarkably lame excuse. "My Lord," I told him, "there is only one police officer in the dock and he is completely innocent until he is proven guilty. He could reasonably object to any reference to rotten apples before this case has even begun."

There was a heavy silence. I had turned to look at my client in the dock and I saw what I took to be a small shadowy smile of gratitude. Ballard sat immobile, as though waiting for sentence of death to be pronounced against me.

"Members of the Jury," Graves turned stiffly in the direction of the twelve honest citizens, "you've heard what Mr. Rumpole has to say and you will no doubt give it what weight you think fit." There was a welcoming turn in the direction of the prosecution. "Yes, Mr. Marston Dawlish. Perhaps you may continue with your opening speech now that Mr. Ballard's Junior has finished addressing the Court."

Marston Dawlish finished his opening speech without, I was pleased to notice, any further support from the learned Judge. Doctor Petrus Wakefield was the first witness and he gave, I had to admit, an impressive performance. He was a tall, still, slender man with greying sideburns, slightly hooded eyes and a chin raised to show his handsome profile to the best possible advantage. When he took the oath he held the Bible up high and projected in a way which must have delighted the elderly and hard of hearing in the audience attending the Chivering Mummers. He smiled at the Jury, took care not to speak faster than the movements of the Judge's pencil, and asked for no special sympathy as a betrayed husband and potential murder victim. If he wasn't a truthful witness, he clearly knew how to play the part.

An Old Bailey conference room had been reserved for us at lunchtime so that we could discuss strategy and eat sandwiches. Ballard, after having done nothing very much all morning, was tucking into a prawn and mayo when he looked up and met an outraged stare from Commander Durden.

"What the hell was the Judge up to?"

"Gerald Graves?" Ballard tried to sound casually unconcerned. "Bit of an offputting manner, I agree. But he's sound, very sound. Isn't he, Rumpole?"

"Sound?" I said. "It's the sound of a distant foghorn on a damp night." I didn't want to depress the Commander, but he was depressed already, and distinctly angry.

"Whatever he sounds like, it seems he found me guilty in the first ten minutes."

"You mean," I couldn't help reminding the man of his denunciation of defence barristers, "you found the scales of justice tipped towards the prosecution? I thought you said it was always the other way round."

"I have to admit," and the Commander spoke as though he meant it, "I couldn't help admiring the way you stood up to this Judge, Mr. Rumpole."

"That was standing up to the Judge, was it?" I couldn't let the man get away with it. "Not just another courtroom trick to get the Jury on our side and give the scales of justice a crafty shove?"

"I don't think we should discuss tactics in front of the client, Rumpole." Soapy Sam was clearly feeling left out of the conversation. "Although I have to say, I don't think it was wise to attack the Judge at this stage of the case or indeed at all." He'd gotten the last morsel of prawn and mayo sandwich on his chin and wiped it with a large white handkerchief before setting out to reassure the client. "From now on, I shall be personally responsible for what is said in Court. As your leading counsel, I shall do my best to get back on better terms with Graves."

"You mean," the Commander looked distinctly cheated, "he's

going to get away with calling me a rotten apple?"

"I mean to concentrate our fire on this man Luxford. He's got a string of previous convictions." Ballard did his best to look dangerous, but it wasn't a great performance.

"First of all, someone's got to cross-examine the good Doctor Petrus Wakefield," I reminded him.

"I shall be doing that, Rumpole. And I intend to do it very shortly. We don't want to be seen attacking the man whose wife our client unfortunately—"

"Rogered." I was getting tired of Ballard's circumlocutions. "Misconducted himself with." Ballard lowered his voice, and his nose into a paper cup of coffee. This was clearly a part of the case on which Soapy Sam did not wish to dwell.

"You'll have to go into the whole affair." I told him. "It's provided the motive for the crime."

"The alleged victim is a deceived husband." Ballard shook his head. "The Jury are going to have a good deal of sympathy for the Doctor."

"If you ask him the questions I've suggested, they may not have all that much sympathy. You got my list didn't you?"

I had given my good learned leader ten good points for the cross-examination of Doctor Petrus. I had little faith in his putting them particularly clearly, or with more force or power of attack than he might have used if he'd been asking the Doctor if he'd driven up by way of the M25 or had his holiday yet. All the same, the relevant questions were written down, a recipe for good cross-examination, and Ballard only had to lob them out across the crowded courtroom.

"I have read your list carefully, Rumpole," my leader said, "and quite frankly I don't think there's anything in it that it would be helpful to ask Doctor Wakefield."

"It might be very helpful to the prosecution if you don't ask my questions."

"I shall simply say that, 'My client deeply regrets his unfortunate conduct with your wife,' and sit down."

"Sit down exhausted?" I couldn't help asking. "Don't you want to get at the truth of this case?"

"Truth? My dear Rumpole," Ballard was smiling, "I didn't know you were interested in the truth. All these questions," he lifted my carefully prepared list and dropped it on the table, "seem like nothing but a sort of smoke screen – irrelevant matter to confuse the Jury."

"You read about my meeting with Knuckles Huckersley in the Black Spot Pub?"

"I did, and I regretted the fact that a Member of the Bar would go to such lengths, or shall I say depths, to meet a potential witness."

"You're not going to ask the good Doctor about his practice in the East End?"

"I think the Jury would find that quite counterproductive. It could look like an attack on his character."

"So you won't take the risk?"

"Certainly not." Ballard's thoughts had strayed back to his lunch. "Are those sandwiches bacon and lettuce?"

"I rather imagine corned beef and chutney," Mr. Crozier, our instructing solicitor from Chivering, made a rare contribution to the discussion.

There was silence then. Ballard chewed his last sandwich. No doubt I had broken every rule and shown a lamentable lack of faith in my learned leader, but I had to make the situation clear to our client, the copper who had shown complete lack of faith in defending counsel.

"Well, Commander," I said, "you've got a barrister who's going to keep the scales tipped in what you said was the right direction."

"Towards justice?" Bob Durden was trying to stick to his old convictions as a drowning man might to a straw.

"No," I said, "towards a conviction. If it's the conviction of an innocent man, well, I suppose that's just bad luck and part of the system as you'd like it to work."

There was a silence in the lunchtime conference room. Ballard was at ease in his position as the leader. No doubt I was being a nuisance and breaking most of the rules, but he seemed to feel that he was still in charge and could demolish the corned beef and chutney in apparently contented silence. Mr. Crozier looked embarrassed and the Commander was seriously anxious as he burst out, "Are you saying, Mr. Rumpole, that the questions you want asked could get me off?"

"At least leave you with a chance." I was prepared to promise him that.

"And Mr. Ballard doesn't want to ask them?"

"I've told you. They'll only turn the Judge against us," Ballard mumbled past the corned beef.

"And why do you want to ask them, Mr. Rumpole?" The Commander was puzzled.

"Oh, I'm just one of those legal hacks you disapprove of," I told him. "I want you to walk out of Court laughing. I know that makes me a very dubious sort of lawyer, the kind you really hate. Don't you Commander Durden?"

In the silence that followed our client looked around the room uncertainly. Then he made up his mind and barked out an order. "I want Mr. Rumpole's questions asked."

"I told you," Ballard put down his half-eaten sandwich, "I'm in charge of this case and I don't intend to make any attack on a reputable Doctor whose wife you apparently seduced."

"All right." In spite of Ballard's assertion of his authority it was the Commander who was in charge. "Then Mr. Rumpole is going to have to ask the questions for you."

I was sorry for Soapy Sam then, and I felt, I have to confess, a pang of guilt. He had behaved according to his fairly hopeless principles and could do no more. He rose to his feet, left his half-eaten sandwich to curl up on his plate, and spoke to his friend Mr. Crozier who looked deeply embarrassed.

"Under the circumstances," Ballard said, "I must withdraw. My advice has not been taken and I must go. I can't say I expect a happy result for you, Commander, but I wish you well. I suppose you're not coming with me, Mr. Rumpole?"

As I say, I felt for the man, but I couldn't leave with him. Commander Durden had put his whole life in the hands of the sort of Old Bailey hack he had told the world could never be trusted not to pull a fast one.

"Doctor Wakefield, you're suggesting in this case that my client, Commander Durden, instigated a plan to kill you?"

"He did that, yes."

"It wasn't a very successful plan, was it?"

"What do you mean?"

"Well, you're still here, aren't you? Alive and kicking." This got me a little stir of laughter form the Jury and a doom-laden warning from his Lordship.

"Mr. Rumpole, for reasons which we need not go into here, your learned leader hasn't felt able to continue with the case."

"Your Lordship is saying that he will be greatly missed?"

"I am saying no such thing. What I am saying is I hope this defence will be conducted according to the high standards we have come to expect from Mr. Ballard. Do I make myself clear?"

"Perfectly clear, my Lord. I'll do my best." Here I was looking at the Jury. I didn't exactly wink, but I hoped they were prepared to join me in the anti-Graves society. "Of course I can't promise anything."

"Well do your best, Mr. Rumpole." The old Gravestone half closed his eyes as though expecting to be shocked by my next question. I did not disappoint him.

"Doctor Wakefield, were you bitterly angry when you discovered that your wife had been sleeping with Commander Durden?"

"Mr. Rumpole!" The Grave's eyes opened again, but with no friendly expression. "I'm sure the Jury will assume that Doctor Wakefield had the normal feelings of a betrayed husband."

"I quite agree, my Lord. But the evidence might be more valuable if it came from the witness and not your Lordship." Before Graves could utter again, I launched another question at the good Doctor. "Did you consider divorce?"

"I thought about it, but Judy and I decided to try to keep the marriage together for the sake of the children."

"An admirable decision, if I may say so." And I decided to say so before the doleful Graves could stir himself to congratulate the witness. "You've produced the letter you found in your wife's handbag. By the way, do you make a practice of searching your wife's bag?"

"Only after I'd become suspicious. I'd heard rumours."

"I see. So you found this letter, in which the Commander said they might be happier if you vanished from the face of the earth. Did you take that as a threat to kill you?"

"When I heard about the plot, yes."

"When you heard about it from Luxford?"

"Yes."

"But not at the time you found the letter?"

"It occurred to me that it might be a threat, but I didn't believe that Bob Durden would actually do anything."

"You didn't believe that?"

"No. But I thought he meant he wanted me dead."

"And it made you angry?"

"Very angry."

"So I suppose you went straight round to the Commander's house and confronted him with it?"

"No, I didn't do that."

"You didn't do that." I was looking at the Jury now in considerable surprise with a slight frown and raised eyebrows, an expression which I saw reflected in some of their faces.

"May I ask you why you didn't confront my client with his outrageous letter?"

"I didn't want to add to the scandal. Judy and I were going to try and make a life together."

"That answer," the sepulchral Grave's voice was now almost silky, "does you great credit, if I may say so, Doctor Wakefield."

"What may not do you quite so much credit, Doctor," I tried to put my case as politely as possible, "is the revenge you decided to take on your wife's lover. This letter," I had it in my hand now and held it up for the Jury to see, "gave you the idea. The ingenious revenge you planned would cause Bob Durden, and not you, to vanish. Isn't that the truth of the matter?"

"Are you suggesting, Mr. Rumpole," the Judge over-acted his astonishment, "that we've all got the case the wrong way round and that it was Doctor Wakefield who was planning to murder your client?"

"Not murder him, my Lord. However angry the Doctor was, however deep his sense of humiliation, he stopped short of murder. No. What he planned for Mr. Durden was a fate almost worse than death for a senior police officer. He planned to put him exactly where he is now, in the Old Bailey dock, faced with a most serious charge and with the prospect of a long term of confinement in prison."

It was one of those rare moments in Court of absolute silence. The clerk below the Judge stopped whispering into his telephone; no one came in or went out, opened a law book, or sorted out their papers. The Jury looked startled at this new and extraordinary idea. Everyone seemed to hold their breath, and I felt as though I had just dumped my money on an outside chance and the roulette wheel had started to spin.

"I really haven't the least idea what you mean." Doctor Petrus Wakefield, in the witness box, looked amused rather than shaken, cheerfully tolerant of a barrister's desperate efforts to save his client, and perfectly capable of dealing with any questions I might have the wits to ask.

Graves swooped to support the Doctor. "Mr. Rumpole, I presume you're going to explain that extraordinary suggestion?"

"Your Lordship's presumption is absolutely correct. I would invite your Lordship to listen carefully while I put my case to the witness. Doctor Wakefield," I went on before Graves could summon his voice back from the depths, "your case is that you learnt of the alleged plot to kill you when Luxford called to warn you. We haven't heard from Mr. Luxford yet, but that's your story."

"It's the truth."

"Luxford warned you because he was grateful for the way you treated his mother?"

"That is so."

"But you'd known Len Luxford – The Silencer as he was affectionately known by the regulars in the Black Spot in Bethnal Green – long before that, hadn't you?"

Doctor Wakefield took time to think. He must have thought of what The Silencer might say when he came to give evidence and took a gamble on the truth. "I had come across him, yes."

"Because you practised as a doctor in that part of London?"

"I did, yes."

"And got to know quite a lot of the characters who lived on the windy side of the law?"

"It was my job to treat them medically. I didn't enquire into the way they lived their lives."

"Of course, Doctor. Didn't some of your customers turn up having been stabbed, or with gunshot wounds?"

"They did, yes." Once again the Doctor took a punt on the truth.

"So you treated them?"

"Yes. Just as you, Mr. Rumpole, no doubt represented some of them in Court."

It was a veritable hit. The Jury smiled, the Gravestone looked as though it was the first day of spring, and I had to beware of any temptation to underestimate the intelligence of Doctor Wakefield.

"Exactly so. And, like me, you got to know some of them quite well. You got to know Luxford very well in those old days didn't you?"

"He was a patient of mine."

"You treated his wounds and kept quiet about them."

"Probably."

"Probably. So would it be right to say that you and The Silencer Luxford went back a long time, and he owed you a debt of gratitude?"

"Exactly!" The Doctor was pleased to agree. "Which is why he told me about your client's plan to pay him to kill me."

"I'm just coming to that. When you're not practising medicine or patching up old gangsters, you spend a great deal of time acting, don't you?"

"It's my great passion." And here the Doctor's voice was projected and enriched. "Acting can release us from ourselves, call on us to create a new character."

"Which is why you encouraged acting in prisons."

"Exactly, Mr. Rumpole! I'm glad that you understand that, at least."

There was a moment of rapport between myself and the witness, but I now had to launch an attack which seemed, now that I was standing up in a crowded courtroom, like taking a jump in the dark off a very high cliff.

"I think you encouraged Len Luxford to act?"

"In the old days, when I did some work with prisoners, yes."

"Oh, no, I mean quite recently. When you suggested he go for a chat with Commander Durden about police informers and come out acting the part of a contract killer."

The Doctor's reaction was perfect – good-natured, half amused, completely unconcerned. "I really have no idea what you're suggesting," he said.

"Neither have I." The learned Gravestone was delighted to join the queue of the mystified. "Perhaps you'd be good enough to explain yourself Mr. Rumpole."

"Certainly, my Lord." I turned to the witness. "It was finding the letter that gave you the idea, wasn't it? It could be used to support the idea that Commander Durden wanted you dead. You were going to get your revenge not by killing him, nothing as brutally simple as that, but by getting him convicted of a conspiracy to murder you – by finishing his career, turning him into a criminal, landing him, the rotten apple in the barrel of decent coppers, in prison for a very long time indeed."

"This is absolute nonsense." The Doctor was as calm as ever, but I ploughed on doing my best to sound more confident than I felt.

"All you needed was an actor for your small-cast play. So you got

Len Luxford, who owed you for a number of favours, to act for you. All he had to do was lie about what Commander Durden had said to him when he arranged a meeting, and you thought that and the letter would be enough."

"It's an interesting idea, Mr. Rumpole. But of course it's completely untrue."

"You're an excellent actor, aren't you, Doctor?" I took it slowly now, looking at the Jury. "Didn't you have great success in the Shakespeare play you did with the local Mummers?"

"I think we all did fairly well. What's that got to do with it?"

"Didn't you play Iago? A man who ruins his Commander by producing false evidence?"

"Mr. Rumpole!" Graves' patience, fragile as it already was, had clearly snapped at what he saw as my attempt to call a dead dramatist into the witness box. "Have you no other evidence for the very serious suggestions you are making to this witness except the fact that he played, who was it..." he searched among his notes, "the man Iago."

"Oh, yes, my Lord." I tried to answer with more confidence than I felt. "I'd like the Jury to have a couple of documents."

Mr. Crozier had done his work well. Having surrendered Bob Durden's bank statements to the young man from the Crown Prosecution Service, he seemed to take it for granted that we should get Doctor Wakefield's in return. Now the Judge and Jury had their copies, and I introduced the subject.

"Let me just remind you, Luxford saw Commander Durden on March the fifteenth. On March the twenty-first you went to Detective Inspector Mynot with your complaint that my client had asked Luxford to kill you for a payment of five thousand pounds – two and a half thousand down and the balance when the deed was done."

"That's the truth. It's what I told the Inspector."

"You're sure it's the truth?"

"I am on my oath."

"So you are." I looked at the Jury. "Perhaps you could look at your bank statement. Did you draw out two and a half thousand pounds in cash on March the twenty-first? Quite a large sum wasn't it? May I suggest what it was for?"

For the first time the Doctor missed his cue. He looked about the court hoping for a prompt, and, not getting one, invented. "I think I had to pay...I seem to remember things were done to the house."

"It wasn't anything to do with the house was it? You were paying Len Luxford off in cash. Not for doing a murder, but for pretending to be a part of conspiracy to murder?"

The Doctor looked to Marston Dawlish for help, but no help came from that quarter. I asked the next question.

"When does he get the rest of the money? On the day that Commander Durden's convicted?"

"Of course not!"

"Is that your answer?" I turned to the Judge. "My Lord, may I just remind you and the Jury that there are no large amounts of cash to be seen coming out of Commander Durden's account during the relevant period."

With that I sat down. Counsel for the prosecution suggested that as I had taken up such an unconscionable time with Doctor Wakefield, perhaps the Court would rise for the day, and he would be calling Mr. Luxford in the morning.

But he didn't call The Silencer the next morning or any other morning. I don't know whether it was the news of my cross-examination in the evening paper, or a message of warning from Knuckles, but in a fit of terminal stage fright Len failed to enter the Court. A visit by the police to the house from which he carried out his window-cleaning business only revealed a distraught wife who had no idea where he had gotten to. I suppose he had enough experience of the law to know that a charge of conspiracy to murder against the Commander might change into a charge of attempting to pervert the course of justice against Doctor Wakefield and himself. So he went with his cash, perhaps back to his old friends and accustomed haunts, his one unsuccessful stab at the acting profession over.

When Marston Dawlish announced that without his vital witness the prosecution couldn't continue, Mr. Justice Graves gave a heavy sigh and advised the twelve honest citizens.

"Members of the Jury, you have heard a lot of questions put by Mr. Rumpole about the man Iago. And other suggestions which may or may not have seemed to you to be relevant to this case. The simple fact of the matter is that the vital prosecution witness has gone missing and Mr. Marston Dawlish has asked me to direct you to return a verdict of 'not guilty'. It's an unfortunate situation but there it is. So will your foreman please stand?"

I paid a last visit to the conference room to say goodbye to my client and Mr. Crozier. The place had been cleaned up, ready to receive other sandwiches, other paper cups of coffee and other people in trouble.

"I suppose I should thank you." The Commander was looking as confident again as he had on the telly. Only now he was smiling.

"I suppose you should thank me, the shifty old defence hack, and a couple of hard cases like Knuckles and Len Luxford. We doubtful characters saved your skin, Commander, and managed to tip the scales in favour of the defence."

"I shall go on protesting about that, of course."

"I thought you might."

"Not that I have any criticism of what you did in my case. I'm sure you acted perfectly properly. You believed in my innocence."

"No." I had to say it, but I'm afraid it startled him. He looked shocked. His full lips shrank in disapproval and his forehead furrowed.

"You don't believe in my innocence?"

"My belief is suspended. It's been left hanging up in the robing room for years. It's not my job to find you innocent or guilty. That's up to the Jury. All I can do is put your case as well as you would if you had," and I said it all in modesty, "anything approaching my ability."

"I don't think I'd ever have thought up your attack on the Doctor," he admitted.

"No, I don't believe you would have."

"So, I'm grateful to you."

It wasn't an overgenerous compliment, but I said thank you.

"But you say you're not convinced of my innocence?" Clearly he could hardly believe it.

"Don't worry," I told him. "You're free now. You can go back to work."

"That's true. I've been suspended for far too long." He looked at his watch as though he expected to start immediately. "It's been an interesting experience." I was, I must say, surprised at the imperturbable Commander who could fall passionately in love, wish an inconvenient husband off the face of the earth, and call his own criminal trial merely "interesting". "We live in different worlds, Mr. Rumpole," he told me, "you and I."

"So we do. You believe everyone who turns up at Court is guilty. I suspect some of them may be innocent."

"You suspect, you say, but you never know, do you?"

And so he left with Mr. Crozier. I fully expect to see him again in his impressive uniform, complaining from the television in the corner of our living room about the scales of justice being constantly tipped in favour of the defence.

"You had a bit of luck in *R. v. Durden*." Ballard caught me up in Ludgate Circus one afternoon when we were walking back from the Old Bailey. "I gather Luxford went missing."

"That's right. I told him. "Are you calling that luck?"

"Lucky for you, Rumpole. From what I read of your cross-examination, you were clearly irritating the Judge."

"I'm afraid I was. I do have a talent for irritating Judges."

"Pity, that. Otherwise you are, in many ways, quite able."

"Thank you, Ballard."

"No, I should thank you for getting me out of that unpleasant case. Our clerk fixed me up with a rating appeal."

"Good old Henry."

"Yes, he has his uses. So, you see I have a lot to thank you for, Rumpole."

"You're entirely welcome, but will you promise me one thing?"

"What's that?"

"Please don't hug me, Ballard."

"I told you Rumpole, that I could tell at once that there was something fishy about that client of yours." Hilda's verdict on the Commander was written in stone.

"But he was acquitted."

"You know perfectly well, Rumpole, that that doesn't mean a thing. The next time he turns up on the telly I shall switch it over to the other channel."

Forget Graves, I thought, leave out Bullingham; you'd search for a long time down the Old Bailey before you found a Judge as remorseless and tough as She Who Must Be Obeyed!

"Ah, interesting," said Lesley Henderson, her mouth contorting to articulate the words around the impediment of a half-masticated Bourbon biscuit. "That must be Roger Rabbit's mum."

The three women crunching biscuits and nursing plastic cups of tea craned their necks. A small, unremarkable, dark-haired woman waited in line at the trestle table for her own refreshment, her head turning occasionally to gaze at a wall barnacled with grotesque paintings of oversized heads entitled 'my mummy' that glared down on the hall's occupants like a surveillance device. Holding her hand was a small boy with curly hair and prominent front teeth.

Lesley leant forward conspiratorially. "Well, we're honoured indeed. Mrs Rabbit has clearly found time in her busy diary to come and see what young Roger does in her lengthy absence."

The other two women smiled and moved their shoulders as though shrugging off invisible perching birds. Dorothy Stevens gesticulated at Rosemary McKendrick beside her. "Move Lesley's coat off that seat, Rose. Get her over here."

A grey wool coat and an orange silk scarf adorned with a child-like pattern of bumble bees was hastily shifted from the one remaining vacant plastic seat to the floor beneath an occupied one. The dark-haired woman accepted a cup of tea from a plump parent helper behind the trestle, then bent down and kissed her son on the forehead. He ran off towards a group of boys at the back of the school assembly hall, his slapping feet joining the muted thunder that the boys' cavorting drummed on the scoured oak floorboards. She watched him go, then her shy gaze roamed the room in search of refuge before coming to rest on the three women staring at her. With a pause that betrayed it as a considered effort, she smiled with an accompanying upward nod of the head. Lesley raised a hand. The gesture was returned.

"Sorted," said Dorothy under her breath.

Cautiously, the dark-haired woman threaded her way through the labyrinthine obstacle course of formally and sensibly arranged plastic stacking chairs, that had been informally and ludicrously rearranged by the groups of women who now occupied them, gabbling together like startled geese and booby-trapping the way between them with handbags and jackets. In this sea of shrill femininity, only one or two ugly, gangly men, whose beards, wire-rimmed spectacles, cagoules, and bicycle-clipped trousers advertised a very particular kind of personal failure, indicated that this was a parents' open day rather than a mothers' one. The dark-haired woman arrived at her destination and stood awkwardly, like a child called to a stern father's study waiting to be asked to sit. All three seated women noted her discomfort with pleasure and said nothing.

"Hello," said the standing woman quietly to Lesley. "Are you Sandy's mum?"

Lesley grinned. "Guilty!"

The dark-haired woman laughed politely, trying to look amused despite the weakness of the joke. Regardless of its disingenuous provenance, it was a nice laugh. "I'm Thomas's mum, Irene. I think Thomas plays with Sandy quite a lot."

The seated women exchanged furtive and amused glances.

"Why don't you sit down?" suggested Lesley, neither confirming nor denying Irene's statement.

"Thank you."

"We don't see much of you at the school gates," said Rosemary as Irene sat down on the prepared chair.

"No. I work. My mum drops off and collects Thomas most days. A child minder on the days she can't manage."

"Ah," said Lesley.

"Do you work?" asked Irene, pressing a finger to the top lip she'd just burnt by sipping the unpleasant tea.

"At the hardest job they've come up with yet," said Dorothy.

Irene raised her eyebrows in polite enquiry, her head inclined to invite fuller explanation.

"It's called being a full-time mum."

Irene nodded sagely, ignoring the heavy theatrical emphasis on the last three words. "Yes, no one realises how tough it is, all this, do they? Not until they do it themselves."

Lesley snorted.

Irene looked at her quizzically.

"So what is it that you do then?" demanded Lesley in a voice that was rather too rough for a pleasantry.

"I work in computers," said Irene, her eyes drifting to the group of boys at the back of the hall, pushing and jostling by the tables where the projects they'd been working on were laid out for their parents to admire. The boys were growing rowdy, the high-pitched yelling giving way to a subtle but audible drop in key and tempo.

"Keep you busy?" enquired Rosemary with a barely concealed sneer.

Irene sipped her tea again, eyes still on the boys. "Yes. I have to travel a lot. It's hard sometimes."

Dorothy crossed her arms over the large breasts that were fighting to get out of a zippy-up fleece that advertised her husband's polytechnic by way of a badly designed embroidered logo. "Well of course there's hard and there's hard isn't there?"

"Yes," said Irene. "There certainly is."

A shout rang out from the back of the hall and then a scuffle. Irene was on her feet and over to the boys with a speed and agility that surprised the seated women. Thomas was already on the floor, Sandy Henderson standing triumphantly amongst a small group of hooting admirers. Irene picked up her son and straightened out his crumpled uniform with a quiet motherly efficiency. Neither mother nor son spoke, but instead looked intently at each other as the group of boys watched with shining eyes to see what Sandy would do next. But Sandy was looking at Thomas's mother's face. She moved her gaze slowly to meet his and his cheeks coloured.

"Buck-toothed freak," he muttered to his nearest companion as he turned and walked away.

Irene waited until she and Thomas were alone in the small space they had defined with crouched bodies, then put an arm around his shoulders and said something quietly into his ear. Thomas looked into her dark eyes, moved off, head bent, and began looking at the scrapbooks, poking at them to turn the pages with a limp disinterested finger.

The three women were quiet as Irene rejoined them and sat down, smoothing her grey suit skirt over short muscular legs. Lesley looked at her friends. All three exchanged mirthful glances, trying hard not to laugh.

"The projects are rather good, aren't they?" said Irene in a steady voice.

Alasdair Henderson didn't kiss his wife goodbye in the morning any more. Nor did he kiss or hug his two boys. For the last two years he had worked hard at making his exits from number fifteen Churchill Avenue as swift as he could manage, and now after a breakfast that had been punctuated with the usual sly contemptuous insults from his sullen brutish sons, fuelled by tiny encouragements from his wife, he was free and happy behind the wheel of his car. Sonya's flat had been broken into last night and he was going straight there to act as her saviour. His whispered comforts to her over the mobile in the garden last night at midnight had been well received, and his crotch ached at the prospect of the many ways he would relieve her anxiety when he got inside the small and trendy Hyndland apartment that he paid for.

He was not disappointed. She had calmed down, mostly because nothing had been taken and it looked like kids had just kicked in the door. They took an hour to make each other feel better about the whole thing and the Alasdair that kissed her goodbye, and left for work for the second time that day, was a man who felt the world was on his side. As he accelerated through an amber traffic light and glanced in his mirror at some pathetic little white Japanese car behind him that hadn't his kind of horsepower to make it through, he felt like a real man, and one to be reckoned with.

Lesley walked a few steps out of her prime territory by the main gate and sidled up to the elderly woman. "Am I right in thinking you're Thomas's granny?"

The older woman turned and regarded her over the top of her spectacles without warmth. "Yes?"

"I'm the mum of one of his friends."

"Which friend exactly?" said the woman curtly and with an accent of upper class origin that took Lesley by surprise. This wouldn't do. Surely everyone realised that in the school gate hierarchy grandparents were only one step up the food chain from nannies, who were undisputed pond scum and not to be acknowledged under any circumstances. This granny was clearly getting above herself. Who did she think she was? After all, Lesley had made an effort to come and speak to her in full view of the troops. Gratitude would be appropriate. A snippy response was quite wrong, and the surprise of the woman's class had thrown her.

Lesley's pulse quickened. "One of the few he has, I believe," she said, working hard to elevate her middle class status to a slightly higher plane with a mannered and clipped diction, her gaze deliberately leaving the woman's face as though already bored. "Well, considering his rather noticeable orthodontic problems," she added. "You know how cruel children can be."

"Indeed," replied the older woman non-committally while consulting an elegant and expensive wristwatch, thereby trumping the semblance of boredom to a considerable degree.

Lesley fumed. How dare the old cow treat her like this?

She glanced over at the girls, still waiting, whispering to each other and smiling, anxious to see what titbit she would return with. Lesley composed herself. "Is Irene working today?"

"What do you think?"

A rage boiled in Lesley's belly that threatened to affect her voice. That couldn't happen. The placid delivery of slights and covert insults was essential to their efficacy. She must remain calm. She breathed deeply. "I imagine it must be rather hard, that's all. You know, for mothers who don't get to do much mothering."

The elegant and expensively dressed old woman looked once more at Lesley over the top of her spectacles, her eyes and nose screwed up as though examining an offensive piece of graffiti on a wall. "What are you anyway? A dentist or something?"

Lesley could feel colour rising in her cheeks. "No."

"Then what is it you do exactly?"

"I'm a mother."

"As are we all. But what do you do?"

"Isn't that enough?" There was a nervous laugh in Lesley's voice.

The old woman wrinkled her nose again and turned her gaze back to the playground with an air of finality. "Self-evidently not."

Thomas Barker's *Monsters Incorporated* lunch-box travelled at least fifteen feet before coming to a rest against the wall. It split open and spilled its contents onto the wet concrete. The small comforts of home, the ham sandwich and round wax coated cheeses, the chocolate bar and hardboiled egg his mother had packed that morning as they'd laughed at something on breakfast telly, all lay like crash casualties in a muddy puddle as Thomas viewed them side on from his own prone position in a similar body of water.

"Get up, you fucking rabbit-faced twat!"

Thomas pushed himself up on his palms and knees. His trousers were wet through and black with mud. His anorak had at least saved his torso from a soaking. Sandy Henderson kicked at the puddle and splashed Thomas in the face. Thomas stood up, wiping his eyes.

"Say it. Go on."

Thomas shook his head.

Sandy's eyes narrowed. He gripped the smaller boy by the hair. "Say 'my mum has to work because she can't keep a man and she's a fucking moron'."

Thomas shook his head, eyes fixed on the ground. "My dad's dead."

Sandy snorted, just like his mother. "Yeah? My mum says yours just works because she's a stupid lazy tart who can't be bothered doing the proper job of being a mother."

Thomas didn't react. This was what Sandy hated the most. As he contemplated another kick to Thomas's stomach just to get a response, Mr Strang appeared around the corner of the canteen block. The crowd of boys dispersed like mayflies on the wind.

Thomas Barker watched them go, then wiped his mouth with the back of his arm and went to fetch his lunch-box.

Lesley and Alasdair Henderson shook hands with the Reverend Patterson and exchanged a few pleasantries, mostly about the Scotland versus England rugby match the day before, while Sandy and his younger brother Andrew kicked at the gravel.

"Well, I tell you this my old son, we'll give them what for next time," said the reverend as he gripped the big man's elbow.

"Here now! Could you not have put in a word with the boss upstairs?" grinned Alasdair.

Lesley hit her husband playfully. She was about to add her own little *bon mot*, but the reverend was already pumping the hands of the next exiting congregation member, making a joke about sailing. She composed herself and walked down the gravel drive of the church a few paces behind her children, concentrating on not ruining the heels on her new kitten-heeled shoes from Princes' Square. As they stepped out onto the street Sandy booted Andrew's ankle and he screamed.

"Stop that! Right now!" hissed Lesley through bared teeth, her eyes scanning the crowd of church goers to check no one was witnessing this insubordination, only adding "You little bastards!" when she was sure it was safe to do so. The children ran off down the street and started to swing on the low branches of a flowering cherry, pulling off the blossom in handfuls and throwing it on the ground to wither and die. Following their progress made her miss Irene Barker's appearance from the door of a small white Nissan Micra, and so it took her by surprise when Irene stepped in front of her, her face calm, hard to read.

"Hello Lesley."

"Irene," cooed Lesley. "Were you in church? We didn't see you."

"No."

Alasdair slipped in beside his wife and took her arm, the grin of the village idiot painted across his face.

"This is my husband Alasdair."

Irene shook his hand.

"Irene's in computers, Alasdair. Thomas's mum."

"Ah!" grinned Alasdair. "Computers. Bloody brilliant. Keep telling Lesley that's the kind of thing she should be studying. Get her up off her bloody backside instead of drinking coffee in Fraser's all day with her pals while she spends my money."

Lesley pulled her arm free of her husband's and ground her back teeth together. If he noted the movement then Alasdair didn't register it, on his way as he was to slap the back of another church member standing on the kerb shaking some keys to a new BMW estate.

"Is Thomas with you?" said Lesley coolly.

"No," said Irene. "But I'd like to talk to you about him if I may."

This was good. Lesley liked this very much. She was coming to her to beg. That was the way it should be. It was the way it had to be. Lesley smiled, beatific understanding. "Do you want a coffee? We're just here." She indicated one of the neat identical terraced Edwardian houses stretching away from the church that made up this dependably middle class Glasgow district.

"Thank you," said Irene. She locked the car with a key, as Lesley noted with pleasure the absence of central locking on the tiny vehicle, and together they walked quietly down the street.

"So what brought you to Jarrowhill then?" said Lesley as she placed the mug of coffee on the glass top of the low table.

"Well, I'm sure you know yourself the school has a very good academic reputation. And luckily my mother lives in the catchment area."

"Lesley sat down heavily and pushed a biscuit into her mouth. "So you live with your mother then?"

"Just since John died. We're looking for something more permanent."

"That must be hard," said Lesley without feeling, as she washed down the biscuit with a gulp of coffee.

"Yes."

"And where were you before?"

"We moved around. John's job, and now mine I suppose, takes us wherever the work is."

"Ah," mused Lesley. "Difficult for Thomas."

"Not really. He settles quickly."

"Does he?" said Lesley sitting back, enjoying herself.

Irene looked at Lesley, unblinking, and Lesley looked back, trying hard to do the same. She really was a very plain woman, thought Lesley. The kind of face you would never remember in a crowd. Pretty enough, but so very ordinary. It made her feel good that she was considerably more attractive and certainly more notable in appearance. But then she worked at it. You had to.

"May I ask you a great favour?" Irene said quietly.

"Of course. Anything I can do to help." Lesley hugged herself. Power was a wonderfully intoxicating thing. She knew what was coming and she was going to saviour it.

"I have to go away for ten days. To the States, on business."

You show-off cow, thought Lesley. "How exciting," said Lesley.

"I wonder if while I'm gone, Sandy could perhaps be a little kinder to Thomas."

She had planned for this moment. It was a beautiful and delightful thing when an anticipated pleasure came to fruition so perfectly. Lesley savoured it before raising her eyebrows in surprise and leaning back as if in horror. "I don't know what you mean, Irene."

"I think there's a little tension between them."

Lesley adopted a posture of placation, hand shoulder-high, patting the air. "I'm sure you've got that wrong. It must be just schoolboy scrapping. Sandy thinks of Thomas as one of the gang."

Irene nodded. "Perhaps you're right. But if you could just ask him to be kind for this very short trip, it would mean a great deal to me."

"Well, I mean, I'll have a word, but I really don't…"

Irene leant forward. "When I'm working away from Thomas," she said in a voice so low that Lesley had to strain to hear it, "I have to concentrate one hundred percent on the job. One hundred percent. It's important to me that I don't worry about what's going on at home. I don't like to make mistakes at work."

Lesley was slightly discomforted by the peculiar and measured emphasis on her last sentence, but she sat back and half smiled. "Then perhaps you shouldn't work away from home."

"Perhaps not."

"We all have choices, Irene," said Lesley and drained her cup. Irene Barker sat very still, waiting. It unnerved her. "Yes. Well, of course I'll have a word with Sandy. But don't be surprised if he hasn't a clue what I'm talking about. He's a very friendly and popular boy, you know."

Irene continued to stare for a moment, then got up. "Thank you, Lesley."

She left the room and Lesley followed.

As Irene's small figure walked back down the tree-lined road to her tiny cheap car, Lesley Henderson reflected on how good life was. It was good to be the strong one, the one in control. The one who'd done well for herself, with the wealthy popular husband, the two expensive cars, and two strapping boys. The one who people had to ask for help, who had the power to grant respite or the power to turn up the heat. It was good, in fact, just to be alive.

Sonya Fergusson fumbled through her drawers looking for the red lace bra and pants set that Alasdair had bought her, until she remembered with a smile what they had been through and knew they'd be in the wash. But curiously, she didn't remember putting them in the washing machine. She thought for a moment with a mind befuddled with sleep and then dismissed it. They'd turn up. She opted instead for a black silk teddy, slipping it over her shoulders before looking at herself in the mirror to admire the way her small upturned breasts protruded through the smooth black material.

Sonya yawned and went to start the coffee machine. Behind her in the quiet bedroom, the rummaged drawer remained open, and to an owner who might have been more interested, it revealed that not only was it short of a bra and pants set, but also of some six letters that Alasdair Henderson had clumsily composed, written and sent in the heat of his passion for the recipient. But more than that. Beneath the chest of drawers on the floor, in the dark shadows against the skirting board, lay a crumpled orange scarf with bumblebees.

Irene Barker looked in on her sleeping mother and then kissed her restlessly sleeping son goodbye before she left the house for

Glasgow airport.

She carried only a small holdall as hand luggage as she caught the 6.15 shuttle to Heathrow. On arrival at Heathrow she went directly to Costa Coffee and sat on a high stool at the only beechwood table that was out of the range of the video camera covering the catered area, on account of it being behind a pillar. The man sat beside her within five minutes. He read his paper from cover to cover, finished his coffee and left the envelope on the table. She picked it up and walked to the ladies' room. In the cubicle Irene Barker sat on the closed toilet seat, removed her new passport, the coded instructions and the three credit cards in the name of Mrs Lindsey Scott.

On the flight to Denver she talked to a woman beside her who was going to visit her sister. She had the chicken, watched a movie about some rich people in a big country house and then slept for four hours. In Denver, Irene hired a small car and drove to the address she had been given. The bag with her equipment and the mark's file was concealed in a log pile at the back of the house. In the car she read the file before destroying it. Cats, she thought.

Seven and a half hours later at a Holiday Inn in Colorado Springs, Irene phoned home.

"How are you darling?" she said to Thomas.

"I'm fine. How are you?"

"Fine." There was a silence.

"Is everything okay at school?"

"Yes," said Thomas.

"We'll be moving on again soon darling."

"When?"

"Very soon. Mummy's big contract is nearly finished and then we'll live a little. I promise."

"With Granny?"

"Yes. Granny's coming too this time."

"He ripped up my spelling book today."

Irene stared at herself in the smoked hotel mirror. "That will stop."

"I miss you."

"I miss you too."

The safe house was in a quiet street with neat square lawns but few trees for cover. It was clever and she admired it. He would see a car coming for miles. Irene stopped at the hydrant outside his house to let the mongrel dog she'd just picked out from the town dog pound pee against it. She committed the layout of the house to memory, calculated the distance between the front door and the sidewalk, and paid special attention to the garage door. Then she walked on with the happy animal, an unremarkable housewife walking a dog that couldn't believe its luck.

When he heard the cat screaming, he looked out for the side window of the study. The animal lay half on the sidewalk, half on the road, its back legs twitching. He felt his heart atrophy. The stupid fucking Americans and their fucking cars. Couldn't they see an animal when it crossed the road? He'd seen those bumper stickers, the ones that proudly declared I DON'T BRAKE FOR CRITTERS and they made him feel sick. They had no respect for life. For a second he hesitated. But he was a professional. He could smell danger. No one knew he was here, and this was simply a cat that needed help. He thought of Gammshead, his wife's white Persian at home, and how he would feel if someone failed to come to their beautiful pet's aid in such circumstances.

Carefully, he opened the front door, looked up and down the street, then walked forward quickly to the stricken cat. The neighbour across the road was watching him as usual from the window. He always watched. Of course, he had routinely searched that man's house when he was out and found it safe. An old nosey interfering redneck, just irritated that the new neighbour who lived across the street had a better lawn mower and pick-up. Nothing to cause concern. He waved at the man and the figure stepped away from the window, embarrassed to be caught. The animal was in a bad way. By the time he bent down and gently picked it up, Irene was in the house, her latex gloves already on.

She let him close the front door and then stuck the needle into the back of his neck. His hand and arm flew up in the beginning of a killer defensive move but she was already three steps back and the drug was instantaneous. He fell, his legs folding beneath him like a shot deer. Irene quickly snapped the neck of the cat she'd maimed. It had done its job. No need to let it suffer. She took out two tiny castors from a deep pocket, placed them under his heels, then wheeled the man's body through the house to the garage and opened the car door. They could tell from the shoes these days when a body had been dragged. He was overweight and she was small, but she had been trained how to lift. She re-pocketed the wheels, propped him at the wheel, inserted the hosepipe to the exhaust and brought it round to the driver's side. Taking off her small rucksack, she opened it and found the bottle of vodka, the nasal gastric tube and the syringe. Inserting the greased tube up his nose and feeding it carefully down his throat she syringed in half the bottle of vodka, taking her time, spilling nothing. She glanced at her watch. It was important he stayed alive long enough for the alcohol to enter his bloodstream. Removing the tube, she put the hose between his legs, wrapped his hands around them, turned on the ignition and shut the door.

Back in the house Irene checked her watch, quickly found the computer, inserted the disc and watched for a moment with mild curiosity to see what had been chosen to incriminate their target. As the files of hardcore paedophile porn downloaded onto the hard drive she raised an eyebrow, glancing over his desk and around the room at the tiny clues that told her instantly that this was unlikely to be the man's vice but would mean nothing to the lumpen FBI dolts who would be crawling over the house in the next twelve hours. It was the detail that mattered to Irene. The enigmatic decisions she acted upon without question, and the variety of the challenges kept her interest, but the detail was what kept her alive. As the computer continued to consume pictures of inhuman depravity, she moved to the kitchen, fetched a glass he'd just used and filled it with a generous measure of vodka. She returned to his study, sat it by the computer as the disc finished its business, and then carefully knocked it over. She watched the vodka spill over the desk and dribble onto the floor as she removed the disc and pocketed it. Irene folded the dead cat into her bag, checked that all the doors and windows were locked and secure from the inside and returned to the garage. She looked out through the dusty strip of glass that revealed the street and the house opposite and checked it was clear. Reassured, she opened the car door, pressed the remote garage door-opening device on the car keys and then closed the car door again. It took her seconds to slip out as it opened, and minutes while she hid, to watch it close again automatically, the engine of his modest Lincoln ticking over innocently on the other side. She walked away.

On the plane home Irene had the beef. She sat beside a man who had been on a fly-drive holiday and had very much enjoyed it. She watched a movie about wizards and elves, and before she went to sleep she took out her calculator. After this job, that would make her total savings in the bank accounts in Switzerland and the Caymans come to nearly nineteen and a half million pounds. It was enough. It was nearly time to stop.

"So, Thomas tells us you're moving on then?" said Lesley, adjusting her sitting position to the posture they taught at her Pilates class.

"Yes," replied Irene, smiling. "Next month."

The stage in front of them started to fill with small boys and girls, clattering and shoving in their excitement about their impending performance. Thomas looked smart and proud, his curly head just visible in the back row of the choir. Rosemary and Dorothy came breathless along the row and sat down in the seats that Lesley had kept.

"Sorry," said Rosemary.

"God," said Dorothy. "Nearly didn't make it. Who'd be a bloody mum, eh?" She glanced sourly at Irene. "I don't know how we manage, I really don't," she said pointedly.

Irene smiled sympathetically. Lesley watched the choir assemble for a moment, studying Irene's face from the corner of her eye and registering the pride that shone there. Sandy hadn't made the choir. Sandy was handing out programmes. Sandy was only good at rugby, allowing him as it did to use his skills at knocking people over and hurting them. But even then he was only average. No one made Lesley proud. She relied on herself to do that. Lesley leant into Irene's ear. "I don't want this to sound the wrong way, Irene," she whispered, "but have you ever considered getting Thomas some cosmetic dentistry?"

"Yes," said Irene, still watching her son. "I have."

"And?"

"There's plenty of time."

Lesley raised her chin. "Well, I don't know. You don't want him being made fun of again wherever it is you're going next, do you?"

Lesley sat back with a cruel smile playing on her lips. Maybe it would or wouldn't happen where they were going. She didn't care. But it was up to her if it was going to happen or not in the next month before snivelling Roger Rabbit and his smug working mum left for pastures new. But then the most intoxicating thing about power was the ability to withhold it. Would she withhold it? Would she call Sandy off or encourage him? It was up to her. Power. She pulled in her pelvic floor muscles and relished the choice, although she already knew which it would be.

Alasdair Henderson turned off the television and took his whisky glass through to the dishwasher in the kitchen. He could hear Lesley thumping around upstairs getting ready for bed. He wondered if they should try and have sex tonight in case she started to suspect him, then decided against it. The memory of Sonya's twenty-eight-year-old tongue licking the inside of his thigh quickly turned the idea of wrestling with Lesley's spongey bulk into a horror he couldn't face. He needn't have worried. Lesley had other things on her mind than the dull predictable sex offered occasionally by her dull and predictable husband. She was thinking about strategy, about the thoughts that so absorbed her that she fell asleep without noticing that the kitchen knife she'd used to make a repulsive chicken casserole was not in the dishwasher where it belonged, but lying in the dark beneath her bed. Nor did she know that a dusty hat box on her wardrobe contained more than simply the garish green velvet affair she had bought for Amanda Findlay's ghastly cheap little wedding, but in fact a semen-soiled set of red lace underwear and some badly written love letters.

But then her husband's attention was no more acute than hers.

As Alasdair Henderson ripped open a dishwasher tablet, leaving the packet on the worktop in a habit that he knew annoyed Lesley, stacked his glass, turned on the dishwasher and put out the lights, his thoughts were very far away. So far indeed, that as he closed the dishwasher and went to lock and chain the front door, he failed to register the tiny breeze from the kitchen window that had been propped open with a pebble, the breeze that as he left the room nudged the discarded wrapper off the worktop and made it flutter gently to the floor.

'Trade,' said Nathan, his scowling face darkened further by the over-hanging olive trees, 'couldn't be worse.'

'Trade is rock bottom,' agreed Shem, clutching the sack.

'I don't know what this government think they're doing,' muttered Ehud.

'The situation for gentlemen of the road is abysmal,' said Shem, 'but I don't suppose any of them worry about that.'

Hunched in one of the clumps of trees that dotted the Jerusalem (via Bethlehem) to Cairo highway, they presented an unenticing spectacle. Shem and Ehud were lumbering figures, useful enough in a fight, useless in a chase. Nathan was gaunt, with an acute five o'clock shadow and a brooding expression which made most people, including himself, think he must be the brains of the gang.

'The truth is there's hardly been a soul all evening, and those that have been were obviously economic migrants or bogus asylum seekers.'

'That sort is next to useless,' said Nathan bitterly. 'They ought to be flattered we consider robbing them at all. All you get is a couple of brass denarii and a packet of sandwiches... Mind you, who wouldn't seek asylum in Egypt, rather than stay here under King Herod's benevolent rule? I'd go like a shot if I could get a lift. There's a country that's well run, stable, with plenty of people rolling in money that they're practically asking to be relieved of. Am I right or am I right?'

'You're right,' chorused Shem and Ehud, knowing their place.

'Whereas here...'

'Here anyone with money's been picked off by Herod as a possible rival. Show him a crowd of a thousand and he sees five hundred traitors and five hundred possible rivals.'

'That's what you get,' said Nathan, 'when you have a ruler who's not even a Jew.'

Shem and Ehud thought about that.

'But he's sort of Jewish, isn't he?' asked Ehud.

'He's got the religion, but not the certificate from the Racial Purity Board,' said Nathan, who collected odd little facts.

'Pity it's not the other way round,' said Shem.

'That would suit you, wouldn't it?' said Nathan. 'I saw you two nights since dining at the White Meat Eating House.'

'So what? I just fancied chicken,' protested Shem.

'The meat you were eating had never flapped a wing,' said Nathan sardonically. 'The High Priest would have had your guts for garters if he'd considered you one of the Faithful.'

'I'm as faithful as the next man,' said Shem. 'I've just never been that worried about my diet.'

'All you worry about is getting what you fancy, which is mostly food and sleep. You'll never be a first-rate bandit because you're too soft in your lifestyle.'

Having delivered himself of this damning verdict he turned on Ehud, who had been silent for more than a minute – always a bad sign: if he was thinking he couldn't talk, and vice versa.

'So what's up with you, Socrates?'

'Nothing, what should be up?'

'You're holding yourself a bit apart. Not matey, that.'

'I'm under the weather. I haven't been too regular lately.'

'You were regular this morning. Too bloody regular. It sounded like a volcano erupting. Oh well, it can wait. You'll soon tell us what's biting you.'

And ten minutes later Ehud ended his exile and came over to the other two.

'There's talk in the souks.'

'Oh yes?'

'Talk about Herod.'

'There's always talk about Herod. If a man has had ten wives, mostly simultaneously, there's plenty to talk about.'

'This isn't sex. It's violence.'

They were unimpressed.

'Can't even say it makes a change,' said Nathan. 'Not with his record. If it was you or me it would be mass murder, but if you're a king it's called strong rule. So what's the little charmer got up his sleeve this time?'

'They say he's planning a cull.'

This took even Nathan some time to digest.

'A cull?' he said at last. 'Has High Priest Aristobulus ordered him to slaughter all pigs?'

'Not animals. Human beings – they say he's going to slaughter all the first-born sons of Israel.'

'That's rank sexism!' protested Shem. 'Why not all the first-born daughters? Or say fifty-fifty?'

Nathan had been thinking.

'When you first said violence I wondered if there mightn't be something in it for us. And you know there could be. It would be easy work.'

'Easy work!' said Shem. 'Anybody'd think you'd never met a Jewish mother!'

'If they could be persuaded to bring them to some kind of centre it would be a piece of cake. We would call it a clinic maybe.'

'With the gossip that's going round? No way. Even without the gossip they'd smell a rat. Herod and rats seem to go together.'

'True... What's behind it, then?'

'Oh, he's got hold of some magician, some soothsayer or other.' There was a general groan.

'The curse of the ruling class,' said Nathan.

'Someone called Belisarius is feeding him stories about plots and conspiracies, forecasts of future prosperity if he does this or that, future disaster if he does the other. Herod calls him his Prime Minister.'

'All these newfangled titles,' grumbled Nathan. 'Why doesn't he call him his charlatan in residence?'

'Anyway, the Prime Minister says he has become aware of a new star in the sky, which signifies that a child has been born who will rule the people of Israel.'

'I don't see a new star,' said Shem.

'Course you don't,' said Nathan. 'You never look at the sky unless you're dead drunk and horizontal. Go on, Ehud.'

'Well, naturally Herod's not best pleased. He's going to have a general cull of new-born boys, just to be on the safe side.'

'Sounds logical,' said Nathan. 'Nasty, but logical.'

'They don't call him Herod the Great for nothing.'

'He calls himself Herod the Great. Nobody else calls him anything printable.'

'He'll need a big workforce,' concluded Ehud, 'and he'll pay well for the job.'

'They always say that when dodgy jobs are in the offing,' said Nathan. 'I've experience of jobs like this, believe you me. They employ trash to do it, promising rich pickings because they're "just the men for the job". Then, when it's done they say: "Oh no. You're just trash. We don't pay top rates to trash."'

'Are you saying we're trash?' Shem demanded.

'Of course we're trash. If we were caught on one of our usual jobs, Herod wouldn't even bother to crucify us. We wouldn't be worth the nails or the wear and tear on the timber. He'd tie us in a sack and chuck us in the Jordan.'

'Still,' said Ehud, harking back to the cull, 'it'd be money.'

'Oh yes, a bit,' conceded Nathan.

'Damn sight more than we're getting on the road.'

'True,' Nathan conceded, regretful at giving the idea the thumbs-down. 'But think of the aggro and the awful reputation we'd get. Baby-killers? Practically anyone in the country would sign up to do a bit of tit-for-tat killing. Everyone loves a baby, particularly when someone else is holding it. At best we'd probably be chased out of Jerusalem.'

'Or, worse, not allowed to leave it,' muttered Shem.

'On consideration, I'd say we shouldn't touch it with a barge-pole,' concluded Nathan. 'I'd rather bide my time, hoping for the Big One.'

'Waiting for Mr Jack Pott?' asked Shem.

'If you like.'

'Mr Jack Pott never comes, in my experience,' said Ehud.

'He's got to come some time,' said Shem.

'There you display your entire ignorance of the laws of gambling,' said Ehud.

'One day he's going to come by,' insisted Nathan. 'And then, why shouldn't it be us who picks him off?'

'And why shouldn't it be this little group coming from Bethlehem?' asked Shem.

'Because nothing worth having comes from Bethlehem,' said Ehud. 'Well, for whatever reason, they're in a bit of a hurry.'

They gazed towards the point where the road dipped towards Bethlehem. Slowly breasting the brow of the hill were a little party, a huddled group the components of which could not easily be discerned. The omens for a jackpot did not look good to the other two.

'They may be in a bit of a hurry,' said Nathan, 'but if they're having to go at foot-pace to Cairo, Herod the Great will be a couple of dates in a history book before they get there.'

'There is an animal of some kind,' said Shem, 'but they're having to go at the pace of the walker.'

'Obviously they've got a beast that can't bear two,' said Nathan.

'Probably a dromedary with a back problem.'

'We could put it out of its misery, along with the others,' said Ehud.

'Very attached to its misery is a dromedary,' said Nathan. 'Only one way of separating it from it.' He and Ehud laughed.

'We haven't decided to kill them yet,' said Shem, who had no taste for slaughter.

'Toss for what to do,' said Nathan. 'Heads we relieve them of their goods, tails we relieve them of their lives as well.'

'And rim we let 'em go in peace and brotherhood,' said Shem. Nathan tossed. The coin landed in the sand with the face of Augustus Caesar pointing towards Ehud and the reverse pointing towards Nathan.

'Rim it is,' said Shem. 'No blood this time.'

'I vote we suspend judgment till the party gets close,' said Ehud. 'Course we do,' said Nathan. 'It was just a way of passing time.'

'Until Mr Jack Pott arrives,' said Ehud.

'This is not Mr Pott,' insisted Shem. 'He'd never ride a beast as slow as that one.'

'It's probably some poor family from some far-flung outpost of this great Roman province who've been to register in the Census,' said Nathan.

'Put your cross where the nice man tells you, and don't argue if you don't want a sore back,' said Ehud.

'All in the cause of psephological accuracy,' said Nathan. 'Which is pretty funny since we never have elections.'

'Speak for yourself,' said Ehud.

'Wait – the picture is beginning to get clearer,' said Shem. 'The man walking beside the beast is wearing a rough blanket or piece of sacking around his shoulders.'

'Surprise, surprise,' said Nathan. 'He's one of the Great Rural Unwashed. A ploughman, a carpenter, a crude metalworker.'

'That kind of person can stash away a goodly sum if he's careful,' said Ehud.

'Maybe. But he wouldn't bring it to Jerusalem for the Census, would he?'

'And he wouldn't wear his best overcoat either,' said Ehud regretfully. 'Or maybe the man holding his hand with the pen in it would decide he hadn't been paying enough taxes and he'd be justified of relieving him of his astrakhan. Either way, whether he's a rich yokel or a poor one, we're not likely to benefit.'

'That's right,' said Shem. 'And the most likely thing is that he's a poor sod with no money, hardly any possessions and...wait a bit... The one riding is a woman.'

'Figures. It's a family.'

'And she's holding a baby. The man is leading the beast – it's a donkey—'

'Just as cussed as a dromedary,' said Nathan.

'—because she can't cradle the baby and hold the reins.'

'Typical of our rural poor,' said Nathan. 'They can't adapt their meagre skills to the needs of the labour market.'

'She's feeding it. It's a nice picture, isn't it?'

'Look nice on a Passover card,' said Nathan. 'Hey – what say they've heard the rumours about a cull and are getting out in time?'

'Too bad,' said Ehud. He and Nathan laughed cynically.

'Remember the coin,' said Shem. 'It fell on the rim.'

'Oh Gawd!' said Nathan. 'We said it was just a way of passing the time.'

'Remember what you said about the popular feeling towards baby-killers.'

'I was talking about a mass cull in Jerusalem. They'd never know who did a one-off on the Cairo Road... That starlight's bright, isn't it? Never known it so bright. We'll get a good look at the bags on this side of the donkey.'

Bathed in a silver, ethereal light the little caravan approached. Ehud began to get excited.

'There's bulges,' he said.

'She's feeding the babe,' said Shem. 'You never seen them before?'

'Bulges in the personal luggage. Look, the saddlebags are just sacking like the man's coat. You can see the outline of everything they've got with them.'

'Including bulges,' said Nathan thoughtfully. 'Look at those three bulges towards the tail, will you.'

They all did, but Ehud for one expressed bafflement.

'Sort of squarish,' he ventured.

'Squarish,' agreed Nathan. 'Wouldn't you say ornamented in some way, especially the lids?'

'They're the family utensils,' protested Shem. 'Saucepans, pots, canisters – that sort of thing.'

'Would you expect a family like that to have highly-ornamented utensils?' demanded Nathan.

'Well, why not? Maybe he's a metal-worker like you said, or has a friend who is... What do you think they are, anyway?'

'I think they are caskets,' said Nathan.

'Caskets? Well, so what? Same difference.'

'Caskets beautifully worked in rich metal, holding rich gifts.'

'Yah!' jeered Ehud. 'You've gone soft in the head. What would that couple be doing with rich gifts? Are you saying their baby will be Lord of Israel?'

'No, of course not,' said Nathan impatiently. 'How would a rural clown like that sire a great ruler?'

'She makes a lovely mother,' said Shem dreamily. He deeply approved of motherhood and apple-pie and all the sentimental ideals of the world. 'A woman like that could produce a boy who could do anything!'

'Get real!' said Nathan contemptuously. 'But what if they're travelling with it for someone else? The local bigwig, for example. He'd be an obvious target for such as us, but the local carpenter or whatever would get past unscathed.'

'What are we discussing them for, then?' asked Ehud.

'Because we're sharp-eyed and intelligent – one of us, anyway,' said Nathan. 'Trash though we are, socially speaking. And because they've packed stupidly, with the precious things pointing outwards, and showing.'

Shem wasn't taking that.

'We're so sharp-eyed and intelligent, one of us anyway, that what we saw was probably pewter boxes with a bit of fancy artwork on the lid, and inside the family supply of dried mutton, matzos and dates from the family orchard. Or maybe one contains the family Bible, with a family tree stretching back to King David, or another contains his mother's wedding shift. Anything is possible, so why are we guessing? I'd rather play Pass the Parcel. Anyway, it's all academic now.'

'What do you mean, "academic"?' asked Ehud.

'Useless and unprofitable speculation. They've gone past. Or do you think it's worth running after them?'

Nathan looked, surprised, at the little group progressing toward Cairo.

'Well, they've not gone far.'

'And what do you think they'd do, when three hulking men start-ed running after them? That donkey, with the mother and babe and the three supposed caskets, would discover a surprising turn of speed and would be over the horizon in a twinkling. The best we'd get would be the man. Fancy his sacking overcoat, do you, Nathan?'

Nathan sighed.

'Give it a rest. It was just an idea. I was just passing the time. We're no worse off than we were before.'

'And no better,' said Ehud.

Perhaps. And then again, perhaps not. After all, if there is a niche in Purgatory for sinners who were saved from committing terrible sins worthy of a more dreadful place by a combination of sloth, incompetence and lack of nerve, perhaps all three had won a place in that niche that night.

Meanwhile the donkey, and the baby and the gold, frankincense and myrrh – as inappropriate as most Christmas gifts – proceeded slowly on the road to Cairo.

Antony Mann

Esther Gordon Framlingham

"How about a late seventeenth-century Russian peasant?" I asked.

Across the room, my agent Myra raised an eyebrow. "North or south?"

"South."

"Been done."

"Ah, I meant north," I said quickly.

Myra shook her head. "Sorry, been done," she said. "Sheila Trescothick's Ivan the Irascible series. Ivan's an irascible Russian peasant, disliked by all and sundry in his small northern Russian village, tolerated only because of his extraordinary ability to solve the most perplexing of crimes."

"Yeah, yeah, I get the idea. Okay. Try this on for size." I read from the bottom of my list. "A nineteenth-century Peruvian goatherd, male, between thirteen and sixteen years old, an amateur sleuth who solves crimes across the local mountain community?"

"Nu-uh. Stan Archer. The Miguel Goatchild books."

I didn't think it was necessary that Myra smile so hugely, but you can't say she didn't have a sense of humour. She all but clapped her hands in merriment. A slim and businesslike thirty-five with wavy auburn hair and sharp, intelligent eyes, she'd been taking fifteen percent of my very little income for three years now.

"Oh yeah." I nodded. "I've heard of them. Vaguely."

"They've won awards," said Myra.

"Of course they have. Works of genius."

The room was as light as the small windows and the overtaxed bulb in the frilly shade would allow. The main office was out the door left. Out there, clacking and ringing noises sank meekly into the thick carpet. This was reception, where Myra sat her writers down for chats. It smelled of my grandfather's aftershave. He was dead.

One wall – floor to ceiling – was devoted entirely to books on shelves, both fiction and non-fiction, hardback and soft. These were the books that over the years Myra had sold on behalf of her clients. It was impressive. It said, *I'm a successful agent, I place lots of manuscripts*, and as always, I was impressed. But not one of them was mine.

I sighed and turned my attention back to my list. I'd started with thirty-six brilliant ideas for crime fiction sleuths that didn't yet exist.

Or so I'd thought. Now, there remained only one not crossed off. "Myra, don't piss me around now, because this is my last shot. Are you sitting comfortably? A dominant Neanderthal male at the time of the Cro-Magnon…"

Myra was already shaking her head.

"No?" I whispered.

"Merlene Trent's Ug Oglog novels. You mean to say you don't know them?"

"They've won awards?"

"They're big in New Zealand."

"Lucky New Zealand. May it sink without a ripple, both islands. Well that's that. By my reckoning, there's now a fictional detective for every profession across every social class from each and every region in the entire history of mankind, including the future, parallel universes and q-space."

"What can I say? Crime fiction's going through a purple patch."

I took my cup from the glass table between us and poured the dark tepid coffee down my throat. Like it was going to quench my thirst. "So unless a writer dies – or gets murdered – there isn't a single opening left for a series gumshoe. And I'm stuck trying to write one-offs."

"No, no, that's no good," said Myra.

"I've got a great idea for one. There's this zeppelin pilot, see, and he gets drunk one night and accidentally kills the son of a wealthy local politician in a bar fight. He panics and runs off, but then this other guy who was at the bar finds him and blackmails him into flying the zeppelin into the Arctic Circle where the rich politician is secretly mining—"

"Nobody reads one-offs," said Myra firmly, stopping me in mid-plot. "If there isn't a recurring central character from book to book, readers simply get muddled and don't know what's happening. Sure, a resilient few can cope, but others tend to lose all sense of direction, even when they're sitting down. They get confused and worried. Some throw up. Do you really want to be responsible for making people ill?"

"Yes."

"I'm sorry, Paul," said Myra as though she'd just told me no, she didn't want to change her gas supplier, not today, not any day. "Maybe if you'd been lead singer of a trendy Britpop band, if you were a stand-up comic or celebrity gardener, you could get away with it."

"So what are you saying? That I'm all washed up before I get started? That it doesn't matter what I write, it won't find a publisher? This sucks. I'm going back to law school."

"I like your writing, Paul. I think you've got potential. That's why I'm going to tell you this. Esther Gordon Framlingham is dead."

"Who?"

"Esther Gordon Framlingham. She wrote the Father Rufus Mysteries."

"Really? The little old lady with curly white hair and spectacles? I thought that was Mary Margaret Whitmore."

"It was Esther Gordon Framlingham too. They both have white hair."

"Oh. Dead, huh? That's a shame. Father Rufus, you say?" Now that I thought about it, I knew those books! Between Father Quentin and Father Septus in the alphabet, sixteenth-century abbot, sixteenth-century Exeter. "Yeah, yeah, I read some when I was growing up. They're kind of fruity, aren't they?"

"Fruity? No. Maybe you're thinking of Father Rastus. This is Father Rufus. There's no fruit. Anyhow, if you'll just let me finish my fucking thought for a change, what I was going to say was, Cantor aren't certain any more that they want Esther Gordon Framlingham dead."

"Publishers can do that now, bring people back to life?"

"No, no, well not the mid-size ones like Cantor anyway. She's dead, but they haven't released the news yet."

"Crikey, does her family know?"

"Not yet. She's been a recluse for decades anyway."

"How did she die?"

"Boredom. Shut up and let me finish. Cantor would ideally like to keep the Father Rufus series going indefinitely, maybe even until the world is destroyed by a giant asteroid or consumed in the final implosion of the universe. Rufus is a brand name, and of course there's the TV series."

I filled Myra's pause, because she just left it out there for me. "And they want someone to step into Esther Gordon Framlingham's shoes, ghostwrite the Rufus books?"

I filled another. "And you want me to do it? Wouldn't that mean writing under her name?"

"To begin with. Esther Gordon Framlingham was frankly churning out shite towards the end there, and sales were drooping like my husband's dick. Cantor want a team player, someone energetic and enthusiastic to become part of the brand."

"Someone who'll write for peanuts and do what they're told."

"You got it."

"I always thought you were a lesbian."

"Married twelve years this March. And so what if I'm gay? You threatened by that? But enough about me. The point is, Cantor might eventually be willing to let a new writer come up with their own books. If said writer can demonstrate increased sales with the ghostwritten stuff. And, of course, when society moves on and new gumshoe professions develop."

"How about lifestyle coach?" I said. "I've always wanted to write about a mystery-solving lifestyle coach, at any rate for the last four seconds. You can't say it's not contemporary, and no one else has—"

"Anne Portman. The Ralph de Silvian mysteries. De Silvian is a lifestyle coach who solves murders while coaching..."

"Yeah, yeah, put a sock in it yourself for a change. I get the picture."

"Good. If you've got it, then don't go losing it. Anyhow, there is just the one other catch that I've omitted as yet to tell you about. Cantor have asked me to audition two writers for the Esther Gordon Framlingham job. You and one other."

And, she could do basic arithmetic.

"Who's the other lucky fool?"

"Jack Pantango."

"Doesn't ring a bell."

"That's the idea. The one who comes up with the best synopsis-and-three-chapters in the next fortnight gets the nod."

"Didn't Esther Gordon Framlingham leave any storylines behind?"

"At least four hundred, but you don't get to see them unless you win."

"What if I don't like the idea of writing Father Rufus books?"

"Have a ball at law school."

Sleuth. Gumshoe. Detective. Private eye. They're all just another name for soft-spoken tonsured fifteenth-century cleric. I didn't do any research. I didn't need to. The more I thought about it, the more I vividly remembered the Father Rufus books from my childhood. It was my Dad who had bought the whole set by mail order, except for the ones that hadn't yet been written. I liked them so much I would always get to them first and devour them in a sitting. *The White Raven. Candlestyx. The False Witch. The Third Chamber.*

I recalled Dad reading them by the fire on chilly winter evenings. Whenever he finished one, he'd toss it into the flames, and reflectively watch it burn. What was he thinking about? Fire? Books? Books on fire? They were big thick volumes, but quick to read, and it wasn't exactly a huge fireplace. We were never cold, though.

It took me no more than a couple of days to thrash out the synopsis. I came up with a clever plot: this ship's captain gets drunk one night in an inn, see? And accidentally kills the son of a wealthy local nobleman during a fight. He panics and runs off, but then this other guy who was at the inn finds him and blackmails him into sailing the ship to the Arctic Circle where the rich nobleman is running a secret mining operation. Then Father Rufus is called in to solve all the assorted murders and associated mysteries that would no doubt crop up from time to time.

I was halfway through Chapter One when Jack Pantango got in touch.

He was ten years younger than me, and that was only the start of what irked me about him. For some reason he'd wanted to meet in The Juniper Tree, a crummy pub a half mile from Liverpool Street Station, which for me meant an inconvenient trek up from Tooting Broadway by tube. The Juniper Tree was undecorated in olive green wall carpet and those stupid bar mirrors covered in swirly bits that reflect life in swirls. The place was replete with fruit machines going ding, and tired-looking blue-collar types at the bar who'd never figured out how to get some expression into their faces.

Pantango himself was lean and boy-faced, good-looking, with his dark hair slicked back behind his ears. "For some reason, I thought you'd be older," I was saying. "What are you? Twenty-two? Twenty-three?"

Across the table, Pantango was using the tips of his fingers to edge his half pint of lime-and-lemonade in a circle, watching the ice try to keep up as the glass moved round it. He was from the East End, and spoke deliberately, as though it was me who was the idiot. "Mr Gadd, it's like this."

"Call me Paul," I said.

"I won't, if you don't mind. It'll make it easier what I have to say, if we keep it on a business footing."

"Ha, that sounds a bit serious." My attempt at a laugh betrayed me somewhat by sticking fast to the insides of my throat.

"Congratulations, by the way, on getting in on this Esther Gordon Framlingham audition. Have you been on Myra's books for long?"

"Who?"

"She's not your agent? Well, congrats anyway. It's very young to be expecting to land this sort of job, so don't be too disappointed if it's me who ends up with the banana. But don't feel you don't have a chance, because I honestly think you do."

"End up with the banana? What the fuck are you talking about?" He stopped spinning the glass and raised his voice, and the heads of blokes at the bar moved the inch required for their eyes to note what was going on. I got annoyed again as I realised I was up against an authentic cheeky chappy Cockney geezer who no doubt didn't baulk at having to punch people in the face. Plus he was probably a super-gifted natural writer who'd be great on TV and radio and look smooth on the back of a jacket sleeve, who'd most likely soon write the definitive London working-class novel on the proceeds of the Esther Gordon Framlingham job. Which should have been mine.

"Is that a South American name?" I said. "Pantango? You do look a bit Spanish."

Though I only meant to a little, I was making him angry a lot, and now, in my general direction, he poked at the air with his finger.

"Mr Gadd," he said, keeping something nasty corked up that I was glad not to see. "Believe me, I want to say this twice, but if it does end up being only once, then you've saved yourself a smashed kneecap. The Esther Gordon Framlingham job is Jack Pantango's, right? It's a payday for me that I am not going to miss, plus apparently there's other perks that go with. Like there's chicks and drugs, yeah? So get it fucking straight. There's no discussion on this that won't lead to some breakage."

The further annoyance of this upstart punk who wanted to steal my big chance referring to himself in the third person as though he could present himself objectively to the world at large – a habit I've always despised, even in myself – was the last straw. Though by his expression he was almost begging me to, I had no choice but to protest.

"Sorry," I said, standing and draining my glass in one. "I've been working towards this Esther Gordon Framlingham thing for the last five years. Actually, I haven't been working towards it at all, but it'll have to do until something better comes along. Do what you have to, but don't forget, a writer writes with his brain, not his kneecaps. I cite as an example that French guy who was paralysed but still wrote a book using his eyelid to press down the keys on his typewriter? Or what was it? Come to think of it, it couldn't have been that." I turned to the assembled heads at the bar, all now facing in my direction, assaulting me with their mild amusement and indifference. "Does anyone remember the name of that book, or the guy's name even? I never read it myself. Anyway, don't forget him!"

With that, I walked out, turning no more than four or five times to see if Pantango was following. But he just sat there, staring at me, a small, hard smile on his face, and I could tell, he would soon be beating my fucking head in.

As it turned out, he didn't want to beat me up. He wanted to kill me. I found out soon enough when, halfway along the darkest stretch of the lane which ran from The Juniper Tree towards Liverpool Street Station, where the only real illumination in fifty yards came from the filthed-up windows of a heat-trap chippie selling last month's grease in tonight's batter, he came at me from the shadows near a roll-up corrugated doorway with a blade that somehow found light enough to glint back into my eyes.

It turned out also that, even supposing he was a young upstart writer of some talent, he was lousy at killing people. Lunging forward to puncture my squawk of surprise, he tripped on the cobbles of the footpath and his feet skittered out from under him. In retrospect, it was comical, the way he twisted as he fell, the way the air and city smog was forced from his lungs with a grunt as he hit the ground. Even funnier, if you're amused by that kind of thing, was the way the knife in his hand went straight through his eye into his brain. Ha ha. Ha.

I would have called the police, or at least simply walked away, but I was still finding Jack Pantango pretty annoying, not least because he'd just tried to stab me. So, avoiding the spreading pool of blood, I searched his pockets for wallet and keys. I had a vague notion of finding out where he lived and breaking in. On the slim chance his Esther Gordon Framlingham idea was superior to my own, I could steal it with impunity.

It was his wallet that told me he wasn't Jack Pantango at all. According to his driver's license, Gardner Beam had been twenty-five years old, and had lived in Bow, and had looked less like a thug in real life than in passport-sized photos. I also found a sheet of ruled notebook paper, folded in four. On it someone had written, in inverted commas, 'Jack Pantango', and an address in Highgate.

It was dark, but early still, so I bought an A-Z from the kiosk at Liverpool Street and caught the tube across town. Pantango lived in a modern block of flats half way up North Hill, a corner place set back behind a laurel hedge – three stories of pocket-sized balconies painted white, faintly luminous in the moonlight amidst the beige brickwork.

I got through the security entrance on the coat-tails of an old man in a black business suit who didn't see me. He was halfway up the first flight of stairs before the front door had gently squeezed against my foot.

It was a woman who opened the door to Flat 9. Maybe because I hadn't buzzed she was expecting to see a neighbour – she opened her mouth to speak, then shut it again, and I saw a shadow of trepidation cross her eyes. "Yes?" She was fiftyish, a short frump in a kitchen-curtain floral dress that was keeping her ample bosom in check. Her hair was stiff and dark and looked like a wooden salad bowl, something you'd maybe pay a tenner for at a craft fair, inverted and plonked on her head.

"Hi," I said. "I'm looking for Jack Pantango." That made her start, and she would have shut the door in my face if I hadn't stuck out a hand and stopped her. "I don't mean to be rude, but it's important. Is he home?"

She didn't turn around and look back into the flat like I thought she might have done if he'd been there. She just stared straight at me, then sighed deeply, and her shoulders sagged along with her face. "You'd better come in."

"It's okay for *you*," she said, not bothering to hide the bitterness. "You're not all that fat and you're not that old."

"Thanks very much."

We sat in her kitchen, at the table, drinking weak tea by the light of the fluorescent tube. The wall tiles were gaudy with cutesy kitten pictures, and there was a plastic water filter near the sink. She was a Jackie, not a Jack, but she was a Pantango.

"Me?" she went on. "I'm fifty-four and plain ugly. I'm a part-time surveyor with an arthritic left knee. Do you really think I could ever make it as a writer? What publisher is going to want to promote *me*?"

"What about your writing?"

"What's it got to do with that? Sure, if I had some claim to fame. Christ, why didn't I become a politician? Or a bus driver?"

"Do something quirky, like wheel a microwave round the Outer Hebrides. Write about that," I said. "Are you a virgin? That'd help."

"Maybe, but only if I was proud of it. That's why I hired Beam, you see? He was going to be my public face, do the interviews and appearances when I got famous, and I was going to pay him a retainer from my royalties. Plus he was a cheap Cockney thug, so I thought he could scare you off into the bargain."

"You didn't tell him that being a writer meant that he'd get lots of women and drugs, did you?"

"I thought that might make the deal more attractive."

"He believed you on that?"

She refilled my cup. "I'm sorry about the knife thing. Did he really try to kill you?"

"I think that was just for his own enjoyment," I said. "Jesus, Jackie, what was the point? The Esther Gordon Framlingham job, it's faceless anyway! It's anonymous hackwork for a few bucks!"

"Oh, but it could lead to other things, don't you think?" she said, almost plaintively.

"Oh, it could do," I said. "But for me, not for you."

It was simple enough. Pantango didn't have a choice. In return for me not going to the police about Gardner Beam, she left the way clear for me to secure the Esther Gordon Framlingham gig.

I finished my Father Rufus chapters, then sent them off to Myra, and a week or so later she called me into her office.

"This is good stuff," she told me as she slapped the typescript down onto the re-ception room table. "The writing is tight. The characters are real. The story is strong."

I was grinning in anticipation.

"And it's funny," said Myra, "because Jack Pantango rang me during the week and told me she was no longer interested. Wouldn't say why. But that leaves just you."

"You knew Jack Pantango was a woman?"

"Of course I knew he was a woman. He's one of my people."

"Christ, why didn't you tell me?"

"Why the fuck should I? What's it to you? Anyhow, you didn't get the job."

There was nothing I could say to that which wouldn't come out all sulky and disappointed and wrong, so I said, "Why not? You just told me yourself you liked what I wrote! What's the problem? This isn't fair!"

"What's the problem?" She slid the chapters over. "I wanted synopsis-and-three-chapters on Father Rufus. You've given me Brother Rufus."

"I've...what?"

"I don't want sixteenth-century Exeter! I want fifteenth-century Bath! I want Esther Gordon Framlingham, not Edna Williams Dickinson!"

Bloody hell, I'd written about the wrong detective. Sure, a mistake anyone could have made, but could I really have *remembered* it all so wrong, those vivid unimpeachable memories, my father by the fire with a book, my father, the book, the fire? How clear it still seemed. "Whoops," I said. "But no harm done. Let's just switch the dates and places, and make it a Father Rufus story anyway."

"What, and destroy the authenticity? No thanks, buster. In any case, I was going to tell you this if you *had* got the job, so I'll tell you now too. Cantor have decided to keep Esther Gordon Framlingham breathing a while longer. So there's no big break."

"What do you mean, keep her breathing and there's no big break? I thought that was the precise reason there *was* a big break!"

"There's another teensy thing I neglected to tell you. The real Esther Gordon Framlingham has actually been dead sixteen years. When I told you that Cantor were looking for someone to ghostwrite the Esther Gordon Framlingham, maybe I should have said they were really looking for someone to replace the Esther Gordon Framlingham ghostwriter who's been churning the books out for the last decade and a half. But now they've changed their minds and keep it to the status quo. Sorry about that."

"Esther Gordon Framlingham has been dead sixteen years?"

"Her flesh has."

"Does her family know?" In a way, I was relieved. I was a big fan of Brother Rufus, but Father Rufus I could take or leave. But I had an idea. "Hey, what about this? Contemporary fifty-something virginal female part-time surveyor from Highgate with an arthritic left knee."

"Part-time surveyor, you say? Because of course you know the Donna Cable Mysteries by Rod Binks, but I think she's full-time ..."

"Definitely part-time," I said.

"Hmm. Interesting. You might have hit on something. Why don't you write me synopsis-and-three-chapters?"

Michael Jecks

No One Can Hear You Scream

'You ever read Sherlock Holmes, Hawk?'

John Hawkwood had a mild hangover, and opened his eyes with reluctance. Rain spattered against the windscreen, almost obliterating the view of grey, grime-streaked Victorian terraces. Another perfect morning in south London, he thought. Christmas lights were going up, tinsel stars dangling between lamp posts, a massive Santa on his sleigh over a store – all added to his depression. This was a time of year for children. As it was, he'd probably spend Christmas day in the pub – unless he could wangle a day in the station. At least there would be company either way.

'He was in a train, right? Heading off into the country, just like we are now, and he says something like, "Nothing and no one in London scares me half so much as the sight of all these sodding fields," right? 'Cos in a town, there's always someone to hear you, right, but in a field nobody's goin' to hear you scream. Sounds good, that: "Nobody's goin' to hear you scream!"'

Curran sniggered. Hawkwood's driver was at least twelve years his junior, a shorter man, maybe five feet ten, and running slightly to tubbiness, with jowls that only served to emphasise the vacancy of his expression. Apparently his father was a lawyer in a big city firm, rich and very clever, but he and Curran never spoke. When Curran mentioned his old man, it was with a cold bitterness that seemed strange in such a bland man.

Bland was being generous. If there was anything in his eyes, even a tiny spark of intelligence, Hawkwood wouldn't have minded, but as it was, Curran's lean, square features under the hard-man's fair crew-cut wore only a permanent dullness like a disappointed child.

Hawkwood turned away and sighed. 'It's been used. More or less.'

'What?'

'Ridley Scott used it. The director.'

The blank expression on Curran's face made Hawkwood grunt briefly. 'The film: *Alien*. They used the strapline, "In space, no one can hear you scream."'

Jimmy stared through the windscreen for a moment, a scowl of concentration darkening his features.

'Nah. Sorry, before me time, that.'

'Get a move on. You want to be late?'

'What, for the murder?' Curran said disinterestedly. 'Can't miss that.'

The house was one of very few in that wealthy area. There were five on the southern side of the road, none opposite, and all were huge. Each had sprawling grounds, walls, trees and thick undergrowth blocking each from neighbours. It reminded Hawkwood of Curran's words – would Sherlock Holmes have been repelled? Certainly few here could witness murder.

As the car surged along the roadway beneath oaks and beeches, Hawkwood found himself staring out over a patchwork landscape, with fields and woods clearly defined. The view made any house up here worth more than Hawkwood would earn in his whole life, a fact which ignited the bitterness of his jealousy. He could have made money if he'd chosen a different career, but nothing else had appealed. There were ways to make money in the police, but he wasn't having any of that, which was why he'd retire with little more than his house. He didn't even have a family now, not since his wife left him over a year ago, taking the girls with her.

Curran muttered: 'This is it.'

'It' was an elegant building maybe sixty years old. The windows were dark wood, the walls painted white, and the driveway curved gently to a triple garage. Whoever built it expected large parties, Hawkwood thought. There was space for at least twelve cars, because that's how many were already parked, their blue lights flickering among the trees like a laser show designed by a hippy on acid.

They parked in the road. Uniformed police demanded their ID and the two had to sign the register before they could enter the large hall. The first floor was galleried, and Hawkwood hesitated. From a door on his left he heard a woman's desperate, hacking sobs. Overhead came a child's thin wailing. Hawkwood set his shoulders grimly and followed Curran.

The sitting room was at least thirty feet long, delicately decorated with a pale carpet and cream furniture. One sofa and two comfortable chairs sat about a fireplace, a second grouping faced a huge plate-glass window that looked over the view. The coffee tables were pale oak, understated but expensive. Cushions matched the floor-length curtains, with gold patterns on a red background. The whole felt comfortably wealthy, but not ostentatious.

Today strangers had taken over. A photographer stood with his camera pointing at the body, a uniformed officer slowly panned a video camera about the room, another scribbled on a clipboard and handed out evidence bags, paper or plastic depending on the materials discovered. Forensic officers squatted, studying tiny particles. A window was smashed, and tiny shards of shattered glass glittered near the window. An officer was carefully collecting it.

On the floor beside the fire there was a section of lifted carpet. When Hawkwood wandered to it, he saw it exposed the circular face of a small safe.

Curran was talking to the officer with the clipboard, who welcomed Hawkwood with a resigned air.

'Hiya, Hawk.'

Hawkwood squatted at the corpse's side. 'What's it look like, George?'

Near at hand was a large cut glass whisky tumbler. A Glenmorangie bottle lay empty beside the sofa, and there was a stain in the carpet that stank of whisky.

'Robbery turned to murder, she says.' George's voice was toneless, like a man describing a snooker match. 'He was down here night. She came down first thing this morning and found him like this. Window gone, safe opened, and maybe a few hundred gone. He never kept more than that in there.'

'Right.' Both he and George had been through this too often. They knew the score.

The dead man was taller than Hawkwood, maybe six one or two, and had kept in good shape. He was about forty, with a pleasant, square face, fair hair that looked as though it would have been hard to tame, blue-grey eyes that wrinkled at the corners, and a full mouth. He had the look of a man who would have been good company. His death was caused by the heavy-bladed, black-handled cooking knife in his breast.

Hearing a familiar voice, Hawkwood glanced at the door.

The pathologist was a small, round-faced, balding, dapper man whom Hawkwood had never seen without a tie. He nodded at Hawkwood, and set about his work, extracting his tools from his briefcase. While thermometers took the room's temperature, and that of the body, Hawkwood asked, 'Anything obvious?'

'I'd guess he died quickly. One wound; not even defensive cuts on his hands. It must have been an entirely unexpected attack.'

Hawkwood nodded at Curran. 'Fine. Where's the wife?'

Elspeth Arnold sat at her dining table with a handkerchief held to her face, the dark-haired WPC at the window looking anxious. She looked too young to be guarding a widow. Hawkwood walked to her and muttered that she should take a seat herself. She gave him a grateful, pale grin, and slumped into a chair.

Hawkwood sat opposite Mrs Arnold. She looked up without emotion.

She was short, five one, five two at most. Perhaps on a good day she would have been pretty, but today wasn't a good day. She had a blotched, round face that looked petulant, with small eyes and a tip-tilted nose. Her mascara had run, and her hair was unbrushed.

Dressed in a pale blue sweatshirt and jeans, she was barefoot, as though she hadn't had time to shower or dress carefully.

'My name is Detective Inspector Hawkwood. This is Detective Sergeant Curran. We have to ask you some questions.'

'Anything. I've already told the others here...'

Her breath reeked from the scotch in the glass before her, a cut glass tumbler like the one on the floor beside her husband's body. The brand of whisky was the same as the empty bottle, he noticed. Perhaps they had bought it by the case. An ashtray sat on the table beside her, with stubs that had a distinctive golden band about their upper part. Each was stained with her pale lipstick.

'Yes. We are here to take your evidence. First...' he reached into his briefcase for his notepad and recorder. 'This is purely in case I miss something. Do you mind?' She waved a hand dismissively and he pressed the record button. 'Good. For the record, then, let me state that...'

He ran through the preliminary details, checking the time from his watch, giving the names of all in the room, and meanwhile he observed the woman, assessing her.

'You found him when you came down this morning?'

'Christ! He was just lying there,' she blurted, 'blood everywhere. And the Sabatier... God, I came out of there, and was sick all over the place.'

'What exactly happened? From when you woke up.'

'Well, I realised he hadn't come to bed. I came down as soon as I woke. I didn't want Amanda to... to wake him if he'd...'

'If he'd what?'

'If he'd got pissed.' She squirmed uncomfortably. It was a tiny movement, but he was aware of it, and so was she. She threw him a look, then averted her gaze, shifting in her seat. 'It happened sometimes. He'd drink a little too much and then...pass out, I suppose you'd say.'

'Had he been drinking last night?'

'Yes. A lot.'

'Why was that, Mrs Arnold?'

'He was a solicitor, Mr... sorry, Inspector Hawkwood. This morning I...' A hand flapped like a released bird.

'Just concentrate on what happened. You say that your husband was a solicitor. Last night he drank a lot.'

'Yes. He was a successful lawyer.' Her eyes rose and gazed about her at the room, up at the ceiling, at the furniture. There was a certain pride in her face then. 'He did very well. He was a company lawyer. High in the Law Society, too. But yesterday he lost another client, and he was... depressed about it.'

'Depressed? In what way?'

She flared, 'How do you think? He came here and got pissed, and... and...' As though realising she'd said more than she ought, she slumped. 'Do you mind if I smoke?'

Hawkwood watched as she took a long Rothmans International from a squashed, dark blue pack in her pocket and lighted it with a gold Dunhill. 'He got pissed?'

Already the story was pulling together in his mind. The sad, bitter, angry man arriving home, pouring himself a large one, shouting at his wife, perhaps punching her, enjoying the only control he had, the control of another person weaker than him. There was no bruising on her, but he knew wife-beaters knew where to hit so that the bruises were hidden – on the breast, the belly, the upper thighs. Abusers knew how to hide their work.

'Pissed?' she gave a bitter chuckle, smoke drifting from her nostrils. 'He was completely wasted. Out of his tree. Fucked! Is that clear enough?'

'So last night he arrived home. Was he already drunk?'

'He'd had a couple,' she said cautiously, and then gave a twisted grin. 'I suppose you aren't going to prosecute him now, are you? All right then, yes, he was several sheets to the wind when he got home.

I've seen him like that before. I wasn't going to... you can't win an argument with a drunk, you know.'

'When he came home, what happened?'

'I handed him a drink at the door and made him supper. I learned that long ago. There's no point asking, "How was your day, dear?" when he was like that.'

'And then what?'

'You aren't asking much about the robbery, are you?'

'I'm just getting a picture about the evening. I need to know everything,' Hawkwood said flatly. He couldn't tell her that the apparent robbery was already fading to an improbability in his mind compared with the other, more likely, scenario.

'Oh, all right. I left the bottle at his side. That was it. I went up to bed rather than suffer any...'

'Suffer any what?' Hawkwood asked, but he didn't need to press her. The cigarette was shaking slightly in her hand. She took a sip of her whisky, stared at the ashtray, and shook her head slowly, then lifted her chin with a certain pride.

'He was abusive. All right? He used to beat me. I took it, because I was petrified he'd turn on Amanda if I didn't let him. Christ, that was stupid, wasn't it? If I'd had any sense, I'd have left him, taken her with me.'

'But if you left him downstairs, you'd be safe?'

'He wouldn't go upstairs while there was a drink in the bottle.'

'What then? What about when the bottle was empty?'

'I hoped he'd be incapable of climbing the stairs. He'd already had a skinful and when I gave him the bottle I was fairly sure he'd sit down until he'd emptied it. I thought I was safe; I couldn't have got upstairs if I'd drunk all that. You know, when he first started beating me, years ago, I used to try to calm him with sex. It never worked. I was daft even to try that when he was drunk. He only grew more violent.'

'Was he all right when you left him?'

'What do you mean.'

'You went to the kitchen.'

'To cook.'

'The murder weapon was one of your knives. A kitchen knife.'

'I didn't...'

'You say that he could be violent. How was he when he was as drunk as he was last night?'

She looked up again, and her voice was choked. 'He was the devil. The devil himself!' Hawkwood studied her, desperate to see a proof of sadness, a hint of regret; but all he could see was self-pity.

'No one likes a wife beater,' Curran said.

They were in the sitting room again and Hawkwood grunted, exchanging a glance with George. They both knew members of the Croydon force who were considered 'good lads' by their colleagues, although rumours of their behaviour to their wives had spread widely. 'Maybe.'

George was about to speak when an officer appeared in the doorway. 'Sir? Thought you'd like to see this.'

'What is it?' George asked.

The officer passed him a photo. 'I was collecting the broken glass outside, and saw this.'

Hawkwood craned his neck and saw what the officer was pointing at. At the corner of the picture was a clean cigarette butt with a golden band around it, like a Rothmans International.

'It proves nothing,' Curran said. 'It could have been there for ages. Maybe she threw it out of the window days ago. Even yesterday.'

Hawkwood nodded. 'Possibly. Anything else?'

The officer nodded and handed him a second and third picture. 'Vomit. Not far from the window. Someone puked his guts up out there.'

Hawkwood was still outside, feeling marginally better, sitting on a bench in the garden and watching the forensic team, when the woman arrived.

She was a large woman – tall, strong, square-featured, with bright, intelligent eyes set in a face which had seen a lot of life. The tabloids would have characterised her as a lady of the manor, a 'toff', someone who was contemptibly unaware of the modern world. Curran appeared just as Hawkwood was introducing himself, and Curran's ill-concealed dislike made Hawkwood warm to her.

'Are you in charge here?'

She was holding two dogs, a Rottweiler and a Boxer, both straining. Curran kept his distance, but Hawkwood held out his hand to them. 'How can I help you?'

'You can't, I expect,' she said crisply. 'I want to see Mrs Arnold and her daughter to make sure that they are all right.'

'I am afraid that they are not seeing visitors. You'll understand why.'

'I live next door,' she said, jerking a thumb over her shoulder. 'I was going to offer to take Amanda away. It can't be good for her.'

'You only just realised that there was something going on?'

'Yes,' she said simply. 'I'm not one to peer between net curtains, officer.'

'Did you hear anything last night?'

'No. And these two were settled, too. Amy is a light sleeper.'

Hawkwood smiled at 'Amy', the Rottweiler. 'Was the marriage happy? In your opinion.'

She eyed him suspiciously. 'Trying to get the inside griff by plugging the neighbours? Yes, I'd say so. Wouldn't have suited me, but you can never tell what makes others happy, can you?'

'Why do you say that?'

'Well, it makes you wonder, doesn't it? In the summer it quite put us off sitting on the terrace. You could hear the shouts and screaming even when they had their windows shut. The poor child – what she had to live through.'

'Who, Amanda?'

'No, you fool. Oh! Sorry, shouldn't call an officer a fool, should I?' she said with a glint of devilment in her eye. 'No, I meant Elspeth. It was her whom he beat. We used to hear him roaring, then her shrieking, again and again. I sent Charles – that's my husband – over there once, and Elspeth came to the door. All but drunk with pain, slurring and tottering. She said she was fine, that she wasn't hurt, and he couldn't see a mark on her.'

'But?'

'I may be older, but I can read PD James and Barbara Vine. The worst abusers can hit without leaving a mark, can't they?'

Hawkwood saw no reason to comment. 'Is there anything else?'

'I suppose I ought to tell you. A couple of times, after we'd heard them having another shouting match, neither of them went out. He stayed behind, didn't go to work. I went to make sure that they were OK, and she came to the door, but she was clearly worried.'

'What did you conclude from that?'

'That he'd beaten her and didn't want her shooting her mouth off until the bruises were gone. He wouldn't want her going to the doctor, would he? So he kept her indoors.'

'What of the child?'

'She's suffered, I think.' Her eyes went to an upper storey window. 'What a life. If we heard their rows, what did Amanda see and hear? Poor girl. It's said that they've had Social Services in here for her. I expect that's all because of the fights. She's not normal. She never even wears make-up!'

Her scandalised voice made him grin as he thanked her and walked back into the house.

'See?' Curran hissed. 'That bastard deserved it anyway. She was an angel to put up with him.'

'She may have been, but if she stabbed him, she's a murderer,' Hawkwood said uncompromisingly.

'After years of abuse? He got what he deserved, like, and I'd...'

'Whether or not he deserved something, is for others to decide. For me, she committed homicide and deliberately put clues around the place to show us a different story. It was amateur, but the sort of thing that someone who watched the TV often enough would try. She lifted the carpet, emptied the safe, maybe, smashed the window. The only thing she did wrong was, leaving that fag butt out there.'

'Like I said, that was probably days old.'

'I doubt it. The woman's house-proud. She didn't routinely chuck fag ends through the window. That was the only one. No, I think she had a cigarette to calm her nerves out there, and puked because of what she'd done. She set about smashing windows and lifting carpets to throw us off the track.'

'She'd just got thumped, or was about to.'

'Maybe,' Hawkwood said. Struck with a thought, he continued, 'That's a good idea. Phone her doctor and ask if she's been prone to accidents – falling downstairs or walking into doors? Perhaps there's some mitigating stuff there. See whether she has a defence.'

There was one more potential witness whom he must reluctantly question, although he had to wait, thank God – a social worker had driven the child away. Instead, he wandered up to her room and leaned against the door jamb. Two days later, when he met her, that room would come back to him.

Only thirteen, she was already a smoker. Smoke had impregnated all her clothes. With the wide east-facing windows open, the smell would fade quickly enough, and since her mother was a smoker she probably wouldn't even detect the subtle odour. Smokers could rarely smell smoke on others.

It was a typical teenager's space. Drawers on the left, a large wardrobe, all painted white, while at her side was a bedside table with a clock radio and remote control for the large colour TV on top of the chest of drawers, next to a glass and pair of pills still enclosed in their bubbles of plastic, torn from a sheet. She hadn't taken the sedatives.

Seeing her for the first time, he thought Amanda Arnold would grow into a stunning woman. She had the best of her father's looks, with only a little of her mother's chubbiness to give her a certain softness. Calm grey eyes stared at him as Hawkwood introduced himself.

'Do you mind my asking you some questions?'

She sniffed. 'I don't know what I can say to help. Daddy's dead.'

'We'll find who did it.'

'That thief, I suppose.'

This was given in an odd, sarcastic tone of voice. It jarred on Hawkwood's ear. 'Did you hear anything odd that night?'

'The window. Yes. I heard that, I think. I didn't realise what it was at the time.'

Hawkwood nodded to himself. If what he had heard was true, she would have been used to hearing shouting and screaming through the night. 'What time was it?'

'I don't know.'

He nodded again and asked, 'Did your parents have an argument?'

'She was always on at him! Never gave him any peace. Said he was having affairs whenever he was working late, and never believed him!'

Hawkwood was shocked into silence. Beside him, he was sure that the WPC was rocked by this sudden bursting of words. It was as though the girl had bottled them up for years, and now was releasing them under an explosive pressure. The social worker at her side put a hand out, but Amanda snatched her own hand away.

'She drinks all the time, and by the time he got home, she was always out of it! She wanted more money always, just to buy stuff.'

Hawkwood was stunned into silence as the girl told of a family sinking into financial disaster. How Mr Arnold's company was failing, how Amanda had been pulled from her expensive public school and sent to a lesser one, how the cars had gone as Mrs Arnold's drinking rose to one and a half bottles of whisky a day, and how her husband tried to persuade her to go to Alcoholics Anonymous, and received more punches for his temerity.

It must have been a hell on earth for the man. Hawkwood could imagine all too clearly how he would have felt. His security gone, financial and marital, all he could do was protect his daughter. Hawkwood had done the same, in his own way. He felt the sympathy growing in his breast.

'You aren't a child, Amanda,' he said after a few moments. 'What do you think happened that night?'

'She killed him. This stuff about a robber – that's bollocks, isn't it? She lost it again and stabbed him.'

'That is a very serious...'

'Come on! She was pissed, almost out cold on the sofa when I got home. She couldn't even make it upstairs. She'd emptied the bottle. Poor dad was late home again. Not back until eight or so. She told me not to say anything, told me to support her story of a thief, but how could I? He was my dad. I loved him, I really loved him. Poor dad!'

Hawkwood stood as her features crumpled and grief washed away her maturity with tears.

'Wait!' she said as he got to the door. 'What will happen to me?'

Hawkwood glanced at the social worker. 'We'll make sure you're looked after.'

'You mean I'll have to go into a home? Why can't I go home? I can look after myself.'

Her voice had an edge of panic. Hawkwood tried to smile, but all he could see were his own daughters' faces as he admitted to those lies just to protect them. He prayed he had been right.

Curran met him in the hallway with a typewritten report. 'No mistake. The hospital confirms it. Mrs Arnold never had a fall. If anything, it was her husband who was the clumsy one. Thought he was good at DIY and often hurt himself. Broke his thumb once, and cracked some ribs when he fell from a ladder.' His face was grim. He had learned that his idol had clay feet.

'Let's ask her, then,' Hawkwood said.

Hawkwood sat heavily across from Mrs Arnold in the interview room. Her ashtray was already full with stubs, each with their own circle of lipstick under the gold band. Next to it was a mug of tea.

He took up his pen and checked the twin tape recorder. After introducing himself and the others in the room, he began.

'Mrs Arnold, I don't need to tell you that the whole story of a thief was fiction. Amanda's confirmed it. Your story of your husband's drinking and abuse were just that, a story. You made it up to conceal your crime.'

She said nothing. As he studied her features, her eyes brimmed, but there was nothing else.

'You abused him over years, didn't you? Once or twice he couldn't even go to work because you'd beaten him so viciously. Was that because you marked his face, or because you had actually harmed him? We know you didn't let him go to the door.'

'It's not true!' She picked up her mug of tea.

'It is. Your neighbours heard the rows. You did a good job, making them think you were the victim, didn't you? But who'd believe a big, strong man like him could be beaten up by a tiny woman? Except he was a gentleman, wasn't he? And he had no idea how to control you. Perhaps that upset you. Did you find him frustrating? Was that the cause of your anger? Was that why you drank? To soothe your frustration?'

She set the mug back down, and it rattled as it met the plastic.

It was an odd, unsatisfactory story, Hawkwood thought.

She had confessed. She had been in the kitchen when he came home, drunk again, and he sneered at her slurring and tottering. She'd reacted irrationally, grabbing a knife and going to him, screaming that he shouldn't have a go at her when it was his fault she drank – he was screwing his secretary every night. It wasn't enough that he was a failure in business, now he was trying to humiliate her. She wouldn't let a slut take her man, she said, and stabbed him.

Only later did she realise what she'd done. She woke in her own bed thinking that she'd had a nightmare, but going downstairs, seeking a hangover tonic, she found him. Rather than confess, she set up the elaborate fiction, breaking the window and lifting the carpet. She didn't even remember the cigarette end when Hawkwood mentioned it.

Curran didn't want to believe her. His face had shown his agitation, as though he wanted to grab her by the shoulders and tell her to shut up, to remember how badly she'd been treated, but still she had carried on, her voice calm apart from the occasional shudder.

'She stabbed him because she was drunk. Just because she was drunk.'

'After abusing him for years.'

'Why'd he let her?'

Hawkwood shrugged. 'He was a big man. How could he admit that he couldn't protect himself from his wife?'

'He could have defended himself.'

'Maybe he tried. But he was old school. His daughter went to public school, and I daresay he did too. Public schoolboys are brought up never to hit a woman. Perhaps that was it. It was easier to accept her violence than hurt her.'

'She was collected enough to go through the charade of the thief breaking in.'

'She can't have been all that collected,' Hawkwood said. 'She couldn't even remember that fag. Damn!'

'What?'

'I forgot to ask her about the vomit. Was she sick before or after breaking the window? How did that fit into things?'

Curran's face twisted. 'Who cares? The drunken bitch murdered her old man for sod-all reason. It's, like, completely sick, right? The whole fucking thing.'

Hawkwood nodded, but absently. He felt distaste for Curran. He'd wanted Mrs Arnold to be a heroine because that suited his own world view because his mother had been a victim of abuse. Anything that deviated from Curran's norms offended him. Mother love! It was why the Madonna and Child had worked so well as Christian propaganda. For Hawkwood there was a poignant perfection about it.

Suddenly another picture presented itself to him: a cigarette butt lying in the grass; and even as he conceived the link, he felt his stomach lurch and a cold shiver attack his spine. 'Jesus Christ!'

'What? Hawk? What's the matter?'

Hawkwood let the door crash back against the wall as he entered the room. 'So, Mrs Arnold. Tell me, where were you sick?'

'What?' Her startled gaze went from him to Curran and back. 'What is this? You've got my confession. I thought you...'

'Answer the question. Where were you sick?'

'I don't know – in the downstairs toilet.'

'And outside, while you were making up your story and smashing the windows? Where were you sick then?'

'I don't know. What does it matter?'

'We found a cigarette outside. You smoke a lot, don't you?'

'So what?'

'Perhaps that's why your daughter smokes.'

'She smokes because teenagers like living dangerously. They can't assess future risks like lung cancer.'

'You didn't see her smoking, did you? You had passed out. Did she put you to bed?"

'I…No, I was…'

'This is all a lie, isn't it?' Hawkwood said, picking up the confession. 'Is there anything you have told us so far which has been true? Any one thing?'

'You have my confession. Do I have to go through this abuse as well? Isn't that enough for you?'

'No. When kids start to smoke, they often pinch their parents' fags, you know. Just like they take booze from the cupboard.'

'So what?'

'That fag outside had no lipstick on it.'

She sneered. 'So what? It was early. Do you think all women put make-up on as soon as they get up?'

'I'll bet your daughter doesn't.'

She paled. 'That's mad!'

'There's one thing a mother will always protect – her child. Even when that child is mad and has killed her own father.'

'I… No. You're wrong.'

'Do you want a lawyer?'

She opened her mouth as though to refuse, and when Hawkwood saw her face crumple, he picked up her mug himself and went to refill it.

She confessed. When the forensic evidence was sifted, there were many traces of Amanda's crime, and the judge agreed to her plea of insanity.

Almost a year later Hawkwood met Elspeth Arnold again. He was leaving the shopping centre, parcels wrapped ready for his girls. Hopefully this year they'd actually open them. Last year they'd returned them unopened. He'd sat and stared at them for a whole morning, slowly sipping from a bottle of whisky. At lunch he'd thrown them away with the empty bottle.

'Inspector.'

'Mrs Arnold.' Here, in open territory, he felt curiously guilty and furtively looked around for an escape. 'I hoped to hear from Amanda, you know. She won't even let me phone her.'

'I'm sorry.'

'I can't understand why she did it.'

Hawkwood succumbed to his better feelings and took her to a coffee bar where he bought them large cappucinos.

'I've not touched a drop since, you know.'

He smiled. Since that whisky, he'd tried to stop too. He hadn't.

'Why did she kill him? Why not kill me? It was me she hated.'

'I think she despised him for his weakness. She helped carry you to bed but she snapped. She'd had enough of looking after you both. That was how she viewed it.'

'Something I never had an opportunity to ask you: how did you realise it wasn't me?'

Hawkwood stared over her shoulder at a mother with a pushchair at the till. 'There were some clues. I didn't think you'd be so slapdash as to invent such a good alibi and then wreck it like that. And I realised that Amanda wasn't actually so upset about her father's death. She didn't even take the tranquillisers the doctor gave her. That was odd. Then again, she wore no make-up and the cigarette didn't have lipstick on it. I didn't think you'd throw a cigarette away in your garden either. It wasn't the sort of thing you'd do even if you were drunk at the time.'

'I won't be again.'

'No, I doubt you will.'

'What else was there?'

'It was your drunkenness. Even Amanda let slip she'd had to help you to bed. If you were that pissed, he'd be able to protect himself. God, he was used to your temper, wasn't he? If you were as drunk as you and Amanda said, he'd have been able to at least throw a hand in the way and get a slashed palm but he had nothing. He obviously wasn't expecting to be stabbed, and that meant it was less likely to be you who killed him. He would have expected you to stab him. There was only one person in the house who could have stabbed him without his anticipating it.'

'I suppose.'

Hawkwood finished his coffee and the two separated. He was glad that he hadn't had to explain the last detail that Amanda had told him.

She had stabbed her father from frustration because he stopped her killing her mother, the source of, as she saw it, her father's impotence and weakness as well as her own miserable existence. Elspeth had been passed out on the sofa when he returned home. Amanda heard him weeping in the sitting room. She went to comfort him, and then fetched the knife and told him to stab Elspeth. They would explain it as a bungled murder, she said. When he refused, she snatched it back, but he stopped her killing her mother, so she struck out at him in frustration.

She carried Elspeth upstairs and put her in bed, before returning downstairs and going outside. She deliberately smashed the window and lit up a cigarette from her mother's pack, leaving it prominently on the grass. She made herself sick and left the vomit there too, making sure that her mother would be the obvious suspect.

Hawkwood stood under a street light and contemplated the scurrying crowds of people preparing for their happy Christmas. God, he needed a drink!

Her murder almost worked. Because even though the neighbours were some distance away, they still heard the screams. It almost worked because they assumed the worst of him, her father. No one could believe the little girl could have killed him. Just as they didn't realise it was her mother who was the abuser in the family.

'So what do you think of that, eh, Holmes?' he muttered and wandered through the twilight towards home and the pub.

The second or third time Kiley went out with Kate Keenan, it had been to the theatre, an opening at the Royal Court. Her idea. A journalist with a column in the *Independent* and a wide brief, she was on most people's B list at least.

The play was set in a Brick Lane squat, two shiftless young men and a meant-to-be fifteen-year-old girl: razors, belt buckles, crack cocaine. Simulated sex and pain. One of the men seemed to be under the illusion, much of the time, that he was a dog. At the interval, they elbowed their way to the bar through louche suits and little black dresses with tasteful cleavage, New Labour voters to the core.

'Challenging,' said a voice on Kiley's left. 'A bit full on,' said another. 'But relevant. Absolutely relevant.'

'So what do you think?' Kate asked.

'I think I'll meet you outside.'

'What do you mean?'

She knew what he meant.

They took the tube, barely talking, to Highbury and Islington, a stone's throw from where Kate lived. Across the road she turned towards him, a hand upon his arm. 'I don't think this is going to work out, do you?'

Kiley shrugged and thought probably not.

Between Highbury Corner and the Archway, almost the entire length of the Holloway Road, there were only three fights in progress, one between two women in slit skirts and halter tops, who clawed and swore at each other, rolling on the broad pavement outside the Rocket while a crowd bayed them on. Propped inside a telephone box close by the railway bridge, a man stared out frozen-eyed, a hypodermic needle sticking out of the scabbed flesh of his bare leg. Who needs theatre? Kiley asked himself.

His evenings free, Kiley was at liberty to take his usual seat in the Lord Nelson, a couple of pints of Marston's Pedigree before closing, then a slow stroll home through the backdoubles to his second-floor flat in a shabby terraced house among other shabby houses, too far from a decent primary school for the upwardly mobile middle-class professionals to have appropriated in any numbers.

Days, he sat and waited for the telephone to ring, the fax machine to chatter into life; the floor was dotted with books he'd started to read and would never finish, pages from yesterday's paper were spread out across the table haphazardly. Afternoons, if he wasn't watching a film at the local Odeon, he'd follow the racing on TV – Kempton, Doncaster, Haydock Park. *Investigations*, read the ad in the local press, *Private and Confidential. All kinds of security work undertaken. Ex-Metropolitan Police.* Kiley was never certain whether that last put off as many potential clients as it impressed.

Seven years in the Met, two seasons in professional soccer and then freelance: Kiley's CV so far.

The last paid work he'd done had been for Adrian Costain, a sports agent and PR consultant Kiley knew from one of his earlier lives. Kiley's task: babysitting an irascible yet charming American movie actor in London on a brief promotional visit. After several years of mayhem and marriages to Meg or Jennifer or Julia, he was rebuilding his career as a serious performer with a yearning to play Chekhov or Shakespeare.

'For Christ's sake,' Costain had said, 'keep him away from the cocaine and out of the tabloids.'

It was fine until the last evening, a celebrity binge at a Members Only watering hole in Soho. What exactly went down in the small men's toilet between the second and third floors was difficult to ascertain for certain, but the resulting black eye and bloodied lip were front-page juice to every picture editor between Wapping and Faringdon. Today the UK, tomorrow the world. Costain was incandescent.

'What did you expect me to do,' Kiley asked, 'go in there and hold his dick?'

'If necessary, yes.'

'You're not paying me enough, Adrian.'

He thought it would be a while before Costain put work his way again.

He put through a call to Maggie Hambling, a solicitor in Kentish Town for whom he sometimes did a little investigating, either straining his eyes at the local land registry or long hours hunkered down behind the wheel of his car, waiting for evidence of some small near-lethal indiscretion.

But Maggie was in court and her secretary dismissed him with a cold promise to tell her he'd called. The connection was broken almost before the words were out of her mouth.

Kiley pulled on his coat and went out on to the street; for early December it was almost mild, the sky opaque and indecipherable. There was a route he took when he wanted to put some distance beneath his feet: north up Highgate Hill, past the spot where Dick Whittington was supposed to have turned again, and through Waterlow Park, down alongside the cemetery and into the Heath, striking out past the ponds to Kenwood House, a loop then that took him round the side of Parliament Hill and down towards the tennis courts, the streets that would eventually bring him home.

Tommy Duggan was waiting for him, sitting on the low wall outside the house, checking off winners in the *Racing Post*.

'How are you, Tommy?'

'Pretty fine.'

Duggan, deceptively slight and sandy-haired, had been one of the best midfielders Kiley had ever encountered in his footballing days, Kiley on his way up through the semi-pro ranks when Duggan was slipping down. During Kiley's brace of years with Charlton Athletic, Duggan had come and gone within the space of two months. Bought in and sold on.

'Still like a flutter,' Kiley said, eyeing the paper at Duggan's side.

'Academic interest only nowadays.' Duggan smiled. 'Isn't that what they say?'

The addictions of some soccer players are well documented, the addiction and the cure. Paul Merson. Tony Adams. Stories of others running wild claim their moment in the news, then fade. But any manager worth his salt will know the peccadilloes of those he might sign: drugs, drink, gambling, having at least one of his team-mates watch as he snorts a line of cocaine from between the buttocks of a four hundred pounds an hour whore. You look at your need, your place in the table, assess the talent, weigh up the risk.

When Tommy Duggan came to Charlton he was several thousand in debt to three different bookmakers and spent more time with his cell phone than he did on the training ground. Rumour had it, his share of his signing-on fee was lost on the back of a spavined three-year-old almost before the ink had dried on the page.

Duggan went and Kiley stayed: but not for long.

'Come on inside,' Kiley said.

Duggan shrugged off his leather coat and chose the one easy chair.

'Tea?'

'Thanks, two sugars, aye.'

What the hell, Kiley was wondering, does Tommy Duggan want with me?

'You're not playing any more, Tom?' Kiley asked, coming back into the room.

'What do you think?'

Watching *Sky Sport* in the pub, Kiley had sometimes glimpsed Duggan's face, jostling for space among the other pundits ranged across the screen.

'I had a season with Margate,' Duggan said. 'After I come back this last time from the States. Bastard'd shove me on for the last twenty minutes – "Get among 'em. Tommy, work the magic. Turn it round."' Duggan laughed. 'Every time the ball ran near, there'd be some donkey anxious to kick the fuck out of me. All I could do to stay on my feet, never mind turn round.'

He drank some tea.

'Nearest I get to a game nowadays is coaching a bunch of kids over Whittington Park. Couple of evenings a week. That's what I come round to see you about. Thought you might like to lend a hand. Close an' all.'

'Coaching?'

'Why not? More than a dozen of them now. More than I can handle.'

'How old?'

'Thirteen, fourteen. Best of them play in this local league. Six-a-side. What d'you think? 'Less your evenings are all spoken for, of course.'

Kiley shook his head. 'Can't remember the last time I kicked a ball.'

'It'll come back to you,' Duggan said. 'Like falling off a bike.'

Kiley wasn't sure if that was what he meant or not.

There were eleven of them the first evening Kiley went along, all shapes and sizes. Two sets of dreadlocks and one turban. One of the black kids, round-faced, slightly pudgy in her Arsenal strip, was a girl. Esther.

'I ain't no mascot, you know,' she said, after Duggan had introduced them. 'I can run rings round this lot.'

'My dad says he saw you play once,' said a lad whose mum had ironed his David Beckham shirt straight from the wash. 'He says you were crap.'

'Your dad'd know crap right enough, wouldn't he, Dean,' Duggan said. 'Living with you.'

The rest laughed and Dean said, 'Fuck off,' but he was careful to say it under his breath.

'Okay, let's get started,' Tommy Duggan said. 'Let's get warmed up.'

After a few stretching exercises and a couple of circuits of the pitch, Duggan split them up into twos and threes practising basic ball skills, himself and Kiley moving between them, watching, offering advice.

No more than twenty minutes or so of that and their faces were bright with sweat under the floodlights.

'Now,' Duggan said, 'let's do a little work on corners, attacking, defending, staying alert. Jack, why don't you send a few over, give us the benefit of that sweet right foot.'

Kiley was sweating like the rest, feeling his forty years. Either his tracksuit had shrunk or he'd put on more weight than he'd thought. The first corner was struck too hard and sailed over everyone's heads, but after that he settled into something of a rhythm and was almost disappointed when Duggan called everyone together and divided them into teams.

Like most youngsters they had a tendency to get drawn out of position and follow the ball, but some of the passing was thoughtful and neat, and only luck and some zealous defending prevented a hatful of goals. Dean, in his Beckham shirt, hand forever aloft demanding the ball, was clearly the most gifted but also the most likely to kick out in temper, complain loudly if he thought he'd been fouled.

When he slid a pass through for Esther to run on to and score with a resounding drive, the best he could muster was 'Jammy cow!'

Game over, kids beginning to drift away, Duggan offered to buy Kiley a pint. There was a pub on the edge of the park that Kiley had not been into before.

'So what did you think?' Duggan asked. They were at a table near the open door.

'About what?'

'This evening, you enjoy it or what?'

'Yeah, it was okay. They're nice enough kids.'

'Most of them.'

Kiley nodded. The muscles in the backs of his legs were already beginning to ache.

'You'll come again, then?'

'Why not? Not as if my social calendar's exactly full.'

'No girlfriend?'

'Not just at present.'

'But there was one?'

'For a while, maybe.'

'What happened?'

Kiley shrugged and supped his beer. 'You?' he said.

Duggan lit a cigarette. 'The only women I meet are out for a good time and all they can get. Either that or else they've got three kids back home with the babysitter and they're looking for someone to play dad.'

'And you don't fancy that?'

'Would you?'

Kiley wasn't certain; there were days – not so many of them – when he thought he might. 'No,' he said.

Without waiting to be asked, Duggan fetched two more pints. 'Where d'you meet her anyway?' he said. 'This ex of yours.'

'I was working,' Kiley said. 'Security. Down on the South Bank. She'd just come out from this Iranian movie.'

'She's Iranian?'

'No. The film was Iranian. She's English. Kate. Kate Keenan.'

'Sounds Irish.'

'Maybe. A generation or so back maybe.'

'You're cut up about it,' Duggan said.

'Not really.'

'No, of course not,' Duggan said, grinning. 'You can tell.'

Kate's column in the *Indie* questioned the morality of making art out of underclass deprivation and serving it up as a spectacle for audiences affluent enough to afford dinner and the theatre, and then a taxi home to their three-quarters of a million plus houses in fashionable Islington and Notting Hill.

Under Duggan's watchful eye and with Kiley's help, the six-a-side team won their next two games, Dean being sent off in the second for kicking out at an opponent in retaliation and then swearing at the referee.

Margaret Hambling offered Kiley three days' work checking up on a client who had been charged with benefit fraud over a period in excess of two years.

'Come round my gaff, why don't you?' Tommy Duggan said one night after training. 'See how the other half lives.'

And winked.

Drained by two lots of child support, which he paid intermittently but whenever he could, Duggan had sold his detached house in Totteridge and bought a thirties semi-detached in East Finchley, half of which he rented out to an accountant struggling with his MBA.

In the main room there were framed photographs of Duggan's glory days on the walls and soiled grey carpet on the floor. Clothes lay across the backs of chairs, waiting to be washed or ironed. On a table near the window were a well-thumbed form book, the racing pages, several cheap ballpoints, a telephone.

'Academic?' said Kiley, questioningly.

Duggan grinned. 'Man's got to have a hobby.'

He took Kiley to a Hungarian restaurant on the high street where they had cherry soup and goulash spiced with smoked paprika. A bottle of wine.

'Good, uh?' Duggan said, pushing away his plate.

'Great,' Kiley said. 'What's the pitch?'

Duggan smiled with his eyes. 'Just a small favour.'

The casino was on a narrow street between Soho and Shaftesbury Avenue, passing trade not one of its concerns. Instead of a bouncer with overfed muscles, Kiley was greeted at the door by a silvered blonde in a tailored two-piece.

'I'm here to see Mr Stephen.'

'Certainly, sir. If you'll come this way.' Her slight accent was Scandinavian.

Mr Stephen's name wasn't really Stephen. Not originally, at least. He had come to England from Malta in the late Fifties when the East End gangsters were starting to lose their grip on gambling and prostitution up West; had stood his ground and received the razor scars to prove it, though these had since been surgically removed. Now gambling was legal and he was a respectable businessman. Let the Albanians and the Turks fight the Yardies over heroin and crack cocaine, he had earned his share portfolio, his place in the sun.

The blonde handed Kiley over to a brunette who led him to a small lift at the far side of the main gaming room. There was no background music, no voice raised above the faint whirring of roulette wheels, the hushed sounds of money being made and lost.

Kiley was glad he'd decided to wear his suit, not just his suit but his suit and tie.

'Have you visited our casino before?' the brunette asked him.

'I'm afraid not, no.'

One of her eyes was brown and the other a greyish green.

When he stepped out of the lift there was an X-ray machine, the kind you walk through in airports; Kiley handed the brunette his keys and small change, and she gave them back to him at the other side.

'Mr Kiley for Mr Stephen,' she said to the man at the end of the short corridor.

The man barely nodded; doors were opened and closed. Stephen's inner sanctum was lined with books on two sides, mostly leather-bound; screens along one wall afforded high-angle views of the casino's interior. Stephen himself sat behind a desk, compact, his face the colour of walnut, bald head shining as if he had been recently buffed.

A few days before, Kiley had spoken to one of his contacts at Scotland Yard, a sergeant when he and Kiley had served together, now a detective superintendent.

'The casino's a front,' the superintendent told him.

'Prestige. He doesn't lose money on it exactly, but with all those overheads, that area, he'd make more selling the site. It's the betting shops that fetch in the money, one hundred and twenty nationwide. That and the fact he keeps a tight ship.'

'Can you get me in to see him?' Kiley had asked.

'Probably. But nothing more. We've no leverage, Jack, I'm sorry.'

Now Kiley waited for Stephen to acknowledge him, which he did with a small gesture of a manicured hand, no suggestion that Kiley should take a seat.

'Tommy Duggan,' Kiley said. 'He owes you money. Not a lot in your terms, maybe, but...' Kiley stopped and waited, then went on, 'He says he's been threatened. Not that you'd know about that directly, not your concern, but I imagine if you wanted you could get it stopped.'

Stephen looked at him through eyes that had seen more than Kiley, far more, and survived.

'Do you follow soccer at all, Mr Stephen?' Kiley asked.

No response.

'With some players it's speed, with others it's power, sheer force. Then there are those who can put their foot on the ball, look up and in that second see the perfect pass and have the skill to make it, inch perfect, thirty, forty yards crossfield.'

Something moved behind the older man's eyes. 'Liam Brady,' he said. 'Rodney Marsh.'

'Right,' said Kiley. 'Hoddle. LeTissier. Tommy, too. On his day Tommy was that good.'

Stephen held Kiley's gaze for a moment longer, then slipped his wristwatch free and placed it on the desk between them. 'Your Tommy Duggan, he owes close to one hundred thousand pounds. Each time the hands of that watch move round, he owes more.' He picked up the watch and weighed it in the palm of his hand. 'You tell him if he makes payments, regular, if the debt does not increase, I will be patient. Bide my time. But if he loses more…'

'I'll tell him,' Kiley said.

Stephen set the watch back on his wrist. 'Do you gamble, Mr Kiley?'

Kiley shook his head.

'In gambling, there is only one winner. In the end.'

'Thanks for your time,' Kiley said.

Almost imperceptibly Stephen nodded and his eyes returned their focus to the screens on the wall.

'Good evening, sir,' said the brunette in the lift. 'Good evening, sir,' said the blonde. 'Be sure to come again.'

'Jack, you're a prince,' Duggan said, when Kiley recounted the conversation.

Kiley wasn't certain what, if anything, he'd achieved.

'Room for manoeuvre, that's what you've got me. Pressure off. Time to recoup, study the field.' He smiled. 'Don't worry. Jack. Nothing rash.'

There was a message from Kate on his answerphone. 'Perhaps I was a little hasty. How about a drink, Wednesday evening?'

Wednesday was soccer training. Kiley called back and made it Thursday. The wine bar at Highbury Corner was only a short walk from Kate's house; from there it was only two flights of stairs to her bed.

'Something on your mind, Jack?'

There was and then there wasn't. Only later, his head resting in the cleft between Kate's bare calf and thigh, did it come back to him.

'He'll carry on gambling, won't he?' Kate said, when she had finished listening.

'Probably.'

'It's an illness, Jack, a disease. If he won't get proper help, professional help, there's nothing you can do.'

He turned over and she stroked his back and when he closed his eyes he was almost immediately asleep. In a short while she would wake him and send him home, but for now she was comfortable, replete. Maybe, she was thinking, it was time for another piece on gambling in her column.

Duggan had returned from his second spell in the States with a pony-tail and a fondness for Old Crow over ice and down home butt-dirty country music, bluegrass and pedal-steel and tales of love gone wrong. Nothing flash, no rhinestones, the real thing.

Back in England, the ponytail lasted until the first time he watched Seaman run out at Highbury and realised how affected it looked; he toned down his new-found love of bourbon but still listened to the music whenever he could. In a music store off Upper Street, less than a week ago, he'd picked up a CD by Townes Van Zandt, *A Far Cry from Dead*. Country blues with a twist.

Sometimes I don't know where this dirty road is taking me
Sometimes I can't even see the reason why
I guess I'll keep on gamblin', lots of booze and lots of ramblin'
It's easier than just a-waitin' round to die

Playing it was like pushing your tongue against an abscessed tooth.

He had seen Van Zandt in London in 'ninety-seven, one of the last gigs he ever played. Standing sweating in the Borderline, a crowded little basement club off Charing Cross Road, he had watched as Van Zandt, pale and thin and shaking, had begun song after song, only to stop, mid-verse, forgetting the words, hearing another tune. His fingers failed to grip the neck of the guitar, he could scarcely balance on the stool. Embarrassed, upset voices in the crowd began to call out, telling him to take a break, rest, telling him it was okay, but still he stumbled on. Dying before their eyes.

Two days before, Duggan had placed the first instalment of his payback money on a four-horse accumulator and, on the small betting shop screen, watched the favourite come through on the inside in the final race and leave his horse stranded short of the line.

Flicking the remote, he played the song again.

The money from the recording, some of it at least, would go to Van Zandt's widow and their kids. Duggan hadn't seen either his daughter or his two sons in years; he didn't even know where one of the boys was.

There were some cans of lager in the fridge, the tail end of a bottle of scotch; when he'd finished those he put on his coat and followed the familiar path to the Bald-Faced Stag.

Ten minutes short of closing, a motorbike pulled up outside the pub. Without removing his helmet, the pillion rider jumped off and went inside. Duggan was standing at the bar, drink in hand, staring up aimlessly at the TV. The pillion rider pulled an automatic pistol from inside his leather jacket, shot Duggan twice in the head at close range and left.

Duggan was dead before he hit the floor.

Several evenings later Kiley called the kids around him behind one of the goals. In the yellowing light, their breath floated grey and clear. He talked to them about Tommy Duggan, about the times he had seen him play; he told them how much Duggan wanted them to do well. One or two had tears in their eyes, others scuffed their feet in the ground and looked away.

'Who cares?' Dean said when Kiley had finished. 'He was never any bloody good anyway.'

Without deliberation, without meaning to, Kiley hit him: an open-handed slap across the face which jolted the boy's head back and round.

'You bastard! You fuckin' bastard!'

There were tears on his face now and the marks left by Kiley's hand stood out livid on his cheek.

'I'm sorry,' Kiley said. Some part of him felt numb, shocked by what he'd done.

'Fuck you!' the boy said and turned on his heel for home.

Dean lived in one of the flats that bordered Wedmore Street, close by the park. The man who answered the door was wearing jeans and a fraying Motorhead T-shirt, and didn't look too happy to be pulled away from whatever was playing, over-loud, on the TV.

'I'm Jack Kiley,' Kiley said.

'You hit my boy.'

'Yes.'

'You've got some balls, showing up round here.'

'I wanted to explain, apologise.'

'He says you just laced into him, no reason.'

'There was a reason.'

'Dean,' the man called back over his shoulder, 'turn that fuckin' thing down.' And then, 'All right, then, let's hear it.'

Kiley told him.

The man sighed and shook his head. 'That mouth of his, I'm always telling him it's going to get him into trouble.'

'I should never have lost my temper. I shouldn't have hit him.'

'My responsibility, right?' Dean's father said. 'Down to me.'

Kiley said nothing.

'What you did, maybe knock a bit of sense into him.'

'Maybe,' Kiley said, unconvinced.

'There's nothing else?'

'No.' Kiley took a step away.

'Tommy Duggan, what happened to him. It was wrong.'

'Yes.'

'Now that he's, you know, you think you might take over the team, the coaching?'

'For a bit, maybe,' Kiley said. 'It was Tommy's thing really, not mine.'

'Yeah. Yeah, that's right, I suppose.'

The door closed and Kiley took the stairs two at a time.

When he phoned Kate, she began by putting him off, a piece to finish, an early start, but then, hearing something in his voice, she changed her mind. 'Come round.'

The first glass of wine she poured, Kiley finished almost before she had started hers.

'If you just wanted to get drunk you could have done that on your own.'

'That's not what I wanted.'

He leaned against her and she held him, her breath warm on the back of his neck. 'I'm sorry about your friend,' she said.

'It's a waste.'

'It always is.'

After a while, Kiley said, 'I keep thinking there was something more I could've done.'

'It was his life. His choice. You did what you could.'

It was quiet. Often at Kate's there would be music playing but not this evening. From the hiss of tyres on the road outside it had started to rain. At the next coaching session, Kiley thought, he would apologise to Dean again in front of everyone, see if he couldn't get the lad to acknowledge what he'd said was wrong: start off on a new footing, give themselves a chance.

Luckily, they uncovered the grave on Day One.

They would only be given five days to finish; their more famous competitors usually had three, but *The Trowel 'Tecs* were beginners and were working up their act. At Mordaunt Castle they were confident of creating good TV, because it had been known since the sixteenth century that there were 'anciente ruines' in the grounds. Sir Mawdesley Mordaunt – the Elizabethan poet, statesman and home owner – had written to Sir Philip Sidney that the stones on which he once stubbed his toe while crossing the paddock might date 'fromme ye tyme of ye grate Julius Caesar'. So *The Trowel 'Tecs* were hoping to discover a previously unknown Roman road. They would settle for that, though their greater objective was to demonstrate that Mordaunt Castle had been continuously occupied since at least the first century of the Common Era (the TV diggers were very postmodern in their terminology) and that it stood on the site of a Roman fort. They always announced objectives of this type, though they were added to the programme last, once it was known whether the team had found anything.

Had the young, sunburned archaeologists looked up while they worked, they *might* have observed above them, peering over the battlements, the distant heads of three curious bystanders. Watching was a quiet group of ghosts. While less real, they were much more realistic than *The Trowel 'Tecs*. Sir Mawdesley Mordaunt was particularly intense, since it was his four-hundred-year-old theory being tested in the trench below and he really did not want to find that he had misled that famed lover of learning, Sir Philip Sidney.

Sir Mawdesley was flanked by his eternal companions. Major Penitence Rackstraw of the New Model Army, who had died in a castle dungeon during the Civil War, and the White Lady, a daft girl who submitted to anorexia when it was called dying of love. Normally the Black Dog gambolled around annoying them, but he was down below, sniffing among the archaeologists, his medieval nose wildly excited by the whiffs of historic rubbish pits that clung to their boots. Ed, the TV director, scratched his groin; however, that was a frequent occurrence and not caused by the Dog.

The Trowel 'Tecs was a new programme from the Bandwagon

Channel. Deliberately set up as part of Bandwagon's youth-flavoured culture strand, it was supposed to be a 'more accessible' rival to its more famous (and perfectly accessible) competitor. A focal group had suggested that the blatant rip-off needed a celebrity presenter, two eccentric archaeologists with vivid accents, and a very attractive, extremely intelligent woman in shorts. *The Trowel 'Tecs* could hire only one senior archaeologist, though Rick 'Plummy' Duff was good value: he spoke of postholes in a warm burr like the molten jam in a microwaved Pop Tart. For glamour, they managed to get the excellent Xenobia Smith, who yearned to be on rescue digs in Mesopotamia, but her mum wouldn't let her go to a war zone. After hiring a couple of cameramen and a snack wagon, the producers had had their hearts set on a TV cook for presenter, but could only afford a reject from *Pets in Peril*. That Darren, the one the goat once bit. He knew nothing about archaeology. No problem: his job was to run about fast and breathlessly read the autocue. He still had post-traumatic stress after the goat incident; they had promised there would be no animals here, but Darren had a funny feeling that someone was winding him up. For once he was right. He was being licked by the ectoplasmic tongue of the Black Dog. It sniffed his trousers intimately. Darren had a funny turn.

Sir Mawdesley huffed in his ruff as the castle's owner appeared, lurking with sleazy intent near the girl caterers as they handed out feta sandwiches to the volunteer archaeologists. Known to the ghosts as the Current Incompetent, he was taking a keen interest in the TV programme, especially where it involved young women in cotton vests. Sir Hardwicke Hall was a dastardly knight of industry who had bought the castle (along with his knighthood) during the decline of stately houses after the war. He had squeezed a great deal of ticket money from the public, but now toyed with reselling to a developer who would turn it into a business conference centre. More recently he had been in email consultation with Ainslie Mordaunt, the once-hippie granddaughter of the last family occupant, now a dotcom millionairess, who wanted to reacquire her heritage. Sir Hardwicke thought she was a boy, which was just as well. His appalling past behaviour included the time he chased a nice young woman from English Heritage all around the Buttery, causing her to go back to the office in tears and – when the Department refused to support her claim of sexual harassment – to ask for a move to Pensions.

To the TV people, nervous property owners were a regular menace. When Sir Hardwicke started hovering, they prepared to keep him out of the way among the potwashers. However, his anxiety caused murmurs of a different kind among the ghosts on the battlements. They had despised most recent owners of the castle, though the Current Incompetent had incurred more contempt than the rest. His modernisation was particularly crass and as a punishment they had subjected him to an array of chills, smells, and bad resonances. Worse, they knew he had something to hide.

They could do nothing about it. Interfering in the future was against the rules.

Xenobia Smith was ecstatic. Trench One contained a skeleton. The Trowel 'Tecs would now have to wait for statutory confirmation that it was old enough to count as archaeology not foul play. The police had been called and the coroner informed. The delays to their filming were outweighed by the fact that having police in attendance would draw the press, while bones always made for good ratings. They were happy. The ghosts could wait too. They had time on their hands perpetually. And *they* could see something even more interesting. A Roman was sitting on the edge of the trench.

He was a clean-shaven, short-haired dark man in coarse woollen underpants and one-toed knitted socks, looking bleary. Coping with daylight again was making him panic. It was obvious he felt a bit bendy as he looked down in puzzlement at his own skeleton, which lay half curled at his feet. He reacted very slowly. He had been there a long time.

Without consultation – for they had been together for centuries and could read each others' minds – the ghosts stepped off the parapet. Sir Mawdesley and the Major disappeared, then rematerialised neatly at ground level. Deprived of sex while living, the White Lady had become hopelessly keen on it since, so she wafted slowly all the way down, just so she could experience the thrill of her draperies moulding themselves to her meagre body. Well, disembody.

Together the ghosts approached the new arrival. He saw them. As a fellow ghost he was bound to. Spirits would be constantly bumping into each other – and passing awkwardly through one another – were not this the norm; there is traffic control in the afterlife. Courteously they stood nearby, allowing him to react in his own time.

'Don't sit there!' snapped a passing archaeologist. More perceptive than his colleagues, he had spotted the Roman. 'Never sit on the edge of a trench; haven't you been taught anything?' In a kinder voice he went on, 'You could crumble the edge, get loose spoil all over the cleaned area. Besides, on a telly set you look untidy.'

Uncomprehending, the Roman struggled to rise; his phantom buttocks sank deeper into the turf, passing down through broken willow-pattern dishes, past an interesting bellarmine jar, and almost as far as the crude grey rim of a basic Bronze Age cooking pot. At once Sir Mawdesley stepped forward and warned him to think himself into motion like a bubble rising in a millstream. The metaphysics were lost on the Roman, but he responded better to some brisk advice from Major Rackstraw. This Roman must have had some military training. It was hard to tell, now he was wearing only underpants, but when ordered to stand to and present his musket, he straightened up. Simpering, the White Lady offered him a hand, but as he gave his mind to wondering what a musket was he climbed out by himself.

Major Rackstraw removed his lobster-tailed helmet so he looked less threatening. 'They dig a puny breastwork, these antiquarians,' he commented.

'A crude *fossa*,' the Roman agreed, gazing back at Trench One, deciding that it would not stop a wave of barbarian spearmen attacking the...*what*? He craned up at the castle, with its enormous towers, crenellated roofs and haphazard Gothic additions; it seemed a mad, overcomplicated fantasy to one who had been used to the economic lines of Roman forts.

'*Salve!*' Sir Mawdesley showed off his fluent Latin until the Roman (a Briton who barely spoke it) felt certain this was some prick from the officer class. The military man in his breastplate and pot had seemed reassuring, but the nymph with the soulful eyes looked as dangerous to health as an amphora of cheap fish pickle that had stood in a back alley too long in a hot summer.

'Will you tell us what happened to you?' asked the White Lady, with what would have been breathless excitement, had ghosts possessed breath. 'We know that *something* happened, or you would not be here now.'

'Death,' stated the Roman, a literalist. He cleared his throat, suddenly unsure of his own voice, which he had not heard for two thousand years.

'Aye, you now hear the buzzing of a thousand souls above Lethe's brine,' Sir Mawdesley sympathised, making a polite allusion to the classical Underworld. It was a curiosity that the Elizabethan was steeped in Virgil's Aeneid, yet the Roman, a provincial farmer, had never read it. However, he had once met a man who had been in a villa where they had a mosaic of Dido and Aeneas, the Queen of Carthage rather pot-bellied with bad hair and her lover looking like a shifty nincompoop.

'Something untoward occurred,' prompted the Major.

The Roman kept silent, not wanting to own up to a stupid quarrel in a tavern over who had to pay the mules' hay bill. Thinking back to it, he started to look warm, though of course he and his immediate environment remained eerily cold. He made up his mind. He wanted the truth known. He wanted public recognition, and if possible an outcry, over his murder.

'Ah, it was murder!' sighed Major Rackstraw, though the Roman had not spoken. 'Well, be of good cheer. Here is the Provost Marshal who will put all to rights for ye!'

The police had arrived.

'Necessary procedure,' oozed Plummy Duff at the Current Incompetent, with the intention of reassuring him about the police presence. Sir Hardwicke Hall, who had once goosed Mrs Thatcher at a Tory fundraiser, had a reputation for knowing no fear. The one long-quashed anxiety he harboured, as the ghosts recognised, was well hidden. 'Bones that we find are usually from animals, but they have to be checked. Pretty damn obvious when there's a whole spine and the skull grinning up at you, though—' A frisson of glee ran around the ghosts as they crowded Sir Hardwicke Hall, watching him react. After years of enduring five-hour board meetings, he managed not to. 'We stop while the cops deliberate,' Plummy went on. 'What happens next depends on context. In close relation to a known ancient site, you can fairly quickly say that you have a historic burial.'

'Then they leave you alone?' Sir Hardwicke demanded narrowly.

'Actually, they often hang around,' Plummy disappointed him. 'Unless they are having a blitz on car-thieves locally, they like to stay and watch us.'

The White Lady nudged Sir Hardwicke's ribs, her sharp elbow passing through his flesh; as she prodded him intimately in the organs, she gave him an unexpected urge to vomit. She had a strong feminist interest in seeing him brought down.

'And does this count yet as a "known ancient site"?' he asked Plummy.

'Well, we may have a bit of road. But there is no building stone, not even robbed-out. This could be a ritual burial of a type we don't understand yet. But it looks as if our John Doe – or our *Junius Delta* —' Plummy Duff quipped heavily – 'was a ritual burial of a type we understand all too well – I mean, the poor shmuck was mugged and then dumped in a ditch.'

Sir Hardwicke Hall wandered over to Trench One. A couple of constables were chatting to some volunteer diggers, mainly about television. Meanwhile the coroner's officer was bending forwards over the trench, inspecting the skeleton from above as she looked for trauma marks on the bones. It was too tempting. The Current Incompetent responded automatically; seeing a well-formed female rump in comfy-fit slacks, he fondled it.

The coroner's officer straightened up. She was a retired police officer, now working from the local station, a job she had won because of her experience, unflappability and tact. These qualities were needed for dealing with suspects and the bereaved, of course, but her selection board had hoped they would assist in enduring the brusque manners and ego of the coroner, a solicitor of the usual single-minded sort.

She gave Sir Hardwicke Hall a look. She was ten years older than he had thought, she taught aerobics in her spare time, and she looked ready to arrest him for assault. Taken aback, he apologised. It was unacceptable for ghosts to snigger, so the bystanders settled on peals of laughter in an off-stage operatic manner.

'What do you think, ma'am?' quavered Sir Hardwicke, not sounding much like a magnate.

'Oh, we won't cause bother.' The coroner's officer jumped nimbly into the trench. Applying a latex glove, she appeared to stick two fingers down the skeleton's throat, a startling manoeuvre from which she withdrew holding a corroded coin between the fingers. 'If this is from the Roman era, he's all yours,' she told Plummy Duff. 'A copper for Charon – to pay the boatman at the Styx, yes?' In her spare time from being a spare-time aerobics teacher, she had taken an Open University course in Classical Studies.

The Roman was encouraged. Placing the coin beneath his tongue was the one kindness his killers had done him. Anyone should now work out that he had met a misadventure: that he was not simply a victim of a heart attack on the road or of hypothermia, and that he lay outside any proper cemetery, with sinister implications. *The Trowel 'Tecs* were too busy perfecting a close-up of the coin.

'Will we have to wait for a pathologist?' called Xenobia Smith.

The coroner's officer shook her head, as she whistled up the constables and went off to make her report. 'Don't wait – but he's coming anyway. He'll say he's keen on archaeology—'

Xenobia laughed. It was not unkind. 'But the bugger is just hankering to be on TV?'

'What is this TV?' enquired the Roman. The White Lady, who loved to play at being flickery lines on the castle caretaker's portable set, explained.

Filming eventually continued, with the experts expertly discussing the skeleton. They were missing the point. The Roman was strangled. That had left no evidence. A knife had been stuck in him. It had failed to graze a rib. All his possessions except his underwear had been stolen. The archaeologists omitted to spot rust marks left by the abandoned weapon or the preserved weave of the vanished pants and socks fabric. He had been poisoned. They had no funding to send the stomach contents to a lab and analyse its contents. With nothing to explain this death, *The Trowel 'Tecs* called it a routine burial and lost interest.

Frustrated, the Roman wanted to call in an expert. He knew the one he wanted too. He had been listening to the volunteers discussing their favourite fiction, particularly 'an ace Roman' called Didius Falco.

'Nay, 'tis an impossibility,' Sir Mawdesley protested. 'If this popinjay, this Falco, digs you up and solves your death for your contemporaries, then you will not be here now to be exposed by the antiquarians.' It was all one to the Roman, who only wanted justice for his battered corpse, but Sir Mawdesley Mordaunt had a vested interest. If there should be no skeleton to excite interest, he feared the programme would never be made. He was proud of his epistolary skills and wanted to hear experts on the Bandwagon Channel discussing his letter to Sir Philip Sidney. Like everyone else, the still-aspiring poet longed to be on TV.

The Roman's dilemma depressed him, but the ghosts of

Mordaunt Castle were exercised by another matter. It was an issue of conscience, although custom dictated they should take no action, leaving all to fate. They decided to give fate a shove.

The *Trowel 'Tecs* had to devise a scene where an ancient art or craft was reconstructed. Petrina, the researcher, who came fresh from her History of Art degree and really wanted a job in Florence where her boyfriend lived, was struggling. 'Something with Roman food?' she offered, tossing her thin blonde hair and gazing at the muscular cameraman as he strutted about with his dead-weight equipment supported on one shoulder. He was keen to dress up in segmented armour and show off his knees and other attributes. 'Stuffed doormice?' Petrina tried gamely.

'Bloody hell, no.' Ed, the director, could see problems. 'Drop the scoff. We don't carry insurance, if anyone gets listeria.'

'Risk it! We could improvise a link into Roman medicine—'

'Over my dead body.' Ed's favourite archaeological joke. 'Didn't the Romans come to Britain because of the pre-Crufts hunting dogs?'

'I know a woman who supplies puppies for adverts.' Petrina was on the right wavelength. 'Mind you, you have to ban them from the Portaloos or they ruin the lav paper.'

'No budget, darling. Find us a freebie. As for training, that bloody Darren can use his *Pets in Peril* skills.'

The ghosts knew this could be their only chance. They put their heads together (being careful not to clash, lest their auras should tangle); good at logistics, the Major took charge. He whistled up the Black Dog, who was enjoying himself digging holes all over Trench Two. 'You will have to materialise.'

'I want to go in my basket,' whined the Dog unhelpfully.

'Don't give us lip, slave!' commanded the Roman. 'Jump to it!' The Black Dog sulkily decided being trained might be a good game.

'Oh what a pooch!' shrieked Ed, as the Dog turned into visible form, slavering as was his habit. 'What a great historic-looking breed!' The Dog's audition was brief; it was enough that no master came forward demanding a fee for using him. The unpleasant peasant who once owned him would have been furious.

Soon *The Trowel 'Tecs* had geared up Darren to reconstruct training Roman dogs. '*Sede! Vene!* Ow, droppit! *Male cane!*'

Filming proceeded, with its usual pauses and apparent chaos. A band of part-time Celts and some freelance legionaries arrived and helped Darren. The Black Dog enjoyed the attention, but he remembered his role. Like the other ghosts, he knew where the bodies were buried. One body, anyway.

The Black Dog fetched a twig, which a re-enactor was calling a centurion's vine stick, then he peed on Ed the producer's trousers and ran off.

Darren, the presenter, followed, with orders to retrieve the Dog for socialisation. It scrabbled into the walled garden, leapt up on a hot bed and started furiously digging. Darren, who happened to be carrying a geophysical survey instrument, turned it on for fun. 'What have you found, boy…?'

Things moved quickly after that. Everyone agreed it was uncanny. That Darren just picked up a machine, and on his first try they discovered something spooky on geophys.

To be precise, the first find unearthed was a lump of brownish material. The coroner's officer identified it: 'A nineteen seventies handbag clasp.'

'How can you be sure?' asked the Current Incompetent.

'I had one when I was a Mod,' she snapped. 'Trust me, it's plastic!' By then the archaeologists had exposed human remains which made her send for a SOCO team. 'I wonder who she is?' mused the coroners officer aloud, before enquiring of Sir Hardwicke Hall, with what passed for a teasing grin, 'You ever been married, sir?'

She knew that he had. She loathed him so much she had looked him up in *Who's Who*. Who Was Who, it should have been, in the case of Madeleine Hall, m. 1976, no death or divorce specified, though now curiously absent from Mordaunt Castle. People reckoned her money had bought Hall's knighthood. A wife, pondered the coroner's officer, who may have worked out what a bastard she had married and fatally tackled him…

How lucky that the pathologist arrived. He set about his grim evaluation of the scene. Satisfied, the ghosts watched.

One was preoccupied. The Roman was trying to interest someone in his own case. 'So it's the usual mess,' complained this apparition wearily. He had good looks, a sharp wit and expert talents. 'You are offering me a job where it is impossible to say what happened, and no chance of being paid?'

'You might get on television,' promised the Roman Briton, pretending he had influence.

'The name's Falco,' replied his companion with alacrity. 'Suddenly I am available.' He took out a stylus and a shadowy note tablet. '*So! Did you have any enemies, and when were you last seen alive…?*'

Heddie had been missing for several days before someone called the police.

Hours later a search party was raised – a dozen or so of the police, and half a hundred or so local residents like myself – and only a few hours after *that* we found her. She was lying naked alongside one of the many baffling stone-age artefacts that litter Dartmoor. Her skull had been battered in, so that her brains were scattered across the grass (pink, not grey as I'd always imagined). She had been sexually assaulted with a sharp instrument. I was third on the scene, after a pair of hardened police sergeants. I was not the first to throw up. The body which had once been so warm and filled with motion was now cold and clammy and still. The blonde hair was no longer something with which to stroke an appreciative body: it was a mat of sodden keratin. I felt very selfish and particularly necrophiliac thinking of her corpse in sexual terms – remembering the few friendly nights we had spent together – but at the same time I couldn't help it. *Yes*, one part of my mind remembered her laugh and the way the wind bullied her hair and made her eyes shine; but at the same time, *yes*, I remembered her soft breasts against my chest.

Somewhere in another universe they'll tell you about Alan. I don't know the story that he belongs to.

After throwing up again, I cried for several minutes until there were too many people gathered around. I wiped my nose on the back of my sleeve and tried to look like an adult.

A little while later the cops sent most of us away. A forensic scientist was arriving. The police set up a tent over the body, so that eager sightseers would have nothing to sightsee. A plain-clothes detective held me back for some moments after the others had gone.

"I believe you knew the murdered woman," he said.

"Yes. She was a family friend."

"A little more than that, I think."

"How do you mean?"

"She was your mistress, wasn't she?" He lit a cigarette. Like his grubby fawn raincoat, the cigarette seemed to be a part of the uniform.

"Only slightly."

"Like being 'only slightly' pregnant – that sort of 'only slightly'?"

"No. We slept together a few times. Only when we both wanted to. It wasn't a regular arrangement. Just when my wife was away and Heddie didn't happen to have a boyfriend. Really, we were just friends. Honestly. Sex was only a sort of pleasant extra. God – you're not going to repeat this, are you?"

"We may have to. At the inquest." However, he looked as if he would be reluctant to destroy my life.

"But Jan! My wife, Inspector— "

"Detective-Sergeant."

"— it would kill her if ever this got out."

"Perhaps you ought to have thought of that before, sir."

"Would you?"

"No." He smiled. It made him look thirty-five rather than fifty. "I'm not *judging* you, you understand. I'm just trying to tell you what might happen. The coroner might think it a piece of material evidence. But God alone knows what coroners are going to think. If you're lucky the subject'll never come up."

"Hope you're right," I said.

"By the way," he said, as if on afterthought, "I don't suppose *you* killed her, did you?"

"No. Bloody hell! She and I weren't passionate enough for a *crime passionel*. Like I said, she was a friend who I sometimes slept with. It was a different sort of relationship. She wasn't the great passion of a middle-aged life. I don't think she was involved with *anyone* that deeply – and certainly not me."

"She might have been threatening to tell your wife?"

"She wasn't. And…she wouldn't. Even if she had, I'd have lived with it."

"I thought you said it would kill Mrs Wethering if she heard about it?" He threw the half-smoked cigarette into a puddle. It hissed and died.

"That was a figure of speech." I looked over his shoulder at one of the tors. "It would just make life very unpleasant for a while, that's all. But Jan and I would get over it. I know it sounds odd coming from someone who's just confessed adultery, but..." I was embarrassed "... I love my wife very dearly." Why in hell is it that we British always feel so bloody ashamed to admit things like this? It was a lot easier to say I'd committed adultery than to say I loved my wife. Surely it should be the other way around?

"Don't worry, sir," he said. "I really don't think it was you. You just don't seem to me to have the guts."

As I left I didn't know whether to be relieved or insulted. I ended up being a mixture of both.

Later I wondered at the man's insensitivity. Someone quicker on the uptake than me might have objected to the term 'guts'. In the context, you understand.

Alan would have understood my qualms.

I didn't really feel like going in to work, but I didn't really feel like doing anything else, either, so in to work I went. Besides, there was the evening show to do, and it would look curious if Mick Wethering was off the air simply because an assumed distant friend had died, however revoltingly. The big electric clock on the wall stared at me as Jim Paxton handed the studio over. He gave me a can of lager as he left.

"Just to keep you happy through the long night hours." He obviously hadn't heard about Heddie. So far as I knew, he was the only one who knew about the depth of our friendship – except, it seemed, for the police. Hm. How the hell had *they* known?

The question tormented me as I slotted in the cassettes for the ads and my own signature tune, and stuck the first couple of CDs on the decks. Jim would never tell anyone – I was sure of that.

Seven o'clock came and with it the news summary, which Andy read from the adjacent studio. I could see his adam's apple bouncing as he read from his scruffy heap of badly typed script. It was, as ever, odd that I couldn't hear anything he said directly, but could hear his voice blasting in from the speakers in my studio as well as pipsqueaking through my cans. I'd had the sensation a thousand times before, but it was still strange. So at first I hardly registered Heddie's name when the speakers mentioned it. Then I realized that this wasn't Andy reading: IRN had picked the item up. Heddie had made the national news by dying. Ironic. She'd tried so hard to make it while alive.

Sorry, some explanations are needed. Heddie was, in life, a painter. In commercial terms, she wasn't a successful one. She might have been if she'd stuck to fussy little watercolours of Dartmoor scenes – twenty-five quid apiece in the Ashburton Arts Centre – but that hadn't been her style. If she'd produced a canvas less than six feet across I'd never seen it. Her pictures took two strong men to lift and could be attached to only the strongest walls. But it wasn't just because of their size that they dominated any room they were in.

They featured exuberant clashes of colour and heavy forms. Somehow they seemed to give out more light than they received. The net result was that her exhibitions got good write-ups from John Dalton in *The Guardian* but hardly ever sold. If Jackson Pollock had painted them they'd have been worth millions, but no one was prepared to pay even £500 for a Heddie Metcalf original.

Except, that is, for me and Jan. We'd been married for about a month when we first saw an exhibition of Heddie's work on a rainy Saturday afternoon in Barnstaple. It was surprising we were out of doors, really. We were still in that stage of early marriage when, aside from the demands of work and shopping for food, we usually left the house only to make love in a field for a change. However it happened, there we were in front of a canvas called, in uncompromising defiance of the Barnstaple magistrates, 'Fucking'. It was an abstract, like all of Heddie's work, and I've *still* never been able to work out why it's so erotic. Maybe it's just that Jan and I were in the right frame of mind, but the two of us were shot instantly into a sort of tingling sexuality the moment we saw it. We were short of money at the time, and convention demanded that we buy ourselves a three-piece suite, but nevertheless we found ourselves asking the attendant the cost of Picture 7 (we couldn't bring ourselves to call it by its real name to the elderly gentleman, who looked like a stalwart of the British Legion). The price was much more than we'd expected, but Jan pulled out the joint-account chequebook anyway. Why? Well, first because we wanted the picture – aphrodisiacs have always commanded a high price. Second, because of the price itself: £499.99. Any artist with a sense of humour's got to be good.

Jan was scribbling the cheque when a pretty girl I'd vaguely noticed hanging around spoke to us. She looked about sixteen, and was dressed accordingly. She had longish fair hair held together in a pony-tail. There wasn't a trace of make-up on her face. Her skirt was grey, made of some soft material I couldn't identify. She wore a white blouse, through which you could see she had on a pale blue bra. She was wearing also a navy-blue blazer-type jacket, which confirmed the general impression that she was a schoolgirl.

"Sorry to intrude," she said confidently, "but I was wondering why you'd decided to buy that picture."

Jan looked annoyed. I certainly felt it. This wasn't so much intrusion as voyeurism.

"Well," I said, "we don't know much about art but we're...er...impressed by the use of colour, and the juxtaposition of hard lines and soft, and..."

"Oh, shut up, Michael," said Jan, squeezing my hand. (She always called me 'Michael'. Most of my close friends did. Actually, I loathe being called 'Mick', but there are professional considerations.) Jan continued: "We like it because we like it. Isn't that enough?"

"Yes," said the girl. "I'm sorry – again. I must seem very rude to you. You see, I have a sort of special interest. I painted it...and I wanted to know *why* you liked it."

"Then you must be..." I said, squinting at the greyly gestetnered catalogue, "ah, Heddie Metcalf?"

"Too true," she said. She looked nervous, her eyes suddenly tracing the pattern of the cigarette-burnt carpet.

"That's fantastic!" said Jan. The attendant handed her a receipt and told her that we could pick up the painting in a fortnight's time when the exhibition closed. Long enough for the cheque to be cleared, a part of my mind reflected. Most of my mind was wondering how quickly we could get home to bed, however, so I was infuriated when Jan impulsively said: "Would you have coffee with us? We'd like to talk to you."

Heddie immediately said yes, with gratitude so obvious that I wished I were somewhere else. So we had coffee, drove to Exeter, ate a meal in the Curry House, and drove back out to Kingsparson-on-the-Moor. During all of this time Heddie explained that this was only the second painting she had sold, despite the fact that it was her eighth one-person show; that she was 26, despite her appearance, and therefore the same age as me and one year younger than Jan; that this was the first time she had had a chance to talk to someone who liked her work enough to pull out a chequebook (I gathered the other purchaser had been an unusually adventurous pension fund); and that she'd painted 'Fucking' because she wanted to try and capture on canvas how much she enjoyed doing just that. We were all a bit drunk by this time, so the final comment was less of a shocker than it might have been had it emerged over the birianis.

Jan and Heddie had been talking together now since five o'clock. I checked my watch and discovered that it was a quarter past ten. During five and a quarter hours I had contributed at most three paragraphs to the conversation.

I swivelled my slightly hazy gaze to Jan's face. She looked readier for bed than I'd ever seen her, which at that stage in our marriage was a spectacular sight.

"It's been a long day," I said to Heddie. "Would you like me to drive you home?"

"Nonsense," said Jan. "Michael, you're in no condition to drive anyone home. Come to that" – she giggled – "neither am I. Heddie, would you like to kip here? I'm afraid all we can offer is a camp-bed and a sleeping-bag, but..."

I can still remember Heddie's clear, thin voice as she said: "If you don't mind, I'd rather sleep with you two."

Try as I might, I cannot remember all that happened then. At a guess, I turned in shock towards Jan. At another guess, she did the same towards me. Guesses aside, the next thing I knew was that the three of us were more or less naked. I was on my back on the sheepskin rug Jan's mother had given us as a wedding present. The only clear image I have is of opening my eyes to find Heddie eagerly kissing the musty triangle between my wife's thighs.

My wife. Had it been a man doing the same I would have been incensed. As it was a woman, it seemed somehow all right.

Further gaps of memory. I do know that we all reached bed together, but I cannot recall climbing the stairs. I have just one more visual flicker from that night. Jan went to switch out the light, and as she turned to look at Heddie and I sprawled across the bed my eyes focused on the black triangle of her pubic hair. For some reason I found I wanted to check the colour of Heddie's. Was she like so many blondes: fair on the head but dark beneath? As I turned to look, Jan switched out the light.

In the chilly hungover morning, over a dismal breakfast, we all agreed that the night before had been a product of the booze, and that it should never, *never* be repeated. It was six weeks later that I found out that Heddie's pubic hair was almost as blonde as that on her head.

I *had* to phone Jan. Even though, to her, Heddie was nothing more than a good friend with whom, six years earlier, she had engaged in an episode that was best left unremembered, I knew that she would be upset by Heddie's death. I did not want her to hear about it on the radio news. I had to tell her myself. As the ads finished – with the inevitable carpet sale – I pulled the new Backstreet

Boys single off the deck and put Al Stewart's *Past, Present and Future* album on instead. I'd just changed the speed control when it was time for me to speak.

"The cock of the evening to all of you listening to Dart Radio," I said. "This is Mick Wethering speaking, and I'm going to be with you right through till closedown at midnight. At ten we'll have the sports round-up from Jenny Judson, at eleven we'll have the Independent Radio News from Andy Mulveen, but aside from that it'll be music all the way. And we're going to start with a golden oldie that's as popular now as it was when it first came out in the 1970s, Al Stewart's 'Nostradamus'. I'll be right here, listening with you. Hope it brings back happy memories..."

I switched the mike off. Nine minutes of 'Nostradamus' would give me enough time to call Jan. Without really thinking I stuck Meat Loaf's *Bat Out of Hell II* into the other deck; 'I'd Do Anything For Love' would give me an extra twelve minutes, if I needed it – it was going to be a good show for golden-oldie lovers. Thank God there wasn't a fucking *guest* on tonight: most nights I was stuck with spending half an hour pretending to be interested in some touring author and his lacklustre book. Dart Radio doesn't pay its visiting 'celebrities', and so has to make do with whatever the publicists send it.

I felt Alan almost.

I put the earphones around my neck, so that I would know how Al Stewart was getting on without actually having to listen to him, and picked up the phone. I'd expected a direct line out, but Denise had obviously decided to linger around the switchboard for a few extra minutes. (Denise is another story, but one that happened so long ago that I can't remember any of the details. It was long before I met Jan, and it was only a one-nighter. Denise was now unhappily married with two kids, and occasionally told me firmly to keep my hands to myself when they weren't even remotely near her. This was her way of trying to be tantalizing. If I'd been the one behaving like that towards *her* she'd probably have called the vice squad.)

"Hi, Mick," she said sweetly.

"Oh, uh, hi, Denise," I said. "I thought you'd have gone by now."

"A woman's work is never done." She was fond of clichés, and this was one of her all-time faves.

"I wanted an outside line," I said.

"Outside line coming up," she said, and my ear was filled with the purr of the tone. The trouble was, I wouldn't have put it past Denise to listen in. I dithered. Al Stewart was into the central section of 'Nostradamus'. The minutes were ticking away. I pulled the Meat Loaf CD off the deck, hunted for the remastered *Tubular Bells* only to find that someone had liberated it, and instead dragged out an ancient copy of the Incredible String Band's *Changing Horses*. 'Creation' lasts eighteen – count 'em, eighteen – minutes.

Another golden oldie. No one would like it much, not even me, and I'd have to put on seven ads in a row at the end of the track, but I didn't care any longer: I had to speak to Jan.

I listened with one ear to the mind-numbing purr of the phone and with the other to the squeaky version of Al Stewart I could hear directly from the stylus. He finally finished, and I switched my own mike on. "Takes you back, doesn't it?" I said, filling my voice with synthetic friendliness. "This is Dart Radio and I'm Mick Wethering, and I'm glad to know that you – yes, *you* – are listening to the show tonight. And I'm sure you'll be just as glad to know that I'm going to follow that track with another from the same period. Yes, it's one for all of you out there who love the Incredible String Band. Here it is: 'Creation'." Listen to the first few bars. Switch the mike off.

Denise *must* have gone home by now. Dial. Listen to the dialling tone. Was Jan in the bath?

Finally: .

"Kingsparson 364. Jan Wethering speaking."

"Jan. It's Michael here. Something terrible has happened."

"Let me sit down." She wasn't joking. I could hear her pulling up a chair. "OK, tell me."

"It's Heddie. She's dead."

"What?"

"Dead. She's been murdered."

"Oh God. Who by?"

"Darling, I don't know. I don't think the police do, either. I was one of the first to find her. It was...not good." Robin Williamson was speaking intently into my neck and I couldn't make out a word of what he was saying.

"Do they think it was one of us two?"

"I don't believe so," I said, "Why should they? There must have been thousands of other people who knew her."

"Yes, but..." She was thinking about that night, six years back.

Her thoughts were very loud down the line, drowning even the crackles and hisses that we always referred to as the MI5 tappers lighting up their roll-your-own cigarettes.

"That was a long time ago, darling," I said. "It doesn't make any difference now. She's been involved with a dozen people since then. Remember, there was that biker she brought to dinner, and Hector the Lie-Detector Tax Inspector, and..."

"I know, Michael, but we were the only *couple* she..."

"We don't know that." I said, trying not to snap. Jan was on the verge of tears. I could hear. "The whole thing is nothing to do with us."

"I'm sorry, lovie," she said, her voice thickening. "The news hurts, that's all. I'm being selfish. Who killed her isn't really important. I'm just so upset for Heddie, that's all. She's...she was so young."

"Too young to die," I muttered. Denise would have been proud of that one. But it was true: Heddie at 32 had still looked like a schoolgirl. Even dead on the cold, wet moor, with a great gash from her genitals to her breasts, she had looked like a schoolgirl. I gagged.

"Can we stop talking?" whispered Jan.

"What? Oh. Yes. If you like."

"I want to go and...I don't know... say a prayer, or something. I want to have a quiet time to weep for Heddie. Very primitive. I..."

"I know what you mean. I'll be home as early as I can. Don't get too sad."

"I love you," she said.

"I love you too," I said. "*Je t'aime, moi non plus*. I'll be with you soon."

"Yes," she said. "I think that would be best."

She hung up. I started to concentrate on trying to retrieve a few listeners.

Jan. (Alan has nothing to do with this.)

The only woman I have ever deeply loved in a man-loves-woman sense. My wife. My lover. My mistress. My whore and my ever-new shy virgin bride. The exact centre of my Universe. The person with whom I was utterly infatuated. But, unfortunately, only my second-best friend.

Equally unfortunately, my first-best friend was female.

Which was why I'd ended up leading a curious form of double life – not the usual sort of double life, in which there is an element of falseness in at least one relationship, if not both. No, both of my relationships were genuine and profound. On the one hand, there was Jan, who was everything to my soul. On the other, there was Heddie, who was everything to my intellect, so that the intellectual satisfaction of her company somehow spilled over into the emotional part of my mind, too. When she and I were in bed together, which was surprisingly less often than you might think, we weren't just fucking, we were genuinely making love...except that it was a different type of love from the one which Jan and I shared. I never once felt that there was any betrayal involved in my adultery (a silly, cold word). With both women, the interaction of my body with theirs was merely a physical rendition of the love I had for them. With Jan, love-making was a complete and utter surrender of the self. Yet, oddly, with Heddie there were fewer inhibitions: I doubt whether there was a square centimetre of her body that I had not at one time kissed. And yet...and yet, in a way, with Heddie there was less *involvement*. I'm not sure that I quite understand why this was the case, but it was. Perhaps there were fewer inhibitions because whatever we did physically was less important than it would have been between Jan and me. As I say, I don't really understand it.

I often wondered what I'd have done had some King Solomon figure come along and told me that I must give up one or other of the relationships. I never did – and still cannot – work out which of the two was more important to me. They were just...*different*. Ideally, I guess I should have tried to talk Jan into allowing Heddie to live with us: that would probably have been the best thing, now that I use hindsight. But now is now and then was then. At the time, I was caught up in both relationships. It was as if both of the women were two different aspects of the same person. Heddie was the one with whom I walked the shoreline of the Exe estuary talking about Post-Impressionism – a subject of which I knew nothing, but about which I liked to think I sounded knowledgeable. Jan was the one with whom, in the cold hours of the early morning, I muttered about how particle physics seemed incapable of explaining the phenomenon of love. Particle physics was another subject of which I knew nothing.

So who *was* Jan? I realize, guiltily, that I've told you a lot about Heddie and next to nothing about Jan.

Oddly, I find it hard to describe Jan's physical appearance. Oh, yes, the particulars are easy enough: long dark hair, oval face, five foot six, trim figure, looked best in tight blue jeans. But aside from that I'm stalled. I could give a better description of a woman I'd seen and idly fancied on the train than I could of Jan. She just *was*, as far as I was concerned. She was there. She was everything.

In bed together it was less as if we were making love with each other, more as if we were a single organism confirming its identity: there was a great deal of physical ecstasy, but it was almost incidental.

Jan was a virgin when we met – a 'late developer', she used to say. She was no longer a virgin by the time, eighteen months later, we went to bed together; but she might as well have been. She had gone through a very rapid phase of promiscuity, during which she'd lost count, she always said, of the men she'd been screwed by. I use the expression carefully. She had made love with no man; she had screwed no man; she had been screwed by many. None of her 'lovers' had paused to make love with her.

When she and I first made love it was a first time for her.

As far as she was concerned, beforehand, I was simply a prestige one-night stand – local-radio DJ, and all that – while, for me, it was rather different. We'd met because she was an astronomer at Exeter University and Dart Radio, ever desperate to find people who would come and be interviewed for free, had asked her to speak about the new supernova the Hubble had spotted in M31. For half an hour, interrupted by the ads and two puerile records, we discussed super-novae on air. I pretended that I was being the 'voice of the people', whereas the truth was that I didn't know what the hell she was talk-ing about. The interview was really killed in the first few moments when she pointed out that astronomers are constantly spotting supernovae in other galaxies – this one was no big deal.

After the show I asked her out for a drink, but she declined the offer. She had things to do at home, she said, and I felt that the excuse was a real one, not just a polite put-off. Dart Radio not wor-rying too much about repeat performances, she was invited onto the show several times and invited out for that drink the same number of times before, one night, she agreed. The intensity of my interest in her can be gathered from the fact that, during those eighteen months, I went to bed with a woman only one time. That was the sad time with Denise, and for me (and for her too, I think) it was mere-ly a case of releasing tension. It was mindless fucking. Jan was the person with whom I wished to be the whole night long.

The first night Jan and I had a drink together – in the Horse and Groom – was also the first night we made love together. The transition from pub to her flat in Polsloe Road was a swift one: we never finished the first drink. The transformation in her personality was spectacular. As soon as we were inside the peeling-paint blue door she flung her spectacles at the worn couch and the studious astronomer disappeared.

She almost strangled me as she ripped the T-shirt from me. We had the usual tussle with her brassiere as we worked our way like a pair of professional wrestlers into her somewhat seedy bedroom, where the sheets and blankets lay on the bed like a scale model of the Andes. She threw herself down.

"Go on," she said. "Do it. Now."

"Not yet," I said, easing myself down beside her and gently kissing her left breast.

"Let's wait a little."

Although it was a long while later that we had intercourse, it was at this early moment that she started to make love for the first time.

To hell with it, I thought for the umpteenth time that night as I looked around the studio. Time had passed. The usual crap singles had been played. Jenny had done her stuff and gone, as had Andy: people who wanted to know about sports and/or news would either have to switch over to the Beeb or wait until the morning. Forty-five minutes to go before I and Dart Radio could knock off for the night, too. The listeners in their hundreds would just have to accept that the Mick Wethering Show was concentrating almost to exclusion on golden oldies – *long* golden oldies – this time. Made a change from the usual top-twenty drek, anyway.

"Bob Dylan," I said. "A lot of people feel he's lost his way over the last few years. Well, maybe he has and maybe he hasn't." (That's the art of the DJ – to use a lot of words to say nothing.) "Perhaps you think he has. I don't know. Perhaps you think he hasn't. But, whatever you think, I'm sure you'll agree that he hadn't lost his way all those years ago when he recorded that magnificent double album, Blonde on Blonde. And here's what's probably the best track from it." I finished speaking as the opening bars of the satisfyingly thirteen-minute-long 'Sad-Eyed Lady of the Lowlands' sounded tinnily from the pick-up. I switched my mike off, and then began to think about me, and Jan, and Heddie... all over again.

The phone rang. I jumped. Jesus – that could have happened while I was on air! I stared at the instrument. Normally I was punctilious about turning the volume-control down to zero while working, but tonight I'd forgotten. Still, I had an excuse...

I picked up the receiver.

"Mick," said a voice. It was vaguely familiar.

"Michael Wethering," I said. "How did you get this number? Who are you?"

"I've known the number for years," said the voice. "A Dart Radio DJ gave it to me. He's a cunt. My name's Alan. That's all of my name you need to know. Alan."

"Who *are* you?" I asked again.

"I've told you my name."

Curiosity turned into uneasiness. This telephone call should never have come through.

"I don't want to know your name. I want to know who you are and why you're calling me. This number's for emergencies only."

The man at the other end of the line giggled, shrilly, like a young girl. "I'm surprised you have to ask," he said eventually. "You know me very well."

I thought hard. I couldn't think of any Alan that I knew outside Rider Haggard. Oh, yes, there was Alan behind the counter in the post office, but three months ago he'd gone off to live in Finland or somewhere. I was suddenly very conscious of the emptiness of the building. I was alone. I was supposed to lock up after closing down the studio. It was foolish, but I began to think about ghosties and ghoulies and things going bump in the night. We often had phone calls from crackpots, but this 'Alan' didn't sound like the average pub loonie to me. He sounded sinister. There was a timbre in his voice that suggested he knew exactly what he was doing, and the inflection of his words reinforced the impression.

Besides...besides, there *was* that something in his voice I recognized...

"I don't know you at all," I said.

"Do you know the second-rate, stuck-in-a-shit-filled-rut DJ who gave me the number of the direct line into the studio?"

"I probably do, if he's at Dart," I said. In my more honest moments I'd have admitted the description could be applied to any of us on your soaraway local radio station.

"But do you know *exactly* who this fucking shit was?"

"No."

"I'll give you some clues. He's about six feet tall and he has a silly-looking little moustache that for some reason he's very proud of. Perhaps he thinks it suits his image of being virile and manly, cock-swingingly bollock-laden like all the other guys."

I winced. I was the only person at Dart Radio who fitted the physical description. The taunt about sexual neuroses was all too accurate – Jan and I had often joked about it. So had Heddie and I. Both of them had said it was OK, not to worry, and that anyway, it didn't matter, what was important was that I was good in bed. I'd have been more convinced if both of them had not, independently, thought to mention the fact.

"You're talking about me, I think," I said. It was difficult getting the words out. Bob Dylan was having no trouble getting the words out, I thought absent-mindedly, as I heard him buzzing away into my neck.

Alan responded immediately. "Right on the button, *and* you get the ceegar. But shall I tell you a little more about this DJ?"

"What?"

"This turd has been screwing my lover, on and off, for six years now."

"You mean you're Heddie's boyfriend? But I thought she... She always told me there was no one special."

"Well, there was, buster. Me. For six years now I've been with her, loving her, caring for her, sleeping with her whenever I could. And then last week..." Alan began to cry. I looked despairingly across at the timer. Thank God. Two-thirds of 'Sad-Eyed Lady of the Lowlands' still to go. Hardly thinking, I stretched for a CD and got Pat Benatar in concert. Six minutes of 'Hell is for Children' would be better than nothing.

"Pull yourself together, man," I said. "Heddie's dead, so it would make a lot more sense if you and I got together as friends and drank to her memory. She'd like that. She wouldn't want us to go for each other's throats...especially since I never even knew you existed."

"You *shit!*" came the scream. "You bastard shit! You fucker! God, how can you speak like that? You killed her, you cunt! I told the fucking fuzz. You. Killed. Her. You. Cunt."

There was only the one phone-set in the studio – the same one served for calls routed through the switchboard and those coming in on the direct number. I might make a dash for the switchboard, but the blackness of the corridor I could see through the heavy glass door was almost as terrifying as Alan had become. I felt as if someone had stapled me to my swivel-chair. "I didn't kill her," I said limply.

Alan's voice was a whisper this time. "Yes...you...did," he hissed. "I held the knife but it was you who killed her, cocksucker. You and the filth you spread all over her. What do you think it was like for me to hold her in my arms and know that some man had been with her, imagining her still sticky from being with you. But I didn't know who the man was until last week, when she said the wrong name in bed. And then I knew it was you."

"How did..."

"It was easy, arsehole. Have you ever thought how rare your name is? There are thousands of 'Micks' and 'Mikes' for every 'Michael'. When she said 'Michael' to me I was sure, but I made her tell me, anyway. You'd better put on another record. 'Sad-Eyed Lady' is nearly over."

I thought I was going to be sick as I voiced the link. I had to keep this...psychopath... on the line, but I also had to contact the police. I couldn't do both. If I went on air to summon the police Alan would surely hear me – clearly he had Dart Radio playing somewhere near. I didn't want him to hang up. My reasons were not just the logical ones. Some masochistic part of me *needed* to go on listening to him.

Once 'Hell is for Children' was well under way I noticed that I'd forgotten to switch my mike on. Dart devotees had just been treated to a three-minute silence. I grabbed the phone. Had Alan interpreted the silence as me taking time out to call the police?

"Don't worry, wanker," said his almost reassuring voice. "I know what happened. It's not the first time. I listen to your show a lot. Only this time I would guess that you're not going to break into the song and apologize with a laugh. No, not this time. And not ever again."

Sod that, I thought. I broke into the record and laughingly apologized for my little mistake. "Must be getting later than you think," I said to the listeners, who probably totalled two necking teenagers and a taxi driver.

And Alan.

"OK," he said, and I was startled by the increased bitterness in his voice, "so you've had your tiny triumph. Enjoy it. You don't have long. You killed Heddie, with me as your instrument. Now you're going to kill yourself the same way." Abruptly he burst into tears again.

This time I was – definitely was – going to slam down the phone and dial 999, but then a new voice came on the line.

"Darling – Michael, darling."

"Jan," I said. "What for Jesus's love are you—"

"Michael, please Michael – please. I can't stop him. I know all about you and Heddie, and it's all right, I don't mind, we can live with it. But Alan – he's…he's *insane*. He means it when he says he's going to kill you."

"Jan," I said, trying to sound calm. "If you're with that fucking homicidal maniac, then get away from him. Right now. At once."

"Oh God, Michael," she shrieked. "I *can't*. Don't you understand? I *can't*!"

Pat Benatar was off the airwaves. So was Dart Radio. I didn't care.

"What do you mean, you can't?" I said. "Darling, he's nuts. You *must* get away from him. Are you tied to him, or something? Has he got a knife on you?" A picture of Heddie's gutted body flashed into my mind. Jesus! The way I loved Heddie I could live with her death. The way I loved Jan…

"No, it's not that. Michael," and her voice was momentarily icy-cool, "I can never never never never get away from Alan. Don't you understand?"

And then, of course, I did understand. I understood why Alan's voice had seemed so familiar. It was Jan's, but in a lower register.

"Dearest," I said, "I'm going to put the phone down and I'm going to call some doctors, and I'm going to drive out to the house with them. There's no need to be frightened. The police may come with us, but I'll be there and I'll make sure they're gentle with you. You mustn't panic."

"But – but," she said, and then, with one of those maddening inconsequentialities with which we litter our lives: "You can't come away now. What about the show?"

"Oh, dear heart, to hell with the show." There were tears in my eyes. They stung, too: I'd always thought they only stung in books.

"Anyway, Dart has been off the air for nearly four minutes now" – instinctive glance at the electric clock – "and so it can just stay that way till tomorrow. Nobody minds. Probably nobody's even listening. I don't mind. Just let me call the doctors, and we'll come for you."

Privately, I was worried about how quickly the psychiatrists would come. A friend of ours had waited two days while her husband, talking about being the reincarnation of Benito Mussolini, had systematically smashed every object in the house.

"There's no need to come for me," said a voice which was Alan's on a couple of the words and Jan's for the others. "No need to call the doctors. I'll come to you."

"But you can't drive when you're like this, darling."

"No need to drive," said the voice. "I'm just downstairs."

I put the phone down. I switched on my mike, and then realized it was now after midnight: studio transmission had automatically been cut off and we were carrying Radio 2 for the night owls. No more access to the airwaves for Dart Radio this night. I picked the phone back up again. The person who was Jan/Alan had cut it off at the switchboard.

I looked around me for a weapon, but there was nothing I could see. Fend off a murderer with an empty lager can? – no way. I looked at the glass door, and it was as staunchly boltless as ever. I saw Heddie's brains on the moss of the moor, her intestines glistening on the same moss. I decided my only chance was to move. I made for the door but, before I got there, it opened. Framed in it was the woman I loved.

Except that she was a man.

I don't mean that she was dressed any differently from normal – in fact, she was in a skirt, the short skirt I'd bought her a couple of birthdays ago because I'd always fantasized about making love up against a wall with a woman who still had her skirt on. (We'd done it, too. On a holiday we couldn't really afford we'd made love leaning against the Great Wall of China. At the time it had seemed funny, and hence intensely erotic; now the memory brought acid to my mouth.) Costume aside, however, Jan/Alan was male. There was no five o'clock shadow on her/his face, but I could almost see one there.

I could see, also, the carving knife that Aunt Edith had given us for Christmas. It reflected a sparkle from the studio's fluorescent lighting at me. The reflection was not from the steel but from the bright redness that covered the blade, as well as the whole of Jan/Alan's front. There was even a spatter of blood on her nose. It looked incongruously fetching.

"Jan," I said.

"I'm Alan."

"Alan. Alan – look, you're invading Jan's body. I mean, fuck off out of there and let me speak to Jan."

To my surprise, he did exactly that. All at once the figure in front of me was female. I took a step towards her. The knife stayed pointing at me, so I stopped. "Darling," I said, loving her.

"Stay there," she said. "This is very difficult for me."

For a moment it seemed like a domestic quarrel. "It's pretty bloody difficult for—"

"Shut up," she said. "I can't keep Alan down for long. Not now. He wants to kill you. He's already killed Heddie. And Denise, downstairs. She was waiting for you. Her marriage was all fucked up and she thought she might seduce you to Prove Something to her husband. Well, she'll prove something to him, all right, when he has to identify her." Jan began to cry.

Instinct: I moved towards her. The knife gestured me back.

"I want to tell you the truth," said Jan, "before I let Alan come back. You see…while it was Alan who killed Heddie, it was *me* who was her lover. Making love with her was like nothing you can imagine. The very first time, when the two of us were in bed with you, you were nothing but a sort of…impediment. You were the second-best. We kept you happy, and it was something of a vague turn-on, but most of the time we just wanted to be *together*. You were…you were…you were an *excuse*. Yes, I enjoyed making love with you when we were on our own. Yes, I loved you. I loved you, but I was not *in love* with you. I was in love with Heddie. And she was in love with you…and with me. I'm…I'm sorry."

"So you killed Heddie," I said. A knife couldn't kill me now.

"No," Jan corrected, "*Alan* killed Heddie. When he discovered she'd been betraying us, all these years, he took her out on the moor and he smeared his saliva all over her and he stuck his knife into her and he ripped her. And then he beat her brains out with a rock, to make sure she had died."

The way Jan was telling it, the whole episode seemed somehow logical. The memory was clearly hurting her. Tears came to her eyes.

Her face crumpled. One moment it was Alan's, the next it was hers. Both faces expressed the horror of the killings she/he/they had done.

The knife dropped to the floor.

I picked it up. And here I am. The judge said I was evil. He said any confessed adulterer who slaughtered his mistress, his wife, and a casual girlfriend from long ago, all because he was worried about his sexual adequacy, deserved to be put away for life.

Really life – none of your out-in-a-few-years jobs.

He didn't believe me, and I can see that neither do you, which is why you're all going to have some recreational fun kicking the shit out of me. Again. Just like him, you think that people are either good or evil, that Jan was Jan and I killed her because she'd found out about me and Heddie. That I killed Heddie because she was going to tell or had told Jan. That I killed Denise – poor, godforsaken Denise – because she'd eavesdropped on some of my phone conversations with Heddie.

Jan: I touched the upper part of your arm, just above the elbow, and I loved my fingertips against your hairless skin.

I explain myself sometimes.

It was only Alan I killed.

And I killed him to defend myself.

My *self*.

They were halfway to Tunbridge Wells when Alan Pomeroy broke the news to her.

"Oh, by the way," he said casually, "Mary is coming today."

"Mary Millfield?" she gasped.

"I'm afraid so."

"Why on earth didn't you tell me?"

"I just did, Enid."

"You should have warned me in advance."

"That would have been fatal," said Alan with a quiet smile. "You'd have cried off immediately. And I wanted you to be there. You enjoy your lunches so much."

She snorted. "There's not much chance of that today!"

"Enid!"

"Mary Millfield will ruin everything."

"Not necessarily. She's mellowed with age."

"Don't fool yourself," said Enid through gritted teeth. "Women like that never mellow. They simply acquire a coat of moss to hide their granite exteriors. Mary will never change. Anyway," she added scornfully, "what is Mary Millfield bothering to consort with lesser mortals like us for? I would have thought she would be up on Mount Olympus, preening herself in a full-length mirror or receiving her latest undeserved award for services to mystery writing."

"Let's not be catty," he advised.

"She will *patronise* us."

"Not if we jolly her out of it!"

"Alan, it's St. Valentine's Day."

"Then we should show a little love to our fellow creative artist."

"I'm beginning to wish I'd stayed at home."

"Well, I'm not," he said, shooting her an affectionate glance. "These occasional lunches are the only chance I get to see you these days. A hundred Mary Millfields won't deprive me of the pleasure of driving you to the White Horse." He gave a chuckle. "With my heart condition and your stomach ulcers, the only other place we are likely to meet is in a hospital ward."

"Heaven forbid!"

Enid Smale blenched. Poor health was conspiring with the march of time to limit her social life. Bad eyesight had forced her to sell the car and to rely on the kindness of people like Alan Pomeroy, a fellow author who had become a good friend and, in the nicest possible, way a tame suitor. The unsigned Valentine card that had been slipped under her door the previous night was almost certainly from him. Now in his early seventies, Alan was hardly a threat to her long-preserved virginity but he could still give her the odd conversational *frisson*. He was a true gentleman.

In her estimation, an Alan Pomeroy detective story was ten times better than one written by the egregious Mary Millfield. Alan had wit, style and originality. Yet it was Mary who was the worldwide bestseller while he – and Enid Smale, for that matter – toiled relentlessly on for modest rewards. What puzzled her was why her companion was driving her to lunch with controlled enthusiasm when he had particular cause to hate Mary Millfield.

"Her review of your last novel was sadistic," she recalled.

"At least I *was* reviewed," he said with a sigh of resignation. "You know what they say. Better to have been looked over than to be overlooked."

"You weren't looked over, Alan. That harpy slaughtered you."

"She's entitled to her opinion."

"It was a wonderful book."

"Thank you."

"And Mary Millfield knew it. That's why she attacked you. Sour grapes."

"I don't hold it against her."

"Well, I would. She's *evil*."

Until that day, Enid had always looked forward to the meetings of the Southeast Authors and Artists Association, held at a delightful pub in Tunbridge Wells and enabling the assembled scribes and painters to eat, drink, be merry, trade gossip, compare their agents and generally have a good time. The presence of Mary Millfield would change all that. She would be the spectre at the feast. Enid brooded in silence.

The White Horse was an Edwardian construction halfway down a country lane on the outskirts of the town. Built on several levels, it had a precarious car park that narrowed sharply towards its end and obliged one row of vehicles to park within inches of a small precipice. Alan Pomeroy showed no fear as he slid his ten-year-old Ford Fiesta between a Volvo and a gleaming Jaguar. He and Enid got out and went down the steps together. When they entered the build- ing they found that most of the others had already arrived. Drinks were ordered and the convivial atmosphere helped Enid to relax. There were no signs of Mary Millfield, the most famous member of the association. Hopes were raised.

"Maybe the old witch is not coming," said Douglas Harlow mis- chievously. "Or maybe her broomstick overshot the runway at Gatwick."

"Douglas!" hooted Clare Thomason, the resident giggler.

"Then again," speculated Harlow, "she may still be trapped in a list of bestsellers somewhere. Did you see the *Sunday Times* today? Mary has got two books in the top ten. Hardbacks. Just like her. Though she's hard at the front as well as the back."

Clare was seized by another fit of giggling.

"Now don't be unkind, Doug," said Alan Pomeroy, the convener of the group. "We should be honoured that Mary has seen fit to join us. She is a busy woman."

"Yes," retorted Harlow, "she's got all that money to count."

"Good for her!" Barry Weller said defensively. "I take my hat off to her. Whatever you may think of her books, Mary is an undoubt- ed star."

"She's also a paid up member of the association," Alan reminded them, "and thus perfectly entitled to join our meetings. Are you lis- tening, Doug?"

Harlow nodded. "I'll give the old bat a welcome," he said, taking out his cigarette lighter and flicking the flame into life. "You look cold, Mary dear. Come and sit on this while I drive a stake through your heart."

Douglas Harlow was the self-appointed clown of the outfit, a small owlish man in his forties with an impish sense of humour that found full expression in the series of comic novels about a Welsh policeman called Dai the Death.   In spite of his exotically ugly appearance, he was something of a Lothario, and the giggling Clare Thomason was rumoured to be his latest conquest. Why else did a young woman whose insipid watercolours hardly ever sell still come so regularly to the meetings and always contrive to sit next to Harlow? Barry Weller, a retired army man, was a jovial character in his fifties, the author of seven historical mysteries set in the Napoleonic War. He was the group's wine expert.

Enid Smale liked them all, even loud, laughing, paint-spattered Claude Cockspur, the hirsute artist, forever locked in his Picasso Period, and the weird Stephen Rudry, a pale, lonely, badly dressed, introverted young man whose book on Kentish murders revealed a worrying penchant for gruesome detail. Claude was a genial extrovert but Stephen was a watcher, a silent observer, a creature of sly smirks and glinting eyes. Enid could not recall his ever managing a complete sentence. Stephen was the newcomer to the group. His presence was another reason why she hoped that Mary Millfield would not turn up. The latter would never tolerate Stephen's idiosyncrasies nor his delight in the macabre.

It fell to Alan to shepherd them all out of the bar and up the stairs to the Red Room. Enid made sure she sat between Alan and Barry, two decent men who would act as reliable buffers if Mary Millfield did deign to visit them. When they all were seated Douglas Harlow counted the heads.

"Twelve of us," he noted. "Mary will make it thirteen. That's an omen."

"I hope that she comes," said Weller earnestly. "We can congratulate her."

"On what?"

"Her continued success," Alan said jumping in before Harlow could deliver a quip to dispatch Clare into another bout of giggles.

"Now, let's have no more carping about Mary," he went on looking around the table. "She's one of us remember." Enid bit back a tart remark. She was still simmering with anger but she wanted to do nothing to upset Alan. He was such a nice man that he only wanted to see the good qualities in people. While understanding the feuds and resentments that animated the others, he never took sides. Alan Pomeroy, she decided, was a species of saint. Enid wished that she had met him thirty years earlier, before she dedicated her life so recklessly to the teaching of classics in a girls' school, an experience that soured her love of Greek and Latin while draining her energy until it almost expired. A romance with Alan would have rescued her from all that. It was far too late now of course.

But she could still dream.

They were in the middle of the first course when Mary Millfield breezed in.

"Hello, everyone," she said, waving a hand that was encrusted with diamond rings. "No, don't get up, Alan. Barry, how nice to see you. Good lord, it's Douglas. Are *you* still writing? What about you, Claude? Still marooned in your Picasso phase, I daresay." She peered at Enid. "Ah, I do believe that's Enid Smale."

And on she went around the table like visiting royalty. Mary Millfield had timed her entrance for maximum impact. While the rest of them had shared cars to the pub or come – in Stephen Rudry's case – on a battered motorcycle, she had been chauffeur driven in a Daimler that could be summoned again instantly on a mobile phone. She was a big, full-bodied woman with exquisitely styled hair and a handsome face set in a smile of utter condescension. Her clothes and her manner reflected her enormous wealth. As she lowered herself into the remaining chair, she glared at the youngest person in the room and spoke with lofty disdain.

"Are *you* a mystery writer, young man?"

"Yes," Rudry murmured shrinking back into his imitation leather jacket.

"What have you written?"

"Stephen is an expert on Kentish murders," explained Alan, eager to deflect Mary's fire from the most vulnerable target. "But we must raise our glasses to you, Mary. Two books in the top ten. Well done!"

"Hear, hear!" shouted Weller, patting the table with his palm.

Mary beamed at the others. "Thank you, thank you."

Glasses were raised – reluctantly in most cases – and the lady of the hour was duly toasted. Clare Thomason was clearly in awe of her and sat there with her mouth agape. Douglas Harlow was less respectful.

"I should have thought you'd retired by now, Mary," he said.

"Dear me, no," she replied. "What would my public do?"

He grinned boldly. "Cheer, I expect."

Claude Cockspur chortled, Enid suppressed a laugh, Alan shot Harlow a look of reproof, and Clare did not know whether to giggle or be outraged. The rest of the members were torn between amusement and shock. None of them would have dared to make such a remark. Mary Millfield rose above it all.

"You're probably right, Douglas," she said calmly. "Which would be a precedent in itself, of course, because you've made such a career out of being wrong. Especially in your choice of subject matter for your books." She saw him wince. "Perhaps it is time for Mary Millfield to rest her laurels. But my publishers won't hear of it. Every time I write a bestseller, they bind me hand and foot with more contracts. I'm helpless."

"You're the least helpless woman I have ever met," said Alan with old world gallantry. "You could do *anything*, Mary."

"Except write a book," muttered Harlow.

"Thank you, Alan," said Mary with a gracious nod in his direction. "The simple fact is that I'm self-supporting now. Since my husband died, I have to rely entirely on my own income. I can't afford to stop writing."

Enid Smale squirmed in her seat. Mary Millfield earned more in a year than the rest of them put together. Not only were her books sold in large numbers, they had been adapted into long running television series that had achieved global success. It was like hearing Croesus plead poverty. There was a long silence. It was broken, improbably, by Stephen Rudry.

"I'm going to self-publish my next book," he announced.

"Whatever for," sneered Mary.

"So that it looks exactly the way I want it to look."

"What's the title of the new book, Stephen?" asked Alan.

"*Sex crimes in Victorian Canterbury*."

"Don't do it, young man," warned Mary. "Vanity publishing is so pathetic."

"Not in every case," said Alan, trying to support Rudry.

"Have *you* been reduced to that as well, Alan."

"No, no, Mary."

"I was surprised that your last book found a publisher, I must say."

Alan took the insult on the chin. "I just think that you're being unkind to Stephen. He's still new to this game. We all try to help each other in this group, not to make any disparaging remarks."

Mary widened her eyes, "Was I being disparaging?"

"When are you ever anything else?" said Harlow under his breath.

"I do apologise, young man," she said, gushing over Rudry. "I can't pretend that I would ever buy a book on such a ridiculous subject, but I wish you well. Please forgive me."

Stephen Rudry was too crushed to reply. He retreated once more into the safety of his synthetic leather and would not even raise his eyes. Sensing disapproval from some quarters, Mary sought to palliate her critics with a display of charm.

"Let me give you some advice," she said with exaggerated sweetness. "Stephen, isn't it? Believe it or not, Stephen, I, too, was once a raw beginner. I, too, wrote with an 'L' plate tied to my backside. Getting started is hard work, I know, but I kept at it. And do you know how I carved out a successful career as a writer?"

Her lecture continued through the whole of the main course. Stephen himself was not listening but Clare Thomason hung on her every word as if she was hearing the Ten Commandments of writing. She even toyed with the idea of giving up her failed career as a painter in order to emulate Mary and to have a shared interest to discuss in postcoital moments with Douglas Harlow. Alan Pomeroy and Barry Weller took it in turns to indicate agreement with the sage counsel being offered. Others tried to set up their own conversations but Mary's sermon eventually drowned them out.

Enid was quivering with fury. A pleasant meal had been turned into a personal appearance of the phenomenon that was Mary Millfield. Instead of enjoying St. Valentine's Day in the company of her elderly admirer and her friends, she was compelled to listen to the specious words of wisdom. Enid took refuge in drink, and hoped that it would dull her brain and block out the insistent boasting of their unwelcome guest.

"And that's how I did it," declared Mary, sipping her Chablis. "I invented characters that people love. There are twenty Inspector Redblood novels now and fourteen Lilian Pyewackets – she's the church organist who solves village murders that baffle Scotland Yard. Othello Johnson has had six adventures so far – he's my black private eye with an assistant called Iago Lorimer. I write those under a pseudonym."

"What is it?" wondered Harlow. "Desdemona Shakespeare?"

"Then, of course," continued Mary, surging over the interruption, "there are cases involving Strawberry the cat, the ones that feature Daphne Unwin, the first female chief constable, and the Sergeant Ali Khan mysteries. Best of all, in my opinion," she added opening her handbag, "is the new protagonist in my new book, Commander Stilgoe, who is assigned to Interpol on a roving commission. By the way, did I tell you I'd just been awarded the Jagged Dagger by way of a lifetime's achievement?" She extracted the object from her handbag and held it up. "Here it is. Vicious-looking weapon, isn't it? But rather appropriate. I've always favoured stabbing. Twenty-five of my victims fell to the knife."

"I prefer strangling during sexual intercourse," said Stephen Rudry.

The announcement stunned everyone momentarily. Eyes aflame, Stephen sat there and thought about some of the more horrendous sex crimes that he had been researching. It was Douglas Harlow who broke the silence.

"No wonder you have difficulty finding girlfriends, Stephen," he said.

Everyone laughed except Mary, annoyed that the limelight had suddenly shifted to the callow young man. Noting her irritation, Alan tried to appease her by showing an interest in her latest award.

"Do you think we might see the Jagged Dagger?" he asked.

"Rather!" said Weller. "It's a magnificent achievement, Mary."

"And well deserved."

"Thank you," said Mary, lapping up the praise.

She handed over the exhibit and it was passed around the table so that each person could study it in turn. It was a long-bladed knife, made of steel but covered in rust-coloured paint for effect. Inscribed in gold leaf on the handle was a dedication to Mary Millfield as the Queen of Crime. It was an award that none of the other writers there would ever aspire to and they scrutinised it with a mixture of awe and envy. Clare Thomason stroked it wistfully and heaved a sigh.

Enid Smale was almost completely insulated by now from Mary. Four large glasses of Beaujolais, combined with the reassuring proximity of Alan Pomeroy, helped to shut out the sound of Mary's voice. The main course was over. Enid only had to survive the dessert and the coffee before she was free again once more. While the chauffeur whisked the new self-styled Agatha Christie to her estate near Rye, Enid would be driven home by her devoted admirer. With that treat in mind, she began to rally.

Mary Millfield cut short her recovery. Having delivered one long lecture, she now took it upon herself to distribute unsought advice to all and sundry, like a lady of the Manor, throwing pieces of stale bread to a cowering peasantry. Nobody escaped her.

"As for you, Douglas," she said, wagging an admonitory finger, "you really must try to get away from the Welsh Valleys. It makes your books so limited, so provincial, and so depressingly *Welsh*." She turned to look at her next victim. "The same goes for you, Barry.

Much as I like the Napoleonic Wars as a backdrop, they are dreadfully overused. As a genre, costume crime is played out. Fresh woods and pastures new, Barry. That's what you should be telling yourself." Her eyes fell on Enid Smale. "When it comes to Enid, I fear, there's not much I can say about her stories except that they lack any real thrust. I mean, who wants to read stories that feature a retired professor of classics? Clever, they are, I grant you, and shot through with a strange irony. But they have nothing to say to the average reader, and the classical allusions are very confusing. Find something new to say Enid," she instructed. "Or do as I do. Say something old in a novel way."

Jerked out of her reverie, Enid writhed afresh. As each author and artist in the group was subjected to acrid criticism, her rage slowly built. It was when her beloved Alan Pomeroy was attacked that she felt the blood rise in her temples.

"I'm sure Alan won't mind me saying this," said Mary with a supercilious smile, "because he is a professional. And the mark of a professional is the ability to take constructive criticism. His first book was almost brilliant, worthy of Margery Allingham at her best or of Dorothy L. Sayers at her worst. That's a great compliment to him. But both Margery and Dorothy have had their day. They're as useless as last Sunday's papers. Stop keeping one foot in the past, Alan. That's what ruined your latest novel," she explained, "and why I felt duty-bound to review it as honestly as I did. The characters lacked interest, the plot lacked credibility and the whole thing was woefully static. Most worrying of all was that your prose seemed so *tired*. I think you need a rest before you tackle another book. Give yourself a year or two off, Alan. Write less and read more. It's time for you to move into the twenty-first century."

And on she went. It was a devastating attack on a man incapable of defending himself. Dear, kind, considerate, gentlemanly Alan Pomeroy, a gifted author with a string of excellent books behind him, was being ruthlessly torn apart in public. It was quite unforgivable. Enid could withstand the unprovoked assault on her own work, but she would not ignore the gratuitous injury to her friend. Revenge stirred.

"No coffee for me," said Mary as the waitress appeared to take orders. "I really must be going. I always answer my fan mail on Sunday afternoon and that takes *hours*. Excuse me while I powder my nose."

When she left the room there was a collective sigh of relief. Claude Cockspur clapped his hands. Stephen Rudry even found the courage to emerge from his leather refuge. Alan tried to make light of the vicious criticism he had endured but Enid did not stay to hear him. With the Jagged Dagger gripped in her hand, she went off in pursuit of her celebrity prey. Douglas Harlow held up an empty glass.

"Hold on, Enid," he joked. "If you ask her Majesty to pee into this we can probably sell it for a small fortune to one of her fans."

But the bristling Enid had gone out through the door. With a speed she did not know she possessed, she stormed into the ladies' toilet at the moment when Mary Millfield was about to enter a cubicle. Mary saw the dagger.

"Thank you so much for bringing it, Enid," she said. As if addressing a servant, "But this is hardly the place to give it to me, is it?"

"It's the best possible place!" insisted Enid.

With strength borne of pure anger and hatred, she thrust the dagger deep into the other's ample bosom. Mary gasped in pain, stared in disbelief, staggered backwards and then collapsed in a heap on the floor. Enid smiled in triumph. "Did you say that you favoured stabbing?"

As soon as it was clear that Mary was dead, Enid went off to the bar and suggested to the landlord that he might summon the police as there had been an unfortunate accident in the ladies' toilet. Returning to her friends in the Red Room, she found them still bubbling with animosity towards Mary Millfield. Notwithstanding the punishment he had taken, Alan Pomeroy was actually trying to speak up for the woman. Enid enjoyed her moment.

"Mary Millfield is dead," she declared. "I've just put that Jagged Dagger through her black heart."

They laughed at first, but the sudden appearance of the landlord stifled their mirth at once. The man was horrified that a crime had been committed on his premises. "I must ask you all to remain here until the police come," he said. "One of your members has been murdered. That famous lady whose picture is always in the papers."

Everyone was shocked. Alan Pomeroy was distraught.

"Enid," he said in dismay. "Why on earth did you do it?"

"Because of the way she attacked you," replied Enid. "She told me that I needed a new departure. Well, I've found one. I've killed off Inspector Redblood, Lilian Pyewacket, Othello Johnson, Iago

Lorimer, Strawberry the cat, Chief Constable Daphne Unwin, Sergeant Ali Khan, Commander Stilgoe, and all the other boring nonentities from the pen of Mary Millfield. In short," she went on, raising both arms in victory, "I'm responsible for a St. Valentine's Day Massacre!"

They stared at her in blank amazement. Alan was aghast. Barry Weller was on the verge of tears. Clare Thomason turned white. Claude Cockspur actually stopped thinking that he was Picasso. Douglas Harlow could, for once, find nothing comical to say. And Stephen Rudry looked disappointed that there was no sexual element in the crime. Enid Smale grinned at them.

"I feel wonderful," she said. "Before the police come to arrest me, let me buy everyone a drink. After all, we have something to celebrate. We've escaped forever from the clutches of that monstrous woman. Now then, what will you all have?"

A slow smile spread across the face of Alan Pomeroy.

"Mine's a bloody Mary!" he said.

Peter Lovesey

The Field

A field of oilseed rape was in flower, brilliant in the afternoon sun, as if a yellow highlighter had been drawn across the landscape. Unseen by anyone, a corpse was stretched out under the swaying crop, attended only by flies and maggots. It had been there ten days. The odour was not detectable from the footpath along the hedgerow.

Fields have names. This one was Middle Field, and it was well named. It was not just the middle field on Jack Mooney's farm. It was the middle of his universe. He had no life outside the farm. His duties kept him employed from first light until after dark.

Middle Field dominated the scene. So Jack Mooney's scarecrow stood out, as much as you could see of it. People said it was a wasted effort. Crows aren't the problem with a rape crop. Pigeons are the big nuisance, and that's soon after sowing. It's an open question whether a scarecrow is any deterrent at all to pigeons. By May or June when the crop is five feet tall it serves no purpose.

'Should have got rid of it months back,' Mooney said.

His wife May, at his side, said, 'You'd have to answer to the children.'

From the highest point at the top of the field you could see more than just the flat cap and turnip head. The shoulders and part of the chest were visible as well. After a long pause Mooney said, 'Something's happened to it.'

'Now what are you on about?'

'Take a look through the glasses.'

She put them to her eyes and adjusted the focus. Middle Field was all of nine acres.

'Funny. Who did that, I wonder?'

Someone had dressed the thing in a raincoat. All it was supposed to be wearing were Mooney's cast-off shirt, a pair of corduroy trousers filled with straw and his old cap.

'How long has it been like that?'

'How would I know?' Mooney said. 'I thought you would have noticed.'

'I may go on at you for ignoring me, but I'm not so desperate as to spend my days looking at a straw man with a turnip for a head.'

'Could have been there for weeks.'

'Wouldn't surprise me.'

'Some joker?'

'Maybe.'

'I'm going to take a closer look.'

He waded into his shimmering yellow sea.

Normally he wouldn't set foot in that field until after the combine had been through. But he was curious. Whose coat was it? And why would anyone think of putting it on a scarecrow?

Out in the middle he stopped and scratched his head.

It was a smart coat, with epaulettes, sleeve straps and a belt.

His wife had followed him. She lifted the hem. 'It's a Burberry. You can tell by the lining.'

'I've never owned one like this.'

'You, in a Burberry? You're joking. Been left out a few days by the look of it, but it's not in bad condition.'

'Who would have chucked out a fancy coat like this?'

'More important,' his wife said, 'who would have draped it around our old scarecrow?'

He had made the scarecrow last September on a framework of wood and chicken wire. A stake driven into the earth, with a crosspiece that swivelled when the wind blew, giving the effect of animation. The wire bent into the shape of a torso that hung free. The clothes stuffed with straw. The biggest turnip he could find for a head. He wouldn't have troubled with the features, but his children had insisted he cut slits for eyes and the mouth and a triangle for the nose.

No question – the coat had been carefully fitted on, the arms pulled through, the buttons fixed and the belt buckled in front.

As if the field itself could explain the mystery, Mooney turned and stared across the canopy of bloom. To the north was his own house and the farm buildings standing out against the skyline. At the lower end to the south-east were the tied cottages, three terraced dwellings built from the local stone. They were still called tied cottages by the locals, even though they had been sold off to a developer and knocked into one, now a sizeable house being tarted up by some townie who came at weekends to check on the work. Mooney had made a good profit from the sale. He didn't care if the locals complained that true village people couldn't afford to live here at prices like that.

Could the coat belong to the townie? he wondered. Was it someone's idea of a joke dressing the old scarecrow in the townie's smart Burberry? Strange joke. After all, who would know it was there unless they took out some field-glasses?

'You know what I reckon?' May said. 'Kids.'

'Whose kids?'

'Our own. I'll ask them when they get back from school.'

The birdsong grew as the afternoon wore on. At the edge of the field closest to the tied cottages more disturbance of the oilseed crop took place. Smaller feet than Mooney's led another expedition. They were his children, the two girls, Sarah and Ally, eleven years old and seven. Behind them came their mother.

'It's not far,' Sarah said, looking back.

'Not far, Mum,' Ally said.

They were right. No more than ten adult strides in from the path was a place where some of the plants had been flattened.

'See?' Ally said.

This was where the children had found the raincoat. Snapped stalks and blackened fronds confirmed what the girls had told her. It was as if some horse had strayed into the crop and rolled on its back.

'So the coat was spread out here?'

'Yes, Mummy.'

'Like somebody had a picnic,' Ally added.

May had a different, less wholesome thought she didn't voice. 'And you didn't see anyone?'

They shook their heads.

'You're quite sure?'

'We were playing ball and I threw it and it landed in the field. We were on our own. When we were looking for our ball we found the coat. Nobody wanted it because we came back next day and it was still here and we thought let's put it on our scarecrow and see if Daddy notices. Was it Daddy who noticed?'

'Never mind that. You should have told me about the coat when you found it. Did you find anything else?'

'No, Mummy. If they'd wanted to keep the coat, they would have come back, wouldn't they?'

'Did you look in the pockets?'

'Yes, and they were empty. Mr Scarecrow looks nicer with a coat.'

'Much nicer,' Ally said in support. 'Doesn't he look nicer, Mummy?'

May was not to be sidetracked. 'You shouldn't have done what you did. It belongs to someone else.'

'But they didn't want it, or they would have come back,' Sarah said.

'You don't know. They could still come back.'

'They could be dead.'

'It would still be wrong to take it. I'm going to take it off the scarecrow and we'll hand it in to the police. It's lost property.'

A full three days later, Mooney escorted a tall detective inspector through the crop. 'You'll have to be damn quick with your investigating. This'll be ready for combining soon. Some of the pods are forming already.'

'If it's a crime scene, Mr Mooney, you're not doing anything to it.'

'We called you about the coat last Monday, and no one came.'

'A raincoat isn't much to get excited about. The gun is another matter.'

Another matter that had finally brought the police here in a hurry. Mooney had found a Smith and Wesson in his field. A handgun.

'When did you pick it up?'

'This morning.'

'What – taking a stroll, were you?'

Mooney didn't like the way the question was put, as if he'd been acting suspiciously. He'd done the proper thing, reported finding the weapon as soon as he picked it up. 'I've got a right to walk in my own field.'

'Through this stuff?'

'I promised my kids I'd find their ball – the ball that was missing the day they found the coat. I found the gun instead – about here.' He stopped and parted some of the limp, blue-green leaves at the base of a plant.

To the inspector, this plant looked no different from the rest except that the trail ended here. He took a white disk from his pocket and marked the spot. 'Careful with your feet. We'll want to check all this ground. And where was the Burberry raincoat?'

'On the scarecrow.'

'I mean, where did your daughters find it?'

Mooney flapped his hand in a southerly direction. 'About thirty yards off.'

'Show me.'

The afternoon was the hottest of the year so far. Thousands of bees were foraging in the rape flowers. Mooney didn't mind disturbing them, but the inspector was twitchy. He wasn't used to walking chest-high through fields. He kept close to the farmer using his elbows to fend off the tall plants springing upright again.

Only a short distance ahead, the bluebottles were busy as well. Mooney stopped.

'Well, how about this?' He was stooping over something.

The inspector almost tumbled over Mooney's back. 'What is it? What have you found?'

Mooney held it up. 'My kids' ball. They'll be pleased you came.'

'Let's get on.'

'Do you smell anything, inspector?'

In a few hours the police transformed this part of Middle Field. A large part of the crop was ruined, crushed under the feet of detectives, scenes of crime officers, a police surgeon, a pathologist and police photographers. Mooney was depressed by all the damage.

'You think the coat might have belonged to the owner of the cottages across the lane, is that right?' the inspector asked.

'I wouldn't know.'

'It's what you told me earlier.'

'That was my wife's idea. She says it's a posh coat. No one from round here wears a posh coat. Except him.'

'Who is he?'

Mooney had to think about that. He'd put the name out of his mind. 'White, as I recall. Jeremy White, from London. He bought the tied cottages from the developer who knocked them into one. He's doing them up, making a palace out of it, open plan, with marble floors and a spiral staircase.'

'Doing them up himself?'

'He's a townie. What would he know about building work? No, he's given the job to Armstrong, the Devizes firm. Comes here each weekend to check on the work.'

'Any family?'

'I wouldn't know about that.' He looked away, across the field, to the new slate roof on the tied cottages. 'I've seen a lady with him.'

'A lady? What's she like?'

Mooney sighed, forced to think. 'Dark-haired.'

'Age?'

'Younger than him.'

'The sale was in his name alone?'

'That's right.'

'If you don't mind, Mr Mooney, I'd like you to take another look at the corpse and see if you recognise anyone.'

From the glimpse he'd had already, Mooney didn't much relish another look. 'If I don't mind? Have I got a choice?'

Some of the crop had been left around the body like a screen. The police had used one access path so as not to destroy evidence. Mooney pressed his fingers to his nose and stepped up. He peered at the bloated features. Ten days in hot weather makes a difference. 'Difficult,' he said. 'The hair looks about right.'

'For Jeremy White?'

'That reddish colour. Dyed, isn't it? I always thought the townie dyed his hair. He weren't so young as he wanted people to think he were.'

'The clothes?'

Mooney looked at the pinstripe suit dusted faintly yellow from the crop. There were bullet holes in the jacket. 'That's the kind of thing he wore, certainly.'

The inspector nodded. 'From the contents of his wallet we're pretty sure this is Jeremy White. Do you recall hearing any shots last time he was here?'

'There are shots all the time, specially at weekends. Rabbits. Pigeons. We wouldn't take note of that.'

'When did you see him last?'

'Two weekends ago. Passed him in the lane on the Sunday afternoon.'

'Anyone with him?'

'That dark-haired young lady I spoke of.'

The inspector produced the wallet found on the body and took out a photo of a dark-haired woman in a blue blouse holding up a drink. 'Is this her?'

Mooney examined it for some time. He eyed the inspector with suspicion, as if he was being tricked. 'That wasn't the lady I saw.'

There was an interval when the buzzing of insects seemed to increase and the heat grew.

'Are you certain?'

'Positive.'

'Take another look.'

'Her with the townie was definitely younger.'

The inspector's eyebrows lifted. 'How much younger?'

'A good ten years, I'd say.'

'Did they come by car?'

'There was always a sports car parked in front of the cottages when he came, one of them BMW jobs with the open top.'

'Just the one vehicle? The lady didn't drive down in her own?'

'If she did, I've never seen it. When can I have my field back?'

'When I tell you. There's more searching to be done.'

'More damage, you mean.'

Mooney met Bernie Priddle with his dog the same evening coming along the footpath beside the hedgerow. Bernie had lived in one of the tied cottages until Mooney decided to sell it. He was in his fifties, small, thin-faced, always ready with a barbed remark.

'You'll lose the whole of your crop by the look of it,' he said, and he sounded happier than he had for months.

'I thought you'd turn up,' Mooney said. 'Makes you feel better to see someone else's misfortune, does it?'

'I walk the path around the field every evening. It's part of the dog's routine. You should know that by now. I was saying you'll lose your crop.'

'Don't I know it! Even if they don't trample every stalk of it, they'll stop me from harvesting.'

'People are saying it's the townie who was shot.'

'That's my understanding.'

'Good riddance, too.'

'You want to guard what you say, Bernie Priddle. They're looking for someone to nail for this.'

'Me? I wouldn't put myself in trouble for some pipsqueak yuppie. It's you I wouldn't mind doing a stretch for, Mooney. I could throttle you any time for putting me out of my home.'

'What are you moaning about? You got a council house out of it, didn't you? Hot water and an inside toilet. Where's your dog?'

Priddle looked down. His Jack Russell had moved on, and he didn't know where. He whistled.

Over by the body, all the heads turned.

'It's all right,' Mooney shouted to the policemen. 'He was calling his dog, that's all.'

The inspector came over and spoke to Priddle. 'And who are you exactly?'

Bernie explained about his regular evening walk around the field. 'Have you ever seen Mr White, the owner of the tied cottages?'

'On occasion,' Bernie said. 'What do you want to know?'

'Ever seen anyone with him?'

'Last time – the Sunday before last – there was the young lady, her with the long, black hair, and short skirt. She's a good looker, that one. He was showing her the building work. Had his arm around her. I raised my cap to them, didn't speak. Later, when I was round the far side, I saw them heading into the field.'

'Into the field? Where?'

'Over yonder. He had a coat on his arm. Next time I looked, they weren't in view.' He grinned. 'I drew my own conclusion, like, and walked on. I came right around the field before I saw the other car parked in the lane.'

The inspector's interest increased. 'You saw another car?'

'Nice little Cherokee Jeep, it was, red. Do you want the number?'

'Do you remember it?'

'It was a woman's name, SUE, followed by a number. I couldn't tell you which, except it was just the one.'

'A single digit?' The inspector sounded pleased. 'SUE, followed by a single digit. That's really useful, sir. We can check that. And did you see the driver?'

'No, I can't help you there.'

'Hear any shooting?'

'We often hear shooting in these parts. Look, I'd better find my dog.'

'We'll need to speak to you some more, Mr...?'

'Priddle. Bernard Priddle. You're welcome. These days I live in one of them poky little council bungalows in the village. Second on the left.'

The inspector watched him stride away, whistling for the dog, and said to one of the team, 'A useful witness. I want you to take a statement from him.'

Mooney was tempted to pass on the information that Bernie was a publicity-seeking pain in the arse, but he decided to let the police do their own work. The body was removed from Middle Field the same evening. Some men in black suits put it into a bag with a zip and stretchered it over the well-trodden ground to a small van and drove off.

'Now can I have my field back?' Mooney asked the inspector.

'What's the hurry?'

'You've destroyed a big section of my crop. What's left will go over if I don't harvest it at the proper time. The pods shatter and it's too late.'

'What do you use? A combine harvester?'

'First it has to be swathed into rows. It all takes time.'

'I'll let you know in the morning. Cutting it could make our work easier. We want to do a bigger search.'

'What for?'

'Evidence. We now know that the woman Bernard Priddle saw – the driver of the Jeep – was the woman in the photograph I showed you, Mrs Susan White, the dead man's wife. We're assuming the younger woman was White's mistress. We think Mrs White was suspicious and followed them here. She didn't know about him buying the tied cottages. That was going to be his love-nest, just for weekends with the mistress. But he couldn't wait for it to be built. The wife caught them at it in the field.'

'On the raincoat?'

'That's the assumption. Our forensic people may confirm it.'

'Nasty shock.'

'On both sides, no doubt.'

Mooney smiled. 'You could be right about that. So that's why he was shot. What happened to the mistress?'

'She must have escaped. Someone drove his car away and we reckon it was her.'

'So have you arrested the wife?'

'Not yet. She wasn't at home when we called.'

Mooney grinned again. 'She guessed you were coming.'

'We'll catch up with her.'

In a tree in the hedgerow a songthrush sounded its clear notes and was answered from across the field. A breeze was cooling the air.

On the insistence of the police, Mooney harvested his crop a week before it was ready. He'd cried wolf about all the bother they'd caused, and now he suffered a loss through cutting too early. To make matters worse, not one extra piece of evidence was found, for all their fingertip searches through the stubble.

'Is that the end of it?' he asked the inspector when the final sweep across the field was made. The land looked black and bereft. Only the scarecrow remained standing. They'd asked him to leave it to use as a marker.

'It's the end of my work, but you'll be visited again. The lawyers will want to look at the site before the case comes to court.'

'When will that be?'

'I can't say. Could be months. A year, even.'

'There won't be anything to see.'

'They'll look at the positions where the gun was found, and the body and the coat. They map it all out.'

'So are you advising me not to drill next spring?'

'That's an instruction, not advice. Not this field, anyway.'

'It's my livelihood. Will I get compensation?'

'I've no idea. Not my field, if you'll forgive the pun.'

'So you found the wife in the end?'

'Susan White – yes. She's helping us with our enquiries, as we like to put it.'

'How about the mistress? Did you catch up with her?'

'Not yet. We don't even know who she is.'

'Maybe the wife shot her as well.'

'That's why we had you cutting your crop, in case of a second body. But we're pretty certain she drove off in the BMW. It hasn't been traced yet.'

Winter brought a few flurries of snow and some gales. The scarecrow remained standing. The building work on the tied cottages was halted and no one knew what was happening about them.

'I should have drilled by now,' Mooney said, staring across the field.

'Are they ever going to come back, do you think?' his wife said.

'He said it would take a long time.'

'I suppose the wife has been in prison all these months waiting for the trial to start. I can't help feeling sorry for her.'

'If you shoot your husband, you must get what's coming to you,' Mooney said.

'She had provocation. Men who cheat on their wives don't get any sympathy from me.'

'Taking a gun to them is a bit extreme.'

'Quick and merciful.'

Mooney gave her a look. There had been a time before the children came along when their own marriage had gone through a crisis, but he'd never been unfaithful.

The lawyers came in April. Two lots in the same week. They took photos and made measurements, regardless that the field looked totally different to the way it had last year. After the second group – the prosecution team – had finished, Mooney asked if he could sow the new crop now. Spring rape doesn't give the yield of a winter crop, but it's better than nothing.

'I wouldn't,' the lawyer told him. 'It's quite possible we'll bring out the jury to see the scene of the crime.'

'It's a lot of fuss, when we all know she did it.'

'It's justice, Mr Mooney. She must have a fair trial.'

And you must run up your expenses, he thought. They'd driven up in their Porsches and Mercedes and lunched on fillet steak at the pub. The law was a good racket.

But as things turned out, the jury weren't brought to see the field. The trial took place a year after the killing and Mooney was allowed to sow another crop. The first thing he did was take down that scarecrow and destroy it. He wasn't a superstitious man, but he associated the wretched thing with his run of bad luck. He'd been told it had been photographed for the papers. Stupid. They'd photograph any damned thing to fill a page. Someone told him they'd called his land 'The Killing Field'. Things like that were written by fools for fools to read. When a man has to be up at sunrise he doesn't have time for papers. By the evening they're all out of date. An evil thing had happened in Middle Field, but Mooney was determined to treat it as just a strip of land like any other. Personally, he had no worries about working the soil. He put the whole morbid incident to the back of his mind.

Until one evening in September.

He'd drilled the new sowing of oilseed, and was using the roller, working late to try and get the job finished before the light went altogether. A huge harvest moon appeared while he was still at work. He was thinking of supper, driving the tractor in near darkness along the last length beside the footpath, when a movement close to the hedge caught his eye.

If the figure had kept still he would have driven straight past. The face turned and was picked out by his headlights. A woman. Features he'd seen before.

He braked and got down.

She was already walking on. He ran after her and shouted, 'Hey!'

She turned, and he knew he wasn't mistaken. She was the woman in the photograph the police had shown him. Sue White, the killer, the wife of the dead man.

'What the devil are you doing here?' he asked.

'Walking the footpath. It's allowed, isn't it?' She was calm for an escaped convict.

Mooney's heart pumped faster. He peered through the fading light to be certain he wasn't mistaken. 'Who are you?'

'My name is Sue White. Are you all right?'

Mooney wasn't all right. He'd just had a severe shock. His ears were ringing and his vision was going misty. He reached out towards the hedge to support himself. His hand clutched at nothing and he fell.

The paramedics attended to him by flashlight in the field where he'd fallen. 'You'll need to be checked,' one of them said, 'but I don't think this is a heart attack. More of a shock reaction. The blood pressure falls and you faint. Have you had anything like it before?'

Mooney shook his head. 'But it were a shock all right, seeing that woman. How did she escape?'

'*Escape?* Just take it easy, Mr Mooney.'

'She's on the run from prison. She could be dangerous.'

'Listen, Mr Mooney. It's only thanks to Mrs White that we got here at all. She used her mobile.'

'Maybe, but she's still a killer.'

'Come off it. You're talking about the man who was shot in your own field, and you don't know who did it? It was all over the papers. Don't you read them?'

'I don't have time for the papers.'

'It was his mistress that killed him. She's serving life now.'

'His mistress? But the wife caught them at it.'

'Yes, and that's how the mistress found out for certain that he had a wife. She'd got her suspicions already and was carrying the gun in her bag to get the truth out of him, or so she claimed at the trial. She saw red and shot him after Mrs White showed up.'

His voice shook. 'So Mrs White is innocent?'

'Totally. We've been talking to her. She came down today to look at those cottages. She's the owner now. She'll sell them if she's got any sense. I mean, who'd want a home looking out over the Killing Field?'

They helped Mooney to the gate and into the ambulance. Below the surface of Middle Field, the moist soil pressed against the seeds.

I keep a huge ball-peen hammer behind the door. It's one of those elementary precautions a single woman takes when she's feeling insecure. I did not feel exceptionally secure at three o'clock this morning when I heard someone trying to break in, which is why I nearly brained my older brother.

He *said* he knocked and rang the bell before attacking my lock with his credit card. Hah! Breaking and entering is about the only thing his credit card's good for.

"If I don't answer, maybe I'm out."

"At three in the morning?"

"I might've had a date."

"Hah"

"I *might* have, I mean, locked the door, no one answers when you ring. What does that say to you? Come on in? Make yourself at home?"

"You might've been sick or lying injured at the foot of the stairs…"

"It's a *flat*, Robbie. Doesn't the word 'flat' sort of imply no stairs? And don't turn it round. You weren't breaking into my flat for my benefit, were you?"

"Okay, look, I'm here now. Couldn't you just pretend you're pleased to see me?"

Actually in a weird primal way, I'm always pleased to see him. He's my brother: he's been my Robbie forever. It's different for him. For him I was the cuckoo in the nest. Mum told me when she first brought me home from hospital he burst into tears and screamed, "Take it away." But somehow after years of traumatic childhood, we forgave each other. Of course I let him in. I even sat him on the sofa and checked for bruises. But I didn't let him off.

"You in trouble again? Girlfriend chucked you out? Lost your job?"

"No. Well…no. This isn't even about me. It's about Dad."

Oh, right: the sins of the father. Robbie's last refuge. He'd have been okay if Dad had been around to encourage him. Well, all right. But doesn't a girl need her father's love and approval just as much as a boy? Even so, I don't use Dad as an excuse, and no one in his right mind would want him as a role model. What's even more pathetic is that Dad's dead. He died of a dirty needle ten years ago.

"Don't start, Paula, just *don't*. You've got your Ms Perfect Preacher face on and I'm so tired of it. I just want one serious, quiet conversation about Dad, with nobody blaming anyone. I want to ask you, honestly, do you believe Dad was innocent?"

"Taboo subject, Robbie. I'm not listening."

"You've got to now. We say, 'There was no evidence,' as if that proves something. And we say, 'Dad was an addict, not a killer,' as if being an addict is proof of innocence. And we say, 'Dad was too stoned to be competent enough,' like incompetence and innocence are the same thing."

"Hah! If it was, *you'd* be as innocent as a newborn babe."

"Hah, yourself. You're too scared to make anything but jokes. You're always accusing me of not meeting life head-on, of not growing up and taking responsibility, but you're the one who'd rather make smart remarks than have a proper conversation."

I didn't want to talk about the past. Nothing changes there. I wanted to say, "Move on. I have". And I work in a bank, for God's sake. I can't afford a murky childhood. But Robbie had that strungout look – sometimes he needs soothing more than anything else.

"Of course I believe Dad wasn't guilty. We were just kids at the time, but Mum would have known. And she always said it couldn't possibly have been him."

"Paula, she hadn't seen him for a week. We talk as if we had a normal family life when we both know Dad was hardly ever home. Any legitimate income came from Mum. I played hooky all the time, and you—"

"Shut up, Robbie. Everyone nicks something from Top Shop sometime in their lives."

"Right, Sis, shoplifting's normal. Persistent shoplifting, therefore, is super-normal and really, really healthy."

"You're doing it again…turning things round to get at me."

"I'm just saying we weren't as normal as you make out."

"Well, *I* do all right."

"You keep a giant ball-peen hammer behind your door, for Gawd's sake."

"Okay, so I've been a bit unlucky with some of the men I've been out with."

"You're a magnet to every loose screw in a ten-mile radius. What is it with you and violent, unreliable freaks?"

So there we were, sitting one at each end of my sofa, dissing each other, dissecting the family – a game everybody can play. But I don't blame my doomed love life on Dad. It's not as if I've got an irresistible urge to date junkies.

"I've never, ever dated a junkie."

"I said 'violent' and 'unreliable' and 'freak'."

"He was an addict, Robbie, of course he behaved weird."

"'Weird,' Paula? He used to hit Mum. He robbed petrol stations. Weird! I think you're letting him off lightly. You want him innocent so you can be respectable."

"And *you* are being hard on him so that you can let yourself off lightly. You want him guilty so you can be irresponsible."

Then it struck me – Robbie had never been in my flat for this long without asking me for money. What was going on here? He's always on the cadge. Then it occurred to me – all this talk about Dad – what if Robbie is doing drugs? We always swore up, down, and sideways we'd never do drugs. But something had changed. I reached across Robbie to turn on another light.

"What's up, Sis? Why are you staring at me?"

"I'm not staring at you." I was checking him out for the signs I was so familiar with when I was a kid. Let's see your eyes, Robbie, your arms, your receding gums. Are you twitching or nodding? How about those mood swings? Comatose one minute, rampageous the next? Oh, and I forgot to mention – keeping antisocial hours?

"Robbie, I'm tired. I want to go back to bed and I want you to go home."

"I can't go home yet. There's someone out there."

"Who?"

"A girl, Nadine Meneer. Does that name ring a bell?"

"No, should it?"

"Yeah, oh yeah. She's twenty years old and she picked me up in the Ha-Ha Bar."

"Bit young for you."

"Her decision. She's very decisive. And gorgeous. And I'm thinking, wo-ho, my luck's changing."

"Hah!"

"Yeah. So a few drinks and a couple of clubs later, we end up at my place. I'm, like, getting my moves together and hoping the sheets aren't too horrible – when, *zap*, it all goes pear-shaped. She takes out her wallet and shows me her driver's licence. She tells me she's got two friends sitting in a car outside the block. And she's shoving her driver's licence in my face and shouting, 'Don't you know who I am?'"

"Oh, Robbie..."

"I know, because I didn't know either. I mean, she was so pretty and sweet. I thought I'd got really lucky. But she, like, she stayed with me all evening just so she could find out where I lived. So that when she decided to confront me I'd have nowhere to run to."

I didn't want to ask, because I was afraid I already knew the answer: Nadine Meneer must be what's-her-name's daughter. What *is* her name? Why can't I remember? Dad was suspected of beating her to death with a hammer and I can't remember her name. Did I even know she had a daughter? A child called Nadine? Suddenly I'm furious. "How the hell did she find you?"

"I think she went to the police first and then she hired a private detective."

"And what's the point? What gives her the right?"

"Hush, Paula, calm down. Her mother was murdered..."

"What's that got to do with us?"

"That's why I asked if you believe Dad was innocent."

"He was never even charged. Of course he didn't do it. She has no right to come here stalking us, badgering us...and what about the other suspect? He had a green van, too. He didn't have an alibi, either. What about him? Is your precious Nadine stalking him, too?"

"As a matter of fact..."

"What does she *want*? We can't do anything about anything. We couldn't then – with all the neighbours staring when the cops came round and took Dad away. And they came back for his clothes, with yellow bags – could they have chosen a more eye-catching colour? Yoo-hoo, hello neighbours – look what's happening to *our* family."

"Paula, come on, take it easy..."

"How can I? Why are you so calm?"

"I'm not. I freaked out and came here."

"You broke in."

"And you hit me with a hammer. Paula, this Nadine Meneer wants me to take a test. She wants to take a swab of my DNA. She says, 'Don't you *want* to know the truth?'"

"What about the other suspect? Dad wasn't the only one."

"Paula, the other suspect already gave her a sample. It came up negative. He didn't kill anyone. But Dad's dead. He was cremated. They can't test him."

"But *we* didn't do anything. We're innocent. We didn't murder anyone."

"I know, I know. But half our DNA is his. And half, apparently, is enough to tell them if he did it or not."

"That's outrageous – we're supposed to convict our own father?"

"Only if he's guilty. Maybe he isn't – I mean, Paula, I really want to help. But – oh God – he was my Dad."

"You're not considering this, are you, Robbie? I mean the nerve of this woman."

"She said she *had* to know."

"And she thinks you have the answer – or at least half the answer – and you're prepared to give it?"

"No. Yes. Well. He was my *Dad*, but all the time she was talking, I was thinking – yes, the truth is only a swab away, the truth is the most important thing here. Did I say Nadine's really gorgeous?"

I couldn't believe it – my older brother fancied the daughter of the woman his father might or might not have killed. And for this reason he's prepared to betray the whole family. Well, me, actually; I'm the only one left.

But if I calm down and think carefully about it, I'm the one who can turn this around. Because I can't let Robbie risk my peace, my reputation, on a fifty-fifty chance. Do I really think Dad was innocent? Has Robbie got innocent DNA? Fifty percent innocent or one hundred percent innocent? He's already the son of an addict, a bad father, and a worse husband. That should be enough for him. And the other fifty percent – the fifty percent he ignores – his patient, masochistic, hard-working mother, the innocent fifty percent, goes unnoticed. And yet his mother's genetic contribution is the only one he can really count on. We're sure of our mother, Robbie and I. We could always rely on her. But Dad couldn't. Not always. There *is* a way out, provided I ignore the truth. I take a deep breath...

"Robbie, calm down. If you're that screwed up about the truth, *I'll* take the bloody test. Bring Nadine here. I'll do whatever has to be done with her swab. Then it won't be your fault. I'm the one who's positive my father's innocent."

"But are you? Do we really want to know? It's different for Nadine. She wants to close the case – she wants to bury her mother by finding out who killed her."

"Or who didn't. What will she do if I come up negative, too?"

"Then it won't be my fault. I'll have done my best."

Robbie smiles at me hopefully. This, for him, is the most successful outcome he could have hoped for: I have taken the responsibility and he will get the credit. Did I say that Robbie has a very sweet, feckless smile? I wonder who he reminds me of? Can it possibly be the man we both call Dad?

It's a good thing these DNA tests weren't around when I was born, that's all I can say. But they are now. And as long as gorgeous Nadine doesn't think of testing both Robbie and me and comparing the result, I think I can prove the man we both call Dad was not guilty. I'm as sure as our Mum could be when she told me about it just before she died. She said, "Look after Robbie: I know he's older, but you're stronger." And she told me that the man we both call Dad was probably not my father.

Yes, Robbie has a sweet smile. Much sweeter than mine. He *looks* way more innocent than I do. But there is a strong probability that my DNA is way more innocent than his. And I'm being true to our mother's last wish – I'm looking after my brother. I can't be bothered about the truth.

In the distance the surface of the Colorado River shimmered like snakeskin in the late afternoon sun. Small tufts of mist broke on the pebble shores and lifted into the air like tender smoke. On the near bank, the interstate rose out of the mosaic of motels and office blocks at the foot of the Convention Center, stalked across the river and disappeared into the emerald ripples of land that bordered the city to the south.

Dennis Lane stared out across the hill country where it seemed he had spent his entire childhood, alone and afraid, waiting for his father to return home with the latest form of discipline he had discovered to help him in his responsibility as a sole parent. His mother had died when Dennis was three and his father had struggled to look after him on his own. A willing student, he had listened to everyone from the school principal and the local doctor to his unmarried sister down in Galveston and his friends on the bowling team for advice. Not that it made any difference, in the end he had always fallen back on his hands, and Dennis had soon come to resent the people who had made his father feel such a failure: left to his own devices and free from second-hand expectations, he probably would have fared much better and Dennis himself would have been much happier. He closed his eyes for a moment and shook the memories from his head and then turned away from the hills.

Reflected on the side of the Convention Center he could see the dome of the State Capitol, an Austin landmark for over a hundred years. Built from pink granite quarried at nearby Marble Falls, the building had once been the seventh largest in the world and still drew an impressive number of visitors each year, but still nowhere near as many visitors as the building on which he himself now stood.

The sun broke free from the shade of the thunderheads that had started to bunch overhead, and he blinked at the sudden shock to his pupils and dropped his head to look out across the clipped spread of lawn at the foot of the tower. School had been out a couple of months but a number of students still decorated the area. In the far corner of the lawn a man dressed in purple tracksuit pants practised Tai Chi, calm and deliberate in his actions. To his left, a couple of jocks in UT colours hurled a football back and forth to the annoyance of a plump girl in red jeans trying to read a fat paperback. Beneath the shade of a cedar tree a couple of female students chatted quietly, and then all of a sudden one of them tossed back her head and fell flat on her back. She spread her arms in a sudden burst of emotion and stretched her thin limbs into the shape of a star, and at that Dennis felt a chill run up his spine.

On the first day of August 1966, a former marine named Charles Whitman climbed into the observation deck of the University of Texas Tower and, armed with an assortment of weapons, started to snipe at unwary students and teachers on the campus. In what was then the largest simultaneous mass murder in American history, Whitman managed to shoot forty-five people, killing fourteen of them, before a pair of Austin police officers stormed the deck and killed the sniper himself.

Dennis recalled his father telling him about how he had listened to the incident live on KTBC, a cub reporter crouched behind the mobile news vehicle out on Guadalupe telling people to keep away from the UT Tower. Later in the broadcast, the reporter had read out a list of the victims to the anchorman in the studio. The anchor had listened in silence for a couple of moments and then broken in and said: 'Read that list again, please. I think you have my grandson on that list.'

Dennis could tell from his tone that his father had been impressed with the man's dedication to his job, his professionalism, but to Dennis the cold-bloodedness of the anchor's words struck a far greater chill in his young heart than the fatal actions of the killer himself. And it was a feeling that had stayed with him across the years. He took a deep breath and stepped back, reached out and ran his hand across the memorial plaque attached to the inside of the stone balcony. It had taken the people of Austin a long time to come to terms with the tragedy of that day over thirty years ago, and now another mass killer had struck at the heart of their city.

Bonnie Lane: Former Wife

He used to feel my period pains. Every month he'd get these cramps in his stomach at the same time that I started my period. And he always knew when it was going to happen. The same every month, as if he could sense what my body was going through. And I'm not one of those women that're that regular, y'know, so it's not like he could work it out or anything like that. I wouldn't have to tell him, and I never used to turn into some kind of monster with PMS so that it'd be obvious, it was as if he just knew. I mean, I never heard of that before, y'know. You hear about groups of women that live together – nuns, you hear about nuns – you hear about groups of women that live together falling into the same cycle – but guys and sympathetic pains? Uh huh. But Dennis was different. Oh, nothing serious, but a couple of times I remember that he couldn't eat anything for a day or so. And sometimes, sometimes he used to smoke pot to help ease the pain. He said it was as good as any painkillers you could buy in the drugstore. He used to bring home some of the stuff he'd confiscated from kids out on the street. Skim a little off the top, nothing too real, nothing too noticeable. Personal use, y'know. He tried to turn me on to it, but I... The only time I tried it I got sick and I never tried it again.

Griffin Clark, Austin PD: Partner, Homicide Division

I remember driving back to the station with Dennis one night, sometime around the start of the hunt for the Smiler. It had just turned one and it came on the radio that another body'd been found. I don't know, it must've been the second or third, I don't recall. No, that's right, it was the third. Anyhow, it was the time that the press came up with the name – Smiler. The press thought that it might help focus the public and help us out, or at least make people more wary: the guy was still out there, no doubt about that. A couple of lovebirds'd stumbled across the body in a picnic area out in McKinley Falls State Park, hidden behind some cherry trees. Hancock, Blake Hancock. He was a teacher at the junior high on the other side of the park. His neck had been cut from ear to ear, 'like some horrific kind of weird smile,' the kids'd said. And Dennis? Man, I've never seen him so juiced up. When he heard that the guy'd been a teacher he just started in on this shit about how he understood – that's the very word he used, understood – about how he understood what was goin' on in this guy's mind, the Smiler. What was in his head, why he was doin' what he was doin' and how he was now goin' to catch the guy.

Marc Louris, Austin PD: Classmate, Police Academy

Dennis was never the brightest of guys bookwise – he seemed to float around the average the whole time we were in the academy – but he was always the first to pick up on the practical side of things: dismantling *weapons, surveillance techniques, all that kind of stuff. Most times, he just had to watch the instructor once and that was it – he had it.*

Ethan Robinson, Austin PD: Former Partner, Robbery Division
I wouldn't call him a kleptomaniac – that's not fair and it wouldn't be true. But whenever we worked a burglary together, particularly if it was at someone's home, most times he'd end up taking something from the scene. He told me once that it was a way of getting inside the perp's head, tuning into the same vibes that'd stirred him up in the first place. Made him commit the crime. Oh, nothing major – a photograph or a lighter, something small that he could slip into his pocket. Personal stuff. But it's not as if he was the first. No sir, I've worked with guys that'd steal the cash from a dead man's wallet, pocket his credit cards and sell 'em on the street. All kinds of shit like that. But with Dennis it was always personal stuff. And it seemed to work, he always got his man. Dennis was a good cop.

The unmarked police car pulled to a halt in front of the condo on San Jacinto and Dennis Lane climbed out and stretched his arms in the air. He nodded at the uniform in front of the place and then looked up and down the street. The sun had started to set behind the hotels lined up on the shores of nearby Town Lake and the area was bathed in a sulphurous sheen. On the corner a man in a lilac polo shirt and headphones fiddled with a broken sprinkler on his lawn, and across the street a couple of kids in bulky shorts jumped in the heat and rattled the roof of the family car with a basketball.

Ethan Robinson opened his door and flipped his smoke on to the hot tarmac, climbed out of the car and followed Lane into the cool of the condo's lobby.

The door to an apartment on the third floor stood open a fraction, a slice of sun on the carpet outside the apartment like a sundial snapshot of the time of the break-in. Robinson pushed the door open a little further and a sheet of hot air curled around his torso and he felt a catch in his throat. 'Jesus Christ,' he said. 'We should be able to lock this guy up just for havin' no aircon, man, victim or not. 'S like a fuckin' desert in here.'

In the far corner of the room a man in a rumpled T-shirt and blue shorts sat on a chair in front of the window and stared out into the street. At the sound of Robinson's voice he turned and looked at the pair of cops with flat eyes.

'This your apartment?' said Robinson.

The man stood and stepped closer to Robinson. 'That's right,' he said, a touch of defiance in his voice. 'This is my home.'

'And you are?'

'Michael Usher.'

'You live here alone, Mr Usher, there's no...you're not married?'

The man shook his head. 'Just me.'

Robinson looked into the shade that buffeted the walls, the rubble of broken china and furniture that littered the floor. 'You know what happened, Mr Usher?'

Usher hiked his shoulders, pursed his lips. 'No,' he said. 'I just came home and found the place like this.'

'Kids,' said Lane. 'Most likely kids after a quick score.'

Robinson looked across at his partner and let out a short breath, rubbed the heel of his hand across the perspiration on his forehead. He took a notebook and a pencil out of his pocket. 'You know what's been taken?'

'The TV for a start,' said the man, and pointed to a dusty space in the corner.

'I'll check out the rest of the apartment,' said Dennis, and disappeared into the dark stretch of hall that led to the rooms at the rear of the apartment.

Dennis padded into the bedroom, picked up scattered clothes and at once dropped them in the same place. He lifted a slat on the blinds and peered out into the street at the rear of the condo. Heat and dusk had cleared most of the area and all he could see was an Hispanic kid in yellow trunks rolling a watermelon on the sidewalk.

He picked up a photo frame from the sill: a blond boy of about three or four squinted into the sun, a stretch of sun-kissed beach behind him. He had the same flat forehead as the man in the front room: father and son, Dennis reckoned, and slipped the frame into the inside pocket of his jacket.

Couple of hours later, Dennis took a detour on his trip home and headed out past the condo. He pulled into the kerb across the street and peered up at the dark and silent front of the apartment: the man in the T-shirt and shorts had headed out to his local bar to bitch about the fall of the area to his buddies, the invasion of treacherous kids.

Dennis jumped out of the car, lifted a holdall from the back seat and headed into the condo. He took the stairs at a run, and on the third floor took a pocket knife from his coat and popped the lock on the door in less than a minute, slipped into the apartment and left the door ajar.

He stood in the centre of the front room and looked around. The tenant had attempted to clean up the place a little, but it still looked like the local kids had bounced a basketball around the place. Dennis scoped each aspect of the room in turn and then crossed to a bookcase and dropped a silver Buddha statue into the holdall. He ran his hand across a line of CDs on another shelf, pulled out ones that he knew and dropped them in the holdall with the Buddha.

He crossed to the bureau and rifled the compartments, scattered papers and documents across the floor. He came across a passport and a driver's licence and bundled them into the holdall; a pack of unopened photos still in the store's envelope and a pocket calculator landed on top of the passport and the driver's licence.

In the bedroom he added a couple of Ralph Lauren shirts and a pair of faded Levis to the haul; a pair of battered loafers and a fresh pair of white Reeboks trailed the clothes.

He hitched the holdall across his shoulder and left the apartment, leaving the front door open and tilted to ten o'clock, the time of his escape.

Harvey Carter, Lawyer: Racquetball Partner

No matter how busy we were, we always used to try and meet up about once a week to play racquetball. I work for a law firm downtown and use the sport to ease a lot of the stress that builds up in the job. I think Dennis felt the same about being a cop, that he needed some kind of release. I remember one time the game had been pretty competitive, more competitive than usual, and as I went for a low backhand I slipped and fell and sprained my wrist. Dennis took me down to the Emergency Room and then drove me home. But then just before we were due to meet the following week, I had this call from his wife, Bonnie. She said that Dennis still had some pain in his wrist and that he couldn't make it. I didn't know what to say, I didn't understand what she was talking about. I mean, it was me that'd sprained my wrist, right?

Griffin Dark, Austin PD: Partner, Homicide Division

I remember the time Dennis first told me his theories about the Smiler, about the reason he cut people's throats from ear to ear. He told me that it was because... Dennis had this idea that the guy had been abused as a kid and that all he could remember was this smile on his abusers faces as they... y'know, you understand what I'm tellin' you? The smile that told him it was over? That they'd done with him? You do? God, I don't know where that came from; it was never raised in the nine months I worked the case and it was not an idea that made it into the paperwork.

Kent Burke: Crime Reporter, Austin Star
   There was a dark side to Dennis that he kept hidden from most people. It was something that you could maybe catch a glimpse of if you caught him off guard. Fifteen months ago, a friend of mine – his daughter was raped one night after a trip to the movies, right on campus. Nineteen. Straight-A student heading to be a doctor. Pretty, sweet and pretty, just like her mother. She was badly beaten and a couple of bones in her left hand had been broken. I don't know, maybe she put up a fight, but she'd also been hit around the head and suffered a fractured skull. Terrible. Couple of nights later I ran into Dennis out at that cops' bar down near the river, the Lantern. I used to hang out there quite a lot, meet up with a couple of guys who'd tipped me stories in the past. On this particular night someone pointed me in his direction, told me that he was the primary on the case and that maybe I should introduce myself, buy him a beer. Well, I never met this guy before, and he was friendly enough, but there was something about him that made me take a step back. I asked him about the rape case, asked him what had happened and how the investigation was going. I never told him that I was a friend of the family, I didn't want him to feel that he couldn't tell me the truth. I don't know, maybe it was because he was half-cut – he had this kind of dull stare and his breath stank of Jack Black – but the way he talked about the girl, about her breasts and stuff, made me think that maybe his sympathies lay elsewhere.

Dennis took a pull of cold Bud, put the bottle back on the bar and then looked across at the woman in the Ryan Adams T-shirt that had been clocking him for the last hour. She was kind of pretty in a raw way, with thick black hair that fell like a stream at dusk across her shoulders, but her face held a sadness that hinted at a lifetime of mistakes and missed opportunities. Dennis had spotted it the moment he saw her and he had felt no inclination to add to her woes, but after three or four drinks his defences had slipped and he shot her a lop-sided smile and nodded at the vacant stool beside him.

The woman smiled and looked into the faces of her friends for a second, then snaked around the far end of the bar and hitched her-self up on the stool beside Dennis.

'Hey,' said Dennis. 'Get you a drink?'

'Yeah, thanks,' she said, and shuffled around on the stool a little.

'Cold Bud okay?'

'Sure, what else you gonna drink when it's as hot as this?' she said, and blew a jet of air up across her face, flapped her hand in front of her face. She smiled and her teeth reflected neon sparks from the mirror behind the bar.

Dennis turned and raised his hand to the bartender, ordered a couple of bottles of Bud and then spun back around on his stool.

The woman held out her hand to him and said, 'Marnie. Marnie Stead.'

'Ethan,' said Dennis, and took her hand and kissed it.

Dennis followed Marnie up the path that led from the street to a staircase at the rear of the house, his footsteps dull echoes in the moon silence. She had told him that she lived in a studio apartment on the fourth floor, invited him up for coffee after he had treated her to take-out steak burritos from the Little City Café on the ride home. They had eaten in the car and after, she had kissed him and tasted chilli and bourbon on his lips; rubbed the band of soft white skin on the third finger of his left hand to let him know that she wasn't after commit-ment beyond the next few hours.

Sodium lamps cast a pale ochre sheen across the main street, but the foot of the path faded into darkness behind the house and he could just make out her outline ten feet ahead of him, the softness of her ankles and the easy hitch of her buttocks. To his left, knotted rose bushes lined the back wall of a car-parts warehouse, the path itself patched in dusted oil and littered in flattened soda and beer cans. Brilliant stars sparked from a hot, clear sky and the moon looked like a chipped blue marble.

Marnie reached the end of the path, spun on her toes and tossed Dennis a smile just as a security light came on above her head that turned her face the colour of burnt copper. It seemed to hover in the air for a moment, and then she disappeared around the corner and a couple of seconds later he heard her feet hit an iron staircase.

Dennis broke into a run, felt his blood rise in his heart and in his limbs and start to thump in his ears. He chased after Marnie and at the foot of the staircase he reached up and snatched hold of her hair and yanked her back down on to the path.

Marnie let out a startled cry and her limbs bucked in a spastic attempt to hold on to the iron rail, but her efforts were in vain. Her hands clutched at thin air as the back of her head hit the path with a hard and sickening thump. Before she could climb to her feet, Dennis straddled her at the hips, pinned her to the concrete and punched her in the face. Her head hit the path once more and then seemed to shake for a brief second before it slumped to the side; a trickle of blood curled out of her nose and pooled in the hollow of her shoulder, and her eyes rolled up in her head.

Dennis took hold of her ankles and pulled her into the darkness at the rear of the house, shot a look out to the street in both directions. He dropped to his haunches and took hold of the front of her jeans and snatched at the buttons, tore the T-shirt from her chest. He ripped the pair of battered Nikes from her feet and tossed them further into the darkness, slid jeans and panties from hips that felt both hot and cold in his hands and dropped them on the path. His breath came in harsh rasps and he paused for a second and then fell back on his heels and peered out once more at the street for a shift in the atmosphere, potential witnesses to the attack. He looked into the four corners of darkness around him and then, satisfied that he acted in isolation, dropped his hands on to the path and stared into the woman's face. Tortured, bloodied, pained and silent. He lifted a thick bunch of her hair and spread it across her eyes with tenderness, closed her mouth with the palm of his hand.

Griffin Clark, Austin PD: Partner, Homicide Division
Dennis had this idea that the places where the Smiler had picked up his victims held some kind of significance for him, something that reminded him of his childhood. But most of the places were not the kind of places that you'd normally associate with kids – playgrounds, schools, swimming pools, those kinds of places. No, Dennis believed that the killer'd been lonely and abused as a kid and that the places he picked his victims from were the kinds of places that a lonely and abused kid'd hang out – libraries, bookstores, the airport – places where there were loads of other people around, loads of adults, loads of parents. I mean,

like he said, why else would the Smiler pick up his victims in places where sometimes there would literally be hundreds of witnesses? I had the impression that the reason Dennis believed this was because he himself had been a lonely child and that these were the kinds of places that he'd hung out in.

Bonnie Lane: Former Wife

Another thing he used to do – and this'd just drive me crazy – was copy me when we were talking. At home in the den watching TV; having a meal in a restaurant or a drink in a bar; even at my mother's, for God's sake. Gestures, hand movements, the way I sipped a cup of coffee or smoked a cigarette – everything. If I crossed my ankles, he'd cross his ankles; if I scratched my head, he'd scratch his head. It was like looking in a mirror, one of those creepy mirrors that you find at old-fashioned funfairs. I don't think he knew that he was doing it but it used to drive me crazy.

Griffin Clark, Austin PD: Partner, Homicide Division

After we found the third victim – Blake Hancock, the teacher – and we knew we had a serial killer on our hands, Dennis became obsessed with the Smiler and spent all his waking hours on the case. As well as the official reports, he started to keep this scrapbook of all the newspaper clippings that he could find – not just from the local papers but from the New York Times *and the* Washington Post *as well. And every so often he'd tell me about one of the little theories that he'd come up with about the Smiler. Like the fact that all his victims were – and I think this is what he said, but don't quote me – 'figures of assumed authority', although I've no idea what he meant by that. I even heard that he'd turned a room at home into some kind of command centre with crime-scene photos and all that kind of shit pinned to the wall. He never mentioned it to me, so it could just have been a rumour, but it wouldn't have surprised me. I do know that he had this map of the city pinned above his desk in the squadroom with little coloured pins in it where he reckoned the Smiler would strike next.*

Dennis rolled the napkin into a ball and tossed it into the trash can on the sidewalk. He rubbed his hands on his pants and then lifted a pack of Camels from the dash and put a match to one, snapped the flame out of the match and dropped it out on the tarmac. He took a pull on the Camel and behind the smoke he could taste the barbecue smoke that drifted from one of the concession stands on the banks of Town Lake.

Ten minutes earlier he had heard the applause for the final act of the annual Aquafest rise and fall, and people had now started to drift from the site. The moon lit the mass of communal bonhomie that bubbled into the street and split it into smaller and smaller packs until faces started to form out of the darkness. Dennis let his eyes drift across the faces that appeared for a minute or so and then stopped on a couple as they halted to let a '50s Oldsmobile pull out from the kerb in a crescendo of noise and fumes and Buddy Holly.

The pair seemed familiar, but it took Dennis a moment to identify them as the couple that he had come across outside the Continental Club a month or so earlier. He had responded to a disturbance call only to arrive at the bar to find a paramedic bunched over the woman, and the kid already cuffed and in the back of a cruiser. The woman had a fresh bruise on the side of her face that matched the shape of the knuckles on the kid's right hand, but even after Dennis had spoken to her she had still refused to press charges and he had had no choice but to turn the kid loose. The woman had been a trainee parole officer and he remembered wondering at the time if it had been part of her training to date a jerk.

The couple walked down the street to an old blue Honda. The kid unlocked the car and then took hold of the woman's arms and tried to push her inside, but she held her arms stiff at her sides and refused to move, her mouth a firm line of defiance. The kid's mouth opened in a shout lost in the pack and his face turned crimson.

Dennis fired up the car, tapped the pedal and eased across the street, pulled up behind the Honda. He climbed out of the car and walked around to the front of the Honda, rested his hand on the roof as if he intended to hold it back if the kid tried to drive away.

'Hey, haven't I seen this movie before?' said Dennis.

The kid turned to look at him, bunched his face into a question.

'Hey, Detective Lane,' said the woman after a moment, a clear and hopeful smile on her face. He noticed that fear coloured her pupils black. 'Been enjoying the music?'

Dennis felt his head turn from her in embarrassment and he understood at once that he had not misinterpreted the scene. 'You remember what we talked about the last time we spoke?' he said to the kid.

The kid shot a look across the street at the audience that had started to pool on the kerb, turned back to Lane. He opened his mouth to speak, but then he seemed to pull back into himself and he snapped his lips shut.

'This is not —' started the woman, but Dennis cut her off with a raised palm.

'Look,' he said, and pointed at her upper arm where bruises had started to rise in the skin. 'You may not think that you deserve better than this little piece of shit...'

'Hey,' interrupted the kid, but the woman punched him on the arm and he fell quiet.

Dennis smiled and took a step closer to the woman. 'Connie?' he said, and she nodded. 'Look, Connie, you've got a kind face; you look like the kind of person that'd give someone a second chance. But I reckon that this here piece of shit's had just about all the second chances that he could take. That so, kid?'

The kid looked into the cop's face, hit steel, and his mouth crumpled into a sneer.

'Smells like you've had a few drinks, too,' said Dennis.

'Couple of beers or so,' replied the kid.

'And the rest,' said Dennis. 'Still, what the hell do I care if you still want to jump behind the wheel – it's too much like bullshit to write up a DUI on a night like this. But there's no way I'm going to let you drive this lady home. C'mon,' he added, and pointed into the Honda, 'climb in the car and get the fuck out of here before I change my mind.'

The kid reached out to the woman but she stepped aside and his hand snatched at air. 'Travis, no,' she said and turned her back on him. Her shoulders seemed to have lifted a couple of inches and her voice had a clarity and strength that hadn't been there a moment earlier.

The kid snarled at her and then climbed into his car, stoked up the motor and laid rubber on the tarmac as he shot out from the kerb and headed in the direction of the interstate.

Dennis trailed him with his eyes until he disappeared and then turned back to the woman and said. 'That was very brave of you, Connie. But the way you treated him'll prey on his mind, so you'd be wise to bear that in mind the next few days.' He took a pack of Camels from his pocket and offered her one. She declined his offer and he put the pack back in his pocket. 'You need me to call you a cab?' he said.

She looked at his face, turned aside. 'That's okay,' she said. 'I think I saw one of my girlfriends back there. I can catch a ride from her.'

Dennis looked at the tail-enders coming out of the park, the dark spaces behind them. 'You sure she's still here?' he said. 'Looks like most folks've already upped and left. You want me to give you a ride home? It's the least I could do in the circumstances.'

The traffic on Barton Springs Road was thick in the heat of the summer. The tarmac shimmered in front of them like an oasis, and the air that hit his face felt like it had been shot from the tailpipe of one of the semis that roared in the blind distance. Kids in more open-top autos from the '50s cruised the street and, at the junction of Bouldin, Dennis saw a man cross the intersection with a red-faced toddler asleep in the front seat beside him. The man looked like he hadn't slept in a month, ashen and drawn.

For a couple of miles, Dennis chatted about the kind of music he liked to listen to, the fresh bands that had come up in Austin of late, the old-timers he had seen rise and fall and rise once more. Connie listened in silence for a time, but then he noticed that she had started to squirm a little in her seat. 'Hey, don't let the kid rattle you.'

'I just ran into him at the Aquafest,' she said. 'I had no idea he was still in Austin. Last time I spoke to him – after... after that time at the Continental Club I told him I didn't want to see him any more – he told me that he'd been offered a job down in Corpus Christi and he planned to move down there.'

He turned and offered her a smile, noticed a tear on her cheek. 'You want to stop and talk about it? There's a quiet bar...'

'I'm in no fit state to be out in public,' she said.

'Okay, how about Barton Springs?' said Dennis, his tone loose and casual. 'Couple of tins of cool beer from the liquor store before I drop you back home.'

Connie looked at him in surprise – she never expected to be hit on by a cop, even one that had just pulled her out of a difficult situation. She still felt a little jumpy from the encounter with Travis, but as she looked at the cop once more she felt a kind of loyalty come upon her. He's only trying to be kind, she told herself. 'Sure, that'd be nice.'

Dennis purchased some beers at a store near the entrance to Zilker Park and then took the car to a spot that overlooked Barton

Springs, the natural swimming pool in the park. It had been a hot day and three or four people still bobbed in the water on the far side of the lake, brilliant specks under a fresh moon. He parked the car a hundred feet from the only other car in the lot, then popped one of the beers and handed it to Connie. He turned to take another beer from the paper sack on the back seat and took the chance to look around the dirt lot and the rest of the immediate area.

Connie picked up on his actions and said, 'What're you looking for? You expecting someone?'

'No, but you can never be too careful with the Smiler still out there.'

Shock filled her features. 'Hey, you're not using me as some kind of bait, are you? Is that why you brought me out here?'

'Hey, c'mon,' said Dennis. 'You know that's not true. You know why we came out here.'

Connie shuffled in her seat, uncomfortable in the car all of a sudden. She looked out across the lot to where a bunch of people climbed up the hill from the side of the water, towels draped across their shoulders. She took a sip of beer and put the can on the dash. 'Well, thanks for the beer but I really should be getting back.'

'Okay,' said Dennis, and touched her on the forearm. 'Let's not talk about the Smiler no more.'

Connie pointed at a young couple beside a blue sedan. 'Hey, look, there's Reba Ball,' she said, a quiver in her voice once more. 'She lives just across the street from me. That must be her new boyfriend. I heard they were staying with her folks for a couple days.'

'Let's just finish our beer and then I'll take you home,' said Dennis.

Connie opened the door and dropped a foot on to the dirt lot. 'I'll just go ask if I can get a ride home,' she said, and quickly stepped out of the car and started to walk in the direction of the blue sedan.

'Hey, hold on a minute,' cried Dennis, and snapped open the door and hurried around to the other side of the car. He felt his heart thump deep in his chest and his breath came in hard bursts. 'C'mon, I'm sorry, okay.'

But Connie had started to run, and in a moment pulled up in front of the young couple. Dennis could tell at once from their curious faces that they had never seen her before. She started to speak and after a couple of seconds the man peered across her shoulder at him, a look of deep concern on his face. The woman continued to stare into Connie's face, and then she reached out and took Connie's hand and helped her into the back seat of the car and then climbed in beside her. The man shut the door behind them and then slid into the driver's seat. He stoked up the motor and pulled out of the lot in a cloud of dust. Connie did not look back, did not offer him a smile of thanks.

Dennis stood and stared after the car until the red tail-light sheen faded from the pecan trees that surrounded the lot, then shook his head and turned to look out across the lake. The people on the far shore had packed up and left and he found himself alone under the moon. Raccoons and rabbits bundled around in the brittle shrubs beneath the pecan trees, and in the distance he could hear the mournful cries of a bluebird. He strolled around the hill a short distance and tossed some pebbles into the lake and smoked a couple of Camels, kicked at the hard earth in frustration and headed back up to the car.

He had just put his hand on the door handle when he felt his head jerk back and a coldness prick the skin beneath his left ear. On instinct he tried to turn, but before he could shift his feet or lift his hands to his head, the coldness had spread across to his other ear and he felt his throat start to burn. Intense pain spread across his chest and out into his arms, shot across his torso and in seconds he dropped to his knees and then fell flat on his face in the earth. Darkness filled his head and drained across his face, blacked out his vision. His other senses started to fail one at a time, and his last sensation was of the smell of pecans returning to the earth.

Bonnie Lane: Former Wife

Do I think that Dennis was the Smiler? No, of course not. Oh, I know that the murders stopped once that Dennis himself had been murdered, but there's not one shred of physical evidence to prove that Dennis had anything to do with any of the murders.

Ethan Robinson, Austin PD: Former Partner, Robbery Division

No.

Griffin Clark, Austin PD: Partner, Homicide Division

You're asking me if I think that another cop found out that Dennis was the Smiler and took him out? What kind of ridiculous question is that? Dennis just had a hair up his ass on this one and ended up too close to the flame, that's all. End of story.

Laura Wilson

Best Eaten Cold

Soon as Mrs. Fleming said the name, I thought *that's him*, Professor
Stephen Reed: the man who killed my husband. And then I thought,
this is *meant*. Because I believed in justice, and if I get caught – well,
I'll tell you now, there's not a court in the land that would convict
me, not if they knew what I've been through. You might say it's for
God to decide, but I say you make your own justice. In any case, if
you're a believer, then it's God that's given me the opportunity, isn't
it? And I'm taking it. Now.

Professor Reed's daughter's a friend of a friend, of course. They
always are – that's how she gets the business. Fleming's Fine Dining:
Complete Catering Service for Private Parties and Functions.
Dinner parties, all catered, served up, cleaned away – all they have to
do is enjoy themselves. Mrs. Fleming does all the cooking – I'm just
here to dish up and wash up.

I used to like cooking, never do it now – no point in going to all
that trouble just for yourself. I used to do a nice roast, with all the
trimmings – Reg used to love that, right up till the end when he
couldn't keep a thing down…When he'd finished he'd sit back in his
chair with a big smile and say, "Lovely dinner, Mrs. Skinner." And
I'd come round the table and clear his plate and I'd give him a kiss –
just a little one – on the cheek. Seventeen years he's been dead, and
I still miss it. Silly, really, but that's what life's all about, isn't it, the
small things? And I'd have my Reg with me now if it wasn't for
Professor Reed. That's why I'm saying, *it's meant*.

They're all in there, tucking into their dinner. Golden Wedding
Anniversary. We'd have been coming up for ours in a couple of years
if Reg was still alive… He's got his children in there with him.
Grandchildren, as well. We never had children – that can't have been
on my side because I'm one of six and all my brothers and sisters
have families. That was due to Reg's illness, I'm sure of it.

Professor Reed's got silver hair now. Looks good for his age,
though. All plump and pink, not like poor Reg with his face as grey
as stone and so thin you'd think a puff of wind would knock him
over, and he was only forty-eight when he died.

Soon be time for the sweet. Good job it's one of those where they
get the individual bowls…Zabag-lyon-alley-Fragg-ola, it says on the

menu card. Strawberries with fancy custard on top. It was a special request and Mrs. Fleming had to do it all on the spot, so that's made her even more narky than usual. She's just nipped out to the van for something – left it all laid out on the side, so…here we go. Just put them on the tray, and then…it's a round one so I've put a little bit of custardy stuff on the edge to mark the place. I found the bottle in my cupboard at home. Carbon tetra…something-or-other. Dry cleaning fluid. Poison, it says on the label. Do not ingest.

'Course it won't look too good for Mrs. Fleming when her posh friends get wind of how Professor Reed ate one of her dinners and turned his toes up. They won't be so keen to come to her for their little do's after that, will they? It's a shame, though, because one thing I will say for her – she's always paid cash-in-hand, no questions asked, and I could do with the money because I never got a penny after Reg died. They've been saying on the radio there's investigations now into cases like his, saying there might be money for the families – compensation – but if you ask me, it's a waste of time. Professor Reed and his sort, they won't admit they did wrong. People like us don't count, not in their eyes. Half a dozen times I've been in and out of that dining room and he's never once looked at me, let alone recognised me.

There's not been a day since Reg died when I haven't thought of it, it's interfered with my sleep, and there have been times – I don't mind telling you – like after Reg's funeral…ten of us at the crem, that was, and sandwiches, when it's nearly sent me off my head. I found out where Professor Reed lived, you see, and I used to go round there – just when I wanted to talk to him, give him a piece of my mind – night after night, I'd go, but he never opened the door. He got the police onto me, warned me off. They told me I needed help. I said, you'd need help if somebody murdered your husband, but nobody listened.

'Course, he's moved since then. Gone up in the world. Great big house, full of things, nice area…No expense spared, you can see that.

We'd been courting a few months when Reg got the call up, but I knew already he was the one for me. We knew it was coming – National Service, report to such-and-such a place – and none of the boys wanted to do it, but you didn't have a choice. So there he was, doing the training, and he's seen this notice on the board saying they wanted soldiers to help with research about the common cold. Years later, he said to me, "I was a mug, Eileen. I broke the first rule of the army: Never volunteer." He thought it would be a cushy number – decent food, extra pay – so why not? 'Course, now they're saying it never had anything to do with the common cold, but Reg told me he remembered the words as clear as if it was yesterday, and he wasn't a liar.

Professor Reed was the one in charge. They sent them into this chamber with a glass wall so the scientists could watch, and this fan starts going. Reg and the others thought it was germs they were blowing at them because there was nothing to see, and no smell, but he said after a few minutes his nose started to run, and his eyes felt funny and he thought, that's a bit quick…then he noticed this rabbit they had with them, in a cage, it was twitching and jumping about all over the place and he knew something was up.

He said he couldn't see properly, after – they had to lead him back to his billet, and it was like that for three days with terrible headaches and feeling sick and all the rest of it, and then he heard afterwards that it was a nerve gas, but they had to keep it secret and not tell anybody, even a doctor.

We got married as soon as he was demobbed, but he always had a lot of illnesses which he never had before, and I got more and more worried…but it was quite a few years before he even told me what had gone on, and how he thought the health problems must have been brought on by these experiments.

He got a job working for the gas board, reading the meters, but after about five years he started getting dizziness, and not able to breathe properly, and then after that he started feeling sick, and it got so bad he kept having to sit down. Years when it was going on I'd say to him, he'd got to see the doctor and get some treatment, but he said no, because it was a secret – he thought he'd get in trouble if he told anyone. He had to give up work in the end, and by the time he *did* see the doctor, it was too late. Cancer.

So, as I say, I'll miss my extra money, but you've got to take the rough with the smooth, haven't you? Because since Reg died it's stuck in my mind all the time how it wasn't right. What I'm doing won't bring him back, but it'll make it more fair. An eye for an eye, that's what they say, isn't it? And peace of mind – that's worth more than a few quid in your purse.

Well, now…that looks very nice. Just pop the little bottle back in my apron pocket, wash my hands, and it's done.   Better get on and polish the coffee spoons.   Here she is, back again – always in a rush.

"I've got your little bowls all ready, Mrs. Fleming."

"They're *ramekins*, Eileen, not bowls.   And they're not ready, they've got to go back in the oven." And then I see she's got the sifter in her hand and she starts spraying icing sugar like there's no tomorrow, and I'm trying to keep a lookout for my little mark in case it gets covered up, but she's spinning the tray round and before I know it, it's gone and I've got no idea which is which...

She's talking to me, but it takes a minute before I realise she's saying go and clear the plates, and I'm thinking, if I can just keep an eye on the tray, I'll be able to work it out, so in and out I go, fast as I can, but she's got the cooker door open and she's taking the bowls off the tray two by two and shoving them in, and now I can't tell which is Professor Reed's anymore and my mind's spinning round and round like the tray, What do I do, what do I do...

Last plates now, and I'm hurrying as fast as I can, trying to remember if all the bowls looked alike, but she's opening the cooker and bringing them out and they're all glazed on top with the icing sugar and no way to tell...I'm leaning over her, standing too close, and she brushes me out of the way – "fetch me that tea towel," and she's mopping the tray with it. My little mark is gone and I'm watching these bowls, all the same, it could be any one of them, and before I can pick the tray up, she says, "Oh, for heaven's sake," and snatches it up and marches through the door into the dining room, so I go after her and she's putting them down, one for each place, and they pick up their spoons and start to eat and I can see all these mouths opening, red inside, with tongues and white teeth and the shining silver spoons going up and down, and I'm looking, trying to work it out, who it is...Professor Reed or his wife or their sons or their wives or their daughter or her husband or the children, which it'll be, because I don't know how long it takes or what it does and I'm staring at this row of mouths and chins and napkins coming up and glasses of wine catching the light – and I don't know which one will get it or what's going to happen and then suddenly I see myself as if it's somebody else and I start to laugh because this is *my* experiment and it's like Professor Reed and those others when they exposed Reg and his pals to the nerve gas, waiting to see what'll happen and it's a trick like theirs because they think I'm just a waitress and it's just a dinner, and they've got no idea...

And then they stop talking and their heads come up and they look at me because I'm laughing. And I look straight at Professor Reed and he looks back and our eyes meet for the first time and he knows I know and I laugh and laugh and I can't stop, I'll never stop because it's justice and it's perfect and I watch him push back his chair and I know I've done it. Seventeen years it's been, since Reg died, but I've finally done it.

It was Charley Fields, the landlord of the Punchbowl, who started it.

Like his great namesake, Charley didn't much care for dogs or children. In fact, being a Yorkshire publican down to his tap-roots, Charley didn't much care for anything except brass, Geoff Boycott, and his own way.

But if the price of getting the brass out of his customers' pockets into his till was admitting their little companions into his pub, he bit the bullet and said that as long as they didn't yap, fight, defecate or smell too high, they were welcome in the rather draughty and uncomfortable rear bar.

That was the children. The dogs were allowed in the cosy front snug under the same very reasonable conditions.

One misty October evening, Charley peered through the snug hatch to make sure no one was sitting there with an empty glass and he saw a scene to warm a canophilist's cockles.

In one corner, a terrier sat with its bright eyes fixed on the face of its owner, who appeared to be dozing. Stretched out across the hearth in front of the glowing fire lay an aged bloodhound, looking as if it were carved out of bronze till the crinkling of cellophane brought its great head up to receive its tribute of barbecued beef flavour crisps. Beneath the window-nook table a Border collie and a miniature poodle were sharing an ashtrayful of beer while above them their owners enjoyed one of those measured Yorkshire conversations that make Pinteresque dialogue sound like a Gilbert and Sullivan patter song. At the table by the door, a small mongrel by dint of crawling round in ever-decreasing circles was contriving to bind the leg of its blissfully unaware owner to the leg of his chair.

This last was Detective Chief Inspector Peter Pascoe, the newest member of this canine club. The mongrel was Tig and belonged to his young daughter. As the nights drew in, he didn't care to have her wandering the streets even with such a fiercely defensive companion, so he'd taken over the evening walk, whose turning point was the Punchbowl. Observing the bloodhound drooping in behind its owner one damp night, he'd followed suit and over the past couple of weeks had become almost a regular, though he never stayed long enough to exchange more than a polite good evening with the others nor to identify them beyond their dogs.

'Bugger me!' said Charley Field after drinking in the scene for a few moments. 'You lot and your bloody dogs. You'd think you'd given birth to 'em! I bet if there were a fire and you'd only got time to rescue one human being or your dog, you lot would have to think twice!'

'Nay, Charley,' said the poodle. 'If it were thee, I'd not have to think once!'

Before Charley could respond to this sally he was summoned to the bar, leaving the poodle to enjoy the approving chuckles of his fellow drinkers.

As they died away the Border collie suddenly said, 'Hitler.'

'Eh?'

'I'd rescue Floss here afore I'd rescue Hitler, no question.'

The others considered. There was no dissent.

'Joe Stalin,' said the poodle.

'The Yorkshire Ripper,' said the bloodhound.

Both went through on the nod.

The collie looked towards the terrier, who still seemed to be dozing, then turned his gaze on Pascoe. He thought of explaining to them that as a policeman he was duty bound to regard all human life as sacred. Then he thought of trying to explain this to his daughter when he returned home with an incinerated Tig. Then he thought, lighten up, Pascoe. It's only pub talk!

'Maggie Thatcher?' he said tentatively.

This gave them pause.

'Nay,' said the bloodhound. 'She had her bad side, agreed, but she did some good things too. I don't think we can let her burn.'

'I bloody could. Aye, and throw coals on the fire if I could find any to throw,' growled the poodle. 'She closed my pit and threw me and most of my mates on the slag heap, the cow.'

The bloodhound looked ready to join issue, but the collie said, 'Nay, we need to agree one hundred per cent on something like this.'

And the terrier defused the situation entirely by suddenly sitting up straight, opening his eyes, and saying, 'My mother-in-law!'

Over the next few weeks the game took shape, without formal rules but with rules that its participants instinctively understood, and their choice of candidates for the fire gave Pascoe more information about his fellow players than he was likely to get from general enquiry. In a Yorkshire pub a man's private life is a man's private life. You can ask a direct question, but only if you can take a direct answer. Pascoe on one occasion, finding himself alone with the bloodhound, had enquired casually what the man did for a living.

'I'm by way of being an expert,' replied the bloodhound.

'Oh yes. An expert in what?'

'An expert in minding my own bloody business.'

Which was reasonable enough, he decided, and had the up side of meaning he didn't have to tell them he was a policeman.

The one topic on which they all spoke freely was their dogs, and Pascoe, by listening and by observation, was soon familiar with all their little ways. Fred, the ancient bloodhound, had three times been pronounced dead by the vet and three times given him the lie. He loved barbecue beef crisps and howled in derision if offered any other flavour. Floss, the collie, was a rescue dog, having been kicked off a farm when the farmer realised she was frightened of sheep. She was in love with Puff the poodle, who shared her beer but showed no sign of wanting to share anything else, which was why his non-PC owner had changed his name from Percy. Tommy, the terrier, was a genius. He could die for England, stand on his hind legs and offer left or right paw as requested. His pièce de résistance, when given the command *Light!*, was to go to the fireplace, extract one of the wooden spills from a container standing on the grate, insert it in the flame and bring it back to light its master's cigarette. Tig always watched this performance with a sort of sneering yawn. The human race, apart from Rosie Pascoe whom he adored, was there to serve dogs, not the other way round. He didn't want any dog's nose up his behind that had already been up a human's.

The one thing the dogs had in common was that their owners could all find someone, indeed several someones, whom they asserted they would put beneath their pets on a rescue priority list, and the game soon became a regular part of their evening encounter, its rules established by intuitive agreement rather than formal debate.

It was always initiated by someone saying, 'Hitler!' Thereafter the others spoke as the spirit moved them. Approval of a nomination was signified by an aye or a nod, and if unanimous, the game moved on. In the event of objection, the proposer was given a fair hearing, after which objectors either stated their case or admitted themselves persuaded. Unless the vote was unanimous the nominee was declared saved. And the game was usually closed by the terrier declaring, 'My mother-in-law!' though it was possible for someone else to close it by calling out, 'His mother-in-law!'

Pascoe, after his initial failure with Mrs Thatcher, restricted himself to historical characters. Nero was given a universal thumbs-down and he successfully argued the case for leaving Richard the Third to the flames, but when he ventured closer to living memory and suggested Field Marshal Haig, who commanded the British Forces in the First World War, he met surprising resistance and failed to carry the field. On the other hand it was only his unyielding opposition which pulled the fingers of the Hand of God, Diego Maradona, out of the fire.

When he explained the game to his wife, Ellie, she wrinkled her nose in distaste and said, '*Men!*' 'Hang about,' he protested. 'It's only a bit of fun. Anyway, you tell me, you've got the choice between saving Tig and saving George Bush, who do you grab?'

'That's what I mean,' she said. 'This stuff's too serious to make a game out of.' To which he replied, '*Women!*'

One December evening when the frost was so sharp that even Tig's normal indifference to sub-zero temperatures was sorely tested, the pair of them burst into the snug like a pair of Arctic explorers discovering a Little Chef at the Pole.

They got as close as they could to the roaring fire without standing on the bloodhound and gave themselves over to the delicious agony of defrosting. It wasn't till the process was sufficiently advanced to make him admit the wisdom of stepping back a foot or so that Pascoe became aware that the atmosphere in the room, though physically warm, was distinctly depressed. His greeting had been answered by a series of noncommittal grunts, and even the dogs looked subdued.

He went to the hatch and attracted Charley Fields' attention.

'I'll have a Scotch tonight, Charley,' he said. Then, lowering his voice, he asked, 'What's up with this lot? I've seen livelier wakes.'

'You're not so far wrong,' said Charley. 'You've not heard about Lenny then?'

So used was he to thinking about the others only in terms of their dogs, it took Pascoe a moment to work out that Lenny was Tommy the terrier's owner, who was absent tonight.

'No. What?'

'There was a fire at his house last night.'

'Oh God. Is he all right?'

'He's fine.'

'And Tommy?'

'He's fine too.'

Pascoe thought for a second and didn't like where his thoughts were taking him.

'Was anyone hurt?' he asked.

'Aye,' said Charley Fields. 'His mother-in-law. Burnt to a cinder.'

The following morning Detective Superintendent Andy Dalziel sat listening to Peter Pascoe with growing disbelief.

When he'd finished, the Fat Man said, 'I had a dream the other night. Wieldy came to see me to say he were getting married to Prince Charles and it was going to be a white wedding and he wanted my advice on whether he should sell the photo rights to *Hello!* or *OK*.'

'And which did you go for?'

'I went downstairs for a stiff drink. But thinking about it, I reckon my dream made more sense than what you've just told me.'

He looked at the local paper spread out on his desk. Its head-line was THE HERO OF HARTSOP AVENUE over a photo of a man with a terrier in his arms and a blanket round his shoulders being comforted by a fireman outside a smouldering house. The legend below read: *Mr Leonard Gold (38) returned from a meeting at the Liberal Club to find his house in Hartsop Avenue ablaze. Knowing that his mother-in-law, Mrs Brunnhilde Smith (62), was still in the building, despite all efforts to stop him, he rushed inside in an attempt to rescue her. Unhappily his courageous act was in vain, the fire was too far advanced for him to reach the upstairs room from which Mrs Smith's body was later recovered, and it was only the arrival of the fire brigade that enabled Mr Gold himself to make his escape.*

'Let me get this straight,' said Dalziel. 'This guy's a hero, nearly gets burned to death trying to rescue his ma-in-law, ends up in hospital being treated for second-degree burns, and because of some daft game some dog fanciers play in a pub, you want to investigate him for choosing to get his dog out and leaving the old girl to fry? Have I got the gist?'

'That's about it,' said Pascoe.

'And have you got any evidence to support this, apart from this dog game you play?'

'No,' said Pascoe. 'But I haven't looked into it yet. I only heard about the fire last night and I wanted to run it past you first.'

'I think you need to run a lot bloody faster,' said Dalziel. 'Preferably out of my sight. Have you got nowt better to do, like for instance your job? Best keep your hobbies for your own time.'

'In actual fact,' said Pascoe prissily, 'this is my own time. I've got the day off, remember? But in any case, I always thought the investigation of suspicious death was a large part of my job.'

'Suspicious? Has anyone from the fire department been in touch with us to say there's something dodgy about the fire? Or anyone from the pathology lab to say they've got worries about the way the old girl died?'

'No. But it's not that kind of suspicion.'

'So what kind of suspicion is it, Pete? I mean, even supposing what you say is true, where's the sodding crime?'

'I'm sure there's got to be something,' said Pascoe. 'I'll ring up the CPS and talk to a lawyer, shall I?'

'If you must,' sighed Dalziel. 'And while you're at it, ask 'em which they'd go for. *Hello!* or *OK.*'

It wasn't often that the CPS and Andy Dalziel were in accord but this seemed to be one of those occasions.

The lawyer he spoke to was a young woman called, appropriately, Portia Silk, who had what might have been in other circumstances an infectious laugh, which he heard as she quoted at him, 'Thou shalt not kill but needst not strive / Officiously to keep alive.'

'But surely if you let someone die when you could have saved them...' he protested, whereupon she interrupted with, 'Only if you have a professional relationship as in doctor/patient, or a duty of care as in teacher/pupil. But if you're walking along the canal bank and you see someone struggling in the water, it may be regarded by some people as reprehensible of you not to dive in and try to save them, but it's not a criminal act. Even if it were, in the circumstances you cite, proving deliberate choice of dog over woman would be very difficult.'

Pascoe had not survived and prospered under the despotic rule of Andy Dalziel by being easily deterred from a chosen path, and after his disappointing talk with Ms Silk, he immediately dialled the fire station and had a chat with Keith Little, the officer who'd been given the job of looking at the Hartsop Avenue blaze.

'No, nothing suspicious else we'd have been on to you. Fire start-ed downstairs in the living room. Dead woman was a chain-smoker by all accounts. From the look of things, it started in an old sofa, fag end down between the cushions, which pre-dated the fire retardant regulations, and eventually you'd get a nice little blaze going which, once it burnt through to the stuffing, would really explode. After that, well, it's an old house, wooden floors, wooden beams, even wood panelling on some of the walls. Some of them old places are bonfires just waiting for someone to toss a match on to them. Why are you asking, by the way? You got a sniff of something iffy?'

'No,' replied Pascoe honestly. 'Just curiosity. It was in my neck of the woods and I know Mr Gold slightly. You've spoken to him?'

'Yeah. He's still in hospital. Hero they're calling him. Right idiot in my book. Two of our lads had to go in there to get him out. Found him crouched down in the shower room, half unconscious from smoke inhalation. Could have cost them their lives too if things had gone wrong.'

'Did they get the dog out as well? The one he's holding in the *Evening News* picture.'

'No. I gather it were waiting for him when our boys brought him out. They remarked what a fuss it made of him. The paramedics had to let it in the ambulance with him. If you want to be loved, get a dog, eh?'

'Wasn't there a window in the shower room?'

'Aye, but far too small for a grown man.'

'Where did they find the dead woman?'

'Her room was right above the sitting room. Seems her favourite hobby was lying on her bed with a bottle of vodka and listening to music full blast. She'd not have heard anything. In fact it's likely, if she'd drunk enough, she'd have died in her sleep afore the fire erupt-ed through the floorboards. Let's hope so. No way our lads could get to her. They did well to get our sodding hero out.'

When a further call to the pathology lab confirmed that Mrs Smith had indeed been asphyxiated by smoke inhalation before the flames got to work on her, it seemed to Pascoe he'd reached the end of the road. Ellie hadn't been all that pleased when he'd announced that morning that despite having the day off there was something he had to check out at work, so now he made his exit before the Fat

Man found him something to do.

Hartsop Avenue was a mile and a half the far side of the Punchbowl from where Pascoe lived, and there was no reason for him to go anywhere near it on his way home. Nevertheless, some-how or other he found himself parked outside the burnt-out shell of the Gold house thirty minutes later.

He got out of his car and stood looking at the wrecked building. Two women walked by him, carrying shopping bags. As they passed, one said to the other in a deliberately loud voice, 'I think it's disgust-ing the way some people make an entertainment out of other folk's disasters.'

She then turned into the gateway of the house next door while her companion went on her way.

Pascoe hurried towards the neighbour, pulling his warrant card out of his pocket.

'Excuse me,' he called.

She turned an unfriendly face towards him, but when she saw the card her manner became conciliatory.

'I'm sorry what I said just now,' she apologised. 'I thought you were just one of them sightseers. We had a lot of them yesterday, just walking or driving by to take a look. Ghouls, I call them.'

'I agree,' said Pascoe. 'But it's human nature, I'm afraid. You know the Golds well, do you?'

'Oh yes. Greta, that's Mrs Gold, is staying with us till they get something sorted out. Poor woman, she's devastated.'

'I gather she was away when it happened?'

'Down in London, visiting an old school friend and doing some Christmas shopping. *She* wanted to go too, but I think Greta's friend made it quite clear the invitation was for Greta only.'

She Pascoe took to refer to Brunnhilde Smith.

'So you get on well with the Golds then?'

'Oh yes. Lovely couple. Very quiet. At least they were till she came to live with them. But I shan't speak ill of the dead.'

Pascoe's long experience recognised this as the precursor of ill-speaking in the same way as a wassailer in a Danish mead-hall knew that *Hwaet!* signalled the start of *Beowulf*.

Two minutes later he was seated in Mrs Woolley's kitchen drink-ing tea and listening to an account of Lenny Gold's mother-in-law which put her on a par with Grendel's mother.

Mrs Woolley was a friend and confidante of Greta Gold and had got the family background from her. It seemed her mother, Brunnhilde Hotter, a native of Hanover, had married a British soldier in the sixties and on his demob they'd settled in London, where Greta was born. She'd married Lenny Gold in 1985 and they made the error of setting up home only ten minutes' drive from Greta's family home in Kilburn. By 1990, Lenny had had enough. Despite being a Londoner born and bred, he started looking for a job as far away from the capital as he could get, which in the event turned out to be mid-Yorkshire.

'Everything was fine,' said Mrs Woolley. 'She came visiting occasionally, but you can put up with a short visit, can't you? So long as you can see an end. And Mr Smith never liked to be away from home too long. Then five years ago he died. Naturally Greta made her mother come and stay with her for a while to help her come to terms with things. Couple of weeks, she thought. Month at the most. Well, the way Greta put it, there was never a time when they actually asked her to live with them permanently, but somehow it just happened. Hilda – that's what she was known as; Brunnhilde's too much of a mouthful – Hilda had a bad leg. Circulatory problem she said. Fat problem I said. Human limbs weren't made for that kind of load-bearing. She was a big woman, must have cost a fortune to feed. I've seen her sitting where you are now, Mr Pascoe, and watched her eat the whole of one of my Victoria sponges, four slices and it was gone. Plus I had to get my husband to strengthen the chair she sat on, she left it so wobbly.'

As well as her dietary excesses, there were plenty of other strikes against the Widow Smith, according to Mrs Woolley. She was a chain-smoker, she dominated conversations, she often said things in German to her daughter which were clearly comments on others present too rude to be spoken in English, she liked to lie on her bed and play her favourite records very loud ('Wagner, it was,' said Mrs Woolley. 'I know because George, that's my husband, he likes that kind of stuff, but he listens through his headphones, knowing I can't put up with all that screeching and howling.'), and she complained bitterly to any who couldn't avoid listening that it was a tragedy her Greta had married such a useless idle man as Lenny ('One time she said to me,' said Mrs Woolley, 'she said, "Don't you think that's a Jew name, Lenny Gold? All right, they got married in a church but I have seen him coming out of the shower and his thing was like a skinned rabbit." I told her live and let live, she should be ashamed saying such things but she just laughed and tapped her nose.'). Above all she hated Tommy, saying the dog was unhygienic, and she was allergic, and it ought to be put down ('Such a nice little dog,' concluded Mrs Woolley. 'And so clever. I bet if it was one of those things like wolves they had at Colditz, she'd have been a bit fonder of it!').

With the woman's permission Pascoe wandered out into the garden and looked up at the burnt-out shell next door. The garage was on this side, its sloping roof joining the main house wall just below a small square window which was closed, though its glass was cracked, presumably by the heat of the fire.

'Right mess, isn't it?' said a cheerful voice.

He turned to see a round bald man who introduced himself as George Woolley.

'That window,' said Pascoe. 'Is that the shower room where they found Lenny?'

Woolley confirmed that it was.

'Like a door it was to that dog,' he went on. 'Lenny used to leave it open for Tommy so he could get out to do his business when he was shut in the house by himself. A bloody marvel, that dog. Many's the time I've seen him hop out, run down the garage roof, jump down on to the rain barrel there, do the job, then head back in the same way.'

'But the window's closed,' said Pascoe. 'Presumably Lenny didn't bother to open it last night because he wasn't leaving Tommy shut in the house by himself. Mrs Smith was there.'

'Her,' said Woolley with the same intonation as his wife. 'She'd not have bothered to let him out even if she'd noticed he wanted to go. In fact she'd rather he messed up in the house so that she'd have something else to complain about.'

'You don't seem to have liked her much,' said Pascoe.

'Sorry, I know she's dead, but I'm not going to lie. She was a pain and I doubt if even Greta will mind very much that she's gone, not once she gets over the first shock. No, if Lenny had been killed trying to save her, that would have been the real tragedy. I couldn't believe it when he set off into the house.'

'You were there?' said Pascoe.

'Oh yes. I'd been at the Liberal Club with him. Not that we're

Liberals. Who is, these days? But it's a good pint and not too pricey.'

'But he didn't take Tommy?'

'No. No dogs in the club, that's the rule.' He grinned and added, 'And no women either, except on Ladies' Night. Oh yes, it's a grand place.'

'It sounds it. So where did he leave Tommy? He can't have been in the house, can he?'

'I suppose not. He's got a kennel in the garden, sometimes he stays out there when the weather's fine.'

'I see. And you came back together from the club…' prompted Pascoe.

'That's right. In my car. We turned into the Avenue and I said, hello! What's going off? We could see one or two people standing around and it's usually dead quiet. Then Lenny said, oh my God, it's my house! Well, the ground floor was already well alight. I knew that Hilda must still be in there, there was a light on in her bedroom and you could hear her hi-fi system belting out Wagner. Lenny jumped out of the car, I've never seen him so agitated. He didn't seem to know what to do with himself. I asked someone if they'd rung the brigade and they said yes. Lenny ran up the side of the house, I presume to see if he could get in the back, then he appeared at the front again. I got hold of him and said, it's no use, Lenny, we can't do anything, the fire brigade will be here any minute. But he broke loose and before I could do anything he was up the path and going in the front door. I went after him, but the heat was too much for me. I could hear the sirens in the distance and knew that help wouldn't be long, but I really did fear the worst. And what made it worse was Tommy came running round the side of the house, barking and agitated, like he knew Lenny was in there. I've never been so relieved in my life as I was when the firemen brought him out, and I thought Tommy was going to have a fit, he was so happy. He's at the hospital too, you know. Against all the rules, but there was no separating the two of them.'

'Yes, they really worship each other, don't they?'

'That's right. Hey, does that mean you know Lenny and Tommy?'

'Yes. In fact I meet them sometimes when I'm out with my dog.'

'That explains it,' said Woolley, smiling. 'I was wondering what a cop was doing looking around after the fire. So it's just personal interest, is it?'

'Oh yes. I live quite close and I thought, knowing Lenny, that I'd take a look,' said Pascoe, feeling rather guilty as he uttered the lie.

'Understandable,' said Woolley. 'You're not thinking of visiting him in hospital by any chance, are you?'

'I suppose I might, some time,' said Pascoe vaguely.

'It's just that I'd told my wife I'd take her in at lunchtime and we'd bring Greta home and make sure she got a bite of lunch. That's why I'm back here now, but to tell the truth it hasn't gone down too well at work, there's a meeting I should be at in half an hour's time, and there's no way I'd be able to make it...but if you were going to the hospital to see Lenny...'

Why not? thought Pascoe. His morning was knackered anyway, and his suspicions, which had been looking more and more stupid over the past half-hour, had left him feeling very guilty.

He said, 'Yes, I could do that.'

'Great! You're a star! I'll just tell my good lady.'

As they went back into the house, Woolley suddenly laughed and said, 'I know I shouldn't but I had to smile when I thought about it later...'

'What?'

'Do you know your Wagner, Mr Pascoe?'

'A bit.'

'Well, when we got out of the car and saw the house burning, the music blasting out of the upstairs window was *Götterdämmerung*. It was that bit right at the end when they've lit Siegfried's funeral pyre. Brunnhilde gets on her horse and sends him plunging into the heart of the flames. Ironic, eh?'

'Always good for a laugh, old Wagner,' said Peter Pascoe.

At the hospital, they found Lenny Gold fast asleep in a small private room. His wife was with him and so was Tommy, who greeted Pascoe like an old friend.

Greta Gold, a slender, pale-faced woman with more of the Rhine maiden about her than the Valkyrie, said, 'They let me bring him but I have to take him away with me. He doesn't mind. I think he understands he can come back.'

'I'm sure he does,' said Pascoe. 'He's a very clever dog. I know how fond Lenny is of him.'

'Yes, he is,' said Greta, smiling at the terrier. 'Sometimes I'd tell him I thought he loved the dog more than me.'

'Nonsense,' said Mrs Woolley. 'Lenny adores you.'

'I know he does. I was only joking. But Tommy means such a lot to him. Sometimes, if we were out for a long time, he would even ring home, just so Tommy could hear his voice on the answer machine and be reassured. I'm so glad we didn't lose him too, that would have been too much to bear...'

Her eyes filled with tears. Mrs Woolley put her arm round her shoulder and led her aside.

Pascoe stood awkwardly by the bed, looking down at the sleeping figure. Lenny's hands were encased in plastic bags to protect the dressings and his face and head had been scorched too. All this suffered in his brave attempt to save a woman he had every cause to hate, thought Pascoe, his guilt returning with interest.

Mrs Woolley said, 'I'm just taking Greta down to the waiting room for a cup of tea, Mr Pascoe. We won't be long.'

'Yes. That will be fine.'

The two women left. Tommy showed signs of wanting to accompany them but Pascoe called, 'Tommy, come. Down. Stay.'

The dog trotted back, lay down under the bed, and looked up at him, eyes bright, ears pricked, waiting for the next command.

Pascoe thought of Tig's likely reaction to such an instruction. He might obey in the end but it would involve a lot of thought and a great deal of yawning. Much as he loved the little mongrel, it must be nice to have a pet who didn't regard you as inferior, to whom your every word was like the voice of God... God, which is dog backwards... The Game of Dog...the Game of God...

Into his mind came an image of Tommy lying in his basket in front of the fire in the Golds' parlour. The phone rings. After a while the answer machine switches on. The voice of God says, 'Tommy,' His ears prick. He sits up. The voice of God says, 'Light!' He goes to the fireplace, picks up a spill of wood left there, sticks it through the bars of the guard, and when it catches, he takes it to...where? To, say, the sofa, where a cigarette has been left stuck between two cushions. He lights the cigarette, drops the spill, gets back into his basket. And the cigarette burns, and the spill burns, and the cushion... Perhaps a small section of the cushion had had something rubbed into it, one of those cleaning solutions, for instance, which the instructions warn are highly inflammable…

The fire starts. The dog becomes aware of it. After a while he realises this is something it would be a good idea to distance himself from. He wanders up the stairs to his usual exit, the shower room window.

But it is closed.

Brunnhilde, either because she thinks there's a draught, or out of sheer malice and in the hope that Lenny will be confronted by a dog mess on his return, has closed it. As the smoke drifts up the stairs. Tommy starts barking. But his warning cries are drowned by *The Twilight of the Gods* at full belt, and Brunnhilde on her bed is too deep into her vodka bottle and too immersed in Wagner's Germanic flames to be aware of this puny Anglo-Saxon fire building up beneath her.

Lenny comes home. He expects to be greeted by Tommy. When the dog doesn't appear, he rushes down the side of the house and sees that the shower room window has been closed.

And now in panic he returns to the front. The fire roars, the heat is intense. But Tommy is in there. He breaks free from his friend's grasp and rushes into the flames. He knows where Tommy will be. He opens the window, urges the dog out.

And then because he fears, probably foolishly, that the dog's love may match his own, he pulls the window shut again in case Tommy tries to get back in to be by his side. And he sinks to the floor and prepares to die.

A story of great ingenuity…

A story of great villainy…

A story of great courage…

A story of such absurdity that Pascoe shuddered at the thought of Andy Dalziel even suspecting that his right-hand man had let it pollute his mind.

Such ludicrous fantasies belonged, if anywhere, to the world of fairy tales, of escapist movies, of childish parlour games.

Like the Game of Dog.

He mouthed a silent *sorry* at the poor burnt hero who lay before him.

Lenny's eyes opened.

He looked up, focused, and recognition dawned.

He tried to say something.

Tommy, aware his master was conscious, put his front paws on the bed and raised his head to the level of the pillow, his tail wagging furiously.

Lenny reached out one of his bagged hands, touched the terrier's head and winced.

Then he looked at Pascoe and smiled and winked, and tried to speak again.

'What?' said Pascoe, stooping closer.

'Hitler!' said Lenny.

Christopher Fowler

American Waitress

The woman on Table 4 has a laugh like a hen getting sucked into a jet engine. She's been sitting there for hours fooling around with a tuna melt that's gone grey on her. Clearly she has nothing better to do than sit there taking up a whole booth, filling in time between the car-wash and the nail bar, yakking with her friends about what one woman said to another, and how the husband is fooling around on both of them. It never ceases to amaze Molly how small the talk can get toward the tail-end of the afternoon, when the orange light is low and fierce behind the restaurant blinds.

She's managed to keep the four till twelve shift at the restaurant so she can work with Sal, who has more years on her and won't work after midnight, because she has a little girl with a twisted spine who won't let anyone else put her to bed. Sal lives in an EconoLodge near Junction 17N which is filled with frat boys throwing parties and looking to get laid, but it's safe enough for the kid, who feels safer where there's noise. Sal is a classic; she washes her hair in bleach and keeps it filled with pins and pencils in case any guy has a mind to run his fingers through it. Molly likes her; no Ps and Qs but no airs and graces either, so they help each other in the two hours that their shifts overlap.

Molly likes her job, and she's good at it. Her mother was a wait-ress in those chrome-fitted fifties roadside diners that have mostly been demolished now, except in states like Missouri and Florida, where they've been preserved with a kind of airquote-irony she doesn't take to. As a kid, Molly passed her life in diners and family restaurants waiting for her mother to come off duty. She never got bored. She read the books diners left behind, or watched the cook orbiting elliptically between the counter and the grill. Her mother yelled the old diner slang; Adam 'n Eve on a raft, murphy in the alley, shingles with a shimmy, burn the British, hounds on an island, nobody uses that stuff anymore.

Now her mother is gone, and Molly has been a waitress long enough to type any customer within seconds of him coming through the door. That's how she knows the guy on Table 7 is going to be trouble. True, he doesn't have any of the usual tell-tale signs, he doesn't look angry or drunk or both, but there's something about him she doesn't want to get too close to. For a start he looks like he has too much money to be eating in a place like this; forget that crap about family restaurants being great social levellers, you don't eat here unless you're watching the pennies more than the carbs. He's in a blazer, tie and cotton twill slacks, high-top boots and some kind of fancy silver watch peeking out from his sleeve, and it just doesn't feel right. Still, he's in her section so she has no choice.

Molly's worked everywhere, Eat 'N' Park, Chili's, Hooters, Village Inn, Denny's, Red Lobster, Tony Roma's, Chi Chi's, Houlihan's, Applebee's, Red Onion, Lone Star, IHOPs, TGI Friday's, but she prefers the little family places away from the highway, where the regular trade consists of couples who've been coming there for years, local workers and lonely widowers who won't cook for themselves. Plus, you get people passing through who are just looking for a place to eat where the arrival of their eggs won't interfere with their reading of the newspaper. In some places the work is seasonal, so it requires her to move across state. Molly doesn't mind; she has no kids to worry about uprooting, so she follows the job. But the mom and pop joints are disappearing as more people eat on the run. The chain takeouts are carefully situated to cater for office crowds. What they serve is less important than where they're based. The chains purchase tactical real estate, and keep throughput high by avoiding the comfortable familiarity of diners. They expand ruthlessly, encroaching on each other's territory so much that Molly has to look harder than ever to find the places she likes to work. Eventually she'd shifted all the way from Arizona to Florida. She likes warm weather and doesn't want to head up-state, but knows she might eventually have to in order to find a place where she can more easily afford to live.

Molly side-glances the loner as she grabs the coffee pot and swings by his table, dropping the menu in front of him. He's staring at her strangely. Okay, I've got a weird one, she thinks, unfazed. Some eateries attract nothing but crazies, they're situated too close to the bus station, but this place isn't one of those, even though they make you wear pink nylon uniforms that gather more static than thunderheads. She glances at Sal, with her hair like a ball of unravelled blonde wool, stuck through with pens, and wonders how she does it. Sal has five full plates and a coffee pot in her hands. Like Molly, she's on an eight-hour shift making two dollars seventy an hour plus tips, and she never stops smiling. "Honey, I can outsmile anyone if I have to," she tells Molly, "some days it feels like I have a clothes hanger in my mouth." She can handle eight tables at a time, no problem, more if she has to. There are seventeen tables in Mickey's, so the girls take turns to pick up the overlap. She'll give refills on coffee and water but not soda (although her offer to top 'em up gets noticeably slower after three trips) and she takes no shit from anyone.

Molly stands beside the guy at Table 7 and offers: "Hi, what'll it be?" because he's closed his menu.

"What's the special?" he asks, making eye contact and holding the look too long, too deep. He knows damn well what the special is because it's on the board right over the cook's hatch. He's late twenties but going to seed young, too tanned, watery brown eyes, expensive clothes that fit a little too snug. He looks like he doesn't get laid too often.

"Meatloaf, mashed potatoes, onion gravy." Molly stands with her pen poised.

"You have a really pretty face, you could try smiling like your friend over there," he tells her in a refined, not-from-around-here voice.

"I'll smile when I finish my shift. You want the special?"

"No, I'll have the hash and an egg-white omelette."

"We finish breakfast at midday. I can do you the hash as a side."

He sighs and reopens the menu, taking a while to choose, finally settling for chicken-fried steak. Molly checks out his waistline and thinks maybe he shouldn't be opting for the most calorie-laden dish on the planet, but keeps the thought to herself.

"Coffee?"

He nods and she goes to pour when his hand flashes out and grabs her wrist, twisting it hard until she's forced to drop the coffee pot, which bounces on the formica-topped table and cascades scalding liquid into his lap, soaking his crotch and thighs. He doesn't flinch or make a sound. Weirder still, he looks like he wanted this to happen. Then the flicker of a smile vanishes and he explodes, jumping up and patting at his wet pants in mock-horror. "She goddamned scalded me!" he shouts so that everyone turns. "Jeezus!"

"Sal," Molly calls, "some help here."

Sal slides her plates down and shoots over to the table, but so does Larry, the assistant manager, who makes things worse by taking the customer's side without even checking to see what happened.

"I'm burning here, Christ," yells the scalded guy, hopping around, "your waitresses don't even know how to pour coffee, I'm gonna sue you for every fucking penny you've got and put you out of business, man. I have the best lawyers in town, you are *so* history." Sal drops a wad of napkins on the table and throws the scalded guy another wad, saying, "You knocked that out of her hand, mister, I saw you do it you lowlife, you can clear your own damn mess up," and with that all hell breaks loose, with customers taking sides and Larry fighting both of them, standing in front of the scalded guy like a shield. And that's when Molly knows this job is gone, because the customer won't let it go and the management has already decided who's right.

But she can't allow the incident to bug her. You let one misstep like this throw you off and you're sunk. Money runs so tight that it only takes a small miscalculation to drop you into a whole world of ugly-ass debt, and once you fall down you never get back up. So Molly checks in her uniform and says goodbye to Sal, who ruefully promises to stay in touch. Then she begins circling the wanted ads, and the next place she can find that's hiring is called Winnie's Home Cookin', a dozen blocks further to travel from her apartment, twenty-eight tables split three ways, red plastic banquette seats and no tourists, because they stay uptown where there are no burned-out buildings or mean-faced homeboys sitting on the backs of bus benches.

She chooses the place because of the menus, which at Winnie's are bonded carriage trade leather with linings, not sponge-cushioned PVC, and a sign that the place once saw better times. It's as good a way as any to pick a job when one restaurant is so much like another. A few years back, rafia-covered menus became popular, but customers picked the corners off and one pat of butter would ruin them. The public doesn't realise how much of a server's job is side work, clearing and cleaning and replenishing, and one mushed butter-pat can really throw you off. Molly waits tables in places that have cooks, not chefs, where the portions are big and hot, the salads still sweat ice from cold storage, the pie cream comes in a spray can and every other condiment from dressing to creamer is in a fluted plastic pot. She's given a two-to-ten shift with a half-hour break and an unflattering liquorice-red uniform with a nametag she has to get printed herself. The busboy is Indian and speaks better English than her co-workers, Marla and Jeanette, both of whom have allowed their everyday conversation to elide into shorthand order-speak.

The place is really busy tonight, and the table configuration is a bitch to get used to, but she's good at realigning herself to any environment, a homeostatic impulse that serves her well as she moves from job to job across America. Molly knows the secret of staying on top of the work is to be on good terms with the cook, because if he takes against you, your whole shift can go to hell. Unfortunately she got off on the wrong foot with Jomac by accidentally parking in his space. The heavyset cook looks so uncomfortable in his sweat-sheened body that she half expects to see him step out of it like a discarded jumpsuit.

She's keeping busy in a quiet patch, folding cutlery into paper serviettes, thinking about the loss of her last job with some annoyance, when the guy from Table 7 walks right in, bold as a peacock. She recognises him instantly, because you never forget the face that got you fired, but she's careful to act like she's never seen him before, even when he arranges to be seated in her section. Her first thought is: *how the hell did he find me?* The only other person who knows where she's moved is Sal, and she would never tell.

This time he's wearing a blue double-breasted blazer with gold buttons and has blond-frosted hair, a low-rent version of a high roller, like he has money and wants folk to think he's someone special but doesn't have the taste to pull it off. Molly makes sure she keeps the coffee pot well clear of him, and her hand is steady as she pours. He never takes his eyes off her, but she won't be drawn, because if she catches that look he'll know that she recognises him. Her rent is overdue because of the days she lost switching jobs, and she can't afford to screw this one up. She tries to sound casual as she takes his order, which he changes and fools with, trying all the while to connect with her, but she's steel inside, never once letting down her guard.

Placing the order at the hatch, she grabs a glimpse at the table and is shocked to see that he's still staring after her. She wishes Sal was here to back her up. She can't confide in Marla or Jeanette, who share a rented trailer together with Jeanette's boyfriend, so they obviously have no secrets and no time for anyone else's. She'll have to deal with it alone, but forewarned is forearmed, and this time she's not coming anywhere near his reach. When the meal arrives she slips the plate across from the far side of the table, smoothly withdrawing her hand before he can get near her, although he makes no attempt to do so.

She comes back from the table, serves the couple on 12 with lurid emerald slices of Key Lime pie, and is refilling their plastic water glasses when she hears the cry.

She instantly knows where it's coming from, and looks over. He's sitting there clutching his mouth with both hands, and there's a thin trickle of blood coming out of the corner between his fingers. She tries to ignore him but knows he is calling to Marla, who's just passing his table. Her world slows down, because it has suddenly been rendered fragile.

She wonders what could be wrong. He couldn't have burned himself on the plate or found a piece of glass in his potatoes – Jomac is so meticulous in his preparation of the food that the servers are constantly hassled by impatient diners. Her mind flashes back over the service she provided – nothing she's done could have caused him injury; she's in the clear. He's yelling like crazy now, and if she pays no attention it'll look like she has something to hide, so she goes over and stands beside Marla, watching the performance.

The restaurant moves in a strange half-time as she watches Marla trying to convince the man to take his hands from his mouth. He tips the crimson-stained palms away and parts his bloody teeth as Marla probes. Molly sets down the water jug and realises, as her gaze travels up her uniform, that she is no longer wearing her name badge. She washed the outfit last night, as she does most nights, and ironed it before she left the room, pinning the badge in place as she walked down to her side-swiped Nissan, but sometime between then and now it has disappeared, and she has a terrible feeling that it is in his mouth.

Sure enough, the pin is hooked into his gum, but Marla's strong fingers pull it free, she just reaches in there without thinking, not worrying about HIV or anything, she used to be a nurse at the city hospital, and he retches and spits onto the tabletop, the little red badge skittering out in front of him. Molly snatches the thing up, wiping blood from the raised letters to reveal her name. The pin has been jammed in his mouth so hard that it's almost bent double.

Marla's trying to wipe him down with a wadded cloth but he's still yelling blue murder, and now the temporary manager, an ineffectual, almost ghostly Texan kid who goes by the wholly appropriate name of Sketch, is calling her over with a look of anger on his face that's the first genuine emotion she's seen him show.

It's raining hard, the first time in over a month, and it's falling too fast for her wipers to clear, pelting through the smashed window and soaking her shoulder, so she pulls over beside a phonebox. She no longer has her mobile – that was one of the first expenses to go. She's lucky – Sal is just leaving to start her shift.

"How he could even convince people he'd accidentally eaten it, for God's sake, it's a name-tag, he said it had been deliberately pushed into the mashed potato where he couldn't see it, I mean, what is this guy's fucking problem?" She listens to Sal, who's a mix of common sense and Southern toughness, a woman who once went back on a double shift within hours of an abortion in order to pay the doctor.

"No, I didn't report the car window because what's the point? He obviously recognised the vehicle in the restaurant lot, looked in and saw my badge on the seat or the floor. Well it seems pretty obvious to me that's what happened, 'cause I sure as hell didn't come near enough for him to rip it off me in the restaurant." She listens some more. The rain is steaming off the car hood like mountain mist.

"The same as before. Won't press charges if they let me go, yadda yadda, they couldn't get me out of the door fast enough, everyone's so shit-scared of lawsuits. Marla with blood all over her, unbelievable. God, no, I don't want to track him down, I just want to stay the hell out of his path. I wouldn't even be able to give the police a clear description, he looked kind of different this time. Sure I recognise him, but that's because of his manner, you know how you do in this job, complainers stay with you. But I'm going to change the car, that has to be how he found me. I have to anyway, I can't afford to get the window fixed, although what's gonna be cheaper than this heap of junk I don't know. No, I have no idea what car he drives. No, Sal, it's celebrities who get stalkers, I'm just a waitress, but I'd like to know what the fuck he thinks he's doing." She scans the straight wet street as she listens. The sky is darker than the buildings. "Sure, I'll be in touch just as soon as I get something."

After hanging up she goes into the convenience store on the corner and collects the freesheets. She needs to start looking for hirers right now. She can sell the Nissan and go to Rent-A-Wreck until she's back on her feet, the cash will tide her over between jobs, but doesn't know how she'll ever cover the gap and save for another car.

Back in her room at the motel – she swore she'd never rent like Sal, the margin for financial error is just too slight, but there's no alternative now that she's moving around again – she looks at her face in the bathroom mirror, and knows that some restaurants will rule her out. She was always pretty, but the look is getting hard. She's not as light-hearted about the job as she used to be, and it's starting to show. The management want their 'girls' looking fresh, not troubled. She's always been good at hiding her worries behind a smile, has no problem with being on her feet all day and knows the work better than any of the younger ones, her customers always tell her that. If she'd been an executive she'd have risen through the ranks by now, but when you're a waitress there's nothing to be except another waitress, and the older you get the more management start thinking you'll want to use their health plans.

The tips at Winnie's were solid, she needs another place like that. For a while she toys with the idea of taking a second job, just until she's out of this money-hole. She could do mornings in a mall, grab a couple of hours' sleep and keep her regular afternoon shift, or just work one restaurant and pull a double every three days or so, but first she has to find one job, let alone two, and the ads aren't promising.

The first interview she gets is a disaster, a dingy deep-red ribshack staffed by downtrodden-looking migrants with ESL and a scary supervisor called Ethel who warns her that they don't tolerate slackers. The next, which she passes on the spot, is in a diner set behind the graffiti-blitzed bus station, populated entirely by derelicts surviving on handouts of old coffee. Getting in and out of the building involves walking through shadowed no-go zones to an unlit car park; and with her stalker waiting out there somewhere, it's not worth the risk.

Finally she gets a decent slot at Amanda's, a dessert-heavy joint in an unsafe but thankfully well-lit downtown neighborhood where the kids hang out in chicken-wire basketball courts smoking, dealing and constantly shifting loyalties within their social groups. Amanda's desserts are a source of fascination for Molly. They sit in a tall glass cabinet lit spearmint-neon in the middle of the restaurant, and appear to have been manufactured from entirely alien ingredi-ents. The jello is coloured in eye-watering shades that don't exist in or out of nature, the cream is so white that it looks like plastic paint, and the pumpkin pie appears to be made of orange sofa foam.

But hey, it's a job, and the other girls seem okay, if a little distant. They're scared, she can see that, scared of slowing in case they stop altogether, like wound-down clockwork toys. The bad news is she gets the late shift, which is until 2:00am with another half-hour of clearing away after that, but servers can't be choosers and at least night diners aren't so picky about their food. The motel where she's staying smells of damp and fast sex. It has a filthy pool, a scared-looking Mexican cleaner and a weird reception clerk who concen-trates on comic books as though they were Dickens novels. She gets back from Amanda's too tired to wash out her uniform, but it has to be done the night before or it won't be dry in time. The tips are lower because the desserts are cheaper, which is no surprise consid-ering how they taste. Amanda was the original owner, but the place killed her and now it's working on the rest of the staff, who have the bad skin and downbeat demeanor of drug mules.

In the moments when the work eases off, and she looks out through the plate window at the windy, desolate street, Molly some-times wonders how it's come to this. She has no real friends to speak of, no one to share private jokes with, no loyal lover who waits up to tell her things will all turn out fine. And on the bad evenings, when rain weighs down the red plastic canopy and the place is deserted, she asks herself how long she can go on pretending that everything is fine, how long it will be before her ready optimism and her hope-ful smile crack and die with the weight of getting by.

But you think like that and you're already lost. So she covers the burns on her wrist caused by hoisting the coffee pot and shows the surliest diner that she cares, and works on autopilot until at the end of the week, one rainy Sunday night, she doesn't even notice that he's back, the stalker is back, and has slipped into a booth at the end of her section just before the restaurant's due to close.

The lights are dim over the crimson seats, so when she catches his face it's a shock. He looks terrible, like he hasn't slept for a month. He looks like a serial killer haunted by his deeds. His hair has grown out and he's added a moustache that ages him, and she knows she can't ask Rosemary, the other waitress, to take over because her section is empty and she's slipped into the alley for a cigarette.

Ted, the cook, is nowhere in sight. No one can help her. She drops the menu onto his table and beats it, checking that her nametag is in place as she goes. But she has to return to take his order, because that's her job, it's what she does. And he says: "Molly, I've been looking for you everywhere. You're the only one who can help me. Please, don't go, I won't do anything bad."

She wants to go but has to stop and ask. "Why did you get me fired?" She's holding the coffee pot high above him, ready to throw it in his face if he moves an inch toward her.

"You're too special to be working in a diner," he tells her, watching her eyes. "Such big blue eyes, like an angel. You're a good woman, Molly. You know how much it hurt me to let you go? The first time I saw you I knew you could save me from myself, stop me from doing harm to others."

"You're crazy, mister," she tells him. "I can't even save myself."

"Molly—" He reaches out a hand.

"You don't use my name, and if you move one more muscle I swear to God I'll pour boiling coffee over you," she warns. "Now you can either eat and leave or just plain leave, there's no way I'm listening to your bullshit." Her hand is shaking, and she's not sure how much longer she can hold the steel pot aloft.

"Apple pie and coffee," he tells her, as normal as any other diner. "I won't make any trouble in here." She goes to the cabinet and cuts the pie, slipping the knife into her apron pocket, but he's as good as his word. He eats as meekly as a punished child, and leaves a twenty dollar bill on the table without asking for the check. He picks up his raincoat and goes so quickly that she has no time to see which direction he's heading.

She's due off duty in five minutes, and there's no more side work to do tonight because they cleared and reset as the restaurant emptied. Outside, it's raining fit to drown rats. There's a stippled yellow pool stretching across the road where the drains are backed up. No cars, no people, like a movie set waiting for its cue. She thinks of asking Ted to walk her to her car, but doesn't want anyone to think there's something wrong. So she offers to close up for the night, and waits as the others pull their jackets over their hair and head out into the downpour. She douses the lights and watches, but there's nothing happening outside. Finally the waiting gets on her nerves, so she digs out the keys and locks the front door behind her. From the canopy to the car park is a couple of hundred yards max, but she needs to plot the route because parts of the broken tarmac are flooded and her canvas trainers will get soaked.

She negotiates an isthmus through the water toward the Rent-A-Wreck Datsun and already has her keys out when she realises he's sitting in the car, and the headlights come on as he pulls around her, shoving open the passenger door and dropping across the seats to pull her in, but she's fast and lashes out at his face. She's not expecting the pad across her mouth, though, and the gasp of surprise she takes draws chloroform into her lungs. That's the trick, not to put it across the nose like they do in movies, and now it's too late because everything's pressing in on her, and she knows she's losing consciousness. He's going to kill her and leave her body in a ditch, she realises stupidly, and that's not at all what she had planned for herself.

But not before she's pushed her way back out of the car, and although she's disoriented by the rain and the bitter smell in her head, she knows she must breathe clean air fast or she'll go down, and he's slowed up by having to stop the car and come around from the other side. And man, either he's slow or she's fast because she's stumbling back at the door of Amanda's before he comes sliding around the corner toward her. If she can shut the door she'll have won, but his strong hand covers the jamb and pushes back, and all it takes is one clean sharp punch in the face to floor her cold.

"Nurses are strong, of course, but they care in an entirely different way, and they empathise way too much."

She hears him before she sees him. Her right eye is sore and feels swollen shut.

She has a fat lip, a metal taste in her mouth, a jackhammer headache, but at least she's upright in one of the darkened booths, so she can get her bearings.

"You, though—" he shakes a finger at her as he paces about "—you're a real piece of work. I've watched a lot of waitresses, and you're a classic. A dying breed. Like those Newfoundland women who gut fish all day, nothing touches you. I like that. A true *enfant de malheur.*"

"I don't know what that means," she says thickly. She needs a drink of water, something to stop her tongue sticking to the roof of her mouth.

"It means you've had a tough time, Molly. It shows in your face. It's what makes you strong."

"Just tell me what the deal is here." She can't see him clearly. Why the hell doesn't he stand still for a moment? "What's your name?"

"Duane," he says softly.

"Well, Duane, what is it you want?"

"I know you're alone. I know you're broke. Christ, I've seen where you live and I have no *idea* how you can stand it." He angrily throws out his hands. "What is it that keeps you going? You've nothing, nothing at all. But you don't have to be alone. You don't have to fight so hard. I could help you."

"Do me a favour." She points at the counter behind him. "Flick that switch down."

He looks around and sees the steel coffee pot. "Right, sure," he smiles and shakes his head and the orange light goes on, then turns back to her. "I promise you, Molly, I didn't want to hurt you and never will again. But I had to get you to listen to me. All I want is for you to be happy, and if we can come to a deal that will make me happy too, well hey, everybody wins."

She tries to focus, to measure how far she is from the phone, the door, the kitchen knives. "What did you have in mind, Duane?"

"Okay." He perches on a corner of the orange leatherette seat and slaps his hands on his thighs, pleased with himself. "I come from a pretty wealthy family. We owned half the car lots in this city. When my old man died he left me a shitload of money. I can give you whatever you want. You'll never need to worry about making ends meet again. This country favors the wealthy, Molly. If you haven't got it now, there's no way you're ever gonna get it. But I can take care of you."

"You're not in love with me. I got no real education, I got no money, I wait tables and fetch people coffee for God's sake." She glances at the pot. The orange light has clicked off.

"You're strong, Molly. Nothing fazes you. That's what I need, a really strong woman."

"I need caffeine while I think about this. Could you grab me some?"

He rises, then seems to change his mind. "You fetch it. You said it's what you do."

She wonders how nuts he is to let her go near the boiling coffee pot. Maybe it's a trust thing. Maybe he just likes her to wait on him.

That's when she realises the true nature of his proposition. He loves her strength so much that he wants her to use it against him. He wants her to fling the hot liquid in his face, to stab him, to punish him, to make him cry, to expose his helplessness before her.

He's making her an offer. It's a fucked up world, he's thinking, but there are worse deals going. She could be alone for the rest of her life.

She fills the thick white cups that hold less than they look. With a steady hand she carries them together with the pot to the shadowed table. His eyes never leave hers as she sets the cups down and raises the hot steel container level with his face.

He dares her. "Do it, Molly. Do it, and I'll make sure you never have to work in a hellish place like this again. I'll never hurt you. I'll look after you like a princess. There's crazier men than me out there." He licks his lips. "Come on, baby, show me what you're made of."

Molly considers the idea for a moment, then lowers the coffee pot. She absently touches her swollen mouth before she speaks. "You have a hell of a nerve, presuming this is what I need, just because of what I do."

"Everyone wants to feel needed."

She could throw the boiling coffee in his eyes and run out, but then it will never end. Instead, she sets the pot down quietly and walks to the door. "Let me tell you something. I wait at your table, I take your shit, but you can't get inside me. I'm not running across town from you anymore, Duane. You come after me again, I swear I'll end up going to jail for killing you."

"You stupid bitch," he shouts after her, and she realises he's saying that because torture and death at her hands is what he most desires. She wonders what happened to him as a little boy that placed him in the sexual thrall of strong women. "What have you got here? You'll grow old and die serving shitty food to people who don't give a fuck about you. You've got nothing and you'll get nothing."

"That's right, lover," she smiles to herself beneath the rain-sparkled streetlight, "this," she throws her arms wide, "this is what I do. But you only have to do one thing well to have a reason for getting out of bed every morning. And I'm a damn good waitress. What keeps you alive?"

Later, she'll sit in a bar, have a drink, maybe cry. But right now, as she walks away into the night rain, she's already thinking about the ad she saw for the Chicken Lodge downtown, a rundown family joint, good shifts, minimum wage plus tips.

Four months on, there's a two-line piece in the Cleveland Plain Dealer about some rich guy found stabbed to death in a quiet family diner. Police want to interview the woman who served his final meal.

To most of us an iron knife is just an iron knife. Of course, there are different qualities of blade, which is why some of them become almost magical, though I bought one from a pedlar once which would scarcely cut a piece of cheese. Mostly, however, knives are simply things for carrying in one's belt, useful if one is unexpectedly invited out to dine, or as a scant protection against bandits, wolves or bears while travelling. Scarcely a commodity to risk execution for. Yet there is the curious case of Calvus, who did exactly that.

His real name isn't Calvus, obviously. Few people are called "Baldy" legally, but since he hailed from Gaul and had a name which no one could pronounce, Calvus he instantly became. And it was as Calvus the meat-butcher that he sent word to me, when he was captured and locked up in the Glevum market cells.

I knew him only slightly, and liked him even less. He was a small, fat swarthy man, bald as a pig, with a smile as unpleasant as any of his wares. Standing at his *marcellum*, his market stall, with a hatchet in his hand, spattered from head to foot with blood and entrails, and surrounded by bleeding carcasses, he was a fearsome sight. Mothers murmured, "Calvus will get you" when children disobeyed.

It was Junio, my slave, who brought me the news. I'd sent him to collect water from the town fountain, and when he returned, he came panting into my rickety workshop to say, "Master, Calvus the butcher is in jail, and I am sent to ask if you will speak to him."

I put down my selected tiles with a grunt. I was engaged on a complex piece of work, a decorative panel in honour of the impending visit of an ambassador from Rome. I was assembling it on a piece of hessian and was hoping to take it to the council chambers on my handcart the next afternoon. With a little planning, I could take out a section of the existing tiles and put my insert in, while all the councillors were busy at the baths. It is a technique I have perfected over years, and it requires concentration on my part. I was not pleased to be interrupted by a summons from a common butcher who had no rank at all.

I bridled. "He sends a message, does he? I wonder how many guards he had to bribe for that." Common prisoners in the filthy Glevum jail are not usually privileged to summon friends.

Junio gave his cheekiest grin. "You forget, master, he is one of Marcus's *clientes*. No doubt that's why he asked for you."

It was true, I had forgotten that. Calvus had first come to Glevum as a gift, to Marcus Aurelius Septimus (one of the most powerful men in the entire province of Britannia) from a friend. He was then a kitchen-slave, but Marcus had permitted him to buy his freedom shortly afterwards – partly, I suspect, because he didn't like Calvus any more than I did. So Calvus was legally Marcus's freeman – which meant that he had lifelong duties to his patron, naturally, but also that Marcus was more or less obliged to offer protection in return. Which, unfortunately, was where I came in. Marcus Aurelius Septimus is my patron too.

"Marcus suggested it?" I said, knowing what the answer was. I've solved a few crimes for Marcus in the past, and he has formed a habit of involving me. I got up resignedly and gestured for my cloak. No question, now, of my refusing this or I was likely to end up in the cells.

I didn't take Junio with me to the jail. I'd spent a day and night there once myself. The cells are filthy, stinking, dark and damp and men are shackled to the floor like animals: not a place to take an impressionable boy. My decision wasn't very wise perhaps, since, seeing me turn up at the gates tunic-clad and without an attendant slave, the guard on duty almost refused to let me in.

I almost pointed out that I was a full Roman citizen, but remembered that, in that case, I was supposed to wear a toga on business at all times. I let the matter rest. I said, humbly, "His Excellency Marcus Aurelius Septimus required me to come. One of his *clientes* is in jail."

The soldier looked me up and down. "Calvus the butcher, is it? I was warned to expect somebody for him. Through that door there, in the jailer's house."

I should have predicted that. Having a powerful patron won you certain rights. It wasn't like being a citizen, of course (Calvus wasn't born in Glevum, which would have given him automatic rights) but Marcus's name was sufficient to ensure that our interview would not take place in the foul darkness of a cell. Indeed, the room I was shown into was a pleasant one, with a shuttered window space and a rough stool and table set for me. There was even a jug of cheap watered wine, and a few battered-looking dates.

Calvus looked in worse condition than the fruit. His legs were bruised, his clothes were torn, and a bloodied blackness round his eyes and mouth suggested a less-than-gentle arrest. Before they found out who his patron was, the jailers had obviously chained him up "slave-wise", with a collar around the neck linked to his arms and feet. The victim cannot stand upright, nor move without half-strangling himself. Of course, these bonds had been removed by now, but Calvus still walked painfully.

The big guard who had brought him in prodded him towards me with his sword and winked. "All yours," he said. "And welcome to him, too. I was told that you could talk to him alone, on His Excellency's orders, but I'll be right outside the door. If he's any trouble, just give me a shout." He patted his dagger cheerfully and left. I heard the heavy key grate in the lock.

"Well," I said to Calvus, "What's this all about?"

He half-raised his head. "An…n…" he managed, in a voice still cracked with thirst.

I knew I would get nothing from him in this state. I let him have the wine-jug. He lifted it two-handed and drank, straight from the lip, in deep grateful gulps. When he had half-emptied it, I took it from him and said, "Well?" again.

He looked at me. "A knife," he gabbled. "It all started with an argument about a knife. I admit that. But it wasn't me who kidnapped him and tied him up…"

I interrupted him. "Suppose you start at the beginning, Calvus. Who did you have this argument with, and where?"

The butcher heaved a huge sigh. "It was like this…" he said, and launched into his tale. It was a long and rambling version of events, but this – effectively – was what he said.

It happened some months earlier, in Corinium. Calvus had gone there to try and buy a slave to help him with his trade. The slave market at Corinium is a lively one, with slaves from all corners of the Empire – much better than the weekly one held in the forum here. So, Calvus left his brother-in-law to mind the stall, hired a mule, and went to Corinium overnight – to another relative who kept an inn. He wanted to be at the market shortly after dawn to get the best choice of slaves available, and perhaps to make some other purchases.

He didn't find a slave to suit, he said, but he was haggling with the vendor of some wool when an itinerant cutler came into the market-place – a dramatic figure, in a multi-coloured robe, with an impressive beard, long hooked nose, and a huge red turban wrapped round his head. I have seen such men in Corinium myself, they come from the North African Province, and their very appearance draws a crowd at once.

This man did. People were already crowding round as he drew a coloured blanket from his handcart, spread it out, and then reverently lifted down a big, carved box.

He didn't open it at once, but stood admiring it, which only made his audience more curious. They jostled closer.

At last, he opened up the front. It hinged apart like a pair of double doors. The watchers gave a gasp. Inside were knives, cleavers, hatchets, every kind of blade. Then, in a high-pitched sing-song kind of voice, he began his cry – holding a piece of linen in one hand and running a blade down it so it fell in two. "Best knives. Finest in the Empire. Feel the weight. What do you offer me for these amazing blades? Just like those used by the Emperor himself. Twenty denarii? Fifteen? You won't believe it, gentlemen, I'm asking only five denarii. It is a crime. I'm robbing myself at the price. Only twenty left. Who'll buy the first?"

As Calvus described the scene I could imagine it too well. Five denarii was a fair price for a good knife, and some credulous fool in a tunic was soon pressing forwards, eager to part with his hard-earned coin. Then there was another, and another, until all the knives were gone.

"You bought one of them?" I said.

Calvus shook his head. "Not then. I was still bargaining at the buckle stall. But I was listening all the time. Nicodemus – that's what he called himself – sold off the cleavers next. I wanted one of those, but they disappeared more quickly than the knives. Then the hatchets went. By the time I'd finished my business and could get across, there was only one knife remaining in the box. It had a carved bone handle and a wicked blade. He didn't even try to sell us that. Somebody wanted it, but Nicodemus shook his head. That knife was not for sale at all, he said. It was the only one like it in the world, forged in the fires of Vulcan himself."

"You believed that?"

"Of course not, but then he picked it up and started cutting things. It was incredible. I've never seen anything like it in my life, and I've owned scores of knives. Straight through a chicken, bones and all, as if it was a piece of honey cake." Calvus gazed glumly at the stone flagstones on the floor. "I don't know what came over me, but I wanted that knife more than I've ever wanted anything. And Nicodemus knew it. I offered him all the silver in my purse, but he just smiled and shook his head, and made as if to put the knife away."

"So you made him an offer?" I began to see where this might lead.

"A hundred denarii," Calvus admitted.

I gasped. The fact of agreeing on a price – however high – made that a contract enforceable in law.

Calvus shuffled his still-shackled feet. "Of course, it was more than I could realistically afford. But I did want that knife. I had the money saved, to buy a slave, but I wasn't carrying it with me in the market-place – it's always full of pickpockets and thieves. I'd left it, hidden in my mule-pack at the inn, where my relatives could keep an eye on it, but where I could get it if I needed it. And I was desperate to have that knife. Perhaps it really was a magic blade. Certainly it put a spell on me."

I thought I could see what was coming next. "But when you went to get the coins he switched the knife?"

Calvus looked at me indignantly. "I am not quite a fool," he said. "Of course I realized that he might do that. But equally he couldn't let me take it till I'd paid. In the end he offered to put it in the box, under my very eyes, and get one of the townsfolk to sit on it – in full view of everyone – until I came back. I couldn't see the flaw in that. I even picked out the bystander – a young man I slightly knew – so there was no possibility of fraud."

"But…?" I said. There had to be a but.

"I don't know how he did it to this day, but somehow he played a trick on me!" Calvus groaned. "I got the money and came back: he opened the box and gave me the knife – the only one there was. I was delighted. But when I got back to the inn and went to use the blade – merely to cut a piece of barley-loaf – I knew at once that it was not the same. Oh, it looked identical – ornate carved handle and every-thing – but it hardly cut. I took it to the ironsmith straight away – his shop is not so very far away – and he tried to grind a decent edge on it – but to no avail. It was just useless, and I'd paid a hundred denarii for it! I've discarded better knives than that!"

I was beginning to feel quite sorry for the man. "So what did you do then?"

"Went back and confronted him, of course – he was still packing up his things – but the crowd had drifted off by then and he just laughed at me. I was not going to put up with that. I called on the *aediles*, the market police, to have him charged before the magistrates that day."

I nodded. Though a vendor is not liable under the law for the quality of what he sells, a purchaser can sometimes get his money back if he can prove that he was wilfully deceived. "What happened?" I said sympathetically. "Did he avoid arrest?"

That is not unknown. It is the responsibility of the man who brings a case to ensure that both he and the accused appear in person at the town *curia* before noon on the appointed day, otherwise there's no case to be heard. Not as easy as it sounds, if the accused is reluctant to appear!

Calvus surprised me. He smiled, a little bitterly. "Oh, I'd paid the *aediles*. It cost me something, naturally, to have it all rushed through like that, but they seized him and dragged him in before the trumpet blew. They made very sure of that."

I could imagine that. The market police are armed, and – since they are on the first step to higher things – anxious to be noticed by the authorities for their efficiency. They would ensure that Nicodemus came to court "before the trumpet blew".

That was often the hardest part of all. The Romans have this convention of dividing the hours of daylight into twelve equal parts and calling the resultant divisions "hours" (and the same thing for the hours of darkness too). But since most of us humbler citizens have no water-clocks, "the start of the seventh hour" is hard to calculate. So, to mark the official middle of the day, a trumpeter comes out onto the court-house steps and blows – and if you come in after that, you're late. But it seemed that hadn't happened here.

"Did he find some legal quibble, then? Persuade them that they needn't hear the case?"

"On the contrary," Calvus said bitterly, "They heard the case. I lost, that's all."

"But you had witnesses?"

"That was the trouble, in the end. Nicodemus didn't deny the knife was valueless. Instead he turned the whole case on its head. That was the knife that I'd contracted for, he said – contracted properly in front of witnesses – 'Do you solemnly swear to buy this knife for one hundred denarii?' – Which, of course, I had. He didn't ask me to swear the contract till I brought the money back. So technically it was *that* knife that I'd agreed to buy, whatever it was like! The magistrates simply laughed at me and threw me out of court – and I had to pay the *aediles* all the same. It cost me every coin I possessed."

I frowned. "But you did pay?"

"Of course."

"Then I don't understand. This was months ago. Why are you in prison now?"

He gulped, and I thought for a moment he was going to cry. "This is a much more serious affair. They arrested me today. I'm charged with robbery on a public road. Nicodemus's revenge, I suppose."

No wonder he was looking so distraught. If they found him guilty now, that was a crucifying offence. It cost me the remnants of the wine, which he seemed to require to fortify himself, but in the end I got the story of the day.

Calvus had been at his Glevum market stall, as usual – when who should come into the market-place, but Nicodemus, with his box of knives. Calvus was busy with his customers and couldn't leave the stall, but he watched, and it was exactly the same as in Corinium. In no time at all a crowd had formed, and Nicodemus was selling off his knives. Even the patter was identical.

Calvus watched till he could bear no more. The memory of Corinium was still raw. He left his brother-in-law to mind his stall again and made his way to where the cutler was. Nicodemus was selling hatchets by this time – but Calvus noticed there was still a single knife left in the box.

"The same knife?" I interrupted.

"I'm sure of it. The box had been repaired, but the knife looked just the same. I would have known it anywhere – that carved bone handle – it was a work of art. I intended to wait till he began to show it off, and then announce that it was not for sale."

"Because it had been forged in Vulcan's furnaces?"

"Perhaps it was. The way it sliced through everything, it was miraculous. But then someone started bidding for the knife, although the hatchets had not all been sold. The price went up and up, just like before. I don't know what came over me – I was still furious at being made to look a fool. I started shouting that he was a cheat, and people turned to look at me. But the man bidding for the knife was too intent. Then Nicodemus looked up himself. He didn't even recognize my face. It was too much. I strode over and picked up the coloured blanket from the ground, tipped up the box, and sent the whole stand flying." Calvus looked animated, even now, recalling it.

"So *he* called the *aediles*, this time?" I suggested.

Calvus shook his head. "He had no need to call them, they were there. And I was ready with my story too – and then Nicodemus realized who I was. And that's when he sprang his next surprise. He claimed that after the trial in Corinium, when he'd won, he'd gone off to the baths to celebrate before he set off for an *oppidum*, a little village several miles away. But no sooner had he started on the road, than someone came up behind him silently, held a dagger to his ribs and pulled the outer folds of his turban down around his eyes, so that he couldn't see. Then his attacker dragged him off into the trees, stripped him of his purse, pulled off his robes, and left him tied up against a tree. When he came back to his handcart again, he found it had been ransacked, and his knife-box broken into and dashed on the ground."

"It had two compartments, I presume?"

Calvus stared at me. "How did you know that?"

"What other explanation could there be? And what about the knife? The proper knife, that is?"

"He must have had it hidden somewhere else. In any case, it seems it wasn't found. He had it this morning in the market-place, so who knows where it was? But his purse was taken, and he was attacked. And of course, he claims that it was me."

"And was it?"

Under the bruising Calvus turned an ugly shade of puce. "I've been telling them all morning that it wasn't me. I don't have a dagger, anyway. But of course, I'd half-condemned myself by shouting out – in front of everyone in the market-place today – that he'd cheated me in Corinium. And then I turned his knife-stall upside down. That made me seem a violent man. And then he said he recognized my voice."

"Does he have any proof that he was robbed that day?"

Calvus laughed bitterly. "Apparently. A soldier from a passing unit heard his cries – that's how they came and found him stripped and tied up against the tree. The whole detachment thought it was hilarious. No doubt they could be found as witnesses. Oh, Nicodemus was attacked, all right."

I was calculating rapidly. "And what time did you leave Corinium?"

He looked abashed. "That is the trouble, citizen, I can't be sure. A little after the trial finished I suppose. After I'd spent my money at his stall and paid the fine, there was no point in staying any more. In any case, I'd hired a mule – and I had to return that before the town-gates closed."

"That might be important. Where did you hire the mule?"

He gave me the name. Stortus Maximus. I knew the man. He kept a hiring stable just outside the walls. Most of his animals were old and wheezing – as he was himself – but they were cheap. And Stortus was a decent sort of man. He bought his mules and horses broken-down, but he looked after them – some of them went on for years and years. And he was honest too – the town wags said he lacked the intelligence to cheat.

"Very well," I said. "I'll see what I can do. I'll go and talk to Stortus now. And Calvus, when they question you again, give them the answer but say as little as you can. Otherwise you'll talk yourself to death."

He had turned pale now. "What do you mean?"

I looked at him. "You say you had no dagger, Calvus, but you had a knife. You spent all your money on it, didn't you?"

He looked sullen. "That! It would hardly cut a loaf o' bread."

"But a man could hardly see that from behind. Take my advice, Calvus, watch your tongue. Nicodemus is a cunning man. He'll twist your words, just as he did before. Now, I must go if I'm to save your skin. Guard!"

The warder was opening the door, almost before the word was out. "All right, Citizen? He isn't causing any trouble here?"

I shook my head. "Not at all. But you may show me out and take him to the cells."

From the pathetic look on Calvus's face, he must have hoped I'd somehow contrive to free him then and there. But naturally there was no chance of that. I left him to his miserable lot, and made my way – with some relief – back to the freedom of the world outside.

The soldier at the gate grunted a greeting as he let me out.

"There's a message for you from His Excellency. You're to call on him, and tell him how things stand."

"I will," I promised, but I did not go direct. I went first to where Stortus kept his mules.

It was a tumble-down affair, merely a sort of large roofed wooden shed, with a lean-to shack at the back of it. Stortus was with his animals, as usual, giving them fresh water and grooming down their coats, although he stank like a manure-heap himself.

He listened to my question carefully. "It is a long time ago," he said. "But let's have a look. Calvus the butcher – let me see. I gave him old Fatty, I'm sure of it." He went over to the wall, close to a stout little mule with baleful eyes, and looked at a series of scratches he had made. "Here we are. Just before the Ides of Augustus. Just as I thought, he brought it back on time. That's before the shadow reaches the eleventh hour, on the sundial on old Gauss's tomb out there."

He gestured, through the open door, towards the monument. The dead town-councillor had ordered the dial to be built so that every time men looked at the time, they would recall his name.

"That's the time I close the stable door, and settle my beasts for the night. If anyone brings in an animal after that, I charge them for an extra day. That makes them prompt, of course. Naturally, it's more difficult when it's cloudy, like today. Then I just have to guess. All in the contract that is. Here you are, that's my mark for him. Two days – he had it overnight. So he was back in time. That's definite. And it was sunny weather then, as well."

I thanked the old man, slipped him an *as* or two and hurried off, almost as glad to be away from him as I had been to leave the prison earlier. I hoped my tunic hadn't absorbed the smell, as I hastened to the centre of the town, where my patron still maintained a suite of rooms over a wine-shop near the square. I thought of going home to put my toga on, but decided that there was no need for it. I had been visiting the prison, and was already late.

Marcus had me shown into his presence instantly. He was dressed for banqueting, in a toga of dazzling whiteness, set off by the glow of rubies at the clasp and his most glittering rings on either hand. In my smelly tunic, I felt peculiarly ill at ease.

"Well, Libertus, my old friend," he said. The voice was not unkind, but the greeting troubled me. When I am "his old friend",

I'm alarmed. "This is about Calvus, I presume. Have you succeeded in releasing him?"

"Not yet. Excellence," I confessed. "But I think I may have evidence which helps. Who will be presiding in the Calvus case?"

Marcus frowned. "Probably the ambassador from Rome, since he is here. This is a capital offence, so it will fall to a senior magistrate."

I thought of my unfinished pavement piece. "He has arrived then?"

"I am entertaining him to a feast tonight. He is at this moment in the guest room here, preparing for the banquet with his slaves."

I was thinking rapidly. "He has come straight from Rome?"

"Via Londinium and Corinium, of course. He wished to see a little of Britannia. He has never ventured to the northern provinces before. He is quite favourably impressed. You know what rumours circulate in Rome."

I did. Marcus himself had come from Rome originally, and he never tired of telling me about the wonders of the Imperial capital, and how things were different there. However, I had now learned what I'd been hoping for. "In that case, Excellence, there is hope. I believe he will dismiss it out of hand. And if the ambassador presides at the case, the populace cannot accuse you of favouring your own *clientes*, which they might otherwise have done. Calvus is not a very well-liked man."

His face cleared. "You may have a point. I imagine the Ambassador won't mind – and here he is, in fact. Perhaps you would like to speak to him yourself."

The man who was entering the room looked what he was, a man of power. Not only was he elaborately dressed, he had that well-oiled, sleek, self-satisfied air that the rich and favoured always seem to have. He looked at me with something like disgust. I feared a whiff of Stortus hung about me still.

Marcus caught the look and hastened to explain. This was his apartment, after all. "This is one of my *clientes*, Ambassador," he said. "He is a citizen, despite appearances. He has been engaged in an errand on my behalf – and would like to have a word with you." I was not an "old friend" now, I noted with a smile, but Marcus was doing his best for me.

The Ambassador gave me a frosty smile. "About...?"

I had not meant to be catapulted into this, but suddenly there seemed no escape. I took the plunge. "About a case, your Mightiness, that you are scheduled to try tomorrow at the courts."

"That cutler who was set upon and robbed," Marcus put in. "I think I mentioned it to you earlier."

"You did!" the Ambassador said loftily. "It seems to be a cut and dried affair. The man identified his assailant, I believe, in front of witnesses."

Marcus looked at me.

"Ah!" I said. "That is just the point. He identified the voice, but not the face. He didn't *see* the man who tied him up and took his purse. Calvus seems a likely suspect, I agree. He had a grievance, and he had a knife. But did he have the opportunity? We know there was a trial in Corinium – which began just before the seventh hour. They got there just before the noonday trumpet-call, and no doubt the court officials can confirm the fact."

"Well?" the Ambassador demanded testily.

"And then, by the knife-seller's own account, he went off to the baths. It was only afterwards that he was robbed, when he had set off later from the town."

"Well?" again.

"But I have witnesses to prove that Calvus was back in Glevum before the end of the tenth hour. There is no doubt. He hired a mule, and the owner is prepared to swear to it." I sent up a mental prayer to all the gods that no one sent for Stortus to enquire. I did not know that he was "prepared to swear" at all, and he would not make an impressive witness if he did. "And Calvus was back at his market-stall at dawn," I hurried on, pleased to have thought of it. "Anyone in the town will tell you that – which proves that he was back before they shut the gates."

The Ambassador was looking at me with interest.

"Ambassador," I said, "You came that way today. You know how long it takes to travel between Corinium and here. And you were in a swift imperial gig. This man was on a mule. How could he be out-side Corinium at – what? – the ninth hour at least, and be back here in time to manage that?"

"By Hermes," the Ambassador exclaimed. "I do believe you're right. It took me three hours at least to make the trip. It would have taken a man on mule-back more." He scowled. "If this is true, I shall have this Nicodemus flogged and fined for wasting the court's time."

Marcus stepped forwards as if to intervene, but caught my eye. "And Calvus the butcher? What of him?"

"We'd better hold him, since he is arraigned. But see that he has fairer lodging, overnight – on my authority. Tomorrow we'll hear what Nicodemus has to say. It is preposterous. Attempting to identify a robber by his voice."

"As you say, Excellence," I murmured.

Marcus said, "I'll send a messenger to the jail at once – if you would seal the order, Mightiness." He nodded to one of his attendant slaves. "Fetch me some bark and writing ink at once. Best octopus, none of your watered soot." The boy scuttled off to do as he was told, and Marcus turned to me. "Well done, Libertus. Wait here for the letter and you can deliver it."

I did more. Once Calvus was released into the jailer's house I found the inn where Nicodemus was. That wasn't difficult. The whole town was abuzz with news of this colourful visitor. Nicodemus eyed me doubtfully.

"I have a warning for you, knife-seller," I said. "The Ambassador from Rome is here, and he has heard about your case. He has unchained Calvus, on new evidence, and plans to have you flogged and fined when you appear."

Nicodemus laughed. "Don't be foolish, townsman. I have proof. The man threatened me in court, and robbed me afterwards."

"You will find it hard to prove," I declared. "Of course, you know the law – it's clear you understand it very well, that's why you make your contract as you do. But if this comes to court, I promise you, I will be a witness in the case. And I will tell them, if Calvus does not, how you have two sections to your box. You put the good knife into one, get some simple bystander to sit on it, then sell the poor knife from the other side. Isn't that the case?"

His smile faded, but he still said, "What if there are two sections? Both are empty. Anyone may look."

"No doubt they are, at present. That knife is too precious to leave there, in case someone works out your trick. But I know..." I leaned forward and whispered in his ear.

It was a guess, but he confirmed it by the way that he turned pale.

I pressed my advantage remorselessly. "I shall tell them about that, if you appear. It will be the gossip of the town – and rumour spreads like fire before the wind. Before you have reached the next town your reputation will be ahead of you."

His voice was almost a whisper. "And if I don't appear?"

"Then I say nothing. Although, of course, some of the story's out. Calvus accused you of cheating him – that will have spread for miles by this time. If I were you, knife-vendor, I wouldn't try to sell my knives round here again. Now, it is getting dark. If you – for any reason – wish to leave, it would be wise to do it very soon."

I am not good at threats, but that one worked. The next morning there was no Nicodemus at the court, and without him, of course, there was no case to bring. Calvus was released without a charge.

I had turned up at the court to see, and Marcus came across. "Well done, Libertus. You did well. I confess I was surprised myself. I didn't think you'd prove him innocent. I was convinced he did it all the time."

I looked at him. "Of course he did it, Excellence. I didn't prove him innocent at all. I simply persuaded the Ambassador of that, which isn't the same thing. Surely you realised the trick I played? The Ambassador has spent his life in Rome – he doesn't realise that in Britannia, when you divide the daylight into twelve, it varies so much with the time of year. You told me how surprised you were yourself. An hour three months ago, when the attack took place, was naturally far longer than an hour yesterday."

Marcus stared. "That's why Nicodemus spent time in the baths after the trial in Corinium, before he set off for the *oppidum*? I wondered about that."

I nodded. "There was obviously still a lot of daylight left. But Calvus was furious at the legal trick. He waited till Nicodemus left the town, and then crept up and jumped him from the rear – threatening him with that useless knife he'd bought. Ironic really. He wanted to find the other knife, but though he broke the cutler's box in two and discovered how it worked, there was no knife. He betrayed himself there, incidentally. He knew there was a secret. He might have deduced that, possibly. I did myself. But he also told me that the thief hadn't found the knife and that the soldiers laughed when they found Nicodemus by the tree. So he must have been nearby. How could he have known that otherwise? I'm quite sure Nicodemus didn't report it to the *aediles*."

"So Calvus stole the money?"

"He was really looking for the knife. I'm sure of it. That's why he stripped Nicodemus to the skin – why else would a robber strip his victim bare, but leave the clothes, and break up that lovely box as well? Much more sensible to steal it all. Anyway, most of the money in that purse was his – Nicodemus tricked him out of it."

Marcus looked doubtful. "So what happened to the knife? Nicodemus had it yesterday."

I smiled. "That was the interesting part. It was Calvus who gave me the clue. He pulled down Nicodemus's turban to blindfold him. 'The outer folds,' he said. So obviously, he left the turban on. I believe the knife was under it, wrapped in the inner folds. Probably Nicodemus always carried it that way when travelling. I imagine Calvus was not the first to waylay Nicodemus on the road and try to get the knife he'd bargained for – but Nicodemus would just show the box and demonstrate that it was empty. He virtually admitted that to me last night."

Marcus said, "I see," again, and turned to go. Then all at once he turned back to me. "So – why did you save Calvus from his fate? I didn't think you even liked the man."

I didn't rise to that. "You asked me to, Excellence," I said. "Besides, though he was legally at fault, I am not sure that he merited that fate. I had a certain sympathy with him."

I didn't add, although I might have done, that I bought a knife from a pedlar once. A credulous fool in a tunic, eager to be parted from his coin. I think I may have mentioned it before.

A knife that would scarcely cut a piece of cheese.

Mark and Howard were an upwardly mobile couple in an increasingly obsessive search of an upwardly mobile neighbourhood.

At first Dalston appealed to them. There were all those ethnic shops, restaurants and cafés, and, yes, all those Turks, with the sort of bristly moustaches that made Mark gasp with delight, even if they also made Howard groan with horror. Prices could only go up. During their prospecting they were particularly taken with a straggly street of semi-detached Thirties houses. But then they noticed the black teenagers sprawled across a cracked rise of front-steps, while passing around a joint with indolent furtiveness. And, more serious, there was no underground, to take Mark to the council office at which he worked or Howard to his dental surgery.

Acton? Acton was whizzing up. But there was something depressing about the quiet, even sombre streets, with so few people in them. Balham? A chum of theirs – well, more an acquaintance – had been mugged there when merely going out to buy bananas in mid-afternoon. So, after a lot of discussion, they had decided, reluctantly, to rule Balham out.

Eventually, they opted for Stepney. It was a first view of Tredegar Square that clinched it. Oh, if only, if only! Mark, the older of the couple, who knew about such things, having once lived briefly and unhappily with a morose architect, was particularly enraptured. 'I love those giant recessed columns,' he sighed.

'Way beyond us.' Howard was always the practical one, apt to be tight when Mark was wanting to be generous.

'Yes, I know, sweetie, I know, don't I know! But one day... That's what we're going to aim for. Once again he gazed up at an elegant façade. 'You bet all the people living here are *very* grand. No council tenants.' His elderly parents still lived in a high-rise, much vandalised council block.

What clinched the matter was their finding of an estate agent who at once, as Mark put it, came up with the goods. 'Just call me Thelma – I hate formalities,' she told them at their first meeting. At that meeting she was already referring to them, flattering, as 'you boys'. Black and buxom, with a wide space between her front teeth and extremely long fingernails, she at once adopted them as her friends.

They reciprocated.

'I'm not sure how much this is going to appeal' she told them at a second meeting after that first one had yielded 'nothing quite right'. 'It's just come in. You'll be the first people to view it.' It was a house unusually capacious for what, she had to admit, was still a neighbourhood largely occupied by Bangladeshis. Period. Well, Edwardian. The owner, an old lady, had had to go into a home, poor dear, after a stroke. The price was amazingly low for a property of that size, but that was because there were – 'I have to come clean to you boys' – two drawbacks that might put people off. Firstly, the old lady had let the house become a perfect tip. Secondly, there was a sitting tenant.

'A sitting tenant?' Mark pulled a face. He was good at faces.

'I'm not sure I'm encouraged by that,' Howard said.

'Oh, he's a perfectly harmless old boy. A retired army man – captain, major, I can't remember. I don't think you boys will have any trouble with him.'

'Well, let's take a dekko.'

'That's the spirit!' Thelma exclaimed, plunging downwards, arm outstretched for her vast red handbag and then lurching to her feet. 'It's a terrific bargain. And I don't think that old chap is going to last all that long. You've only to look at him to realise that. On his last legs.'

Thelma panted up the uncarpeted stairs ahead of them. 'He has the attic area,' she explained superfluously between gasps. 'I'm afraid the higher and higher you climb, the worse and worse it gets.'

Mark did the face, expressing revulsion, that involved wrinkling his nose, pulling his upper lip upward and to one side. 'There's a distinct pong,' he said.

As they reached the final landing, both Mark and Howard were dismayed to find the tenant's quarters were not self-contained. There was a door open onto a lavatory, its linoleum worn here and there to holes. An ancient washbasin reared up in a corner. One pane of the dusty, cobwebbed window had been clumsily patched with cardboard now coming adrift at the edges.

Thelma wrapped on a closed door beyond the open one. Silence. She rapped again. 'Major Pomfrey!'

'Yes, yes. Come in. Come in!' The voice was high-pitched and nasal.

The major was seated on the edge of a narrow unmade bed, with a half-smoked cigarette held at a jaunty angle between forefinger and middle finger, amber from kippering with nicotine over many years. He was in striped flannel pyjamas, his feet, with their talon-like toe-nails, bare. 'Ah, Mrs Lucy. Good to see you. Forgive my *déshabillé*. I overslept. A case of my alarm clock failing – not for the first time – to be alarming. Do sit.' There was one straight-backed chair, with a chamber pot, almost full to the brim, under it, and one armchair, over which some clothes were scattered.

The three intruders remained standing. 'We don't want to take up your time,' Thelma said, 'but as I explained on the blower, these are the two possible purchasers of the house. They just wanted to say a hello to you.'

'They'll be fools to buy this place. Falling down. Rising damp in the basement and ground floor. Mice. Even rats.'

'Now come on, Major, it's not as bad as all that,' Thelma chided, not attempting to hide her annoyance that he should at once try to run down a property that she had every hope of selling. 'Well, let me introduce…'

The major extended a shaky hand but did not get up. As Howard took the hand, he noticed, with distaste, the orange urine stain in the crotch of the major's pyjamas. He, not Mark, was the one who noticed such things.

'Have you been here long?' Mark asked.

'Thirty-two years. Moved here when I lost some money through a daft investment – and my wife died. Two disasters together. Within a month of each other.' He stared fixedly up at Mark with pale blue eyes that suddenly had a glitter of malevolence in them. 'Sitting tenant. Can't be put out. Controlled rent.'

'Yes, we know that,' Howard said. 'I don't see why that should be a difficulty.'

'The old girl tried to get me out. Many times. At one point even cut off the electricity. Never had any luck!' he laughed. 'You won't either!'

After the brief meeting, Mark and Howard invited Thelma to a cup of coffee at the Starbucks opposite to her office.

'I don't think he'll really pose any problem,' Thelma said.

'I noticed that he didn't have a television set,' Howard said. 'Or a hi-fi. So there'd be no arguments over noise.'

'We hate noise.' Mark said.

'Unless we ourselves are making it,' he added with a laugh.

'The house definitely has possibilities.' Howard raised his cup of *latte* and sipped daintily.

'It's an absolute snip,' Mark said. 'I can already see in my mind's eye what we could do with it.'

Thelma wondered whether to mention that although the sitting tenant had his own lavatory and washbasin, he had no bathroom, and was entitled, by a long-standing agreement, to use the downstairs one. She decided not to. After all, it didn't look as if the old boy took a bath all that often.

'Well, you boys must have a good think. I don't want to rush you. But I must tell you, I'm showing round two other interested parties tomorrow.'

'Then we'll have to get our skates on,' Howard said.

'But don't let's rush things,' Mark warned. Howard was so impulsive.

Howard was often kept late at the surgery. Much of the decorating therefore fell to Mark, even though, as he was the first to acknowledge, he was not the practical one of the two and in any case he had a bad back. There were of course, things that even Howard could not do, and so, though anxious about the rising costs of repairs on top of monthly repayments on a substantial mortgage, the couple from time to time had to call in two jolly black builders recommended by Thelma, whose cousins they were.

From the start, the major was all too obviously fascinated by the work going on around him. Usually wearing nothing more than those striped, flannel pyjamas and slippers, he would slowly descend the creeping stairs, crab-wise, a hand clutching on the banisters, and then position himself in a corner of whatever room in which work was in progress. Leaning against the wall, emaciated arms akimbo, he would stare fixedly for a long time before finally making some suggestion or criticism, more often the latter – 'You've got some of that paint smeared on the wainscot', 'That nail's not straight', ' Here, here! Hold on! Hold on! You've forgotten that spot over there!' These interventions unnerved Mark and Howard, who then became even clumsier. They infuriated the builders, who eventually gave an ultimatum – 'That geezer's got to leave us alone or we quit.'

It was Howard, the more diplomatic of the two, to whom devolved the task of telling the major that the work would proceed more smoothly if he did not interfere.

'Oh, dear! Oh-dear-oh-dear! Well, now isn't that sad? So-o-o sad!' The high pinched voice was really sarcastic. 'I'd hate to put you off your stroke. What a sensitive couple you are, aren't you?'

'It's the builders too.'

'The *builders*? Oh, you mean the cowboys. Did I tell you that I saw one of them pinching a packet of your biscuits? Chocolate bourbons. I glimpsed him opening the top drawer of that cupboard in your kitchen, when he didn't know I could see him from the hall.' He chuckled. 'It's amazing how dark-skinned people are so often light-fingered.'

At first Mark and Howard, who were genuinely kind and tolerant, did their best to accommodate 'Pomme Frite' (as they had soon nicknamed Major Pomfrey). They told each other that, with his innumerable prejudices, he was a figure from the past; that, with wife long since dead and his estranged daughter, the only child of the marriage, far away in New Zealand, the poor creature was desperately lonely; that one had to remember that he was suffering from a host of ailments, ranging from the bronchial cough that reverberated through the house at daybreak every morning with all the regularity of a rooster, to the diabetes for which he had to give himself a daily injection. One could not really be unfriendly, much less hostile, to someone so pathetic.

But over the ensuing months Pomme Frite's intrusions became less and less supportable. Soon after they had moved in, he had asked then whether – since his television set had broken down and he was 'too old to go to all the bother and expense of getting another so late in the day' – they would mind if he watched the cricket on theirs when they were out at work. Reluctantly, they had acceded. Entering the sitting room that evening, after a day of hard work, they sniffed angrily at an unpleasant combination of cigarette smoke and urine, before one of them rushed to fling up the windows and the other frantically busied himself with emptying the overflowing ashtray.

Then something even more appalling happened. They were seated before the television set one evening, watching *Who Wants to be a Millionaire?*, when Pomme Frite's head appeared around the door.

'Would you mind awfully if I joined you?' Without waiting for a response, he began to nudge a chair forward with a bony knee. Eventually, unable to stand the alien presence any longer, Mark exclaimed: 'Oh, this is a bore!', jumped up and switched off the set. 'Yes, we ought to be thinking about our supper,' Howard chimed in. But a few evenings later, Pomme Frite once again joined them, clutching a packet of cigarettes and a lighter against his narrow bony chest, even though they had made it amply clear that they could not abide smoking.

Pomme Frite had a way of usurping the bathroom just when they themselves wished to use it before rushing out to work or a party. Eventually, exasperated beyond endurance by the sound of water constantly running at their expense with a counterpoint of violent expectoration, they suggested that it might be more convenient for all three of them if they agreed on fixed hours when the bathroom would be at his sole disposal. To that Pomme Frite responded: 'Oh, lordy, lordy! You two spend *hours* there, while yours truly waits around, sponge-bag and shaving kit at the ready. One might be living with two members of the fairer sex from the time that you take. No, no, I don't think it would be a good idea to fix definite times, I'll just go on slipping in whenever you give me the chance.'

Soon the intrusions extended to the kitchen, 'I hope you won't take it amiss. I suddenly found I had run out of bread, so, transgressing on your good natures, I helped myself to two of those ciabatta rolls that I found in your bread bin. Rather past their sell-by date, but any port in a storm.' Seeing the look of indignation on the two faces opposite, he replied huffily: 'Of course I'll replace them. Though not perhaps with products quite so *recherché*.' He never did replace them. A short while later, when, having for once returned early from work, Howard went into the kitchen to make himself some coffee, he was exasperated to find a saucepan tilted sideways on the range, its sides clogged with a dark-grey deposit, so obstinate that he had to take a brillo pad to it. He decided that it was the remains of a custard left over from the previous night. Pomme Frite must have succeeded in burning it while heating it up for his own consumption.

At first, Mark and Howard had been concerned about the diabetes. One day, returning from one of his rare forays to the local Wop shop (as he called it), Pomme Frite had staggered through the front door, leaving it wide open, and had then collapsed onto the bottom of the staircase. Fortunately, Howard returned home a few minutes later. 'My syringe, syringe. Medicine cupboard. In the WC.' Howard raced upstairs, opened the rusty, dusty medicine cupboard and found a disposable syringe and a phial of insulin. Later, Pomme Frite croaked, 'You saved my bloody life. Not that it was worth saving,' he added. 'You're a good chap. Basically.' Laughter caused his bony shoulders to shake up and down, 'Even if you're a queer one.'

Did that last sentence mean what Howard and Mark thought that it meant? At that stage in the relationship they could not be sure.

Later, they were. The two of them were having one of their intermittent spats in the hall, over an invitation that each of them thought that the other had agreed to answer, when from above them they heard that disgusting phlegmy cough and then the high-pitched nasal voice: 'Girls! Girls! Please? Why not give each other a nice kiss and make up?' Pomme Frite was leaning over the banister, his face a grey disc in the gloom of the attic landing.

When they next had a party, it was clear that Pomme Frite had similarly been surveying the arrivals – and perhaps also the departures – of the guests from above. 'What an interesting crowd,' he commented to Mark the next morning, at the end of a breathless struggle to pick some letters off the doormat. None of the letters were for him. Having carefully scrutinised each in turn, he held out the pile. 'I was hoping to see some popsies, but all I saw…Well, one lives and learns. This has become an odd old world. You two have certainly brought me up to date with a bump.'

A few days later, the old man and Mark coincided outside the bathroom. Mark was wearing a polo-necked cashmere sweater just bought at the Harrod's sale. Mockingly, Pomme Frite looked him up and down. 'Well, you look very saucy in that little number, I must say,' in what sounded like a feeble imitation of Graham Norton. Certainly, Mark had wondered if that pale blue shade was quite right for him, but to be told, at the age of forty-seven and in line for promotion to the head of refuse recollection, that he looked 'saucy' was bloody cheek.

Somehow these oblique aspersions on their sexuality exasperated Mark and Howard more acutely than any of the more flagrant outrages. It was, in fact, those aspersions that finally persuaded them to try to bribe Pomme Frite to leave – ill though they could afford to do so after all the money that they had had to spend on the house.

As so often, it was Howard who was the spokesman. He entered the low-ceilinged attic room, his tall, thin body leaning slightly forward as so often when he wished to ingratiate himself. 'Am I disturbing you?'

'No, no! Liberty Hall. Take a pew.'

Without taking a pew, Howard produced the spiel that he and Mark had prepared together. They were worried that their tenant was isolated up so many stairs. They were also worried that he might fall while they were both out at work. Had he thought that it might be better if he applied to the Council for sheltered housing?

'I can't say that I have. No. I'm perfectly happy here. You two do so much to look after me.'

'If you did decide to go, we'd be only too happy to – to – well, make a contribution.'

'A contribution? What sort of contribution?'

'Well. Five thousand or so.'

'*Five thousand*?'

Useless.

'He's like those cockroaches,' Mark said. 'Quite disgusting and amazingly persistent.'

'If only we could stamp him out of existence like we did them.'

'It wasn't the stamping that finally got rid of them. It was that pest control officer. That gas was awfully effective.'

Looking back later, each of them decided that that was the moment when the idea first began to germinate. But neither ever confessed that to the other.

Howard came home early with a feverish cold and, having made himself a pot of tea, got into his pyjamas and prepared to clamber into his bed. It was then that he noticed that the bedside radio had vanished. It was not the first time that Pomme Frite had borrowed it, his own ancient Roberts set having expired two or three weeks previously. Howard pulled on his dressing gown, thrust his feet into his slippers, and strode out into the hall. From above he could hear the blare, imperfectly tuned in, of a Sousa march. Taking them in twos and threes, he raced up the stairs.

He banged on the attic door and eventually, getting no answer, flung it open. 'You really have a cheek—' he began. Then he saw the emaciated body, naked except for some underpants, lying sideways across the bed. It was like a gigantic grey grub, he often used to recall in horror in later days. Pomme Frite's mouth was open. Without the false teeth it contained only two jagged, orange-black fangs. There was a whistling sound of air being drawn in and then expelled. The prominent Adam's apple bobbed up and down.

Howard began to dash to the lavatory medicine cupboard. As a dentist he was used to giving injections. No sweat. But then he hesitated, turned back and re-entered the room. He stared down at the grub. He could leave Pomme Frite there, in the hope that the diabetic coma would be a fatal one. Or else...? He picked up the pillow in its soiled case, from where it had tumbled to the floor. He cradled it for a moment, like a baby, in the crook of an arm. Then, with a decisive movement he put it over Pomme Frite's face. The grey body stirred, frantically twitched from side to side. The tassel penis dribbled some urine. With sudden ferocity – better to be safe than sorry – Howard jumped onto the pillow and bounced upside down on it. After that, everything was over quickly. He went downstairs, put on his clothes so recently taken off, and let himself out into the street. His feverish cold seemed miraculously to have cured itself. He decided to go to the gym, where on his last visit he had got into conversation with a muscular Bangladeshi attendant. Promising, very promising.

Pomme Frite's death brought with it three surprises.

Firstly, there was the surprise of the size of his estate; £626,000. 'And to think that we thought that the old brute was on the verge of destitution!' was Howard's comment.

Secondly, there was the surprise of what he wrote in his will about his bequest to Mark and Howard: *I had expected an increasingly lonely and unhappy old age. But the purchase of the house by these two gentlemen has totally changed my life. Since they took over the house, I have felt that I once more belong to a family. They have been like two sons to me.*

Thirdly, there was the surprise that the bequest to Mark and Howard consisted of the whole of Pomme Frite's estate.

Mark and Howard, their Renault loaded with the few possessions not taken by the removers the day before, drove towards Tredegar Square. They had sold the horrid old house to a young, spruce, Vietnamese couple, owners of a successful restaurant, with a large brood of children, for a sum almost twice what they had paid for it.

They had haggled over the house in Tredegar Square with its ancient, upper-crusty owners, all but been gazumped, and then emerged victorious.

'I think this is the happiest day of my life,' Howard said.

'Happier than the one on which we first met?' That had been on Hampstead Heath.

'Well, no, not quite,' Howard remarked untruthfully, 'but almost.'

'Tredegar Square – here we come!'

Mark looked across the Square, to those giant recessed columns with proprietary love. Then he gasped, pointed. 'Who – who is that?'

Howard craned his neck, gripping the steering wheel. A hand was raising the net curtain of one of the two attic rooms. Then, with horror and incredulity, both of them made out the figure in the striped pyjamas.

The sitting tenant had arrived ahead of them.

Val McDermid

The Consolation Blonde

Awards are meaningless, right? They're always political, they're forgotten two days later and they always go to the wrong book, right? Well, that's what we all say when the prize goes somewhere else. Of course, it's a different story when it's our turn to stand at the podium and thank our agents, our partners and our pets. Then, naturally enough, it's an honour and a thrill.

That's what I was hoping I'd be doing that October night in New York. I had been nominated for Best Novel in the Speculative Fiction category of the US Book Awards, the national literary prizes that carry not only prestige but also a $50,000 cheque for the winners. *Termagant Fire*, the concluding novel in my *King's Infidel* trilogy, had broken all records for a fantasy novel. More weeks in the *New York Times* bestseller list than King, Grisham and Cornwell put together. And the reviews had been breathtaking, referring to *Termagant Fire* as 'the first novel since Tolkien to make fantasy respectable'. Fans and booksellers alike had voted it their book of the year. Serious literary critics had examined the parallels between my fantasy universe and America in the defining epoch of the sixties. Now all I was waiting for was the imprimatur of the judges in the nation's foremost literary prize.

Not that I was taking it for granted. I know how fickle judges can be, how much they hate being told what to think by the rest of the world. I understood only too well that the *succès d'estime* the book had enjoyed could be the very factor that would snatch my moment of glory from my grasp. I had already given myself a stiff talking-to in my hotel bathroom mirror, reminding myself of the dangers of hubris. I needed to keep my feet on the ground, and maybe failing to win the golden prize would be the best thing that could happen to me. At least it would be one less thing to have to live up to with the next book.

But on the night, I took it as a good sign that my publisher's table at the awards dinner was right down at the front of the room, smack bang up against the podium. They never like the winners being seated too far from the stage just in case the applause doesn't last long enough for them to make it up there ahead of the silence.

My award was third from last in the litany of winners. That meant a long time sitting still and looking interested. But I could only cling on to the fragile conviction that it was all going to be worth it in the end. Eventually, the knowing Virginia drawl of the MC, a middle-ranking news anchorman, got us there. I arranged my face in a suitably bland expression, which I was glad of seconds later when the name he announced was not mine. There followed a short, stunned silence, then, with more eyes on me than on her, the victor weaved her way to the front of the room to a shadow of the applause previous winners had garnered.

I have no idea what graceful acceptance speech she came out with. I couldn't tell you who won the remaining two categories. All my energy was channelled into not showing the rage and pain churning inside me. No matter how much I told myself I had prepared for this, the reality was horrible.

At the end of the apparently interminable ceremony, I got to my feet like an automaton. My team formed a sort of flying wedge around me; editor ahead of me, publicist to one side, publisher to the other. 'Let's get you out of here. We don't need pity,' my publisher growled, head down, broad shoulders a challenge to anyone who wanted to offer condolences.

By the time we made it to the bar, we'd acquired a small support crew, ones I had indicated were acceptable by a nod or a word. There was Robert, my first mentor and oldest buddy in the business; Shula, an English SF writer who had become a close friend; Shula's girlfriend Caroline; and Cassie, the manager of the city's premier SF and fantasy bookstore. That's what you need at a time like this, people around who won't ever hold it against you that you vented your spleen in an unseemly way at the moment when your dream turned to ashes. Fuck nobility. I wanted to break something.

But I didn't have the appetite for serious drinking, especially when my vanquisher arrived in the same bar with her celebration in tow. I finished my Jack Daniels and pushed off from the enveloping sofa. 'I'm not much in the mood,' I said. 'I think I'll just head back to my hotel.'

'You're at the InterCon, right?' Cassie asked.

'Yeah.'

'I'll walk with you, I'm going that way.'

'Don't you want to join the winning team?' I asked, jerking my head towards the barks of laughter by the bar.

Cassie put her hand on my arm. 'You wrote the best book, John. That's victory enough for me.'

I made my excuses and we walked into a ridiculously balmy New York evening. I wanted snow and ice to match my mood, and said as much to Cassie.

Her laugh was low. 'The pathetic fallacy,' she said. 'You writers just never got over that, did you? Well, John, if you're going to cling to that notion, you better change your mood to match the weather.'

I snorted. 'Easier said than done.'

'Not really,' said Cassie. 'Look, we're almost at the InterCon. Let's have a drink.'

'OK.'

'On one condition. We don't talk about the award, we don't talk about the asshole who won it, we don't talk about how wonderful your book is and how it should have been recognised tonight.'

I grinned. 'Cassie, I'm a writer. If I can't talk about me, what the hell else does that leave?'

She shrugged and steered me into the lobby. 'Gardening? Gourmet food? Favourite sexual positions? Music?'

We settled in a corner of the bar, me with Jack on the rocks, she with a Cosmopolitan. We ended up talking about movies, past and present, finding to our surprise that in spite of our affiliation to the SF and fantasy world, what we both actually loved most was film noir. Listening to Cassie talk, watching her push her blonde hair back from her eyes, enjoying the sly smiles that crept out when she said something witty or sardonic, I forgot the slings and arrows and enjoyed myself.

When they announced last call at midnight, I didn't want it to end. It seemed natural enough to invite her up to my room to continue the conversation. Sure, at the back of my mind was the possibility that it might end with those long legs wrapped around mine, but that really wasn't the most important thing. What mattered was that Cassie had taken my mind off what ailed me. She had already provided consolation enough, and I wanted it to go on. I didn't want to be left alone with my rancour and self-pity or any of the other uglinesses that were fighting for space inside me.

She sprawled on the bed. It was that or an armchair which offered little prospect of comfort. I mixed drinks, finding it hard not to imagine sliding those tight black trousers over her hips or running my hands under that black silk tee, or pushing the long shimmering overblouse off her shoulders so I could cover them with kisses.

I took the drinks over and she sat up, crossing her legs in a full lotus and straightening her spine. 'I thought you were really dignified tonight,' she said.

'Didn't we have a deal? That tonight was off limits?' I lay on my side, carefully not touching her at any point.

'That was in the bar. You did well, sticking to it. Think you earned a reward?'

'What kind of reward?'

'I give a mean backrub,' she said, looking at me over the rim of her glass. 'And you look tense.'

'A backrub would be...very acceptable,' I said.

Cassie unfolded her legs and stood up. 'OK. I'll go into the bathroom and give you some privacy to get undressed. Oh, and John – strip right down to the skin. I can't do your lower back properly if I have to fuck about with waistbands and stuff.'

I couldn't quite believe how fast things were moving. We hadn't been in the room ten minutes, and here was Cassie instructing me to strip for her. OK, it wasn't quite like that sounds, but it was equally a perfectly legitimate description of events. The sort of thing you could say to the guys and they would make a set of assumptions from. If, of course, you were the sort of sad asshole who felt the need to validate himself like that.

I took my clothes off, draping them over the armchair without actually folding them, then lay face down on the bed. I wished I'd spent more of the spring working out than I had writing. But I knew my shoulders were still respectable, my legs strong and hard, even if I was carrying a few more pounds around the waist than I would have liked.

I heard the bathroom door open and Cassie say, 'You ready, John?'

I was very, very ready. Somehow, it wasn't entirely a surprise that it wasn't just the skin of her hands that I felt against mine.

How did I know it had to be her? I dreamed her hands. Nothing slushy or sentimental; just her honest hands with their strong square fingers, the palms slightly callused from the daily shunting of books from carton to shelf, the play of muscle and skin over blood and bone. I dreamed her hands and woke with tears on my face. That was the day I called Cassie and said I had to see her again.

'I don't think so.' Her voice was cautious, and not, I believed, simply because she was standing behind the counter in the bookstore.

'Why not? I thought you enjoyed it,' I said. 'Did you think it was just a one-night stand?'

'Why would I imagine it could be more? You're a married man, you live in Denver, you're good-looking and successful. Why on earth would I set myself up for a let-down by expecting a repeat performance? John, I am so not in the business of being the Other Woman. A one-night stand is just fine, but I don't do affairs.'

'I'm not married.' It was the first thing I could think of to say. That it was the truth was simply a bonus.

'What do you mean, you're not married? It says so on your book jackets. You mention her in interviews.' Now there was an edge of anger, a 'don't fuck with me' note in her voice.

'I've never been married. I lied about it.'

A long pause. 'Why would you lie about being married?' she demanded.

'Cassie, you're in the store, right? Look around you. Scope out the women in there. Now, I hate to hurt people's feelings. Do you see why I might lie about my marital status?'

I could hear the gurgle of laughter swelling and bursting down the telephone line. 'John, you are a bastard, you know that? A charming bastard, but a bastard nevertheless. You mean that? About never having been married?'

'There is no moral impediment to you and me fucking each other's brains out as often as we choose to. Unless, of course, there's someone lurking at home waiting for you?' I tried to keep my voice light. I'd been torturing myself with that idea ever since our night together. She'd woken me with soft kisses just after five, saying she had to go. By the time we'd said our farewells, it had been nearer six and she'd finally scrambled away from me, saying she had to get home and change before she went in to open the store. It had made sense, but so too did the possibility of her sneaking back into the cold side of a double bed somewhere down in Chelsea or SoHo.

Now, she calmed my twittering heart. 'There's nobody. Hasn't been for over a year now. I'm free as you, by the sounds of it.'

'I can be in New York at the weekend,' I said. 'Can I stay?'

'Sure,' Cassie said, her voice somehow promising much more than a simple word. That was the start of something unique in my experience. With Cassie, I found a sense of completeness I'd never known before. I'd always scoffed at terms like 'soulmate', but Cassie forced me to eat the words baked in a humble pie. We matched. It was as simple as that. She compensated for my lacks, she allowed me space to demonstrate my strengths. She made me feel like the finest lover who had ever laid hands on her. She was also the first woman I'd ever had a relationship with who miraculously never complained that the writing got in the way. With Cassie, everything was possible and life seemed remarkably straightforward.

She gave me all the space I needed, never minding that my fantasy world sometimes seemed more real to me than what was for dinner. And I did the same for her, I thought. I didn't dog her steps at the store, turning up for every event like an autograph hunter. I only came along to see writers I would have gone to see anyway; old friends, new kids on the block who were doing interesting work, visiting foreign names. I encouraged her to keep up her girls' nights out, barely registering when she rolled home in the small hours smelling of smoke and tasting of Triple Sec.

She didn't mind that I refused to attempt her other love, rock climbing; forty-year-old knees can't learn that sort of new trick. But equally, I never expected her to give it up for me, and even though she usually scheduled her overnight climbing trips for when I was out of town on book business, that was her choice rather than my demand. Bless her, she never tried taking advantage of our relationship to nail down better discount deals with my publishers, and I respected her even more for that.

Commuting between Denver and New York lasted all of two months. Then in the same week, I sold my house and my agent sold the *King's Infidel* trilogy to Oliver Stone's company for enough money for me actually to be able to buy a Manhattan apartment that was big enough for both of us and our several thousand books. I loved, and felt loved in return. It was as if I was leading a charmed life.

I should have known better. I am, after all, an adherent of the genre of fiction where pride always, always, always comes before a very nasty fall.

We'd been living together in the kind of bliss that makes one's friends gag and one's enemies weep for almost a year when the accident happened. I know that Freudians claim there is never any such thing as accident, but it's hard to see how anyone's subconscious could have felt the world would end up a better or more moral place because of this particular mishap.

My agent was in the middle of a very tricky negotiation with my publisher over my next deal. They were horse-trading and haggling hard over the money on the table, and my agent was naturally copying me in on the e-mails. One morning, I logged on to find that day's update had a file attachment with it. 'Hi, John,' the e-mail read.

You might be interested to see that they're getting so nitty-gritty about this deal that they're actually discussing your last year's touring and miscellaneous expenses. Of course, I wasn't supposed to see this attachment, but we all know what an idiot Tom is when it comes to electronics. Great editor, cyber-idiot. Anyway, I thought you might find it amusing to see how much they reckon they spent on you. See how it tallies with your recollections...

I wasn't much drawn to the idea, but since the attachment was there, I thought I might as well take a look. It never hurts to get a little righteous indignation going about how much hotels end up billing for a one-night stay. It's the supplementaries that are the killers. Fifteen dollars for a bottle of water was the best I came across on last year's tour. Needless to say, I stuck a glass under the tap. Even when it's someone else's dime, I hate to encourage the robber barons who masquerade as hoteliers.

I was drifting down through the list when I ran into something out of the basic rhythm of hotels, taxis, air fares, author escorts. *Consolation Blonde, $500*, I read.

I knew what the words meant, but I didn't understand their linkage. Especially not on my expense list. If I'd spent it, you'd think I'd know what it was.

Then I saw the date.

My stomach did a back flip. Some dates you never forget. Like the US Book Awards dinner.

I didn't want to believe it, but I had to be certain. I called Shula's girlfriend Caroline, herself an editor of mystery fiction in one of the big London houses. Once we'd got the small talk out of the way, I cut to the chase. 'Caroline, have you ever heard the term "consolation blonde" in publishing circles?'

'Where did you hear that, John?' she asked, answering the question inadvertently.

'I overheard it in one of those chi-chi midtown bars where literary publishers hang out. I was waiting to meet my agent, and I heard one guy say to the other, "He was OK after the consolation blonde." I wasn't sure what it meant but I thought it sounded like a great title for a short story.'

Caroline gave that well-bred middle-class Englishwoman's giggle. 'I suppose you could be right. What can I say here, John? This really is one of publishing's tackier areas. Basically, it's what you lay on for an author who's having a bad time. Maybe they didn't win an award they thought was in the bag, maybe their book has bombed, maybe they're having a really bad tour. So you lay on a girl, a nice girl. A fan, a groupie, a publicity girlie, bookseller, whatever. Somebody on the fringes, not a hooker as such. Tell them how nice it would be for poor old what's-his-name to have a good time. So the sad boy gets the consolation blonde and the consolation blonde gets a nice boost to her bank account plus the bonus of being able to boast about shagging a name. Even if it's a name that nobody else in the pub has ever heard before.'

I felt I'd lost the power of speech. I mumbled something and managed to end the call without screaming my anguish at Caroline. In the background, I could hear Bob Dylan singing 'Idiot Wind'. Cassie had set the CD playing on repeat before she'd left for work and now the words mocked me for the idiot I was.

Cassie was my Consolation Blonde.

I wondered how many other disappointed men had been lifted up by the power of her fingers and made to feel strong again? I wondered whether she'd have stuck around for more than that one-night stand if I'd been a poor man. I wondered how many times she'd slid into bed with me after a night out, not with the girls, but wearing the mantle of the Consolation Blonde. I wondered whether pity was still the primary emotion that moved her when she moaned and arched her spine for me.

I wanted to break something. And this time, I wasn't going to be diverted.

I've made a lot of money for my publisher over the years. So when I show up to see my editor, Tom, without an appointment, he makes space and time for me.

That day, I could tell inside a minute that he wished for once he'd made an exception. He looked like he wasn't sure whether he should just cut out the middle man and throw himself out of the twenty-third-floor window. 'I don't know what you're talking about,' he yelped in response to my single phrase.

'Bullshit,' I yelled. 'You hired Cassie to be my consolation blonde. There's no point in denying it, I've seen the paperwork.'

'You're mistaken, John,' Tom said desperately, his alarmed chipmunk eyes widening in dilemma.

'No. Cassie was my consolation blonde for the US Book Awards. You didn't know I was going to lose, so you must have set her up in advance, as a stand-by. Which means you must have used her before.'

'I swear, John, I swear to God, I don't know...' Whatever Tom was going to say got cut off by me grabbing his stupid preppie tie and yanking him out of his chair.

'Tell me the truth,' I growled, dragging him towards the window. 'It's not like it can be worse than I've imagined. How many of my friends has she fucked? How many five-hundred-buck one-night stands have you pimped for my girlfriend since we got together? How many times have you and your buddies laughed behind my back because the woman I love is playing consolation blonde to somebody else? Tell me, Tom. Tell me the truth before I throw you out of this fucking window. Because I don't have any more to lose.'

'It's not like that,' he gibbered. I smelled piss and felt a warm dampness against my knee. His humiliation was sweet, though it was a poor second to what he'd done to me.

'Stop lying,' I screamed. He flinched as my spittle spattered his face. I shook him like a terrier with a rat.

'OK, OK,' he sobbed. 'Yes, Cassie was a consolation blonde. Yes, I hired her last year for you at the awards banquet. But I swear, that was the last time. She wrote me a letter, said after she met you she couldn't do this again. John, the letter's in my files. She returned her fee for being with you. You have to believe me. She fell in love with you that first night and she never did it again.'

The worst of it was, I could tell he wasn't lying. But still, I hauled him over to the filing cabinets and made him produce his evidence. The letter was everything he'd promised. It was dated the day after our first encounter, two whole days before I called her to ask if I could see her again.

Dear Tom, Thanks for transferring the $500 payment to my bank account. However, I'm enclosing a refund check for $500. It's not appropriate for me to accept money this time. I won't be available to do close author escort work in future. Meeting John Treadgold has changed things for me. I can't thank you enough for introducing us.

Good luck. Cassie White.

I stood there, reading her words, every one cutting me like the wounds I'd carved into her body the night before.

I guess they don't have awards ceremonies in prison. Which is probably just as well, given what a bad loser I turned out to be.

He was always Vincent at home.

At school there were a few boys who called him 'Vince', and 'Vinny' was yelled more often than not across the playground, but his mother and father never shortened his name and neither did his brothers and sisters whose own names, in turn, were also spoken in full.

'Vincent' around the house then, and at family functions. The second syllable given equal weight with the first by the heavy accent of the elder members. Not swallowed. Rhyming with 'went'.

Vincent was not really bothered what names people chose to use, but there were some things it was never pleasant to be called.

'Coon!'

'Fucking coon…'

'Black coon. Fucking black bastard…'

He had rounded the corner and stepped into the passageway to find them waiting for him. Like turds in long grass. A trio of them in Timberland and Tommy Hilfiger.

Not shouting, but simply speaking casually. Saying what they saw. Big car. Hairy dog. Fucking black bastard…

Vincent stopped, caught his breath, took it all in.

Two were tallish – one abnormally thin, the other shaven-headed – and both cradling cans of expensive lager. The third was shorter and wore a baseball cap, the peak bent and pulled down low. He took a swig of Smirnoff Ice, then began to bounce on the balls of his feet, swinging the frosted glass bottle between thumb and forefinger.

'What you staring at, you sooty cunt?'

Vincent reckoned they were fifteen or so. Year eleven boys. The skinny one was maybe not even that, but all of them were a little younger than he was.

From somewhere a few streets away came the noise of singing, tuneless and incoherent, the phrases swinging like bludgeons. Quick as a flash, the arms of the taller boys were in the air, lager cans clutched in pale fists, faces taut with blind passion as they joined in the song.

'No one likes us, no one likes us, no one likes us, we don't care…'

The smaller boy looked at Vincent and shouted above the noise,

'Well?'

It was nearly six o'clock and starting to get dark. The match had finished over an hour ago but Vincent had guessed there might still be a few lads knocking about. He'd seen a couple outside the newsagent as he'd walked down the ramp from the tube station. Blowing into bags of chips. Tits and guts moving beneath their thin, replica shirts. The away fans were long gone and most of the home supporters were already indoors, but there were others, most who'd already forgotten the score, who still wandered the streets, singing and drinking. Waiting in groups, a radio tuned to *5 Live*. Standing in lines on low walls, the half-time shitburgers turning to acid in their stomachs, looking around for it...

The cut-through was no more than fifteen feet wide and ran between two three-storey blocks. It curled away from the main road towards the block where Vincent lived at the far end of the estate. The three boys who barred his way were gathered around a pair of stone bollards, built to dissuade certain drivers from coming on to the estate. From setting fire to cars on people's doorsteps.

Vincent answered the question, trying to keep his voice low and even, hoping it wouldn't catch. 'I'm going home...'

'Fucking listen to him. A posh nigger...'

The skinny boy laughed and the three came together, shoulders connecting, forearms nudging one another. When they were still again they had taken up new positions. The three now stood, more or less evenly spaced across the walkway, one in each gap. Between wall and bollard, bollard and bollard, bollard and wall...

'Where's home?' the boy in the cap said.

Vincent pointed past the boy's head. The boy didn't turn. He raised his head and Vincent got his first real look at the face, handsome and hard, shadowed by the peak of the baseball cap. Vincent saw something like a smile as the boy brought the bottle to his lips again.

'This is the short cut,' Vincent said. 'My quickest way...'

The boy in the cap swallowed. 'Your quickest way home is via the airport.' The smile that Vincent had thought he'd seen now made itself very evident. 'You want the Piccadilly Line to Heathrow, mate...'

Vincent chuckled softly, pretending to enjoy the joke. He saw the boy's face harden, watched him raise a hand and jab a finger back towards the main road.

'Go round.'

Vincent knew what he meant. He could walk back and take the path that led around the perimeter of the estate, approach his block from the other side. It would only take a few minutes longer. He could just turn and go, and he would probably be home before they'd finished laughing.

'You heard.' The skinny boy leaned back against a bollard.

He could *easily* turn and go round...

'Now piss off...'

The edges of Vincent's vision began to blur and darken, and the words that spewed from the mouth of the boy with the shaven head became hard to make out. A distant rhythm was asserting itself and as Vincent looked down at the cracked slabs beneath his feet, a shadow seemed to fall across them. A voice grew louder, and it was as if the walls on either side had softened and begun to sway above him like the tops of trees.

The voice was one Vincent knew well. The accent, unlike his own, was heavy, but the intonation and tone were those that had been passed on to him and to his brothers and sisters. It was a rich voice, warm and dark, sliding effortlessly around every phrase, each dramatic sentence of a story it never tired of telling.

His father's voice...

Looking out from his bedroom window, the boy could see the coffee plants lying like a deep green tablecloth across the hillside, billowing down towards the canopy of tree tops and the deep, dirty river beneath. If he raised his eyes *up*, he saw the mountain on the far side of the valley, its peaks jutting into the mist, the slopes changing colour many times a day according to the cloud and the position of the sun. Black or green or blood red. Other colours the boy had no name for.

A dozen views for the price of one, and he'd thought about all of them in the time he'd been away. He'd tried to picture each one during the bone-shaking, twelve-hour bus ride that had brought him home from school five days before.

'Hey! Stand still, boy. This is damn fiddly...'

Uncle Joseph, on his knees in front of him, his thick fingers struggling with the leather fastenings, as they had every morning since they'd begun. It was hard to tie the knots so that the strings of beads clung to the calves without slipping, but not so tightly that they would cut into the flesh.

When he'd finished with the beads on the lower legs, Uncle Joseph would move on to the thick bands of dried goatskin, each heavy with rows of bells and strapped around the thighs. These were expensive items, handmade like everything else. Lastly, Joseph would wrap the dark, highly polished belt round the boy's waist. On three out of the last four mornings, much to the boy's amusement, he'd sliced a finger on one of the razor-sharp shells sewn into the leather.

Behind him, Uncle Francis worked on attaching the beads that crossed his back and chest in an X, like brightly coloured bandoliers. Francis was always cheerful, and the boy imagined that he too looked forward to that moment when Joseph would cry out, curse and stick a bleeding finger into his mouth. It was always Francis and Joseph who dressed him. The rest of his uncles waited outside. He'd been amazed at quite how *many* uncles he had, when they'd gathered on the night after he'd got back; when the family committee had met to organise it all.

There had been lots to decide.

'Do we have drummers?'

'Of course. This is important. *He* is important...'

'Grade A. Definitely Grade A...'

'These drummers are not cheap. Their damn costumes alone are a fortune...'

'I think they should come *with* their costumes. It isn't fair. We shouldn't have to pay for the costumes separately...'

'We should have *lots* of drummers!'

And on and on, deep into the night, arguing and getting drunker while the boy listened from his bedroom. Though he didn't understand everything, the passion in the voices of these men had caused excitement to swell in his chest. Yes, and an equal measure of dread to press down on it, like one of the huge flat stones that lay along the river bed at the bottom of the valley. He'd lain awake most of that night thinking of his friends, his age-mates in the other villages, wondering if they were feeling the same thing.

'All set, boy,' Uncle Joseph said.

Uncle Francis handed him the headdress, rubbed the back of his neck. 'Feeling fit?'

Outside, he was greeted with cheers and whoops. This was the last day of gathering and there was more noise, more gaiety than there had been on any day previously. This was the eve of it all: the final glorious push.

He took his place in the middle of the group, acknowledged the greetings of his brothers, of uncles and cousins whose names he could never remember. Though no one was dressed as extravagantly as he was, everyone had made the necessary effort. No man or boy was without beads or bells. The older ones were all draped in animal skins – monkey, zebra and lion. All had painted faces and strips of brightly coloured cloth attached to the edges of their leather vests.

A huge roar went up as the first drum was struck. A massive bass drum, its rhythm like a giant's heartbeat. The smaller drums joined then, and the whistles, and the yelps of the women and children, watching from the doorways of houses, waving the gatherers good-bye.

The boy cleared his throat and spat into the dirt. He let out a long, high note, listened to it roll away across the valley. The rhythm became more complex, more frantic, and he picked up his knees in time to it, the beads rattling on his legs and the shells clattering against the belt round his waist.

He began to dance.

The procession started to move. A carnival, a travelling circus, a hundred or more bare feet slapping into the dirt in time to the drummers. A cloud of dust rose up behind them as they picked up speed, moving away along the hard brown track that snaked out of the village.

The mottled grey of the slabs was broken only by the splotches of dogshit brown and dandelion yellow.

Vincent looked up from the floor of the walkway.

The eyes of the two taller boys darted between his face and that of their friend. It seemed to Vincent that they were waiting to be told what to do. They were looking for some sort of signal.

The boy in the cap raised his eyes up to Vincent's. He took a long, slow swig from his bottle, his gaze not shifting from Vincent's face. Then he snatched the bottle from his lips, wiped a hand across his mouth and glared, as if suddenly affronted.

'*What?*'

Vincent smiled, shook his head. 'I didn't say anything.'

'Yes you fucking did.'

The boy with the shaved head took a step forward. 'What did you say, you cheeky black fucker?'

The smaller boy nodded, pleased, and took another swig. Vincent shrugged, feeling the tremble in his right leg, pressing a straight arm hard against it.

'Listen, I don't want any trouble. I'm just trying to get home…'

Home.

Vincent blinked and saw his brother's face, the skin taken off his cheek and one eye swollen shut. He saw his mother's face as she stood at the window all the next afternoon, staring out across the dual carriageway towards the lorry park and the floodlights beyond. He saw her face when she turned finally, and spoke. 'We're moving,' she'd said.

One more blink and he saw the resignation that had returned to her face after a day doing the maths; scanning newspapers and estate agents' details from Greenwich and Blackheath. As the idea of moving *anywhere* was quickly forgotten.

'I've already told you,' the boy with the bottle said. 'If you're so desperate, just go round.'

Vincent saw the face of his father then. As it had been that day when his brother had come home bleeding, and then, as he imagined it to have been twenty-five years before. In a country Vincent had only ever seen pictures of.

The boy sat at the back of the house, beneath the striped awning that his father had put above his bedroom window. Rose rubbed ointment on to his blisters. They stared across the valley at the sun dropping down behind the mountain, the slopes cobalt blue beneath a darkening sky.

He knew that they should not have been sitting together, that his uncles would not have approved. Contact with young women was frowned upon in the week leading up to the ritual. He would regret it, his uncles would have said, in the days afterwards, in the healing time after the ceremony.

'Talk to young women…' Joseph had told him, 'let them smile at you now and shake their hips, and you will *pay*.'

He didn't care. He had known Rose since before he could walk and besides, Joseph, Francis and the others would be insensible by now. They had sat down around the pot as soon as they had finished eating supper. Talking about the day, filling in the elders on how 'the boy' was doing and getting slowly drunker. Sucking up powerful mouthfuls of home brew from the pot through long bamboo straws.

The boy had watched them for a while, no longer jealous, as he would have been before. Once it was all over, he would have earned the right to sit down and join them.

'Fine, but not yet, you haven't,' Rose had said when he'd mentioned it to her.

It had been a hard day and the boy was utterly exhausted. He reckoned they had danced twenty miles or more, visited a dozen villages, and he had sung his heart and his throat out every step of the way. He was proud of his song, had been since he'd written it months before. Even Rose had been forced to concede that it was pretty good. He'd practised it every day, knowing there was prestige and status attached to the best song, the best performance. He'd given that performance a hundred times in the last week and now his voice was as ragged as the soles of his feet.

It had been a successful day too. Uncle Philip had not announced the final tally, but it had certainly been a decent haul. Relatives close and distant in each homestead had come forward dutifully with gifts: earthenware dishes piled high with cash; chickens or a goat from cousins; cattle from those of real importance. Philip had made a careful note of who'd given what, in the book that was carried with them as they criss-crossed the district, each village ready to welcome them, each able to hear them coming from a mile or more away.

Everyone had been more than generous. By sundown the following day, the boy would be a rich man.

'Are you scared?' Rose asked.

He winced as she dropped his foot to the floor. 'No,' he said.

The boy wasn't sure why he lied. Being frightened was fine, it was *showing* the fear that was unacceptable, that would cost you. He remembered the things that had scared him the most that day, scared him far more than what was to come the following afternoon. He had been sitting with the elders in the village where his father had been born. Squatting in the shade, stuffed full of roasted goat and green bananas, with barely the energy to nod as each piece of advice was given, each simple lesson handed out.

'You will not fear death…'

'You will defend your village against thieves…'

Then he'd been handed the baby.

'There are times when your wife will be sick, and you must look after yourself and your children.'

'You will learn to cook...'

'You will learn to keep a fire burning all day…'

They roared as the baby began to piss on his lap, told him it was good luck. They were still laughing as the boy danced his way out of the village. All he could think about, as he began his song again, was how being unafraid of death and of thieves sounded easy compared with taking care of children…

He thought about telling Rose this, but instead told her about what had happened in the first village they'd visited that day. Something funny and shocking. A distant cousin of his father's had been discovered hiding in the fields on the outskirts of the village. Trying to dodge the handover of a gift was a serious matter and not only had the offering been taken from him by force, but he had brought shame upon himself and the rest of his family.

'Can you believe it?' the boy said. 'That man was Grade A! Cowering in the tall grass like a woman, to avoid handing over a bowl. A *bowl* for heaven's sake…'

Rose pushed her shoulder against his. 'So, you think you're going to be Grade A? Grade B maybe? What d'you think, boy?'

He shrugged. He knew what he was hoping for. All he could be certain about was that this was the last time anybody would call him 'boy'.

The one with the bottle stood a foot or so forward from his two friends. He reached over his shoulder for the lit cigarette that he knew would be there, took three quick drags and handed it back. 'What team do you support anyway?'

'Fucking Man U, I bet…'

For a moment, Vincent thought about lying. Giving them their own team's name. He knew that he'd be caught out in a second. 'I don't follow a team.'

'Right. Not an *English* team…'

'Not any team,' Vincent said.

'Some African team, yeah? Kicking a fucking coconut around…'

'Bongo Bongo United FC!'

'"Kicking a coconut", that's classic...'

'Headers must be a nightmare, yeah?'

The skinny one and the one with the shaved head began to laugh. They pursed their lips and stuck out their bumfluffy chins. They pretended to scratch their armpits.

'You know what FC stands for, don't you? Fucking coon...'

Vincent looked away from them. He heard the monkey noises begin softly, then start to get louder.

'Look at him,' the one in the cap said. 'He's shitting himself.' He said something else after that, but Vincent didn't hear it...

Dawn, at the river, on the final morning.

Dotted for a mile or more along the flat, brown river bank were the other groups. Some were smaller than his own, while others must have numbered a hundred, but at the centre of each stood one of the boy's age-mates. Each ready to connect with the past, to embrace the future. Each asking for the strength to endure what lay ahead of him.

The boy was called forward by an elder. As he took his first steps, he glanced sideways, saw his age-mates along the river bank moving in a line together towards the water.

This was the preparation.

In the seconds he spent held beneath the water, he wondered whether a cry would be heard if he were to let one out. He imagined it rising up to the surface, the bubbles bursting in a series of tiny screams, each costing him grades.

He emerged from the river purified and ready to be painted with death.

The sun was just up but already fierce, and the white mud was baked hard within a minute or two of being smeared across his face and chest and belly. The mist was being burned away, and looking along the bank, the boy saw a row of pale statues. A long line of ghosts in the buttery sunlight.

He watched an old man approach each figure, as one now approached him. The elder took a mouthful of beer from a pumpkin gourd and spat, spraying it across the boy's chest. The beer ran in rivulets down the shell of dried mud, as prayers were said and his uncles stepped towards him.

The group that had been nearest to him jogged past, already

finished, and he looked at his age-mate, caked in white mud as he was. The boy had known him, as he'd known most of them, for all of their sixteen years, but his friend was suddenly unrecognisable. It was not the mask of mud. It was the eyes that stared out from behind it. It was the eyes that were suddenly different.

The boy was nudged forward, was handed his knife, and the group began loping away in the same direction as his friend. Drumming again now, and singing, heading for the market place. All of them, all the ghost-boys, moving towards the moment when they would die and come back to life...

'Shut up!' Vincent shouted.

After a moment or two the skinny one and the one with the shaved head stopped making their monkey noises, but only after a half-glance in their direction from the one in the cap.

'Turn your pockets out,' he said.

Vincent's hands were pressed hard against his legs to keep them still. He slowly brought each of them up to his pockets, slipped them inside...

'Maybe we'll let you *pay* to go home. Let me see what you've got.'

Vincent's left hand came out empty. His right emerged clutching the change from his train ticket. He opened his hand and the one in the cap leaned forward to take a look.

'Fuck that, mate. Where's the notes?'

Vincent shook his head. 'This is all I've got.'

'You're a fucking liar. Where's your wallet?'

Vincent said nothing. He closed his hand around the coins and thrust his fist back into his trouser pocket.

The one in the cap took a step towards him. He was no more than a couple of feet away. 'Don't piss me about. I don't like it, yeah?'

He could easily turn and go round...

'Where's his phone?' the skinny one said.

'Get his fucking phone, man. They always have wicked phones.'

The one in the cap held out his hand. 'Let's have it.'

It suddenly seemed to Vincent that the phone might be the way out of it, his way past them. Handing it over, giving them something and then trying to get past was probably a good idea...

The mobile was snatched from his grasp the second he'd produced it. The one in the cap turned and swaggered back towards his friends. They cheered as he held it up for them to look at.

The three gathered round to examine the booty and Vincent saw a gap open up between the far right bollard and the wall. He thought about making a run for it. If he could stay ahead of them for just a minute, half a minute maybe, he would be virtually home. He reckoned he could outrun the two bigger ones anyway. Perhaps his mother or father, one of his brothers might see him coming...

He took a tentative step forward.

The one in the cap wheeled round suddenly, clutching the phone. 'Piece of cheap shit!' His arm snapped back, then forward and Vincent watched the phone explode against the wall, shattering into pieces of multi-coloured plastic.

The crack of the phone against the bricks changed something.

By the time Vincent looked again, the gap had been filled. The three stood square on to him, their bodies stiff with energy despite their efforts to appear relaxed. The space between them all was suddenly charged.

Vincent had no idea how he looked to them, what his face said about how he felt at that moment. He looked at *their* faces and saw hatred and excitement and expectation. He also saw fear.

'Last chance,' the one in the cap said.

The boy was stunned by the size of the crowd, though it was nothing unusual. He could remember, when he'd been one of the onlookers himself as a child, thinking that there couldn't possibly be this many people in the whole world. Today, as at the same moment every year, those that could not get a clear view were standing on tables and other makeshift platforms. They were perched on roofs and clustered together in the treetops.

He and his age-mates were paraded together, one final time, carried aloft like kings. His eyes locked for a few seconds with a friend as they passed each other. Their Adam's apples were like wild things in their throats.

While the boy moved on shoulders above the teeming mass of bodies, the dancing and the drumming grew more frenzied. Exhausted, he summoned the strength to sing one final time, while below him the basket was passed around and each relative given a last chance to hand over more money or pledge another gift.

Now, it was only the fizzing in the boy's blood that was keeping him upright. There were moments – a sickening wave of exhaustion, a clouding of his vision as he reached for a high note – when he was sure he was about to pass out, to topple down and be lost or trampled to death. He was tempted to close his eyes and let it happen...

At the moment when the noise and the heat and the *passion* of the crowd was at its height, the boy suddenly found himself alone with Joseph and Francis at the edge of the market place. There was space around him as he was led along a track towards a row of undecorated huts.

'Are you a woman?' Joseph asked.

'No,' the boy said.

The boy wondered if thinking about his mother and father made him one. He knew that they would be waiting, huddled together among the coffee plants, listening for the signal that it was over. Did wishing that he was with them, even for the few moments it would take to shake his father's hand and smell his mother's neck, make him less than Grade A?

'Are you a woman?' Francis repeated.

'No!' the boy shouted.

His uncles stepped in front of him and pushed open a door to one of the peat latrines. 'This will be your last chance,' Joseph said.

The boy moved inside quickly, dropped his shorts and squatted above the hole formed by the square of logs. He looked up at the grass roof, then across at his uncles who had followed him inside. He knew that they had sworn to stay with him until the final moment, but honestly, what did they think he was going to do? Did they think he would try to kill himself by diving head first into the latrine?

Did they think he would try to run?

Joseph and Francis smiled as the shit ran out of him like water. 'Better now than later,' Francis said.

The boy knew that his uncle was right.

He stood and wiped himself off. He felt no shame, no embarrassment at being watched. He was no more or less than a slave to it now.

A slave to the ritual.

The beer can hit him first, bouncing off his shoulder. It was almost empty, and Vincent was far more concerned by the beer that had sprayed onto his cheek and down his shirt. The can was still clattering at his feet when the cigarette fizzed into his chest. He took a step back, smacking away the sparks, listening to the skinny one and the one with the shaved head jabbering.

'I don't believe it, he's still fucking here...'

'Is he? It's getting dark, I can't see him if he isn't smiling...'

'He said he wasn't looking for trouble...'

'Well he's going to get a fucking slap.'

'He's just taking the piss now...'

'We gave the cunt every chance...'

'They're *all* taking the piss...'

'He's the one that's up for it, if you ask me. It's *him* who's kicking off, don't you reckon? He could have walked away and he just fucking stood there like he's in a trance. He's trying to face us down, the twat. Yeah? Don't you reckon?'

'Come on then...'

'Let's fucking well. Have. It.'

Vincent became aware that he was shifting his weight slowly from one foot to the other, that his fists were clenched, that there was a tremor running through his gut.

A hundred yards away, on the far side of the estate, he saw a figure beneath a lamp-post. He watched it move inside the cone of dirty, orange light. Vincent wondered if whoever it was would come if he shouted...

His eye darted back to the boy in the cap, and to the boy's hand, which tilted slowly as he emptied out what drink there was left in his bottle.

The noise in the market place died as each one stepped forward, then erupted again a minute or two later when the ritual had been completed.

It was the boy's turn.

The crowd had moved back to form a tunnel down which he walked, trancelike, his uncles slightly behind. He tried to focus on the two red splodges at the far end of the tunnel and when his vision cleared he saw the faces of the cutters for the first time. Their red robes marked them out as professionals – men who travelled from village to village, doing their jobs and moving on. They were highly skilled, and had to be. There were stories, though the boy had never seen such a thing happen, of cutters being set upon by a crowd and killed if a hand was less than steady; if a boy were to die because of one of them.

The boy stopped at the stone, turned to the first cutter and handed over his knife. He had sharpened it every day on the soft bark of a rubber tree. He had confidence in the blade.

In three swift strokes, the knife had sliced away the fabric of the boy's shorts. All he could feel was the wind whispering at the top of his legs. All he could hear was the roaring of the blood, loud as the river, inside his head.

He was offered a stick to clutch, to brace against the back of his neck and cling on to. This was the first test and with a small shake of the head it was refused. No Grade A man would accept this offer.

He was hard as stone...

His hands were taken, pressed into a position of prayer and placed against his right cheek. His eyes widened and watered, fixed on the highest point of a tree at the far end of the market place.

Repeating it to himself above the roaring of the river. Hard as stone...

The boy knew that this was the moment when he would be judged. This was everything – when the crowd, when his family would be watching for a sign of fear. For blinking, for shaking, for shitting...

He felt the fingers taking the foreskin, stretching it.

Focused on the tree...chalk-white ghost-boy...stiff and still as any statue...

He felt the weight of the blade, cold and quick. Heavy, then heavier and he *heard* the knife pass through the skin. A boom and then a rush...

This was when a Grade A man might prove himself, jumping and rubbing at his bloody manhood. The crowd would count the jumps, clap and cheer as those very special ones asked for alcohol to be poured into the wound...

The boy was happy to settle for Grade B. His eyes flicked to his uncle Joseph who signalled for the second cutter to come forward. The knife was handed across and, with three further cuts, the membrane – the 'second skin' – was removed.

A whistle was blown and the boy started slightly at the explosion of noise from the crowd. It was all over in less than a minute.

Everything took on a speed – underwater slow or blink-quick – a dreamlike quality of its own as the pain began...

A cloth was wrapped around the boy's shoulders.

He was gently pushed back on to a stool.

He lowered his eyes and watched his blood drip on to the stone at his feet.

There was a burning then, and a growing numbness as ground herbs were applied, and the boy sat waiting for the bleeding to stop. He felt elated. He stared down the tunnel towards the far side of the market place, towards what lay ahead.

He saw himself lying on a bed of dried banana leaves, enjoying the pain. Only a man, he knew, would feel that pain. Only a man would wake, sweating in the night, crying out in agony after a certain sort of dream had sent blood to where it was not wanted.

He saw himself healed, strutting around the market place with other men. They were laughing and talking about the different grades that their friends had reached. They were looking at women and enjoying the looks that they got back.

The boy looked down the tunnel and saw, clearer than anything else, the baby that he'd been handed the day before. He watched it again, happily pissing all over him.

He saw its fat, perfect face as it stared up at him, kicking its legs.

The skinny one and the one with the shaved head were drifting towards him.

Vincent knew that if he turned and ran they would give chase, and if they caught him they would not stop until they'd done him a lot of damage. He felt instinctively that he had a chance of coming off better than that if he stood his ground. Besides, he didn't want to run.

'I bet he's fucking carrying something,' the skinny one said.

The one with the shaved head reached into his jacket pocket, produced a small plastic craft knife. 'Blacks always carry blades…'

Vincent saw the one with the cap push himself away from the bollard he was leaning against. He watched him take a breath, and drop his arm, and break the bottle against the bollard with a flick of his wrist.

Vincent took a step away, turned and backed up until he felt the wall of the block behind him.

Hard as a stone…

'Stupid fucker.'

'He can't run. His arse has gone…'

'I bet he's filling his pants.'

Vincent showed them nothing. As little as his father had shown when the blade sang against his skin. He tensed his body but kept his face blank.

'Three points in the bag, lads,' the one with the broken bottle said. 'Easy home win…'

Vincent had learned a lot about what you gave away and what you kept hidden. They could have his phone and whatever money they could find. He would give them a little blood and a piece of his flesh if it came to it, and he would try his hardest to take some of theirs.

Vincent looked down the tunnel and saw them coming. He would not show them that he was afraid, though. He would not give them that satisfaction.

He was Grade A.

Stephen Volk

Indicator

In all my memories of my father, I cannot remember him once telling me a story. There were few books in the house: sports magazines collected in binders, the odd political memoir, a few non-fiction books about aviation, an unopened, unwanted gift or two, and newspapers, always newspapers, but hardly any books. I think he was probably rather like the accountant overheard by John Mortimer on a holiday beach who couldn't see the point in reading anything that wasn't true.

There are many possible stories. Even now, I am not sure which this is to be. There is the story of my father's life. Of course, that has been told, and will be told, *ad infinitum*, in some cheaply printed paperback by some tabloid gnome, or in tiresomely creative television documentaries. Close up, the exhaust with the pipe running from it. Close up, the fumes filling the car. Close up, a bulky, indistinguishable actor slumped over the wheel.

Then there is my story, meagre though it is for any kind of drama, which I am presently negotiating with a publisher friend of Dad's. My brother has got a damn good advance from HarperCollins, and I confidently expect a few k more than that. After all, he is a bachelor, and I have a wife and kids. Added interest. We've been in *Hello* magazine, for Christ's sake.

Then there is the story of the abominable trial. Everyone seems to tell that one differently. According to the judge I'm innocent. According to the man in the street, "He got away with it, didn't he?" The poor old man in the street who can just about understand his bank balance or his betting slip.

Today we heard the verdict. Perhaps that's why I'm in this kind of mood. We came out to face the phalanx of lenses, the massed ranks of BBC and ITN, chattering like baboons in a cage. I took my wife's hand in mine, tightly, giving them time to frame up and focus on it. Then I delivered my statement. Handwritten.

"The last five years have been a protracted hell not only for myself and my brother, but for those around us, completely uninvolved parties nevertheless affected by the relentless and malicious pressure of media accusation. Also those accusations were perniciously directed at my father in his role as Treasurer of the Inner

London Development Council and the man directly and personally responsible for those funds." I faintly emphasised the word *personally*. "He, sadly, tragically, is no longer with us to answer to those charges in a court of law." A quaver came to my voice. The requisite flashes strobed. "I am glad and feel vindicated at last that the judge has said categorically that my brother and I at no time acted unlawfully. Were we naive not to ask where the funds came from which our father invested in our construction companies? Yes. Was there nepotism? Arguably. Were there back-handers? No. Was there any sort of criminal collusion? No. Did I believe my father? Yes. Did I trust my father? Yes. Was my father a difficult man to say no to? Absolutely.

"I do not believe however that he had any selfish interest at heart. I do believe, on the contrary, he was doing what he thought best to rescue an impossibly difficult financial situation. Sadly he is not here to defend his reputation. I however have defended mine. I am not a crook. I am not a liar. I am innocent."

Simon is waiting for the car with Dougal McRae in the back seat. We get in and he says, so much for the press release. I say, it's much better from the horse's mouth. The Daimler snails along Fleet Street and turns at Ludgate Circus, its indicator ticking like a metronome.

"Are you all right?" says Dougal. His starched collar cuts into his red shaving-raw neck.

"Fine," I say.

"You look wrecked."

"I'm meant to be," I say. I flip the drinks cabinet open and take out one of the two Monte Cristos. "I didn't shave or wash my hair this morning. Does it look all right?"

"They'd never let you in the bloody Garrick."

As we drive across Blackfriars Bridge, there is a white van in front with CLEAN ME finger-written in the dirt. I look out at the happy throng and their simple lives. The cigar smoke slowly fills the car, like burned earth, like ashes, like Christmas. The interior of the car is muggy again after the sobering chill of the pavement. I run my words through my head, editing them this way and that for *News at Ten*. I am reasonably satisfied that they can't do too much of a hatchet job, but I am inured to that now.

When the car stops again, I look behind to see that my brother is still there in his BMW, alone. I ask Dougal what Kenneth is doing tonight. Dougal says he is booked on a flight to Goa. Booked? That took more optimism than I gave him credit for.

On his own, I ask? He says he doesn't know.

Arabella, whose short, tight dress is riding up her stockings, says, "Are you coming to the country?"

I say, "No, I don't think so. There are a few things to see to. I promised Ronnie Philp a celebratory binge at Wheeler's. I'll stay in the flat tonight. I'll be down first thing tomorrow."

She looks out of the car window. She tucks a strand of ash blonde hair behind each ear. "Do you want Simon?"

"You take Simon. I'll come down in the XJ. Helps me unwind, the XJ."

"Call me," she says. "Won't you?"

The cigar smoke prickles my eyes. I remember how I used to sneak one from Dad's cigar box and suck it, unlit, trying it for size. Somehow the smell was always the smell of his breath, his goodnight kiss.

You know you're famous when people make up jokes about you. There's a joke going round about Dad.

— Did you know that Geoffrey Cush has invented a new car?

— Oh really? How many gears has it got?

— Four. First, second, third, and (teller of joke lapses into a coughing fit).

Boom boom. There are plenty of others. Then there are plenty who don't find the jokes funny. I don't suppose the rate payers down in the docklands who feel that my family took the Christmas stuffing out of their mouths think they're very funny either.

I arrive at Butler's Wharf alone and the flat seems more than usually empty. I rattle round my privacy, the air around me suddenly empty of manic, slanging or sycophantic voices. I have only the sound of my own voice. I almost expect accusations from the furniture, a haranguing from the wall coverings. The silence is like someone who knows, but won't say.

I turn on the telly and pour myself a small Calvados. I recognise the figures of Bogart and Bacall in *To Have and Have Not*, an ironically appropriate title. As Donald Trump said when he owed 600 million, that bum on the street is better off than me – he's just skint. But the truth is, whether Donald Trump has 600 million or owes 600 million, the same number of bankers follow him round by his shirt tails and laugh at his jokes. And I daresay he eats at the same restaurants.

I phone the direct line to Nina Hopkins's office.

"Did you watch the news?"

"How are you?"

"Great."

"Congratulations."

"I'll catch it on the six o'clock," I say. "How did I come across?"

"Tired. Relieved. On the edge of tears," then after a pause, the word I most want to hear: "Honest." She must hear the tinkle of ice cubes against my teeth, because she says: "Are you on your own?"

"I am."

"I'll come round."

I hang up. I immediately ring the office. I've received a bundle of faxes, mostly well wishers. I tell Siobhan to bin the rest, and fire off some three line thank-yous, apart from two which would need to be personal.

I roll up my tie in a ball. It is unbelievable to think that it is all over. On the first day, when I came into the light, I raised my hand, palm outwards, to shield the sun, and that was the image that greeted me, cropped, blown up, doctored, from every broadsheet and tabloid front page the following morning. I was panned, zoomed, freeze framed, exploded into pixels and whizzed into a box, parrot-like, over the shoulder of Trevor McDonald.

Of course, they said in the beginning, "He must have known." As I'm sure they said as the Daimler sped away, "The bugger must've known. How could the sons not know?"

I telephone Philp and wriggle out of dinner. I say the emotion of the day has taken it out of me, just feel completely drained. He understands. Get an early night, old boy. I shall, I say. Well done, he signs off, uncertainly stumbling over each word, great relief to us all.

"Bless you," I say in a hushed tone, immediately aware it is my father speaking. His smile stays on my lips till I wipe it away. I'd seen him hang up the phone so many times with a blown kiss like that. But what did I expect? I learned at the knee of the master.

Now, I realise, the master is me.

I almost always, in my hour of need, over the past five years, have heard my father's voice in my ear. That trout-tickling basso profundo that so often accompanied his monolithic rise over the board-room table, usually before his hand-kissing charm turned like a knife into a weltering verbal demolition. "Power was the only thing in the world that stopped him feeling useless." This I found myself saying to ITN the day after my father's suicide. Kenneth, my brother, as became habitual, kept a low profile. (As a result, the research poll we commissioned privately found that whilst the public 'despised' me, it merely 'felt sorry' for him.) The newspapers said that the Cush brothers seemed 'remarkably composed' that day. I don't know. I once read that when a person falls from a great height they look to all intents and purposes unharmed, but when they do the autopsy, every organ is ruptured, every bone shattered, inside they're a complete write-off. That's what it felt like to me.

Dad was alive when my mother found him in the car. When my brother and I were informed, he was already being hurtled in an ambulance to a place in West London where they train deep sea divers. The policeman explained to me that, apparently, the only way to treat carbon monoxide poisoning is to de-pressurise the body, and this was the closest place they could do it. So we arrived at this grotty industrial estate protected by Rottweilers, at this ramshackle Nissen hut in Southall, with a colourful mural of a deep sea diver surrounded by fish over the walls. The place was padlocked and the lights were out. We became suddenly optimistic: obviously he had recovered and they'd taken him to the nearest hospital to recuperate. We were wrong. Dad had never recovered. He'd died in that concrete shed surrounded by badly painted fishes. By the time we'd reached the hospital, he was in the morgue. The nurse we collared used a wonderful euphemism, 'Rose Cottage'. "He's been taken to Rose Cottage," she said to the policeman. Not to me.

Dad was a Quaker, and if you've ever been to a Quaker funeral, it's a peculiar business. It begins in absolute silence, and there are spoken contributions from anyone and everyone who wishes to speak. In this day and age, to sit in 'silent reflection' for any period of time is shamefully agonising. As the seconds tick by, one finds oneself thinking not of the deceased, but of whether one has set the car alarm, or whether one's mobile phone has any messages. I loved my father, but I found myself examining with immense scrutiny the polished toe-cap of my shoe rather than thinking of him. The Meeting House was foetid with macs and morning coats and stillness. Most disconcerting of all, I found my eyes wandering to an object on a desk to one side of the room, marked with a Sellotaped label reading boldly OUT TRAY.

Several people spoke ministries. Outside a *Sun* reporter's mobile
rang, and crates of bottles were being delivered to the Bunch of
Grapes. Someone afterwards told me that that was the origin of the
term Quaker: that people would quake with fear before standing up
and speaking at a meeting. Ever since, I've thought it curious that a
whole faith should be based on stage fright.

At the graveside – the family only now – one of Dad's jokes came
back to me. "Dead centre of town," he'd say, expecting us to look
puzzled. "Graveyard," came the punchline as he tapped the car window, followed by his over-loud, ghost train laugh. My brother and I
came to anticipate this joke every time we drove down the Holt
Road. He used to tell it anyway, and it would invariably be capped by
his own laughter. Eventually, it had a kind of comfort attached to it:
the joke that is no longer funny.

I could see him, driving, smiling.

Mum always said that if Dad saw one of his cronies and waved
when he passed them in Market Street, he'd still be grinning like a
fool ten minutes later when we got to Trowbridge Road. That was
the public Geoffrey Cush that everyone knew and loved, not his private face. To the outside world he was always "A hell of a nice feller,
Geoff." I often saw his arm around the shoulders of a councillor or
a mate, but never around his wife's. He kissed her only at times when
it could clearly be seen by others. I suppose my mother came to
make the most of these sparse shows of affection when she could. It
was never a particular priority to him.

One priority he did have, always, was winning. Six years old, he
never allowed us to score goals. When we played Monopoly he was
always the Banker and he always cheated, sneaking money from the
box whilst our eyes were misdirected elsewhere. It was "All part of
the fun." Once when I got fed up with him and upset the board and
made Kenny cry, my father said, "You have to grow up and learn to
be a good loser."

Nina Hopkins arrives at four thirty. She lets herself in with her
own key. The straggling residue of the hack pack outside think she's
another resident of the block, they ignore her. I am already
undressed. She seems harassed to begin with, or she is uptight on my
behalf. I have a Scotch ready for her and I ask how her day was. She
says, "Shitty." She works as a feature writer for *The Guardian*, small
and Welsh, well-muscled and squat like a female scrum half, dressed

like a social worker in Camden Town haggles and rattling Bombay jewellery. She takes off her clothes and jumps into bed. Her skin is cold and her lips taste of whisky. Her Peter Pan hair is bleached blond, and her pubic hair black as seaweed in a Chinese restaurant.

"You've started without me," she says, finding my erection under the sheets.

"Almost," I say.

She pulls back my foreskin and I'm like a rock. It pleasantly surprises me.

"You're excited," she says. "I thought I might have my work cut out this afternoon."

"Fuck 'em," I say, rolling on top of her. "Fuck the lot of them." Her vagina is loose and wet. I wonder if she masturbated in the ladies at *The Guardian* before she got in a cab. It's a mad fiction, I know. I run it through my mind like a film clip, behind my closed eyes, and I'm there in the cubicle with her when I come – it's ridiculous.

As we lie in the bath, later, I hear the music of the six o'clock news to the smell of *Angels on Bare Skin*, from Lush. Hopkins drops her cigarette in the toilet bowl and reaches out to pull the flush. The long hairs in her armpit fan and then close. Her attention is focused on a blackhead on my knee, which she anoints with soapy water.

"Daniel and Kenneth Cush have today been acquitted of all charges of fraud. They had been living with the threat of criminal proceedings since the suicide of their father Sir Geoffrey Cush and the scandal surrounding the alleged misappropriation of Inner London Development Council funds..." I climb out of the water and drip into the bedroom, turning up the volume on the remote control. "...Daniel said he regretted the huge investment of time and money by the SFO in their bid to convict him..." A pink-nosed reporter outside the Law Courts. "It felt close to madness, he said, when everything you do and say is construed only as deception, and it particularly offended him that his father had been branded a liar, a cheat, and some kind of despotic monster..."

I see Dad's face up on the screen. No, it isn't Dad in the blue shirt and white collar behind the desk: it is me, the docklands outside the office window. My lips are moving.

"The whole idea that the public, if we are to believe the media, had in their head, that there was this grand conspiracy to divert funds to the sons' companies, that my father was somehow skimming off the cream to line our collective pockets..." Mixed bloody metaphor. A touch of humanity. Not bad. "...it's simply repugnant. It's simply, terrifyingly untrue. This notion that rate payers' money which was supposed to be helping amenities, housing in the inner city, getting the homeless off the street, keeping pensioners warm, et cetera, was finding its way into my father's cheque book, is arrant nonsense."

Hopkins lays down a bath towel and sits naked on the bed beside me. She lights a Marlboro Light. I can smell the bath-water on her. With one hand she manipulates my penis, and she puts her open mouth to my shoulder and blows. I think it is meant to arouse me. Almost immediately after coming, I realised, I wanted to be alone. Even while I was still inside her, I wanted her not to be there.

My close up says: "Dad made a foolish...a series of foolish, bad decisions, but he was doing his job, as he saw it, to manage the funds at his disposal, so that a potential disaster could be overcome. He was guilty of bad judgement, bad practice, hubris – and if I was guilty of anything at all, I was guilty of not standing up to him and saying, what is going on, Dad? But nobody, including myself, was able to say to Sir Geoffrey Cush, are you sure this is not a mistake? That was simply a foreign language to him."

Interviewer: "Do you wish that you could turn the clock back?"
Me: "Of course."
Interviewer: "Would you have done things differently?"
Me: "Of course. Of course I would. My father is dead. Of course I would. Hundreds of millions of pounds were lost, and many, many people suffered considerable loss and hardship as a result. Of course I would."

I reach to the bedside table and put on my watch.

Hopkins stands on the other side of the room, catching herself unwillingly in a full-length mirror. She picks up her own watch and looks at it, then dries herself and pulls on her knickers and leggings. Her knickers have seen better days. Without asking, it's a ritual now, she calls the usual number from my phone's memory and within a few minutes I hear a black cab purring up outside.

"Give me a call," she says.

She understands the situation and she is happy with it. We have discussed it many times.

Unexpectedly, she moves to the bed where I lie naked. She pulls at my flaccid penis as a person tweaks the rubber of a balloon. Then she kisses my cheek, pulls on her various layers of outer covering, Eskimo like, and leaves.

Dad's picture comes up. The beetle brow, the broken veins in his cheeks, the big pancake roll fingers. If Dad had been in that court, he'd have had the SFO for breakfast. Crook, liar, double-crosser – to his face? I don't think so. Never in a million years. That's the great, deep, shifty cowardice of it all.

He was worth ten times any of them, and they knew it. He'd been through more than they could even contemplate. He'd been one of the first soldiers to step through the gates of Belsen. I don't remember him ever talking about it. I first knew when I was fifteen, from my mother. All the times we'd been watching *633 Squadron* or *Colditz* and he'd say "Rubbish" or "Shut up" and switch channels suddenly made sense. My mother told me he'd had a nervous breakdown shortly afterwards and got invalided out of the army. Once, I asked him why he didn't like watching war films, and his answer was typically evasive, but precise. "The actors," he said, "It's the *acting*."

Within thirty-six hours of him dying, surprise surprise, the SFO suddenly thought they had a case. My brother and I sat through seventy days of prosecution evidence. I was shaking by the end of it. I was white. It was like a witch hunt. The pressure was on them for someone to pay. I stuck to the facts: that every action taken by us was a legitimate and legal action. But I never lost sight of the possibility I could be in jail by Christmas, and neither did my wife or my children that they could have their husband and dad taken away from them.

The BBC *Nine O'clock News*: "Daniel and Kenneth Cush have been cleared of conspiracy to defraud over 100 million pounds of ratepayers' money from regional council funds..."

I remember the way Arabella threw her arms around me earlier today, so tight I thought that she might literally break my neck.

"I love you," she said.

"...The Cush brothers will not face further prosecutions. The Judge said that subsequent charges would be unjustified and a flagrant abuse of power..."

I decide to go to Hamley's tomorrow and get Kit and Zoe a pre-Christmas treat, and something for Arabella. A perfume a little less exotic perhaps. Arabella says the children are spoiled. She's hard on them, being with them all day, every day, she's always the one to blow her top. And daddy comes in as the big softie to wipe the tears. It makes her so mad sometimes, that their dad can do no wrong.

In my dressing gown now, I look out of the picture window across the black of the Thames at Alderman's Stairs, at the lights of the Tower Hotel and St Katherine's Wharf, and Wapping. Beyond my grey reflection, I think of the black-and-white PR photos of Dad, shirt sleeves rolled up, hairy arms, gorilla-like, meaty knuckles pressing down the conference table. A Neanderthal baby, more built for a donkey jacket than a Savile Row suit.

As I raise the telephone receiver to my face and listen to the ringing tone I can smell the spermicide from Nina Hopkins's cap on my fingers.

"Hi. Did I wake the kids?"

"No, they're watching a video." Down-to-earth Arabella, cleverly avoiding them watching TV. Kit had already been in punch-ups in the playground with yobs who called his dad a swindler and a crook who murdered old age pensioners who couldn't pay their heating bills.

"What are they watching?"

"*Childsplay 3*," she jokes.

A breath goes through my nose, a kind of laugh.

"You didn't ask if you woke me."

"Did I?"

"No."

"Listen," I say. "I'll be down tonight."

"Are you sure?"

"It'll be an easier drive. The roads'll be deserted."

"How was dinner?"

"Oh, Philp chickened out. I was quite relieved. Ended up sleeping for about six hours, spark out."

"Poor sweet, you must be shattered. Will you be OK to drive?"

"I'll be perfect. I'm wide awake now."

"Shall I wait up? When will you be here?"

I looked at my watch. It was getting on for ten. "About midnight. Don't worry if you're asleep. I'll try not to wake you." I have an image of slipping out of my clothes, leaving them in a pile in the dark, and squeezing into the creaky cottage bed with its clean sheets.

I am driving down the M4 with the needle fidgeting under 70, aware that the Calvados is still in my system, though I don't feel it. I feel a kind of out-of-body remoteness now. The car doesn't seem to exist, the dark of it melding into the surrounding night, the only thing hinging it to reality being the lights of the dashboard, like the points in a dot-to-dot puzzle not yet completed.

The road is empty. I do not have the radio on, the tarmac under me providing a rumbling, abstract melody. I watch cars loom up in my rear view mirror, indicating, and overtaking, tail lights disappearing into the dark.

It's remarkable. When we used to go for a run in my grandfather's Hillman Hunter, we used to think we were speeding at 35.

I used to have one of those toy steering wheels when my father had his first car. It was yellow. You'd stick it to the dashboard with spit and pretend it was you who was driving. "Stirling Moss," he called me. With my free hand I'd make up arbitrary gear changes. And I remember, when *Goldfinger* came out we'd all want stick-on bullet holes for the car windows, except Dad wouldn't let us have those. Or a nodding Boxer dog in the back window, like my cousin had.

A Volvo overtakes me. Its indicator seems bright and insistent, a warning, an asterisk, an accusation.

It's funny how things come back when you least expect them. The memory comes up like a fish out of water, a flash at first, then so clear I can touch it.

I was eight. I must have been eight, because we were on our way to Bradford hospital and the only reason I can think for going to Bradford hospital was when my brother was born, and he's eight years younger than me. My mother was in the car, so she must've been pregnant with Kenny at the time. I presume she was going for a check-up.

I remember Dad asking me if I'd like to give the baby its middle name. I'm pleased as punch. I ask for him to be called Gregory, because Gregory Follows was my best friend in school. (I fell out with Gregory that summer, and I never saw him again once I left primary school. So Kenny was landed with a stupid middle name nobody liked, including me. It was the name of a friend I didn't have any more.)

On this day, we are driving to Bradford hospital in Dad's first car, the green Morris Minor. It is sunny. Dad is smiling. Perhaps he's seen one of his cronies ten minutes ago, I don't remember, but he has one of those grins which was nothing to do with my mother in the passenger seat or me in the back.

I say I feel really happy and I can't remember why. Dad laughs and says it's because I'm going to have a baby brother. I say, oh yes. But I think to myself the real reason is that I've got an afternoon off school.

We are going down the Winsley Road and come up to the T-junction with the Bath Road, and stop at the broken white lines. I am asking Mum if Gregory can come round for tea and play Scalextric and my dad looks right and left and pulls out to turn left and suddenly smash. A van has gone right into the side of us, or for a second it seems as though it has. In fact it has clipped the driver's side wing and bumper, crunching and sprinkling the glass from the headlight all over the road. It makes a sharp bang and my mother, of a nervous disposition at the best of times, shrieks and holds her arms stiffly against the dashboard. "Oh, hell!" she says, her voice drawing it out musically like an opera singer. I am sure she is going to faint.

I, on the other hand, feel calm. I quickly realise that the worst is already over. My mother's fear and panic is retroactive, almost as if reliving the anticipatory graph of horror she has missed by the suddenness of the crash.

"Are you all right, Mum?"

"Of course she's bloody all right," says dad.

"Daniel?" says my mum, her voice rising shrilly. She turns and reaches out her hands to me. I am not sure whether she is going to comfort me, or me her.

"Sit down," says Dad. I am standing up in the gap between the driver's and the passenger seat. I see his face from a three-quarters angle from behind. A redness begins to seep from his collar upwards, his lips are pulled tight, and I can tell from the crow's feet vanished from his cheeks that he isn't smiling any more. He asserts a kind of terrifying calm over himself and methodically moves the gear stick into neutral and switches off the engine, completely oblivious to my mother's stifled sobbing. My mother's emotionality was never a serious consideration. Beyond him, I can see the van framed in the Cinemascope of the dusty windscreen, sunlit, a hefty vehicle pockholed with rust, the automotive equivalent of the kind of boys in school who my mum tells me not to play with.

"Quiet," my dad says.

"Oh Geoff. What happened, love…?" My mother's voice flirts with tears. There's a suggestion of blame in her sympathetic tone. My father doesn't ask if she was hurt, or comfort her in anyway. He doesn't even look at her. His unblinking eyes are on the van door as it opens and creakily slams shut.

"Leave this to me."

He opens the car door and my mother says, "Now don't start anything, Geoff, for goodness sake. Please, promise me you won't." She reaches out towards him, her fingers not quite touching the sleeve of his royal blue blazer in the second before there is emptiness behind the steering wheel and the door is slammed in our faces.

"Who's the bloody idiot, then, eh?" I can hear my father booming dully outside our car. Mum cringes.

He stands with his hands on his hips, his trilby on head, shirt tight across his pot belly and his cricket club tie, a maroon squiggle, dancing in the wind. The man from the van, a good six inches shorter and thin as a whippet, is a builder of some sort. He has overalls caked in white limey residue, cement or plaster, which salt his face and sticky-up Stan Laurel hair. The lines in his face seem to all point to his powder-blue eyes. Some plastic twine ties his overalls together at the hip, where a button is missing.

"Is anybody hurt?" says the man, quietly spoken, and obviously shaken and trying to peer into our car. He hunches down, catches sight of Mum and me and looks concerned.

"No thanks to you there isn't," says my dad. Dad has his back to us.

The man looks at him now. "What? What are you talking about?" He sounds genuinely baffled. He sounds like somebody picked on for something they didn't do. "What are you on about?"

"On about!"

"You're in the wrong, pal, not me," the small man says, a slight tremor in his voice. Not somebody used to or relishing confrontation, this chap. He shifts from foot to foot as if trying to avoid it. "You want to read your Highway Code."

"You what?"

"Well. Coming out into a main road without looking. Christ. Who the hell's fault do you think it is?"

"You must be bloody joking!"

"Me? I'm not joking, no. You're the joker."

"I've got a pregnant woman in that car!" says my dad with an expressive gesture in our direction.

"What, I suppose that's my fault too, is it?" says the man. "I wouldn't be surprised."

"Oi. You watch it!" My dad shuffles closer to him, making the most of his height advantage to intimidate. "You watch what you're saying, you. That's my wife in there, that is."

"God, God alive..." breathes my mother against the car window. She has turned her head away from the confrontation, only to be faced by two passersby, a woman with a shopping trolley and another with a pram, transfixed as the altercation gets more and more heated. My mum closes her eyes. "Geoff. No. Please. Don't..." she prays under her breath, in vain. But she knows her husband of old and since she can't prevent it, what she really wants is for this to be over as soon as possible. Please. Please.

Outside the car, his stubby index finger is stabbing at the small man's chest.

"Hey. Don't point that finger at me, pal."

"What?"

"I said don't point that bloody finger at me, *all right*?"

"I'll do what I want with my finger. It's my bloody finger. If I want to point it at you I'll bloody *point* it at you. Who are you to tell me what to do with my finger!"

The small man does the only thing he can do. He laughs, and turns away, shaking his head. My father goes after him as if to grab him by the arm or the throat. The man turns, unexpectedly. Disarmed, my father backs up a step, a coward, his neck as maroon as his cricket club tie. His chin is in the air, Mussolini-like now, hands on hips, a big strutting cock.

My eight-year-old mind races with the question: *Is this what dads do?*

This was not a hero and baddie, like in the pictures. This was not John Wayne and Sitting Bull, this wasn't even Ernest Borgnine and Richard Widmark – this was something I recognise all too well, just a big blow-up version of a scrap in the playground. I think: this is how it is. This is how it will be, then. The playground just gets bigger.

Mum dabs her nose with a hankie and puts it back up the sleeve of her cardigan. She sniffs.

I say, "I'm all right," quietly – not to her, but as a statement of fact, to myself, to convince me.

Outside the mute chorus of onlookers is growing, none of them with the slight intention to either arbitrate or interfere. They are like cows in a field.

It seems like we have been there for hours but it is probably less than five minutes. My dad is putting on a laboured tone of voice now, as if talking to a congenital idiot: "You were coming down that road, let's face it. And you indicated to turn left. I *saw you*. A hundred yards away. Your left indicator was merrily flashing away, I saw it! *That's why I pulled out*. Because *you* were indicating to turn left. *Except you didn't, did you?* Oh no. You changed your mind and you just...you just came along straight and went straight into the blinking side of me!" He is becalmed now, more considered, so *blinking* replaces the involuntary *bloody*. "Didn't you? Pal. Pally..." A touch of mockery now. Victory in sight, he can smell it. "Go on. Admit it! Didn't you?"

Silence.

The small man whispers something beginning with F under his breath, a bad word I haven't heard a grown-up say before. He looks up and, seeing the wild triumphant gleam in my father's eyes, he says, "You're half cracked, you are."

"Am I? Oh, yes," says my father, showing his teeth. "You would say that, wouldn't you?"

"So I indicated I was turning left?"

My dad laughs incredulously. "You *know* you did!"

"Bollocks did I."

"Are you telling me I don't know what I can see with my own two eyes?" says my father.

"Your bloody eyes need seeing to, mate, if that's what you saw. I'm on my way to the A4. Why the hell would I be taking a turning to go through Winsley?"

"Well, we only have *your* word for that, don't we? We don't know where you're travelling. You could be travelling to *Timbuctoo* for all we know!" The man doesn't move. There is a flicker in my father's face that he might have overstepped the mark. "I – I don't know, do I? For – For all I know you might have flicked the indicator on by accident. All I know is, *that indicator was bloody on!*"

"I didn't do anything by *accident*. Look. Look at my van, look at the front." He moves to his vehicle but my father doesn't follow.

"Look. Is the indicator on? No."

"Not *now*, no! Obviously!"

The skinny man looks at the big man. Not yet the elephant seal who will go to Buckingham Palace to collect his knighthood for services to charity. Not yet the chairman of one of the top five banks. Now, back then, a Co-op man, selling insurance and picking up small change from old ladies in terraced houses once a week, invited in for tea and digestives and to listen to their troubles by the heat of a two-bar electric fire, while his two little sons do their homework.

"You don't believe me. Fair enough. No, fair enough!" says my father, straightening his tie. "We'll ask the boy."

I feel a coldness like tapwater run down my back and suddenly I want to go to the toilet. I'm sure I haven't heard correctly. I couldn't have heard correctly.

"The boy was watching," my father is saying in some distant world. "He saw what happened. Exactly what happened. Didn't you son?" The voice grows louder as it grows closer.

My father's face is up to the window beside me, his enormous palms flattened against the glass. His bushy eyebrows cast caterpillar shadows over his eyes. I see the small black dots of bristle on his top lip, cartoon clear. Behind him, more indistinct, I see the builder looking at the sky, folding his arms, moving his weight from one foot to the other, saying, "Listen, pal..."

"No no. No no," insists my father, holding up a hand. The builder puts his hands deep in his pockets and looks at the clouds, squinting.

My dad's face fills the window. All of a sudden, I can't see anything else. He's filling my eyes and my head. "Now, Dan. You know I want you to tell the truth, don't you?" I can smell the warm leather of the seats.

I nod.

My father says, "You know that, whatever happened just now, you must say the truth. Never mind what you think your dad wants you to say. Your dad – listen to me, son—" I look into his big chocolate coloured eyes "—Your dad wants you to tell the truth, that's all." I can see every pore in the tip of his nose. I am closer to him now than when he tucks me into bed and turns out the light. I watch his lips form the words. "That's all that matters, all right?"

"Wait a minute," says the builder, behind.

Dad straightens up. All I see now is the maroon tie and an expanse of shirt filling the window.

"What's the matter?"

"Come off it…"

"What?" my father sounds pained. Affronted. Hurt. "Are you saying – what? That my boy, that – come on, out with it. If you've got something to say, say it!"

"This is bloody ridiculous and you know it is."

"Is it?" Now my father addresses the pram lady and the four people standing at the bus stop, who have listened to everything. He is playing to the stalls. "*Is* it ridiculous?" He walks over to the bus stop and returns, arms outstretched.

Then the builder silently looks my father from head to toe, inwardly summing him up. I don't know what he thinks he sees, apart from not thinking much of him, but he also looks over to me, and he looks in my eyes for quite a long time. Like he feels sorry for me. Then he looks at my dad, like he thinks even less of him, and folds his arms and says quietly, "All right then. You're the boss. Ask the lad, go on. Ask the lad if he saw the indicator on." He sees my father hesitate slightly and he picks a flake of plaster dust from his sleeve and flicks it away.

"Right then," says my father. He rolls on his heels, nodding at him. "Right then. We'll settle this. Right. We'll settle this once and for all."

He comes closer and wipes the window next to me with his hand, then taps the glass with his hairy knuckles.

"All right, Daniel. You've heard what we're talking about. Have you?"

I nod.

"The truth. Dad won't be angry at you. You won't be in trouble, whatever you say – all right? All I want you to say is what you *know* to be absolutely true, all right?"

I nod.

It is warm and the seat smell is horrible and I want to go for a wee. I don't look at my mum. My mum is no part of this now. I forget she is even there.

"The truth, lad, remember," says the builder. "Nobody will blame you for telling the truth, I promise." He looks in a packet of Woodbines for a cigarette but the packet is empty. He drops it into a nearby gutter, poking it down the drain with his toe. He looks like a nice, kind man. I wonder if he is somebody's dad, if he is one of those dads who take their children to the park, to the swings on a Sunday afternoon.

Dad backs away from the car, away from me, hands raised, as if saying, look, no hands, the boy is on his own. He has no expression on his face now but complete, abject innocence, removing himself from the action, from the equation, from the accusation. He steps the same distance from our car as the builder. I feel abandoned. Alone. Empty. Both are bathed in the same dusty sunlight beyond the smeary glass of the Morris.

The smell of the sun on the leather seats is almost making me sick. I try not to breathe too deeply, because I know it will.

"Just the truth, laddo," says the small man softly. "That's all I want. That's all your dad wants, isn't it?" He looks across at my father, sideways.

I look into my dad's eyes, but I can't find them. I know they are there, somewhere, but the sun is too bright. "That's all I want, son. All you have to do is answer the question. Was it off or was it on?"

"That's all you have to answer," says the builder. "Was the indicator off or on?"

I open my mouth. I hear my breath come out. Except it isn't my breath, it's a word. And I'm curious as to what word it is that has come out of my mouth, and I say it again so that I can listen to it this time. And I say, "On."

My father cups a hand behind his ear. "What? What did you say, Danny? Speak up!"

"On," I hear myself say again, then louder: "*On*." And in my mind I see the word on a blackboard and I am trying to rub it out.

"On! Did you hear that?" says my dad outside, standing in the road, advancing on the man. "Did you hear that, eh? *On!*" The small man's shoulders fall against the side of his van.

My dad asks for the man's insurance company and it turns out the man doesn't have insurance. He looks ashamed, humiliated. He doesn't have a tax disk on his van either. My dad says, "Ho." It doesn't take a genius to work out his vehicle isn't fit to be on the road, and he knows it. And that means just one thing we all know now, Dad, my mother, me: that the man is poor. And that somehow seals it.

They have more words, but I don't really hear any of it, it is like being underwater, maybe for minutes, I don't know how long – then Dad backs off, flattening his tie against his paunch and buttoning his blazer across it.

The man stands propped against his van, his arms hanging. He looks at me. He looks at me as if everything makes complete sense, as if he knows everything, more even than I know or would ever know.

I duck down a fraction, hiding my sight line under the frame of the window. And I hear him laughing. I look up again, and he is shaking his head and laughing. Dad says nothing to him after that.

I look the other way, keep my eyes inside the car, on a copy of *Look and Learn* beside me on the back seat, until I hear the van rev and reverse and clatter away with a miner's lung of an engine. And I hear my father get a dust-pan and brush from the boot and sweep up the broken glass from the front of the car, and as he is doing it he is whistling.

Afterwards, he gets in behind the steering wheel and he shows my mother a fan of twenty pound notes. My mother doesn't say anything and neither does he.

As we drive to Bradford hospital, I can see my dad's big brown eyes in the rear view mirror. It might be the sun, but there are big crow's feet round his eyes and it looks like he is smiling. Without taking his eyes off the road ahead, he says, "Well done, son." I have that feeling again, that I am really happy and I don't know why.

And he has the smile on his face all the way to Bradford hospital, and all the way home. Twenty minutes, because I am counting. One thousand two hundred seconds. That is more than when he sees one of his cronies, even. Much, much more.

Peter Robinson

Shadow on the Water

We were meant to be getting some sleep, but how you're supposed to sleep in a cold, muddy, rat-infested trench, when the uppermost thought in your mind is that you're going to be shot first thing in the morning is quite beyond me.

Albert Parkinson handed around the Black Cats to the four of us who clustered together for warmth, mugs of weak Camp coffee clutched to our chests, almost invisible to one another in the darkness. 'Here you go, Frank,' he said, cupping the match in his hands for safety, even though we were well below ground level. I thanked him and inhaled the harsh tobacco, little realising that soon I would be inhaling something far more deadly. Still, we needed the tobacco to mask the smell. The trench stank to high heaven of unwashed men, excrement, cordite and rotting flesh.

Now and then, distant shots broke the silence, someone shouted a warning or an order, and an exploding shell lit the sky. But we were waiting for dawn. We talked in hushed voices and eventually the talk got around to what makes heroes of men. We all put in our two-penn'orth, of course, mostly a lot of cant about courage, patriotism and honour, with the occasional begrudging nod in the direction of folly and luck, but instead of settling for a simple definition, Joe Fairweather started to tell us a story.

Joe was a strange one. Nobody quite knew what to make of him. A bit older than the rest of us, he already had a reputation as one of the most fearless lads in our regiment. It never seemed to worry him that he was running across no man's land in a hail of bullets; he seemed either blessed or indifferent to his fate. Joe had survived Ypres one and two, and now here he was, ready to go again. Some of us thought he was more than a little bit mad.

'When I was a kid,' Joe began, 'about eleven or twelve, we used to play by the canal. It was down at the bottom of the park, through the woods, and not many people went there because it was a hell of a steep slope to climb back up. But we were young, full of energy. We could climb anything. There were metal railings all along the canal side, but we had found a loose one that you could lift out easily, like a spear. We always put it back when we went home so nobody would know we had found a way in.

'There wasn't much beyond the canal in those days, only fields full of cows and sheep, stretching away to distant hills. Very few barges used the route. It was a lonely, isolated spot, and perhaps that was why we liked it. We used to forge sick notes from our mothers and play truant from school, and nobody was ever likely to spot us down by the canal.

'Not that we got up to any real mischief, mind you. We just talked the way kids do, skimmed stones off the water. Sometimes we'd sneak out our fishing nets and catch sticklebacks and minnows. Sometimes we played games. Just make-believe. We'd act out stories from *Boy's Own*, cut wooden sticks from the bushes and pretend we were soldiers on patrol.' Joe paused and looked around at the vague outlines of our faces in the trench and laughed. 'Can you believe it?' he said. 'We actually *played* at being soldiers. Little did we know...

'One day, I think it was June or July, just before the summer holidays, at any rate, a beautiful, sunny, still day, the kind that makes you believe that only good things are going to happen, my friend Adrian and me were sitting on the stone bank dipping our nets in the murky water when we saw someone on the other side. I say *saw*, but at first it was more like sensing a presence, a shadow on the water, perhaps, and we looked up and noticed a strange man standing on the opposite bank, watching us with a funny sort of expression on his face. I remember feeling annoyed at first because this was our secret place and nobody else was supposed to be there. Now this grown-up had to come and spoil everything.

'"Shouldn't you boys be at school?" he asked us.

'There wasn't much we could say to that, and I dare say we just fidgeted and looked shifty.

'"Well," he said. "Don't worry, I won't tell anyone. What are you doing?"

'"Just fishing," I said.

'"Just fishing? What are you fishing for? There can't be much alive down there in that filthy water."

'"Minnows and sticklebacks," I said.

'"How old are you?"

'We told him.

'"Do your parents know where you are?"

'"No," I said, though I remember feeling an odd sensation of having spoken foolishly as soon as the word was out of my mouth, but it was too late to take it back.

'"Why do you want to know?" Adrian asked him.

'"It doesn't matter. Want to play a game with me?"

'"No, thanks." We started to move away. Who did he think he was? We didn't play with grown-ups; they were no fun.

'"Oh, I think you do," he said and there was something about his voice that made the hackles on the back of my neck stand up. I glanced at Adrian and we turned to look across the canal to where the man stood. When we saw the gun in his hand, both of us froze.

'He smiled, but it wasn't a nice smile. "Told you so," he said.

'Now, I looked at him closely for the first time. I was just a kid, so I couldn't say how old he was, but he was definitely a grown-up. A man. And he was wearing a sort of uniform, like a soldier, but it looked shabby and rumpled, as if it had been slept in. I couldn't see the revolver very clearly, not that I'd have had any idea what make it was, as if that even mattered. All that mattered was that it was a gun and that he was pointing it at us.

'Then, out of sheer nerves I suppose, we laughed, hoping maybe it was all a joke and it was just a cap gun he was holding. "All right," Adrian said. "If you really want to play…"

'"Oh, I do," the man said. Then he pulled the trigger.

'It wasn't as loud as I had expected, more of a dull popping sound, but something whizzed through the bushes beside me and dinged on the metal railing as it passed by. I felt deeply ashamed as the warm piss dribbled down my bare legs. Thankfully, nobody seemed to notice it but me.

'"That's just to show you that it's a real gun," the man said, "and that I mean what I say. Do you believe me now?"

'We both nodded. "What do you want?" Adrian asked.

'"I told you. I want to play."

'"Look," I said, "you're frightening us. Why don't you put the gun away? Then we'll play with you, won't we, Adrian?"

'Adrian nodded. "Yes."

'"This?" The man looked at his revolver as if seeing it for the first time. 'But why should I want to put it away?"

'He fired again, closer this time, and a clod of earth flew up and stung my cheek. I was damned if I was going to cry, but I was getting close. I felt as if we were the only people for hundreds of miles, maybe the only people in the whole world. There was nobody to save us and this lunatic was going to kill us after he'd had his fun. I didn't know why, what made him act like that, or anything, but I just knew he was going to do it.

'"Don't you like this game?" he asked me.

'"No," I said, trying to keep my voice from shaking. "I want to go home."

'"Go on, then," he said.

'"What?"

'"I said go on."

'"You don't mean it."

'"Yes, I do. Go."

'Slowly, without taking my eyes off him, I backed up the bank towards the hole in the railings. Only when I got there, and I had to turn to squeeze through, did I take my eyes off him. As soon as I did, I heard another shot and felt the air move as something zipped by my ear. "I've changed my mind," he said. "Come back."

'Knowing, deep down, that it had been too good to be true, I slunk back to the bank. The man was muttering to himself, now, and neither Adrian nor I could make out what he was saying. In a way, that was even more frightening than hearing his words. He was pacing up and down, too, staring at the ground, his gun hanging at his side, but we knew that if either of us made the slightest movement, he would start shooting at us again.

'This went on for some time. I could feel myself sweating and the wetness down my legs was uncomfortable. Apart from the incomprehensible muttering across the water, everything was still and silent. No birds sang, almost as if they knew this was death's domain and had got out when they could. Even the cows and sheep were silent, and looked more like a landscape painting than real, living creatures. Maybe a barge would come, I prayed. Then he would have to hide his gun and we would have time to run up to the woods. But no barge came.

'Finally, he came to a pause in his conversation with himself, at least for the time being. "You," he said to Adrian, gesturing with his gun. "You can go now."

'"I don't believe you mean it," Adrian said.

'The man pointed the gun right at him. "Go. Before I change my mind and shoot you."

'Adrian scrambled up the grassy bank. I could hear him crying. I had never felt so alone in my life. Inside, I was praying for the man to tell Adrian to come back, the way he had with me. I didn't want to die alone by the dirty canal. I wanted to go home and see my mum and dad again.

'This time my prayers were answered.

'"Come back," he said. "I've changed my mind."

'"Are you going to shoot us?" I asked, when Adrian once again stood at my side, wiping his eyes on his sleeve.

'"I don't know," he said. 'It depends on what they tell me to do. Just shut up and let me think. Don't talk unless I ask you to."

'*They*? What on earth was he talking about? Adrian and I looked at one another, puzzled. There was nobody else around. Who was going to tell him what to do? You have to remember we were only kids, and we didn't know anything about insane people hearing voices and all that.

'"But *why*?" I asked. "Why are you doing this? We haven't done you any harm."

'He didn't say anything, just fired a shot – pop – into the bushes right beside me. It was enough. Then he started talking again, and I think both Adrian and me now had an inkling that he was hearing the voices in his head, and that maybe he was having a conversation with the mysterious "they" he had mentioned.

'"All right," he said, the next time he calmed down. He pointed the gun at me. "What's your name?" he asked.

'"Joe," I said.

'"Joe. All right, Joe. You can go. What's your friend's name?"

'"Adrian."

'"Adrian stays."

'I stood my ground. "You're not going to let me go," I told him. "You'll only do the same as you did before."

'That made him angry and he started waving the gun around again. "Go!" he yelled at me. "Now! Before I shoot you right here."

'I went.

'Sure enough, when I got to the hole in the fence, I heard him laugh, a mad, eerie sound that sent a chill through me despite the heat of the day. "You didn't think I meant it, did you? Come back here, Joe."

'Somehow, the use of my name, the sound of it from *his* lips, on *his* breath, was worse than anything else. For a moment, I hesitated then I slipped through the hole in the railings and started running for my life.

'I knew that there was a hollow about thirty feet up the grassy slope, and if I reached it I would be safe. It was only a quick dash from there to the woods.

'I heard him shout again. "Joe, come back here right now!"

'I ran and ran. I heard the dull pop of his revolver and sensed something whiz by my right side and thud into the earth. My heart was pumping for all it was worth and the muscles on my legs felt fit to burst.

'But I made it. I made it to the hollow and dived into the dip in the ground that would protect me from any more bullets. I heard just one more popping sound before I made my dash for the woods and that was it.'

Here, Joe paused, as if recounting the narrative had left him as out of breath as outrunning the lunatic's bullets. From our trench, we could hear more shots in the distance now and a shell exploded about two hundred yards to the west, lighting up the sky. Further away, somewhere behind our lines, a piper played. I handed around my cigarettes and noticed Jack Armstrong in the subdued glow of the match. Face ashen, eyes glazed, lips trembling, the kid was terrified and it was my guess that he'd freeze when the command came. I'd seen it happen before. Not that I blamed him. I sometimes wondered why we didn't all react that way. There but for the grace of God... I remembered Harry Mercer, who had tried for a Blighty in the foot and ended up losing the entire lower half of his left leg. Then there was Ben Castle, poor, sad Ben, who swore he'd do it himself before the Germans did it to him, and calmly put his gun in his mouth and pulled the trigger. So who were the heroes? And why?

'What happened next?' asked Arthur. 'Did you run and fetch the police?'

'The police? No,' said Joe. 'I don't really remember what I did. I think I just wandered around in a daze. I couldn't believe it had happened, you see, that I had been so close to death and escaped.'

'But what about your friend? What about Adrian?' Arthur persisted.

Joe looked right through him, as if he hadn't even heard the question. 'I waited until it was time to return home from school,' he went on, 'and that's exactly what I did. Went home. The piss stains on my trousers and underwear had dried by then, and if my mother noticed the next time she did the washing then she didn't say anything to me about it. We went on holiday the next day to stay for a week with my Aunt Betty on the coast near Scarborough. Every day I scoured my dad's newspaper when he'd put it aside after breakfast, but I could find no reference to the lunatic with the gun. I even started to believe that it had all been a figment of my imagination, that it hadn't happened at all.'

'But what about Adrian?' Arthur asked.

'Adrian? I had no idea. That whole week we were with Aunt Betty I wondered about him. Of course I did. But surely if anything had happened it would have been in the papers? Still, I knew I had deserted Adrian. I had dashed off to freedom and hadn't given him a second thought once I was in the woods.'

'But you must have seen him again,' I said.

'That's the funny thing,' Joe said. 'I did. It was about two days after we got back from our holiday. I saw him in the street. He started walking towards me. I was frightened because he was a year older than me, and bigger. I thought he was going to beat me up.'

'What did he do?' Arthur asked.

Joe laughed. 'That's the funny thing,' he said. 'Adrian walked up to me. I braced myself for an assault, and he said, "Thank you".

'I wasn't certain I'd heard him correctly, so I asked him to repeat what he'd said.

'"Thank you," he said again. "That was a very brave thing you did, dodging the bullets like that, risking death."

'I was stunned. I didn't know what to say. I must have stood there looking like a complete idiot, with my mouth hanging open.

'"Had he gone?" he asked me next.

'"Who?" I replied.

'"You know. The lunatic with the gun. I'll bet he'd gone when you came back with the police, hadn't he?'

'Now I understood what Adrian was thinking. "Yes," I said. "Yes, he'd gone."

'Adrian nodded. "I thought so. Look, I'm sorry," he went on, "sorry I didn't hang around till you got back with them, to help you explain and all, but I was so scared."

'"What happened?" I asked.

'"Well," Adrian said, "as soon as you made it to the woods, he ran off down the canal bank. He must have known you'd soon be back with help, and he didn't want to hang around and get caught. I probably stood there for a few moments to pull myself together, then I headed off in the same direction you did. I just went home as if I'd been to school and didn't say a word to anyone. I'm sorry," he said again. "I should have stuck around when you came back with the police."

"'It's all right," I said. "They didn't believe me. They thought I was just a trouble-maker. One of them gave me a clip around the ear and they sent me home. Said if anything like that ever happened again they'd tell my mum and dad."

'Adrian managed to laugh at that. I was feeling so relieved I could have gone on all day making things up. How I went back to try and rescue Adrian by myself and found the man a little further down the bank. How I carried the loose railing like a spear and threw it at him across the canal, piercing him right through the heart. Then how I weighted his body with stones and dropped it in the water. But I didn't. It was enough that I was exonerated in Adrian's eyes. Good enough that I was a *hero*.'

Joe began to laugh and it sounded so eerie, so *mad*, that it sent shivers up our spines. Jack Armstrong started crying. He wasn't going anywhere. And Joe was still laughing when the black night inched towards another grey dawn and the orders came down for us to go over the top and take a godforsaken blemish on the map called Passchendaele.

Amy Myers
Murder by Ghost

'The most haunted place in the county. Know that?'

The 9th Earl of Sissingbrook's bleary eyes fixed Auguste Didier with a glare. Auguste sighed. One of the unfortunate side-effects of the magnificent cuisine he produced for the members of Plum's Club for Gentlemen was that there was always one left happily clutching a glass of brandy, far into the night. It was one o'clock, a time when all decent chefs should be in their beds, dreaming of the delicacies they would produce the next day.

'No, your lordship.'

'Ghosts everywhere at Ellincourt Place. That's why I wanted to see you.'

Auguste was instantly wary. So this summons had not been just for another brandy, this one was personal. He was walking on eggshells, and so far he didn't like the look of the omelette.

'Headless horsemen, ghosts chucking stones and crockery, the limping nun – I'm used to all of them,' his lordship continued gloomily. 'This one's different. This ghost is after *me*.'

'Why?' Auguste enquired cautiously.

'It wants to murder me.'

Auguste's instincts had been right. There was trouble brewing here. 'A murdering ghost?'

'Why not?' The earl investigated the bottom of his now empty brandy glass. 'Ghosts get away with murder all the time. They think they're immune, that they can just materialise and announce they want someone's blood, and no one will dare to stop them. They order people's deaths just like that. No respect for the law.'

Extreme caution now. 'Why did you wish to see *me*, your lordship?'

'You've got a reputation for sorting out the truth behind murders, haven't you? I want you to come and tell the blasted thing it's wrong. I'm innocent. You can cook us dinner if you like.'

Dinner for a ghost? Auguste began to retreat hastily out of the room. It was the brandy speaking, he told himself. Tomorrow his lordship would remember none of this.

'Back here,' came an instant roar. 'I'll make it worth your while.'

'Money, sir,' Auguste tried to say bravely, 'is not my concern. My presence at Plum's to cook dinner to other members is.'

'I've fixed that. Had a word with the secretary fellow. You come and do your job at Ellincourt Place and I'll set you up in that cooking school you've always wanted to run.'

Auguste paused in his own dematerialising act. No harm in enquiring further.

'If the ghost wants to murder you, what reason does it have? What exactly does he think you've done?'

'It's not a he. It's a woman. She thinks I murdered her. All long robes and a laugh like a hyena. I know who it is. It's Marie-Antoinette.'

That did it. A headless royal ghost was too much for Auguste even to consider arguing with face to face – if only because there'd *be* no face. It put paid to serving it dinner as well.

'Not the queen,' the earl continued, reading Auguste's expression correctly. 'My Marie-Antoinette was a can-can dancer at one of these Paris night-life places. I first saw her there when I used to go on card-playing sprees. Changed her name to Maria when she married that dull old bore Robert Preston. She's come back to accuse me of having murdered her, and has the nerve to tell me I'll die for it this coming Saturday at midnight.'

Auguste paled. 'Why does she believe you murdered her?' Untactfully he added, 'Does she remember your doing so?'

The earl turned purple. 'She couldn't. I *didn't* do it. Years ago it was, fourteen to be precise, in 1883. Saturday is the anniversary. I met her again in '78, two years after she married Robert. She was still a stunner so I turned a blind eye to her social inadequacies. She and I became – er – much closer friends. Not to put too fine a point on it, I was infatuated with her. All flashing eyes and skirts, if you know what I mean. I was younger then of course, and not married.'

'Did her husband know about your friendship?'

'Certainly he did,' his lordship instantly retorted. 'No complaints there. She'd done her duty by him. Produced two sons – though it's true she claimed one of them might be mine. She kept that from Robert. She only married him because he had money, one of those jumped-up industrialists. Then he lost it all. Until recently, that is.'

Auguste noted that Mr Preston's restored fortunes seemed to give the earl little pleasure, but was relieved that it was he and not the ghost who would be the recipient of his cuisine.

'If you ask me,' the earl confided, 'Robert's grief at Maria's death didn't last too long. Fine-looking woman, but you couldn't take her anywhere. And temper! She could throw more china than all the Ellincourt ghosts put together.'

Auguste endeavoured to make sense of all this. 'You were present when she died?'

'Of course I was. We all were.' The earl glared at him, obviously thinking Auguste's powers of deduction were far below expectations. 'I'd just become engaged, and my fiancée Judith, now my wife, was staying at Ellincourt. Then, damn me, if Maria didn't get wind of it before I'd had a chance to tell her. She insisted on coming to join the party. When I said this would look damned odd, she said she'd drag Robert along too, and for good measure her brother who was staying with them. Otherwise she'd tell Judith all about our little affair.'

Only a very dim earl could have imagined this ensemble would provide an enjoyable house-party. Auguste decided to keep this thought to himself.

'Her brother François Duval was one of those twitchy Frenchmen with a long nose stuck into everything. He's done well for himself considering the parents were provincial butchers. You'll meet him. The same party's coming on Saturday – minus Maria.'

'Apparently not,' Auguste pointed out, while meditating on the earl's ability to stir up trouble for himself.

'Eh? Ah, see what you mean.' The thought of his ghost's reappearance gave the earl no pleasure.

'And what happened on that evening in '83?' Auguste enquired.

'Maria had taken the news that our affair was over surprisingly well, or so I thought. She only broke a few old Chinese vases and a couple of Staffordshire figures. Then I found she'd told Judith, not to mention Robert and François, that her younger son is actually mine. Rubbish of course. He's far too ugly.'

Auguste began to feel some sympathy with the ghost.

'Anyway, next morning Maria was found dead. Not a mark on her. No symptoms of poisoning, nothing. It was put down to a freak illness. Broken heart, I decided. She must have taken our parting harder than I thought.' There was complacency in the earl's voice which put Auguste even more on the ghost's side.

'Where does murder come in then?' he asked.

'It didn't until this hag of a ghost popped up, screeching about my murdering her.'

'Why now?' Auguste asked practically. 'It's fourteen years ago.'

'You tell me. You're the detective, and you're going to prevent my being murdered in my bed on Saturday.'

Auguste wondered how to phrase his next question tactfully, and decided there was no such way. 'Cannot your wife do that?'

A glare. 'I sleep alone. Wish I could say the same about her.'

Auguste decided not to comment, though he longed to satisfy his curiosity about the countess's private life. Instead he satisfied it on another strange facet of this story.

'Might I ask *why* you are inviting the same party to Ellincourt on Saturday? Is it an anniversary ritual?'

The earl snorted. 'Damnfool notion of yours. No. Robert and François are coming to discuss business. Their request. I could hardly say no, especially as they said it's to do with Maria. Robert's second wife Gertrude will be coming too. Probably wants to keep her eye on Judith.'

Even more interesting. 'What exactly do you want me to do, your lordship?'

'Not much,' the earl barked. 'Cook the dinner, and while you're serving it, find out who really murdered Maria, though I still think that ghost's got it wrong. She's turned up twice in the last week to tell me she's going to have her revenge, so on Saturday you can tell her whom she should be murdering instead of me.'

Just like that. Auguste took a deep breath, and prepared to defend his own skin. 'I prefer not to, your lordship. Could you not spend Saturday night at Plum's? I understand ghosts don't travel.'

'A Sissingbrook has never flinched in the face of battle,' the earl roared. 'We shoot only when we see the whites of their eyes.'

Unfortunately, August reflected, it would be he who was facing the whites of the ghost's eyes – if she had any. Balancing this prospect against the financing of his cooking school would be hard. On the other hand, the likelihood of this ghost turning out to be a true phantom, despite the earl's claim about Ellincourt Place's reputation, was small. A laughing and speaking ghost was equally rare. Ghosts, on the whole, were never funny; they wrung their hands in anguish. That was the whole point of them, for they imprinted their grief on the mists of time. Therefore it followed she was almost certainly a very material ghost, who would be intent on murdering her victim and not Auguste. It might therefore be possible to fulfil his duty by talking reason into her. In any case, he would be near to the earl so that the ghost could hardly walk through him into the room.

He recalled that in the previous century a ghost had appeared to a titled philanderer in similar circumstances to complain of her treatment and forewarn of his death, at a precise hour and on a precise day. His friends, invited to spend the night for his safety, advanced the clocks three hours, and the philanderer was much relieved when the apparent hour for his death passed without incident. Unfortunately the ghost would have been a strict adherent of Greenwich Mean Time, had that yet been established, for the wrong-doer duly expired at the correct spectral time.

Even as Auguste began to wage the battle with him over whether to accept the challenge, the earl himself assisted the decision by passing out and ungracefully sliding from his chair onto the floor. A touch of the bell brought two liveried Plum's footmen into the room to pick up the brandy-sodden customer and remove him to a bedroom for the night. Auguste presided over his departure with relief, for it meant he had the night to consider whether or not the financing of his cooking school was worth braving this haunted journey.

Certainly there must have been several possible motives for murder. There was only the earl's word for what had passed between himself and Maria, and he had to protect his position with regard to his fiancée. The husband could have murdered her in jealous fury at finding he was not the father of his own son. The earl's then fiancée could have murdered her out of fury and jealousy. The brother – well, who knew what motives he might have? Money by inheritance was one possibility.

Nevertheless, to discover the truth about a fourteen-year-old murder during the space of a dinner – and still to dedicate himself to his usual high standards of cuisine – was a difficult assignment. Moreover there was another factor that interestingly the earl had not mentioned, though it had been in the newspapers. He had referred to Robert's restored fortunes, but not to how this had been achieved. A large stone had recently been discovered in a chest of his late wife's effects stored in an attic, and had been identified as the missing Star Diamond, discovered a century ago and whose last known owner was an Indian maharajah. At his death in 1874 the stone had vanished and his family denied all knowledge of it. Now it belonged to Robert Parsons, and he and Maria's brother were coming to Ellincourt Place 'on business' connected with her. And then there was Gertrude Parsons to consider, who according to the newspapers had singled out the stone as worthy of checking. Had she a role to play in this?

Could it be, Auguste wondered, that the appearance of the vengeful ghost at such a time was not entirely coincidental?

Ellincourt Place by day was an unprepossessing house, a mediaeval abbey, much altered and expanded. The nuns would hardly have recognised their former home, Auguste reflected, as the earl stomped around the house with him to show him the haunted terrain.

'The ghost materialises out there—' he pointed out over the garden from his first floor bedroom. 'She starts with a fiendish cackle to wake me up, and then shouts out her intentions.'

Auguste looked carefully out of the window. Below him, slightly to the right, was the orangery and beyond that the gardens. Directly below him was a drainpipe on an ivy-covered wall. Auguste could see possibilities in this arrangement and was somewhat relieved. He allowed the cooking school to float back within the realms of practicality – provided of course there was still an Auguste Didier alive to run it.

'Don't the servants hear anything? Doesn't anyone else see it?'

'There's no one except Judith on this side of the house, and she'd sleep through, if the devil himself came to call. Servants are at the back of the house in the attics. The ghost keeps her voice down when she's speaking, but they've complained about the hyena cackles. When they come out to investigate, there's nothing there. Judith thinks I'm out of my mind, of course.'

Auguste felt happier. It must surely be a very human ghost, some Pepper's Ghost illusion perhaps, but it still had to be tracked down. Not to mention a murder solved in the space of an hour or so.

'Do your wife or the servants see the other phenomena?'

'Yes. I've seen one or two myself. The nun limps up and down the yew paths. Headless horseman gallops down to the lake from time to time – oh, and I've spotted the seventeenth-century cook from time to time.'

Auguste froze. 'What happened to him?'

The earl frowned. 'Lot of fuss about nothing. One of the ancestors decided to take over the cooking, took a fancy to the meat cleaver and the blasted cook objected. Damned nerve.'

Auguste eyed the earl very carefully. If there was a tradition of expendable cooks in this family, not even his *Soufflé d'Auguste Didier* would save him. The 9th earl might well be mad. The threat would not be to the earl from a trick ghost, but to a very human maître chef from a temporary employer.

The appearances of other apparitions at Ellincourt was not reassuring, however. No trickster would prepare his ground years in advance by laying on unnecessary illusions in the form of limping nuns and butchered cooks. Therefore it was either a true ghost – or an earl aspiring to follow in his ancestor's tracks.

Auguste decided to turn his mind to the more rewarding aspect of his visit: the preparation of dinner. The least pleasant aspect of his career was that he was often obliged to serve meals to the unappreciative, but Auguste had conquered it by convincing himself that the delights of his cuisine were an art in themselves. Did Rembrandt consider the gaze of the unappreciative public before painting his masterpieces? Did Michelangelo? No. So Auguste Didier too would create for art's sake alone, and consign to the stewpot the thought that it might well be his last great offering to the world.

It was just as well, for the company collected for dinner that evening was not going to be appreciative. The days when de la Reynière gathered his friends together solely to act as juries on his cuisine were long past. The earl and his wife Judith – some years younger than he and a handsome woman in her forties – made a formidable couple. Robert, the industrialist, looked uninspiring, though he displayed the happy confidence of someone whom fate always saves at the last moment. Spectacularly so in his case, Auguste reflected. Star Diamonds did not appear every day. Monsieur François Duval appeared a humble Uriah Heep to whom Robert's slightest wish was his command, although his eyes, Auguste noted, were extremely sharp. Gertrude Parsons, Robert's new wife, seemed the exact opposite of Maria, being a distinctly dowdy lady in her late thirties, though the set of her jaw suggested a strident domestic life. He had gathered that she had married Robert only months before the loss of his fortune, and that consequently her discovery of the Star Diamond was as delightful a surprise to her as it was to her husband.

Auguste remained in an unobtrusive position at the doorway, trying to look uninterested as to the fate of his exquisite goose *á la Dauphinoise* in the mouths of those clearly unappreciative diners. Whatever their thoughts might be centred on, it was not his cuisine, though how anyone could treat his John Dory in champagne sauce with such indifference was beyond his comprehension.

He wished that he could have advanced the clocks as had the friends of the victim last century, for that would at least have established whether or not it was a true spectre. Modern times, however, would have quickly put paid to such a scheme, since there were far too many clocks and pocket watches nowadays for it to work. The ghost and its threat to the earl, moreover, were general knowledge.

'It doesn't exist,' snorted Judith. 'Such illusions are in one's own mind. I believe I heard something once, but when I looked from my window, there was nothing there.'

'You think I'm planning my own murder then?' barked her loving husband.

'Guilt,' she decreed. 'No doubt what the ghost claims is true, and you have merely moved it from within your mind to an imaginary external manifestation. Orestes and the Delphic Oracle, you know.'

The earl clearly didn't, but his reply was forestalled by François Duval. '*Mais non*, Judith. My poor sister would never have sought revenge for her death. Always loving and gentle.'

'You weren't married to her,' Robert retorted calmly. 'You did not know Maria, Gertrude, but she could be a devil. Remember that last evening when you killed her, Gerard?'

'I didn't,' howled the earl. 'And there's no proof she was even murdered.'

'It's my belief,' Robert pontificated, ignoring him, 'that Maria was drugged, probably with laudanum, then suffocated.'

'How very unpleasant,' Judith murmured.

'You should know.' François turned on her with unexpected venom. 'You were there that night.'

'Are you suggesting that I was involved?' Judith flared up.

'*C'est possible, Madame la Comtesse*. You had reason enough – if you believed my poor late sister's deranged wanderings. But it is more likely to have been Gerard himself. My poor sister could be mischievous, I acknowledge, but it meant nothing.'

'It did,' her husband replied curtly.

François took no notice. 'It is possible she might have teased you,

Gerard, with threatening to tell your fiancée Judith about your, shall we say, *amitié* with her.'

'It was over, and Judith knew about it.'

'Not till then,' she sweetly whipped back.

Robert flushed. 'Dammit, Maria *was* my wife.'

'A loved one?' enquired Judith sharply.

'No, but not enough to kill her.' Robert was torn, Auguste could see, between need to reassure Gertrude, and ensure his own safety.

The earl leapt in eagerly. 'Stuff and nonsense, Robert. Hadn't Maria just told you one of your sons was mine? Not that I believe it, of course. But you might have done. If anyone suffocated her, you were best placed, being in the next room to her.'

'Carefully manoeuvred there by you,' Robert snarled.

The earl refused to retreat from his belligerent stance. The whites of Robert's eyes had flashed, and would not find an earl of Sissingbrook wanting. 'This ghost hasn't got a good memory. Of the two of us only you had reason to kill her. I'd told her our friendship was over, gave her a present, and she quite saw my point.'

'Why does that chef remain here?' François Duval threw casually into the conversation.

Auguste decided it was not for him to speak. He retained the impassive look adopted by all servants, cultivated over the centuries to indicate, firstly that they are invisible, and secondly, that nothing said in the dining room would be discussed except in the privacy of the servants' hall and kitchens.

'He's here to find out which one of you two killed Maria in time to convince the ghost she shouldn't kill me, but tackle the real murderer – if any,' Gerard added somewhat anticlimactically.

A silence, broken at last by Robert. 'A clever idea, Gerard, but you killed her. We all know that. We don't need a ghost to tell us.'

'No motive,' howled the earl. 'Who can prove it's true?'

'Maria's ghost.' François changed sides to support Robert.

'I don't believe in ghosts' ability to murder,' the earl replied defiantly, 'any more than they can recall the truth about their own deaths.'

'Twelve o'clock will prove your point,' Judith observed.

'In two hours' time. You'll have time for coffee, Gerard,' chortled François.

'You believe in ghosts, Monsieur Duval?' enquired Gertrude, as if doing her social duty in keeping the conversation going.

'*Non.*'

As if to disprove his point a noise suspiciously like a shower of stones raining against the windows startled the assembly.

Auguste moved quickly to the curtains, and drew one aside. It was growing dark, and a stiff breeze was stirring the bushes. A branch or two gently rapped against the glass; a cat was strolling across the lawn, a pot had fallen on the gravel path. Any of them could conceivably have caused the noise, but it was not a good omen for the night ahead.

At half past eleven a highly annoyed Auguste was standing in the gardens outside the orangery, his eyes peeled for ghosts rising over the bushes ahead of him. Secondly they were peeled for any intruders making for the drainpipe on the ivy-clad wall below the earl's bedroom. A hefty manservant was guarding the drainpipe itself.

Auguste was not happy for two reasons. Firstly, he had expected his vigil to take place outside the earl's bedroom *in* the house, not here, and secondly, this position hardly seemed ideal for his mission. True, the glass roof of the orangery behind him was unlikely to bear the weight of anyone hoping to approach the earl's room that way, but the huge windows were slanting open, which might allow someone access to the orangery and the cover of the bushes inside.

The earl had refused to allow him to stay in the house. The door into the corridor was locked and so was the door to the adjoining bathroom he shared with his wife; he gave Auguste a key to each. Any intruder would come via the window, the earl claimed, and Auguste and the manservant would make sure she didn't succeed. It was a moot point as to what would happen if it really was a ghost, who had no need of drainpipes. Presumably only Auguste's impassioned plea of the earl's innocence could then prevent catastrophe.

Moreover, before he left the earl, Auguste had had to confess that as yet he had no idea as to the cause of Maria's death.

'Her husband had reason to kill her, because although he knew of your relationship with his wife, he was unaware until that night that his younger son might be your child and not his. Your then fiancée could have taken revenge after learning so cruelly about your affair, but the brother would seem to have no reason unless he benefited from the will? Was Maria rich? Under the Married Women's Property Act, she would be able to leave her money to whom she wished.'

'Robert was a rich man then. I believe Maria said she'd leave what she could to François to aid their family in France, but it wouldn't be much. But don't ask damnfool questions about Maria. *Tell* me who murdered the woman, and then tell her ghost. Otherwise I won't be alive in the morning to find out what this precious business is that they're so eager to discuss. Robert was all for meeting this evening, but I wouldn't have it. How could I have concentrated on business when a ghost was threatening to kill me an hour or two later?'

'Did she ever mention the Star Diamond to you? Did the Maharajah give it to her during her stage career, perhaps?' Auguste had been interested that no mention of this had been made at dinner, although it had apparently been in Maria's possession at the time other death. Revenge was a powerful motive but money, in Auguste's experience, beat it. He received a quick answer.

'That's enough. I'm tired. Get out of here and do your job!'

Auguste obliged, and here he was, outside as requested, doing it. The vehemence in his lordship's reply – if reply it could be called – was interesting. It suggested the 'business' did have something to do with the diamond. If so, the whole perspective of what might have happened that night in 1883 was changed – which provided a discussion point, with the ghost.

Auguste was aware he was ignoring the fact that the ghost, if immortal, might know exactly what happened, and be entirely uninterested in Auguste's wish to discuss it. Nevertheless it gave him the right to ask for at least a stay of execution for the earl; he was relieved to have something to offer in the earl's defence.

He shivered. It was not warm, and very dark out here. It was also eerie, and the notion of discussion with a ghost took on an all-too-real aspect now that the time was coming. Would the ghost stand still and listen? Did one speak to a ghostly lady as to an earthly one? Would she reply or just screech? Would this murdering ghost chop down anything and anyone in her way? Would she even – terrible thought – send a deputy to do her dirty work? Jack Ketch the hangman, for example? Robespierre equipped with guillotine? A Medici to force poison down his throat?

'There are no such things as ghosts...' he muttered. 'There are no such things as —'

And then he saw it. A misty light over the dense bushes in front of him, no, a *shape*. A shape within the light. Feverishly he began to run through his list of a hundred favourite recipes, a formula that usually sent him contentedly to sleep. Not tonight. Not with this thing dancing up and down before his eyes. A woman's shape, a grotesque grimace of fury on her face.

'Phantasmagoria,' he told himself. 'A trick. An illusion.' But he could not convince himself. It was coming nearer. And nearer.

'*Courage*,' he cried at it, '*le diable est mort*.' Or was the devil dead? Was it not he in disguise coming for him now?

How could he *plead* with this thing? 'Go away,' he croaked inadequately. 'The earl's innocent. Stop!'

She didn't.

'I need more time,' he shouted. She halted for a moment, and encouraged, he tried again.

'You had a sad death,' he shouted. 'I shall discover the truth for you if you were murdered, so please spare the earl tonight.'

As defending council's eloquent last plea he rated it poorly, but the ghost seemed impressed. She retreated slightly, and in a burst of courage Auguste walked towards her, a trembling hand extended in a show of truce. The ghost receded further, and Auguste rushed at her, raising his arm to touch her – but there was nothing there. No substance, then no misty light, no ghost. Only a screeching peel of laughter.

He was alive. Weak from relief, Auguste rushed to the white-faced manservant by the drainpipe. He was gabbling in fear, and Auguste had to cut across him. There was no doubt he too had seen the apparition.

'Anyone come this way?'

'No,' came the reply, just as the man collapsed onto the flowerbed.

Auguste had to leave him there. His first duty was the earl. He hurried upstairs, and produced his key to unlock the earl's door as arranged. Inside one dim oil lamp lit the room. The earl was quiet, and fearfully Auguste approached. He was not breathing. He had not been suffocated. He had been strangled.

'It seems,' Robert observed, as Auguste wearily joined the small group in the morning room, 'that you didn't do a very good job in persuading the ghost of poor Gerard's innocence.' They had all returned to their beds for a few hours' sleep, but Auguste had been present while doctors and police conferred over the late earl during the night.

'Perhaps he wasn't innocent.' Too late, Auguste realised that Judith was present, and that this possibility was hardly tactful.

'My poor husband,' she half sobbed, half shouted at him. 'He is lying here dead, and I had told him I didn't believe in ghosts. You were supposed to defend him. What incompetence! Tell me what is happening, please.'

'An inspector from Scotland Yard has been called.' Auguste decided not to point out that only a few hours ago she had virtually been accusing 'her poor husband' of murder. Nor would he mention that it had been at his suggestion that he should telephone to Inspector Rose. It had been a short, and for him, not sweet conversation. Through the crackles and hisses on the line, Egbert Rose had as usual come straight to the point.

'Who did it, Auguste?'

'A ghost.'

Silence greeted this remark, but Auguste could guess the inspector's reaction.

'So it appears,' he added unhappily. This unfortunate choice of words brought back vivid memories of his own spectral experience.

'You nail it down. I'll bring the handcuffs.'

The inspector would not arrive for several hours, time which might be valuable in determining what had happened. Auguste forced himself to concentrate on it. He had failed the earl, and owed him that much at least. It was all too possible that he had indeed murdered Maria, but why, and who had killed him? The earl had seemed genuinely terrified at Plum's, either because he knew he was guilty of Maria's murder, or because he knew he was innocent and needed that proven to be rid of the threat. If the former, then it seemed strange to ask Auguste to investigate, however, and if innocent, he must surely have had his own ideas about how she died. Vengeance was a favourite cry of returning ghosts, but murder had more practical aspects. Why would the earl have resorted to murdering Maria under his own roof after the damage had been done? Maria had already broadcast her son's parentage, and in her rage and anguish at her rejection had more reason to murder him than he her.

By the time Inspector Rose arrived, Auguste had managed an hour or two's sleep, and his brain informed him it was prepared to start work again.

'Where's this ghost, then?' Egbert asked briskly. 'Lead on.'

By day it was easier to be brave, and hard to recall the near panic that the previous night's illusion had brought. Reason now superseded fear, for the unknown could be made known. Auguste led the way to the high bushes that formed a wall around the rose garden. He walked with confidence because he already guessed what he would find.

'There,' he pointed.

'All I see is a dead rose-bush.'

'A dying rose bush, ashes, and indentations on the ground.'

'That's a ghost?'

'Yes, when brought to life by smoke from a lit brazier, coupled with a magic lantern and a determined murderer.'

Egbert sighed. 'Tell me.'

'Phantasmagoria – an illusion perfected last century. The magic lantern casts up the image on a slide, and the smoke makes the spectre move. Sliding the lantern to and fro makes it advance and retreat. I thought at first the orangery provided the means for a Pepper's Ghost illusion, but the mist – or smoke – put that out of the question.'

'Can you tell me how the murderer can be in two places at once? Playing tricks down here and up there strangling the earl?'

'No, but —'

'Or who it was?'

'No, but —'

'Or who, if anyone, killed Maria Parsons?'

'No, but —'

Egbert grinned. 'Glad I'm going to be of some use.'

'My buts,' Auguste retorted with dignity, 'might be of some slight assistance.'

'We'll start with who killed the earl then.'

'The raw fish comes before the *sole au Chablis*,' Auguste objected. 'The death of Maria Parsons is the root of the dish.'

'Forget about ghosts. My job is the earl. Who killed him?'

'Only one person could in practice. His wife. No one could come through the door from the corridor. His wife would be most likely to have a key to the adjoining chamber.'

'Is she strong enough to strangle her husband silently without at least the dickens of a row?'

'What if she put a sleeping draught in his coffee or brandy?'

'Possible,' Egbert conceded. 'Motive?'

'None that I know of, but —' Auguste eagerly proceeded to out-line his theory on the Star Diamond being the 'business' referred to by the earl. So far there was no evidence to link the earl with the dia-mond at all, but suppose the diamond had been the parting present the earl had made to Maria? It was hardly likely that the earl would knowingly have given such a priceless gem away, but if he had been ignorant of its worth, it came back into the realm of possibility. And if the earl was concerned in 'the business', then his wife as – presum-ably – his heir would be too.

Egbert's eyes gleamed. 'That's a but worth hearing. We'll see what the lady says.'

Lady Judith's face now showed little sign of grief or her earlier passion, though Auguste conceded that iron discipline could be con-trolling her expression until such time as she could be alone. To his pleasure she was forthcoming about the 'business'.

'You are quite right, Inspector. This gathering was to discuss the diamond. It was most unfortunate. My late husband poured out the story to me a few days ago. The diamond had been his, but he, as everyone else, thought it worth very little. He had been given it as payment for a trifling gambling debt in Paris, and he gave it to Maria as a parting present that evening, telling her it was worth a great deal of money. Her maid, after the tragedy of her death, packed her pos-sessions and took them back to the Parsons' home, where they were bundled into the chest in which Gertrude later found the stone. Gerard naturally asked to see Robert to discuss the matter.'

'The late earl told me it was at Mr Parsons' and Monsieur Duval's request that the meeting was arranged,' Auguste pointed out.

The glare from Lady Judith indicated that the arrangement for his cooking school was doomed.

'Naturally my late husband would not tell *you*, Mr Didier, in case you enquired the reason for the gathering. It had nothing to do with the ghost and Maria's death. It was confidential.'

'Not now, your ladyship,' Egbert Rose replied. 'Tell us the reason, if you please.'

'My husband had written to Robert to demand the diamond's return, or at least part of its value in cash. Robert had refused, but he needed Gerard to sign a statement that he had given it to his wife.

I'm afraid Gerard was threatening to contest ownership. He was in a strong position as he could prove he had been given the diamond by the Maharajah, but could claim that Maria had stolen it from him that night. Naturally Gerard could therefore hope for a substantial share of the money it raises. He was, I fear, not always an honourable man.'

'And now that your husband is dead?'

'Robert stands to benefit greatly. There is no one who can deny his right to it, and I stand to lose a great deal of money. Someone in this house murdered my husband last night. A crazed servant perhaps. As I had a key to Gerard's bedroom, you may perhaps be considering me as what I believe is termed a suspect. I trust you will now see that far from wishing my husband dead, I had every reason to keep him alive.'

'We have established that the ghost was a mere illusion,' Auguste told her. 'If, as you gently imply, Mr Parsons might be responsible for your husband's death, he must also have been responsible for the ghost yesterday night, and for her two former appearances. How did he gain access?'

'That is simple. My late husband did not keep dogs, and entrance to the house was not necessary since the illusion appeared in the garden, so Gerard told me. I regret now that I did not believe him.' A tear was permitted to roll down the iron-muscled cheek. 'Do you believe her, Auguste?' Egbert asked. 'This murder required two people, one to work the illusion, one to strangle the earl. She had the key, which she could have lent to an accomplice, but on the other hand the local police have discovered that the housekeeper's master keys have vanished, which opens up a whole menu of choices. The most likely would be Robert and François.'

'Why the ghost?'

'Pardon?'

'Why did the murderers – if there were two – bother to alert the earl to their plans by the ghost illusion if the diamond was the motive for the murder?'

'Leave the ghost out of it,' Egbert said patiently.

'*Impossible*. The garnish is part of the dish as presented to the diner.'

Back in his kitchen after Egbert had left to interview the three members of the houseparty, Auguste hoped the fog in his mind might clarify – until he remembered it wasn't *his* kitchen. Here he was only a passing guest. In *his* kitchen he knew where everything was. Everything fitted into a whole. The creation of a roast turkey *à la Financière* depended on the garnish – the ragout, the sweetbread, the truffles, the quenelles, and the glaze – and of course the timing of the turkey itself.

The timing – there was a stirring in his mind as the facts collected themselves together and slowly came to the boil.

Why had the ghost illusion been necessary? Who had killed Maria? And who had killed the earl? Now they began to set into a perfect soufflé – which all depended on timing.

That evening, Auguste found Egbert morosely contemplating the gardens from the orangery, and suggested they take a walk. 'I know why the ghost was so necessary,' he ventured.

Egbert sighed. 'Forget the ghost.'

'And I know who killed the earl.'

'That's more like it.' A slight stirring of interest.

'It begins with the ghost.'

Egbert glared. 'Quickly then. None of your rigmaroles.'

'The ghost illusion was to draw attention to Maria's death —'

'Rather obvious, isn't it?'

'And its *timing*. Also to concentrate on that parting present the earl told us he gave her.'

'The diamond.'

'We only have Lady Judith's word for that.'

'True.' Egbert looked more interested. 'What about the timing, then?'

'Maria died in 1883, a year after the Married Women's Property Act went through. That provided for any property belonging to the deceased *before* the Act was passed to belong to the husband automatically as before, but any property acquired *after* that date went according to the woman's will.'

'So Robert had every reason to kill the earl, with the help of his wife Gertrude?'

'Yes. But only if the parting present *was* the diamond.'

'Did the earl lie to his wife, or did she lie? She had nothing to gain.'

'No, but her lover did.'

'Robert?'

'If the parting present were not the diamond, and we have no evidence it was save one woman's word, then Robert would need the earl alive, not dead, in order to prove he gave the diamond to Maria much earlier. That was the business the earl told me Robert had asked to discuss. Otherwise François could contest ownership.'

'So who murdered the earl?'

'Underneath the garnish of this dish, I believe Lady Judith operated the ghost illusion. Our murderer was the lover whom the earl implied existed, and who was given a key to the door after Lady Judith removed the servants' master keys to deflect suspicion from herself.'

'Robert?'

'No, François Duval. Together they planned to make it appear that the diamond was only given to Maria after the Married Women's Property Act came into force.'

Egbert Rose considered this. 'There's a flaw in your jewel, Auguste. He would have removed the earl who could knock his claim to kingdom come, but still wouldn't have proof that it was given to Maria that night.'

'No, but Lady Judith, I'm sure, would tearfully back his claim, Robert would be under suspicion of murder and would only have presumption of ownership. At the very least, the value of the diamond would have to be split.'

'I'll take a slice of this dish of yours, Auguste,' Egbert said at last. 'In fact, I'll keep the whole cake. But who killed Maria?'

'No one. There was no murder. The parting present was not the diamond. Nor was there a ghost.'

They were walking into the rose garden as Auguste spoke, and in the twilight something made him shiver. Was it the memory of that terrifying phantasmagoric figure swirling in a cloud of smoke last night? Or was it something else? Was it the stillness of a hot summer evening, as heat supersedes time, and slows it to dream-pace?

From somewhere there floated a faint chuckle, and they saw the indistinct shape of a frou-frou-skirted woman dancing along the path towards the arbour. Auguste could hear the beating of his heart – or was it Egbert's? For a moment he doubted his own reason. This morning he had seen the evidence of a human-created phantasm. What was this ahead of them? A gardener's bonfire, with his own fear superimposing the illusion of last night? Or – no, it was impossible. The earl had mentioned limping nuns, headless horsemen, and butchered cooks. This *thing* ahead of them was none of those. But 'real' ghosts were never seen by more than one person at a time. He glanced at Egbert, who was very pale.

'Something we ate,' Egbert managed to croak.

By the time Auguste looked back towards the arbour, the figure had vanished.

'It is the lobster we had this evening,' Auguste gulped.

'Too rich. Not cooked by Auguste Didier.'

Auguste did not hear him. A second chuckle was coming from the shrub rosebush at his side.

Mat Coward

Room to Move

If you'd seen inside my small flat, you might have guessed that I was a successful burglar, and you might even have offered the opinion that I was too good at my trade.

The place was overflowing. Literally; not only was every square foot of floor space occupied by my takings, but even my tiny balcony was entirely stuffed with boxes of antique clocks and state-of-the-art VCRs, all of them oilskin-wrapped against the weather, and securely anchored by bungee straps.

I have always found burgling so easy, you see; I have always been so very good at it. And there came a time when I just didn't have space in my flat for even the smallest new item.

But even then, I carried on burgling.

One Wednesday afternoon, I made a fenestral entrance to a luxury apartment down by the docks.

At first, I thought I'd got the wrong place. I'd been assured that this was the home of an extremely fashionable lawyer, a man who made more money in an hour than most people spend in a year. Yet here I was, standing in an enormous room, almost empty but for the sunlight streaming through its extravagant glaziery.

The furniture consisted of three floor cushions and a nearly invisible glass coffee table, huddled away in a corner, as if ashamed of themselves. There was no carpet. No curtains. No hi-fi, not even a telly.

A quick scan of the other rooms revealed the same unnerving lack of contents. In the bedroom there was a rolled-up futon; in the kitchen a midget fridge, home to a bottle of mineral water, a bottle of champagne and a carton of orange juice. The champagne had probably cost half a ton, but really – you don't climb up the side of a converted warehouse in broad daylight just for the sake of fifty quid's worth of fizzy wine. Do you?

I was beginning to get annoyed. Did this man have something against burglars?

The main room (you couldn't really call it a living-room, under the circumstances) was dominated by an artwork. I hadn't paid it much heed, because there's little sense in my line of work in devoting time to things which can't be lifted. And this was most certainly a thing which couldn't be lifted. It was about the size of a bed, and probably thirty times heavier. Even if I could have got it out of there, it would never have fitted on my balcony.

Made from onyx, I reckoned, as I gave it an absent-minded kick. Shaped like a teardrop. Sort of Japanesey-looking. Which was when I cottoned on to what was going on.

I looked at the big room again, and this time saw it for what it was: not a cave...but a lifestyle statement. This wealthy lawyer was a minimalist. A room bare, but for the barest of bare necessities – necessities so bare they might have been prosecuted for indecent exposure – and amid all this naked air, a simplistic work of art which had probably cost him as much as the flat itself. I should have spotted it straight away. Probably would have, if I hadn't had all that sunlight in my eyes.

This man was making a statement. He was saying "I own so little, all of it of great value; why would I bother owning things of lesser worth?" And he was also saying "Go on, then; burgle me. Enjoy the orange juice, sucker!"

I was so frustrated, that for a moment I even considered doing something disgusting on his floor. At right angles to the onyx teardrop, and slightly skew whiff of a line from the coffee table to the doorway. That would screw up his minimalist symmetry, all right.

But I couldn't really have done it. I was a burglar, after all; I took things, I didn't leave things behind. Except that this time, there was nothing to —

Yes there was!

The realisation came from nowhere, arrived full-feathered at the forefront of my seething mind.

This flat wasn't empty. The fashionable lawyer wanted people to think it was, he designed it so that it would appear empty; but it wasn't. It was full of the one thing I needed most in the world: not VCRs or antique clocks. I had those, in quantities uncountable. The one thing I didn't have was space.

This flat was full of space. Square yard upon square yard of space.

And I'd almost missed it. In my anger, I'd almost provided the punchline to the minimalist's joke.

Almost, but not quite. I gazed around me in near rapture at the loveliness of my booty; not only at its quantity, but at its clean, fresh, sun-sparkled, high-rent calibre. It was, after all, the property of a man both rich and tasteful.

Which was very much the point. All this space – weaving and snuggling between the invisible coffee table and the rolled futon and the mineral water – had been paid for by a rich man. And one thing I have known, since I was old enough to wiggle through a bathroom window, is that anything which has been bought by a rich man, can be stolen by a poor man.

Whistling softly, and smiling broadly, I began to pack the space into my canvas bag.

I had a busy few days after that. First I had to unpack and install the space I had taken from the lawyer's flat, which involved rearranging the contents of my flat – an immensely difficult and frustrating task, due to the very problem I was attempting to cure. After a while, it became obvious that this would take forever, or perhaps even longer, and so I hardened my heart and made arrangements to rid myself quickly of most of my stock.

Eventually, the lawyer's space was in place, and I made myself a cup of tea and looked about at what I had achieved. It was impossible to tell where his smart, clean space ended and my drab, workaday space began. I smiled at that: perhaps the fashionable lawyer had been conned, had thought he was buying special space but had in fact been palmed off with the ordinary stuff, same as the rest of us have to put up with all our lives. I didn't care one way or the other. I didn't want his space for its resale value, but for its utility.

On that basis, I was more than satisfied. The walls and floors and ceilings of my flat shone with space, which effortlessly swallowed my remaining stock and called out for more.

This was a call I was happy to answer. The next forty-eight hours were amongst the most energetic of my burgling life.

One week later, I was awoken at four in the morning by a hammering of fists on my front door. Two policemen, one in uniform and one in jeans, stood smirking on my welcome mat.

"Better get dressed, chummy," said the plainclothes man. "This is a warrant to search these premises."

"On what grounds?" I asked.

"You were seen leaving the place, old son. We've got a witness. Your likeness was shown to the witness, who identified it as being that of the person he had seen on the day of the offence."

"I see." I was trembling. It was cold with the door open. "You'd better come in."

"Much obliged, pal," said the detective, as he and his colleague eased past me to begin their work.

I put on my clothes, then sat on a box in the hall, thinking about prison. I smoked a cigarette and wondered what might become of me when I grew old. I could hear the two policemen moving around my flat, muttering to each other and cursing to themselves. Now and then, I would hear one or the other of them trip over a box, or stumble over a carton, or tumble into a tarpaulin.

The search took a long time, while I grew more and more afraid. Was it worth sending for a lawyer? Probably not; my spirit was leaving me, and I felt then that I would admit to whatever they accused me of.

"Right. Sign here." I hadn't heard the detective approach, and I jumped, dropping my cigarette, as he leaned over me, holding out a document and a pen. His face was sweaty with exertion, and red with anger. I signed. The officers left.

It took me a few minutes to understand what this meant; they hadn't found what they were looking for. Two police officers, armed with a warrant and a lifetime's supply of evidence bags, had searched every inch of my flat and somehow they had failed to uncover —

It had gone.

I looked around me and realised why the police hadn't found the space I'd taken from the rich lawyer. They hadn't found it, because it was no longer there. I'd been robbed.

As I stood again in that huge room, with its absurd teardrop and its extravagant windows, I felt my anger returning. This time, it was accompanied by shock.

I hadn't taken all the space on my first visit; nothing like. I'd taken only what I thought I could use, and what I thought I could carry. I had returned there with the intention of replenishing my depleted stocks of space. What I hadn't expected to find was this: that the lawyer's luxury apartment contained just as much space as it had before!

I was frozen in place by a kind of crushing comprehension of my own puny insignificance. I had walked out of here with as much of this man's space as I could physically lug away, and yet I hadn't made so much as a dent in the bastard's wealth. Not so much as a kitten's scratch on the surface of his self-assurance.

Had he even been inconvenienced by my previous visit, this

fashionable lawyer? Not likely. He'd probably just made a phone call, and his new space had been delivered within the hour. Insurance companies always cough up uncomplainingly for his type.

Unless...could it be, could it possibly be, that this was the same space; the exact same space?

Once it had me in its teeth, this idea wouldn't let me go. Could the rich lawyer have stolen the space I'd taken from him? Or hired someone to do so on his behalf? Not probable, no; but undeniably plausible.

And what did the smug sod need all that space for, anyway? He didn't use a quarter of it!

To be absolutely frank, this last thought – which I believe I spoke out loud, in that full and empty room of sunshine and floorboards – pretty well tipped me over the edge.

Early the following morning, after a sleepless night, I went out and hired a large van. I loaded it, and drove to the lawyer's apartment.

It took me all day, and all my strength, and more ingenuity than I had ever known I possessed, and it shattered, probably forever, every burgling instinct I had developed over a lifetime, but as the sun fell and the city streets filled, I was done.

A petty satisfaction, it might be said, but it was the best I could do and it healed me to an extent. I couldn't take this rich man's space away from him, I understood that now; I couldn't own it, except briefly, and he couldn't be deprived of it, other than for the time it took him to flex his wealth and replace it. But if I couldn't take it away from him, I could at least fill it up.

By the time I was finished, the rich lawyer's space was as invisible as his fashionable floorboards and his tastefully blank walls and his pointlessly high ceilings. From up to down and from side to side, there wasn't an inch of that foul, beautiful place that wasn't occupied, with brazen rudeness, by top of the range VCRs, and other people's heirlooms, and mid-nineteenth century china models of English sheepdogs.

All, that is, but for a few, clear yards. A single navigable path led from his front door, across his living-room, all the way to his onyx bloody teardrop. How was that for a minimalist statement?

I knew him by now, I thought; knew him the way I knew myself, which is to say not intimately, but at least accurately. I knew that what I had done to his space would ruin it for him permanently.

Happy, or at any rate somewhere in that vicinity, I went home. As I turned the key in my front door, I was chuckling, wondering what sort of insurance policy, even for a rich and fashionable and valued client, could possibly cover that.

I stepped into the hallway of my little flat – and I simply could not believe what I saw. Was this some cruel joke? Where on earth had it all come from?

The whole place was crammed to the rafters...with space.

Not everyone realised that the thing about Assistant Chief Constable Desmond Iles was he longed to be loved. Among those who did realise it, of course, a good number refused to respond and instead muttered privately, 'Go fuck yourself, Iles'. A very good number. On the other hand, there was certainly a young ethnic whore in the docks who worshipped the A.C.C. unstintingly, and he would have been truly hurt if anyone said it was because he paid well.

What Iles totally abominated was people who came to esteem him only because he had contributed or helped in some way: say a piece of grand, devastating violence carried out by the A.C.C. for them against one of their enemies. He despised such calculating, *quid pro quoism*, as he called it. Once, he had told Harpur he utterly disregarded love that could be accounted for and reckoned up. Harpur felt happy the A.C.C. received from his docks friend, Honorée, and from Fanny, his infant daughter, the differing but infinite affection he craved. Also, Iles's wife, Sarah, definitely possessed some quaint fondness for him, quite often at least. She had mentioned this to Harpur unprompted in one of their quiet moments.

To Harpur it seemed that much of Iles's behaviour could be explained by this need for completely spontaneous, instinctive, wholehearted devotion. Think of that unpleasant incident at the Taldamon School prize-giving, for instance. Although Iles would regard the kind of physical savagery he was forced into there as merely routine for him, it had made one eighteen-year-old girl pupil switch abruptly from fending off the A.C.C. sexually to offering an urgent come-on. This enraged Iles. He had been doing all he could to attract the girl, probably as potential stand-by in case Honorée were working away some time at a World Cup or Church of England Synod. Totally no go. And then, within minutes, the Taldamon girl suddenly changed and clearly grew interested in Iles, simply because he had felled and disarmed some bastard in the stately school assembly hall, and kicked him a few times absolutely unfatally about the head and neck where he lay on the floor between chair rows. Colin Harpur instantly knew the A.C.C. would regard this turnaround by the girl as contemptible: as grossly undiscerning about Iles, as Iles. That is, the essence of Ilesness, not simply his rabbit punching and kicking flairs, which could be viewed as superficial: as attractive, perhaps, but mere accessories to his core self. Harpur saw at the end of this episode that the A.C.C. wished to get away immediately from the girl and return to Honorée for pure, unconditional adoration even, if necessary, on waste ground.

It was some school: private, of course, and residential, and right up there with Eton and Harrow for fees. In fact, it cost somewhere near the national average wage to keep a child at Taldamon for a year, and this without the geology trip to Iceland, the horse riding and extra coaching in lacrosse and timpani. Harpur and Iles – Iles particularly – were interested in Taldamon because the police funded one of its pupils during her entire school career. This was an idea picked up from France. Over there, it had long been police practice to meet the education expenses for the child or children of a valuable and regular informant, as one way of paying for tipoffs. The scheme convinced Iles and others. It was considered less obvious – less dangerous – than to give an informant big cash rewards, which he/she might spend in a stupid, ostentatious way, drawing attention to his/her special income. That could mean the informant was no longer able to get close to villains' secrets because the villains would have him/her identified as a leak. It could also mean that his/her life was endangered. A child out of sight at a pricey school in North Wales would be less noticeable. Or this was the thinking.

They had put Wayne Ridout's daughter, Fay-Alice, into Taldamon, from the age of thirteen, and now here she was at eighteen, head prefect, multi-prizewinner, captain of lacrosse, captain of swimming and water polo, central to the school orchestra, destined for Oxford, slim, straight-nosed, sweet-skinned, and able to hold Iles off with cold, foul-mouthed ease until…until she decided she did not want to hold him off, following a gross rush of disgusting gratitude: disgusting, that is, as Harpur guessed the A.C.C. would regard it.

Harpur and Iles would not normally attend this kind of function. The presence of police might be a give-away. But Wayne had pleaded with Iles to come, and pleaded a little less fervently with Harpur, also. It was not just that Wayne wanted them to see the glorious results of their grass-related investment in Fay-Alice. Harpur knew from a few recent conversations with Wayne that he had felt down lately. Because of her education and the social status of Taldamon,

Ridout sensed his daughter might be growing away from him and her mother, Nora. This grieved both, but especially Wayne. His wife seemed to regard the change in Fay-Alice as normal. Harpur imagined she probably saw it on behalf of the girl like this: when your father's main career had been fink and general crook rather than archbishop or TV game show host, there was only one way for the next generation to go socially – up and away. Regrettable but inevitable.

Wayne could not accept such sad distancing. He must reason that if he were seen at this important school function accompanied by an Assistant Chief Constable, who had on the kind of magnificent suit and shoes Iles favoured, and who behaved in his well-known Shah of Persia style, it was bound to restore Fay-Alice's respect for her parents. And it would impress the girl's friends and teachers. For these possible gains, Wayne had evidently decided to put up with the security risk in this one-off event. Harpur doubted Fay-Alice would see things as her father did and thought he and the A.C.C. should not attend. But Iles agreed the visit and addressed Harpur for a while about 'overriding obligations to those who sporadically assist law and order, even a fat, villainous, ugly, dim sod like Wayne'. The A.C.C. was always shudderingly eager to get among teenage school-girls if they looked clean and wore light summery clothes.

It was only out of politeness that Wayne had asked Harpur. As Detective Chief Superintendent, Harpur lacked the glow of staff rank and could not tog himself out with the same distinction as Iles. In fact, the A.C.C. had seemed not wholly sure Harpur should accompany him. 'This will be a school with gold-lettered award boards on the wall, naming pupils who've gone on not just to Oxbridge or management courses with the Little Chef restaurant chain, but Harvard, Vatican seminaries, even Time Share selling in Alicante. There'll be ambience. Does ambience get into your vocab at all, Harpur? I know this kind of academy right through, from my own school background, of course. I'd hate you to feel in any way disadvantaged by *your* education, but I ask you, Col – do you think you can fit into such a place as Taldamon with that fucking haircut and your garments?'

'This kind of occasion does make me think back to end of term at my own school, sir,' Harpur reminisced gently.

'And what did they give leaving prizes to eighteen-year-olds for there – knowing the two-times table, speed at dewristing tourists' Rolexes?'

'Should we go armed?' Harpur replied.

'This is a wholesome occasion at a prime girls' school, for God's sake. Col.'

'Should we go armed?' Harpur said.

Iles said, 'I'd hate it if some delightful pupil, inadvertently brushing against me, should feel only the brutal outline of a bolstered pistol, Harpur.'

'This sort of school, they're probably taught never to brush inadvertently against people like you, sir. It would be stressed in deportment classes, plus during the domestic science module for classifying moisture marks on trousers.'

Iles's voice grew throaty and his breathing loud and needful: 'I gather she's become a star now as scholar, swimmer, musician and so on, but I can remember Fay-Alice when she was only a kid, though developing, certainly…developing, yes, certainly, *developing*, but really only just a kid…although…well, yes, *developing*, and we went to the Ridout house to advise them that she should —'

'There are people who'd like to do Wayne. He's helped put all sorts inside. They have brothers, colleagues, sons, fathers, mothers. Perhaps the word's around he'll be on a plate at Taldamon, ambience-hooked, relaxed, unvigilant.'

'A striking-looking child, even then,' Iles replied, 'despite Wayne and his complexion. A wonderful long, slender back, as I recall. Do *you* recall that, Harpur – the long slender back? Do you think of backs ever? Or was it the era when you were so damn busy giving it to my wife you didn't have time to notice much else at all?' Iles began to screech in the frenzied seagull tone that would take him over sometimes when speaking of Harpur and Sarah.

Harpur said, 'If we're there we ought at least to —'

'I mean her back in addition to the way she was, well —?'

'Developing.'

This long back Fay-Alice unquestionably still had, and the development elsewhere seemed to have continued as it generally would for a girl between thirteen and eighteen. A little tea party had been arranged on the pleasant lawns at Taldamon before the prize-giving, out of consideration for parents who travelled a long way and needed refreshment. It was June, a good, hot, blue-skied day. 'Here's a dear, dear acquaintance of mine, Fay-Alice,' Wayne said. 'Assistant Chief Constable Desmond Iles. And Chief Superintendent Harpur.' Iles gave her a true conquistador smile, yet a smile which also sought to hint at his sensitivity, honour, beguiling polish and famed restraint. Fay-Alice returned this smile with one that was hostile, nauseated and extremely brief but which still managed to signal over her teacup, *Police? So how come you're friends of my father, and who let you in here, anyway?* Was it just normal schoolgirl prejudice against cops or did she have some idea that daddy's career might be lifelong dubious – even some idea that her schooling and Wayne's career could be unwholesomely related? This must be a bright kid, able to win prizes and an Oxford place. She'd have antennae as well as the long back.

'Fay-Alice's prizes are in French literature, history of art and classics,' Wayne said.

'Won't mean a thing to Col,' Iles replied.

'I wondered if there'd been strangers around the school lately,' Harpur said, 'possibly asking questions about the programme today, looking at the layout.'

'Which strangers?' Fay-Alice replied.

'Strangers,' Harpur said. 'A man, or men, probably.'

'Why would they?' the girl asked.

'You know, French lit. is something I can't get enough of,' the A.C.C. said.

'Mr Iles, personally, did a lot with education, right up to the very heaviest levels, Fay-Alice,' Wayne said. 'Don't be fooled just because he's police.'

'Yes, why are you concerned about strangers, Mr Harpur?' Nora Ridout asked.

'Are you two trying to put the frighteners on us, the way pigs always do?' Fay-Alice said.

'I recall Alphonse de Lamartine and his poem "The Lake",' Iles replied.

'Alphonse is a French name for sure,' Wayne said 'There you are, Fay-Alice – didn't I tell you, Mr Iles can go straight to it, no messing? Books are meat and drink to him.'

Iles leaned towards her and recited: '"Oh, Time, will you not stop a while so we may savour the swiftly passing pleasures of our loveliest days?"'

'Meat and drink,' Wayne said.

'Don't you find Lamartine's plea an inspiration, Fay-Alice?' Iles asked. 'Savour. A word I thrill to. The sensuousness of it, together with the tragic hint of enjoying something wonderful, yet elusive.' He began to tremble slightly and reached out a hand, as if to touch Fay-Alice's long back or some conjoint region. But moving quickly towards the plate of sandwiches on a garden table, Harpur put himself between the A.C.C. and her. He took Iles's pleaful, savour-seeking fingers on the lapel of his jacket. In any case, Fay-Alice had stepped back immediately she saw the A.C.C.'s hand approach and for a moment looked as if she was about to grab his arm and possibly break it in some kind of anti-rape drill.

'Or the history of art,' Wayne said. 'That's another terrific realm. This could overlap with French literature because while the poets were writing their verses in France there would be neighbours, in the same street most probably, painting and making sculptures in their attics. The French are known for it – easels, smocks, everything. It's the light in those parts – great for art but also useful when people wanted to write a poem outside. In a way it all ties up. That's the thing about culture, especially French. A lot of strands.'

'And you'll be coming home to live with Mother and Father until Oxford now, and in the nice long vacations, will you, Fay-Alice?' Iles asked.

'Why?' she replied. Iles said, 'It's just that —'

'I don't understand how you know my father,' she replied.

'Oh, Mr Iles and I – this is a real far-back association,' Wayne said.

'But how exactly?' she asked. 'He's never been to our house, has he? I've never heard you speak of him, Dad.'

'This is like an arrangement, Fay-Alice,' Nora Ridout replied.

'What kind of arrangement?' Fay-Alice asked.

'Yes, like an arrangement,' Nora Ridout replied.

'A business arrangement?' Fay-Alice asked.

'You can see how such a go-ahead school makes them put all the damn sharp queries, Mr Iles,' Wayne said. 'I love it. This is what I believe they call intellectual curiosity, used by many of the country's topmost on their way to discoveries such as medical and DVDs. What they will not do, girls at this school – and especially girls who do really well, such as Fay-Alice – what they will not do is take something as right just because they're told it. Oh, no. Rigour's another word for this attitude, I believe. Not like rigor mortis but rigour in their thoughts and decisions. It's a school that teaches them how to sort out the men from the boys re brain power.'

'So, does the school come into it somehow?' Fay-Alice asked. 'Does it? Does it? How are these two linked with the school. Dad, Mum?' She hammered at the question, yet Harpur thought she feared an answer.

'Linked?' Iles said. 'Linked? Oh, just a pleasant excursion for Mr Harpur and myself, thanks to the thoughtfulness of your father, Fay-Alice.'

'A business or social arrangement?' Fay-Alice asked.

'No, no, not a business arrangement. How could it be a business arrangement?' Wayne replied, laughing.

'Social?' Fay-Alice asked.

'It's *sort* of social,' Wayne said.

'So, if it's friendship why do you call him Mr Iles, not Desmond, his first name?' Fay-Alice asked.

'See what I mean about the queries, Mr Iles? I heard the motto of this school is "Seek ever the truth", but in a classical tongue which provides many a motto around the country on account of tradition. You can't beat the classics if you want to hit the right note.'

The A.C.C. said, 'And I understand swimming has become a pursuit of yours, Fay-Alice. Excellent for the body. You must get along to the municipal pool at home. I should go there more often myself. Certainly I shall. This will be an experience – to see you active in the water, your arms and legs really working, wake a-glisten.' Beautifully symmetric circles of sweat appeared on each of his temples, each the size of a two-penny piece, although the group were still outside on the lawn and under the shade of a eucalyptus. 'The butterfly stroke – strenuous upper torso exercise, but useful for toning everything, don't you agree, Fay-Alice? Toning everything. Oh, I look forward to that. Wayne, it will be a treat to have Fay-Alice around in the breaks from Oxford.'

'Aren't you a bit old for the butterfly?' she said. 'I hate watching a heart attack in the fast lane, all those desperate bubbles and the sudden incontinence.'

Iles chuckled, obviously in tribute to her aggression and jauntiness. 'Oh, look, Fay-Alice —'

'We don't really need *flics* here, thank you,' she replied. 'So why don't you just piss off back to your interrogation suite alone and play with yourself, Iles?' Harpur decided that, even without pre-knowledge from its brochure, anyone could have recognised this as an outstandingly select school where articulateness was prized and deftly inculcated.

In the fine wide assembly hall, he appreciatively watched Fay-Alice on the platform stride out with her long back et cetera to receive prizes from the Lord Lieutenant. He seemed to do quite an amount of congratulatory talking to and handshaking with Fay-Alice before conferring her trophies. All at once, then, Harpur realised that Iles had gone from the seat alongside him. For a moment, Harpur wondered whether the A.C.C. intended attacking the Lord Lieutenant for infringing on Fay-Alice and half stood in case he had to move forward and try to throw Iles to the ground and suppress him.

They had been placed at the end of a row, Iles to Harpur's right next to the gangway, Wayne and Nora on his left. To help keep the hall cool, all doors were open. Glancing away from the platform now, Harpur saw Iles run out through the nearest door, as if chasing someone, fine black lace-ups flashing richly in the sunshine. He disappeared. On stage, the presentations continued. Harpur sat down properly again. The A.C.C.'s objective was not the Lord Lieutenant.

After about a minute, Harpur heard noises from the back of the hall and, turning, saw a man wearing a yellow and magenta crash helmet and face-guard enter via another open door and dash between some empty rows of seats. At an elegant sprint Iles appeared through the same door shortly afterwards. The man in the helmet stopped, spun and, pulling an automatic pistol from his waistband, pointed it at Iles, perhaps a Browning 140 DA. The A.C.C. swung himself hard to one side and crouched as the gun fired. Then he leaned far forward and used a fierce sweep of his left fist to knock the automatic from the man's hand. With his clenched right, Iles struck him two short, rapid blows in the neck, just below the helmet. At once, he fell. Iles had been in the row behind, but now clambered over the chair backs to reach him. Harpur could not make out the man on the floor but saw Iles provide a brilliant kicking, though without thuggish shouts, so as not to disturb the prize-giving. Often Iles was damn fussy about decorum. He had mentioned his own quality schooling and this intermittent respect for protocol might date from then.

But because of the gunfire and activity at the rear of the hall, the ceremony had already faltered. Iles bent down and came up with the automatic. 'Please, do continue,' he called out to the Lord Lieutenant and other folk on the stage, waving the weapon in a slow, soothing arc, to demonstrate its harmlessness now. 'Things are all right here, oh, yes.' Iles was not big yet looked unusually tall among the chairs and might be standing on the gunman's face. A beam of sunlight reached in through a window and gave his neat features a good yet unmanic gleam.

Afterwards, when the local police and ambulance people had taken the intruder away, Harpur and Iles waited at the end of the hall while the guests, school staff and platform dignitaries dispersed. Wayne, Nora and Fay-Alice approached, Wayne carrying Fay-Alice's award volumes. 'Had that man come for me?' he asked. 'For me? Why?' He looked terrified.

'My God,' Nora said.

'Someone hired for a hit?' Wayne asked.

'I'd think so,' Iles said.

'All sorts would want to commission him, Wayne,' Harpur said. 'You're a target.'

'My God,' Nora said.

'Someone had you marked, Wayne,' Harpur said.

'He'd have gone for you in the mêlée as the crowd departed at the end of the do, I should think,' Iles said.

'But how did you spot him, Mr Iles?' Nora asked.

'I'm trained always to wonder about people at girls' school prize-givings with their face obscured by a crash helmet and obviously tooled up,' Iles said. 'There was a whole lecture course on it at Staff College.'

'Why on earth did he come back into the hall?' Nora asked.

'He would still have had a shot at Wayne, as long as he could knock me out of the way,' Iles said. 'He had orders. He's taken a fee, I expect. He'd be scared to fail.'

'Oh, you saved Daddy, Mr Iles,' Fay-Alice replied, riotously clapping her slim hands. 'An Assistant Chief Constable accepting such nitty-gritty, perilous work on our behalf, and when so brilliantly dressed, too! It was wonderful – so brave, so skilful, so selfless. I watched mesmerised, but *mesmerised*, absolutely. A privilege, I mean it. Thank you, Mr Iles. You so deserve our trust.' She inclined herself towards him, the long back stretching longer, and would have touched the A.C.C.'s arm. He skipped out of reach. 'We shall have so much to talk about at the swimming pool back home,' she said. 'I do look forward to it.'

'Let's get away now, Harpur,' Iles snarled.

'Yes, I must show you my butterfly, Mr Iles,' Fay-Alice said. 'Desmond.'

'Let's get away now, Harpur,' Iles replied.

H.R.F Keating

Majumdar Uncle

Whenever Inspector Ghote saw tourists from the West idling along Bombay's tumultuous streets he was apt to think that, although the common man got no long vacations, there were instead holidays dotted and dimpled all along the calendar. There was Republic Day, with in Delhi its huge march-past. There was Holi, marking the end of winter, the day when even the mightiest are permitted to be squirted with coloured water and dusted all over with puffed-out powders. There was Diwali, festival of lights, marking also the end of the financial year. There was Naag Panchami, festival of snakes, hundreds of them dancing to the music of the pipe. There was Bombay's own Ganesh Chaturthi, when the huge plaster images of the elephant god at the end of their brief day are at last immersed in the sea. And there are many, many others, even among them from the West Christmas day.

On each and every such holiday, he thought, out come the crowds, rejoicing, making music, dancing, feasting. Everyone delighting in the brief respite from toil. Except myself.

Partly, he knew, this was because as somehow permanently juniormost officer in Headquarters Crime Branch he frequently found himself alone there in charge on such days. But even when he was at home on leave the holidays were almost always ruined for him by the presence of Majumdar Uncle. Heavy-set, sixty-year-old, maharajah moustached, always knowing himself to be right Majumdar Uncle.

It is not even, he thought viciously, that he is my uncle itself, though he is always claiming and claiming that status. He is my wife's Bengali uncle, and with his first name being Amit he ought to be called as Amit Uncle. But, no, he is invariably called by the more resounding name. Because he is an altogether more resounding man. And he is not even Protima's full uncle. He is cousin by marriage only, and a distant one also.

Yet none of this is stopping him exercising full uncle rights each and every time he is visiting this distant cousin of his and her police inspector husband. And that is always on a day of holiday. On days when there is business to be done he is doing business all the day long in that big department store he has until, as they say, gold is dripping from his fingers. But when he is coming to us he is always asking questions, even the sort of question no one should ask. He is drawing conclusions also, and, whether they are right or wrong, in his eyes they are becoming hundred-percent truth.

'So, Protima Cousin, you are getting altogether fed up with this lazy good-for-nothing husband of yours?'

'But, no. No, Majumdar Uncle, I am not at all fed up. Why should I be? He is one good man.'

'But you are saying he is always and always not at home. What is he doing? That is what I am asking. And I am telling you, he is idling and drinking and consorting with bad women also.'

'No, no, Majumdar Uncle.'

But no number of *noes* alter Majumdar Uncle's opinions once he has pounced on them. Protima's mention of my long working hours becomes altogether forgotten under the weight of that gold-heavy pronouncement.

There it is lying below all the statements he has made over the years. Holiday by holiday the burden has grown and grown. Majumdar Uncle may have altogether forgotten opinions he has uttered and trumpeted in that elephant's voice of his, but, forgotten by him or remembered, they are in my mind piled up one on top of the other.

Protima, when at last Majumdar Uncle has left our flat, may have freed herself of that burden. She is, after all, a member of that big extended Bengali family – however distant is the branch she has blossomed upon. But I have no magical family mantra, passed down from one generation to another, transmitted from branch to branch, to be repeated and repeated until the dark shadow has shifted. Also, I can never ask if she has freed herself from the gold-heavy weight. To speak about Majumdar Uncle in words that, once uttered, will be there engraved on our life for ever, it is more than I am daring to risk.

No, do what I may, any tiny thing that is reminding me of Majumdar Uncle brings the monsoon cloud of the man's mixed and mangled opinions down on my head. It may be just only a glimpse of one ad in the paper for some giant sale on the next-coming holiday, and at once I am thinking that the day may bring him to our door. Or it may be the sight, which I am seeing from time to time, of an elephant standing patiently in the road at a red signal, and I am thinking that no red signal howsoever bright will stop that man's elephant progress. Or, if it so happens that a fire engine is passing, blaring its klaxon as the driver tries to thread his way to a distant conflagration, then I am thinking of Majumdar Uncle announcing with klaxon voice whatsoever opinion he has just hit upon.

Nor am I able ever to persuade myself that in face of the man I am being altogether too much of fearful. However often, here in my cabin at Headquarters, I am stating and stating that I am an officer used to command, I am knowing at once that Majumdar Uncle is not at all a person I will ever be able to order to be silent. Yet when some miscreant is in front of me I can tell him without hesitation to shut his mouth. And that mouth is shut then, *ek dum*.

And worse, worse. Whenever a holiday is drawing near when I am not to be on duty and the notion is entering my head that we might take a trip somewhere, to Powai Lake, to Elephanta Island, or even just only to the Hanging Gardens a bus-ride away, I know I cannot put the idea to Protima, Yes, I am believing she would at once agree. She does not welcome Majumdar Uncle's visits. I know it. I have seen her wriggling and wriggling under his questions. But I have heard also Majumdar Uncle trampling over her protests like one elephant marching through breast-high swaying grass, and I know I cannot bring myself even to mention such an act of defiance.

It is altogether timid. It is ridiculous. It is unbefitting an officer of Crime Branch.

But...

The round of holidays dotting the calendar went onwards. At Vasant Panchami as on every year Protima, as a good Bengali, had dressed herself from head to foot in yellow to welcome Spring. But Majumdar Uncle paid them no visit. Ghote, however, spent the day with ears pricked for the robust thump on the door that always heralded a descent upon them. At Holi he was on duty once again, and only when he got back home late did he learn Majumdar Uncle had come, had squirted pink water all over little Ved so plentifully that the boy had at last burst into tears. On Rath Yatra, when in distant Orissa the great chariot of God Jagannath is rolled along its celebrated ceremonial path by a hundred straining human legs, Ghote, at home as it happened, had felt that he, like the victims of old, was being crushed by the juggernaut of Majumdar Uncle's rolling-onwards presence. At Dusshera, its ten-days-long festival ending with burning on huge bonfires of the wicked God Ravana, Ghote, caught once again, was able to do no more than wish and wish he could build a fire big enough to consume, to the last spoonful of fat, his bulky booming bugbear.

But then, with Diwali approaching, at last and at last, a notion of how he might deal once and for all with the gold-dripping Bengali came unexpectedly into his head. It had arisen when, with his customary dread, he was thinking of all the past visits Majumdar Uncle had paid on this particular day of festivity, one which he himself as a boy had always especially delighted in.

In those village days he had revelled in the way that on the fifteenth day of the moonless dark half of the Hindu month of Kartik the obscured sky had been lit up at Diwali by a hundred sparkle-trailing fireworks. Down on the ground below little lamps in their dozens had traced out the shapes of the houses. And there had been the loving exchange of sweets, and new clothes to wear and all the promise of a year ahead unsullied by care.

But ever since he had had a home of his own, shared with his wife and later with their son, that wonderful day had been overshadowed as if the dark half of the month of Kartik had been halted in its tracks, black night for ever. This was a holiday when Majumdar Uncle never failed to appear. His big air-conditioned car, driver at the wheel, would issue a horn-thrumming blast and into the flat its overwhelming owner would burst, followed by the downtrodden driver, arms laden with gifts. And even these, magnificently generous though they might seem to be, were, Ghote reckoned, no more than Majumdar Uncle's opinions of the family and its ways boomed out not in words but in lavish and useless objects. When on an earlier visit Majumdar Uncle had got it into his head, on no evidence, that Protima was a bad cook, then the gift he brought her was what he claimed to be a new superior make of stove. Or when he had decided that whatever shirt Ghote had been wearing on his last visit was 'altogether a disgrace', then a new silky slithery nylon one in foully garish colours was handed over. To be worn at once.

But, besides the lavish gifts, there were also two objects which Majumdar Uncle particularly wished to display before his wretchedly impoverished – as he thought – cousin. These were his glossy black leather-bound, gold-dated account books, about to be closed at the end of this financial year.

There were, of course, two books. There was the one ready to be inspected by any tax officer who chose to ask, its profits neatly modest. Then there was the other, an exact replica in appearance detailing precisely the totals, week by week, month by month, of how much the thronging customers at *Majumdar's* had actually paid for their purchases, and how little the store's proprietor had paid for what they had bought, let alone how seldom he had paid out the due tax. And this was the book that would be shown, in full boastfulness, to Protima, wife of a man who earned no more than the salary of a police inspector.

How Majumdar Uncle must despise me, Ghote thought, as by royal command he was forced to look on as the pages were turned. Year after year knowing altogether well that Protima will not betray a family member to the hated *taxwallas*, he displays the evidence in front of myself even pointing out how he is always careful as a precaution against accident to mark his private book with a tiny dot of white paint on the bottom corner of its back cover.

But – and this was the thought that had suddenly bloomed in his head – what if, at some convenient moment during the big balloon of a Bengali's visit that white dot was somehow obliterated? And then transferred to the other book?

All right, he thought, it is not at all the act of a gentleman to play a trick like that. But when has Majumdar Uncle ever behaved like a gentleman to myself?

Yes, I will do it. And I do not think Protima will be too much of unhappy when her Majumdar Uncle is sent to prison.

As soon as he had left his cabin that very day Ghote paid a visit to the pavement booksellers at Flora Fountain. There he searched and searched until he spotted a volume – it was in fact, an American collection of crime-story parodies called, *The Hair of the Sleuthhound* – with a cover of an almost identical black to Majumdar Uncle's annually appearing two account books.

Next, as he rode homewards on his motor-scooter, he stopped beside the glaring plate-glass windows of that money-spinning department store *Majumdar's*. If that man is using white paint to make those year by year dots on the covers of the books he must not at all show the *taxwallas*, he had reasoned, then where else would he obtain same but from his own store, cost free?

Eyes alert for any sign of the huge proprietor wandering about to keep alert his ill-paid assistants, he hurried to the basement and there bought a small pot of *Majumdar Quick-drying White*, and a small pot of *Majumdar Quick-drying Black* – '*Majumdar Black Covers Any Colour*' – happy for once to be adding to the store's profits.

At home, when he found Protima busy in the kitchen and little Ved out playing with the neighbours' children, he experimented on *The Hair of the Sleuthhound*. A sleuthhound, he thought, that is what I am being also. He worked carefully away with a fine brush borrowed from Ved's paintbox until eventually he was able in less than two minutes to get on to the book's black cover a warning white spot of exactly the shape and size he remembered so well from Diwali visit after Diwali visit. Then he practised blotting out his trial dots in dense black. Yes, he said to himself, *cover any colour* is one promise Majumdar Uncle is making and keeping.

Before long Diwali was just a day away once again. Ghote, as soon as he had arrived home, had taken Ved to the Chinese firework shop and bought a good quantity of rockets. I will be having some extra special celebrations, he whispered to himself. And at once asked: or will I? To the rockets he added, to Ved's delight, a large handful of crackers to be burst under everyone's feet. Then, just before a sleepy Ved tumbled into bed, they watched as one by one the houses round about were strung all along their roof lines with little coloured electric lights, ready for the next evening when there would come – Ghote felt the muscles of his shoulders tighten in anticipation – the looming presents-bearing form of Majumdar Uncle.

And come he did. For a moment as his huge shape blocked up the doorway booming out 'Your neighbours have not put up enough of lights', Ghote thought he would not be able to do it. But then he made himself pass before his eye the whole procession of holidays ahead when Majumdar Uncle would come crashing in on them, and he made up his mind. He would put his plan into action, just as he would give the word of his poised and waiting *jawans* when surrounding the hide-out of a gang of *dacoits*.

Somehow he would contrive within the next half-hour to take away the two account books. Then, swiftly as a pickpocket slipping his haul to an accomplice, he would blot out the warning white dot on the book the tax inspectors must never see and he would place another one on the book Majumdar Uncle had filled with safely concocted reasonable figures. In no time at all he would put the two books back where Majumdar Uncle had carelessly put them down in the way he always did after displaying them to Protima and himself.

So, within days Majumdar Uncle would find himself in custody, accused under Indian Penal Code, Section 420, Cheating. And all my troubles would be over.

Of course, as at every Diwali, Majumdar Uncle, as soon as he had ordered his driver to put down the pile of presents he has brought – Ghote, watching, thought he could make out the embarrassing shape of an unregulation pistol, his own gift no doubt – opened up his account books for Protima to be shown how clever he had been.

'This year I am putting down more of profits for the *taxwallas* to see,' he boomed. 'Last year they were not too much of happy at the level I was showing.'

'Profits this year are down?' Protima asked guilelessly.

'Not at all, not at all. Up, up. Up by twenty-five percent, more, more. It is just only that I must put a figure those fellows will accept. They are to come tomorrow itself. A Government Servant Class Two, a fellow I am bribing, was telephoning to tell.'

Ghote inwardly rejoiced. The sooner the inspectors asked to see Majumdar Uncle's account book the sooner they would be presented with the one that had – if I am able to do it – its warning white dot covered in *Majumdar Quick-drying Black* guaranteed to cover even *Majumdar Quick-drying White*.

He watched, or made a pretence of watching, while Protima, head studiously bent over the turning pages, made small noises of appreciation.

'Look, look,' Majumdar Uncle's fat finger pointed. 'Look at this sum. More of profit in one day than inspector of police is earning in one year only, yes? Yes? Yes?'

'Well, yes, it must be,' Protima agreed.

'Ved, Ved,' Majumdar Uncle suddenly trumpeted now. 'Come and see how one proper man is making some money-punny.'

Ghote felt a dart of outrage. Not because it had been implied he was not one proper man, he was accustomed to that sort of jibe from Majumdar Uncle, but because the big balloon was proposing to initiate his son, *his* son, into such nefarious ways.

He almost protested aloud.

But he knew he had to stand there and watch while the fellow, giggling, went through his figures, false and true, for the benefit of a boy whose arithmetical skills scarcely exceeded the ability to count to one hundred and one. Because, when the time came, he was going quietly to spirit away those two books and five minutes later return them, transformed into a bomb that would blow away Majumdar Uncle's dominance for ever.

But before long Majumdar Uncle appeared to realise his young audience was not appreciating every nuance of his skilful accounting.

'So what has Majumdar Uncle got this Diwali for a boy who is not at all getting right such simple sums?' he bellowed. 'Nothing at all. Nothing whatsoever. Nothing he is giving to such a boy. Nothing.'

Ved crumpled into tears.

But then, to Ghote's delight, in a sudden burst of revengefulness, Ved grabbed the two heavy books and ran.

In a moment they heard the door of his little bedroom, his sanctuary, close behind him with a defiant bang.

Protima was horrified.

'Ved, Ved, bring back Uncleji's books at once.'

'No, no, no, no' came a tear-choked voice from behind the door.

'Husbandji,' Protima said, or rather ordered, 'go and get those books from that naughty rascal.'

'No,' Majumdar Uncle promptly contradicted. 'That is not the way to do it. You must always with a child just only wait till they are coming to their senses. The boy will come back with my books as soon as he is realising he would then get the fine, fine presents I am giving.'

'Correct, Majumdar Uncle,' Ghote jumped in. 'But I will just only go and make sure the boy is not scribbling on your hundred percent precious books.'

'Very well, very well,' Majumdar Uncle answered carelessly, 'Let Mr Policeman be a good-good officer and be keeping the law and order, yes?'

Ghote went.

In Ved's room he launched at once into a little conspiracy. It involved two pots of Majumdar paints and the fine brush he had borrowed from Ved's paintbox. As that voice boomed on and on from the next room, telling Protima she had all along been buying vegetables from the wrong market and pointing out how much better it would be to have gone, not to *Majumdar's* – 'We are selling them too much damn rotten stuff' – but to a much more distant market, 'best in Bombay', Ghote performed his much practised conjuring trick.

In little more than two minutes the white dot on the private book was obliterated and on the book carefully compiled for the tax officers to examine there had appeared in exactly the correct position a tiny white mark designed to warn Majumdar uncle that this was the one never to be seen.

Then he gave Ved his instructions.

'Stay in here until you have counted to one hundred and one. That will give time for these paints to dry and it will also make Majumdar Uncle believe you have, as he was telling just now, come to your senses. Then when you come back with his books he will give you the presents he has had all the time waiting for you.'

Ved's eyes shone and he at once began to count.

'One-two-three-four-five-six-seven-eight-nine-ten.'

'No, no. Not so fast. Begin again when I am shutting your door and then count slowly-slowly.'

'Yes, Pitaji.'

Ghote, back under the Uncle Majumdar cloud, also began, in secret, slowly counting.

...one hundred and one.

He was a little surprised he had been quicker than Ved. But perhaps, he thought, the boy has truly by-hearted my advice to go slowly.

Time passed.

Majumdar Uncle eventually finished explaining to Protima how wrong she was to go to her nearest market. He turned to Ghote.

'So,' he thundered, 'all your talkings and butterings have done nothing to make that badmash of a son of yours come back with my account books. I was telling, the only way with a boy of his sort is to punish and punish him. A few good twists of his ear and he would come squealing.'

'I will go and fetch,' Ghote replied stiffly, suppressing most of his rage at Majumdar Uncle's contradictory advice.

Hastily he went to Ved's room.

He found him idly dipping his paintbrush into, first, the pot of white paint then the pot of black. At the sound of his father's voice he looked up with a start.

'What have you been doing?' Ghote snapped out. 'I could have counted to a thousand and one in the time you have taken.'

'Oh. Oh, I was forgetting. Must I begin once more?'

'No, no. Pick up the books, jaldi, jaldi, and take them to Majumdar Uncle. Perhaps he will give you some presents.'

Ved carefully carried the two fat volumes into the next room and presented them solemnly to Majumdar Uncle. Who positively snatched them from his hands.

'Now I am going,' he announced. 'Already I have spent too much of time here.'

He did at least leave on the chair where his driver had set down the pile of Diwali presents those presumably intended for Ved. Ghote was grateful at least for that, whether it had been meant or not. He was grateful, too, to see the wrapped un-regulation pistol had been taken away.

Then, as the sound of Majumdar Uncle's big foreign car faded into the distance, a happy, happy thought came to him. In that car were two account books, one marked with a tiny white dot, one not. And that was the one that was going to be shown the next day to the *taxwallas*. With its full account of the huge profits *Majumdar's* had made, taxes unpaid.

'Pitaji,' he vaguely heard Ved saying. 'Pitaji, I am more clever than you. In one minute only I was putting the black paint on the white dot you had left and making a new white dot on the other book.'

It took Ghote almost as long as that one minute to absorb the impact of what Ved had lisped out. But then he realised to its full extent exactly what had happened. When next day the tax inspectors came to *Majumdar's*, after they had been greeted with offered whisky and sweetmeats lusciously laid out, with smiles and guffaws, they would be handed the concocted account book that all along Majumdar Uncle had intended they should see. And on the next holiday that came what would happen? The billowing bugbear would descend on them once more. And on the next and the next and the next.

He felt the whole future black before him.

But then...

Then into the blackness there came, like a Diwali rocket lighting up the dark sky, a thought.

Yes. Yes, this is it. In real truth I have defeated that man. It was, after all, just only one small accident that was upsetting my plan. Yes, I am able to defeat him. Truly I am able. I can do it again, somehow, anyhow, whenever I am wanting.

It was as though the whole black sky on the last day of the dark half of the month of Kartik had in one moment flooded with the light of the new moon, with Diwali light.

Colin Dexter

The Double Crossing

I trust this statement will clarify the situation in which I find myself. It was with some reluctance that I signed the original transcript and think my own version of the relevant facts may perhaps be clearer. DC Watson was very patient and polite when I came into Reading Police Station, but I'm afraid I cannot see him as a serious contender for the Booker Prize. All I am trying to do is to clarify the complex sequence of events which it has been my unhappy lot to experience.

My wife Kathryn and myself (we have no children) had decided to spend a week in northern France. It would have been ungrateful not to invite Kathryn's mother, Mary, to join us. She had been living with us for the past seven years; and although Kathryn and I knew how good it would be to have a holiday on our own, we never seriously considered such an arrangement. Mary was in her mid-seventies – her health progressively going downhill, with her memory sadly degenerating. In any case, she deserved a break just as much as we did. She had been wonderfully kind to us, especially after the death of her husband when she'd sold her Georgian property in Cheltenham and given us £45,000 – money with which we were able to take out a mortgage on our present house at 53, Christie Drive, Cholsey. (You will remember the most illustrious gravestone in our village churchyard?)

The only hiccup in the plan was that Mary insisted, absolutely, that she must fund the whole holiday herself – otherwise she would remain at home and try to look after things while we were away. It was a bit of emotional blackmail, yes; but it was a generous offer and we finally agreed to it. Yet in reality it wasn't *all* that generous. I had recently bought a spanking new three-berth caravan which we parked at the bottom of the drive. Any B&B or hotel bills would therefore be nil. And apart from the three sites into which I'd already booked (car-plus-caravan) the only heftyish expense was the fare for the ferry-crossing: £430 return – irrespective of the number of passengers. But, yes, we did hope to indulge ourselves with cheeses and wines and some of the local specialities. We could hardly wait.

Our local travel agency arranged the holiday, and we were booked for an 8 a.m. crossing – it seems an eternity but it is only two days ago! I followed the advice given quite meticulously: to allow about two and a half hours for the drive down to Dover; to be at the dock-side one hour before the scheduled departure time; and to give our-selves an extra hour, just in case. I decided therefore that we should set off at 3 a.m.; and after checking everything for the umpteenth time, we left Cholsey at 3 a.m. precisely.

With traffic virtually non-existant, we had ample time to take a break for coffee and croissants at a deserted service station. And at Dover we found ourselves drawn up in third place in the ferry queue – wide awake and happily anticipating the holiday. The sky was light now, with the sea calm, and prospects appearing well-nigh perfect.

At 7.05 a.m. the Tannoy informed waiting vehicles that boarding was imminent and that documents should be ready for customs and passport clearance. Seated beside me, Kathryn turned to her mother. 'Give me your passport then, Mum.'

After a minute or so I heard a groan of semi-panic behind me; and after a couple of minutes, a high squeak of semi-hysteria:

'Oh, no! I must have... It must still be... Oh, *no!*' Despair. Tears. Repeated self-incrimination.

Kathryn and I climbed the metallic stairs to the upper deck, where we ordered two Full-Monty breakfasts in the restaurant. As the Met Office had forecast, the crossing was smooth; and we arrived ten minutes early in Calais, where we passed through Customs and Immigration without the slightest difficulty. Things had turned out far better than anticipated.

I should (I now realise) have pulled up at some lay-by on our journey south to St Nicholas-sur-Somme, where I had pre-booked a space for two nights. But I am not too confident a driver on the con-tinent and I was anxious to reach our destination. Just over an hour later, I needed no more than an occasional *oui* and *non* before a spot-ty-faced youth pointed the way towards our plot on the caravan site. When I pulled up the handbrake on the parched little area that would temporarily be our home, my shoulder muscles finally managed to relax. And as Kathryn unfastened her safety-belt I found myself smiling ruefully as she leaned across and kissed me, before opening her passenger door and walking down the side of the Rover to the caravan. When she came back to the car her cheeks were a ghastly white as she spoke the words so slowly:

'She's dead, John! Mum's *dead*.'

Inside the caravan there was a low wooden box, about eight feet long, affixed to the off-side panel, on which three persons could sit reasonably comfortably; and inside this box was ample space for us to store duvets, blankets, pillows, etc. It was here that Mary had reluctantly agreed to conceal herself before our embarkation at Dover. Such reluctance, I believe, had little to do with the dishonesty of her concealment – only with the thought of lying there for the key crossing-time. Yet perhaps this was not quite such an ordeal as it might appear. The lightweight wooden lid would be lying alongside her, to be pulled across and over only in the extremely unlikely event of some shipping official checking for illegal stowaways. 'Still like a coffin, though,' I remember poor Mary saying.

We must have been mad, I agree. Yet we had one slim consolation. When I entered the caravan, it seemed clear to me that she could not have died from suffocation. The lid still lay alongside her, and the expression on her face was free from any trace of pain or panic. We could only hope and pray that she had died comparatively peacefully from – well, from something like a stroke.

What could we do? What should we do? What *did* we do?

After anchoring the seperated caravan, Kathryn and I walked twice around the perimeter of the site, desperately debating the situation and finally agreeing on the most cowardly course of all. We returned to the car and drove off, minus caravan, for the Coq d'Or, some ten kilometres distant, a restaurant I had already earmarked as the best in the immediate locality. But we could peck only occasionally at the veal as our thoughts continued to circle round and round in our heads – although in truth we drank considerably more claret than was wise.

As we drove back, we found we had agreed (at last!) on the course of action we should have taken many hours previously: to report *everything* to the nearest French authorities. We just wanted to tell the truth; to face the music; to accept whatever we had to accept; above all, to be able to arrange, sometime, somewhere, a decent burial service for Mary. Hitherto, perhaps the biggest barrier to such a course had been the wretched language problem. But we were past that now.

It was dark when we were checked in, wordlessly, by the same spotty-faced youth now sporting a pair of bulky earphones. But the site was well lit, and we had no trouble finding our plot, No. 36, just beneath a high beech-hedge.

But there was no caravan in No. 36.

No caravan-cum-corpse in No. 36.

Plot No. 36 was completely deserted.

Luckily a few places (for cars only) were still available on the dawn-ferry at Calais – where I explained as best I could that my holiday plans had been curtailed because of a family bereavement.

'But you 'ad a caravan, monsieur?'

I nodded. 'Left it with my friends – *mes amis – vous comprenez?*'

We were allowed to proceed without further ado.

I drove the Rover up the ramp and soon we were crossing the Channel the other way, the waves now considerably choppier than they'd been the day before. Kathryn said she appreciated the irony – if little else.

Once back home, I rang you immediately, and spent over two hours with DC Watson. I was invited to read through my statement and to initial any changes that I wished made. There were so many changes though that I suggested it might help if I submitted my own version. Watson assured me that he personally would take no offence at such a procedure.

You are reading that version now.

John Graham.

As requested, I attach a sheaf of relevant documents – tickets, bills, receipts, etc.

When Detective Chief Superintendent Stratton first read through the statement, he'd known that the situation would be far from easy to handle. The corpse was in a foreign country; was not even (officially) registered dead; was still nowhere to be found; and might well have been sprinkled with concentrated curry powder in order to confuse any intelligent sniffer-dog – before being fed into some Gallic timber-shredder. And why for heaven's sake should *he* need to be involved? What were those bloody *gendarmes* doing?

Yet now, after a leisurely second reading, he found himself pushing his bifocals a little further down his nose, and then – yes! – even smiling slightly. It was at least well-written stuff, certainly of higher literary quality than he'd come to expect from his own underlings. No spelling mistakes in the whole caboodle...

He reached for one of his telephones and rang the newly appointed Detective Inspector, summoning him into the sanctum sanctorum – pronto.

Stratton held up the stapled pages of the Revised Version: 'You've already, er...?'

'Yessir.'

'Writes well, eh?'

The DI nodded. 'Only those two spelling mistakes as far as I could see.'

'Mm.' Stratton seemed momentarily unsure of himself. 'Just remind me...'

'Well, he can't spell "separated" and he can't spell "non—"'

'Mm. Yes. Those are the only two mistakes I'd, er...'

'It's just my old boss. He was a real stickler about—'

'What do you make of all this?'

'Needle in the proverbial, as far as I can see. Unless those Frenchies come up with—'

'Think they will?'

'Well, they know the reg. of the caravan but—'

'Ever tried to dump a caravan yourself?'

'No, sir. But like I was saying, as far as I can—'

The DCS interrupted him irritably: 'That's the third time in a minute you've told me how far you can bloody well see! But shall I tell you something? I'm beginning to wonder if you can see all that far at all. So just *listen* a minute, will you, Lewis?'

Stratton was soon in full swing!

'Mum-in-law in her mid-seventies, OK?'

'Yessir.'

'Memory going downhill sharpish?'

'Yessir.'

'Selling her posh Cheltenham place at the top of the housing-market—'

'Yessir.'

'—then insisting on paying for a joint holiday?'

Lewis nodded.

'So? Do you reckon there's just a possibility she's got a few spare spondulicks somewhere that some people might want to get their greedy paws on?'

'Well, I—'

'What are the three main motives for murder? Come on!'

'Well—'

'For Christ's sake stop saying "well"!'

'Sorry, sir.'

'Well?'

'Well, jealousy, sex, money – that's what my old boss used to say.'

'Agreed, Lewis. But there's only *one* of that immortal trio that's running right through all this bullshit.' The DCS flicked the statement with a podgy right forefinger. 'Tell me! Why do you think this splendid fellow of ours, Mr Gray—'

'Graham, sir.'

'—left Cholsey at – what was it? – 2.30 a.m.'

'3 a.m., I think, sir.'

'The small hours – the *dark* hours – that's all I'm saying.'

'Yessir.'

'So why— Augh! Forget it! You're new, Lewis, and no one's going to blame you for that. But we've all got to start learning somewhere. So? So what do you do? One, you try to find out how much Mrs Whatsername's got stashed away somewhere. Two, you'll find out as confidentially as you can whether the old gal's last will and testament isn't exactly disappointing reading as far as her only daughter is concerned. Third, you get in touch with—'

But Lewis was bemused: 'You don't mean, sir – you're not saying—?'

'That's exactly what I *do* mean – that's exactly what I *am* saying – and that's exactly what *you're* thinking, Lewis. We've got a *murder* on our hands. Listen!'

Lewis, a comparatively simple soul, was aware of his own inexperience. So he sat back quietly and listened.

'We're never going to find the old gal in France. Know why? Because she never left England in the first place. Just think a minute. Who saw her leaving Cholsey, eh? Nobody. Who saw her on the ferry-crossing? Nobody. Who caught a single glimpse of her once she was over the channel? Nobody.'

Unconvinced but not wholly unimpressed, Lewis sat back meekly as Stratton completed his tutorial.

'Just one further piece of advice, my son. Before you start taking up the floorboards and digging up the flower-beds at 35 Christie Drive—'

'53, sir.'

Stratton let it go at that.

As he walked back to his open-plan office, mentally listing his priorities, Lewis realised that the DCS was a clever enough cop, one who had just put a wholly different perspective on events, but one who could never hold a candle to his old boss.

Sergeant Kate Lucan looked up from her computer screen when he came in. She'd been in the force long enough to make some shrewd assessment of any newcomer. All right, the latest DI was unlikely to become the brightest star in the firmament, but he was pleasant and honest and, well, clever *enough*. As she watched him though, she witnessed a colleague who was not exactly over the moon or over Mars. And very soon afterwards she sensed that he was pretty amateurishly learning next to nothing about whether some recently deceased old lady had bequeathed a healthy bank balance to an only daughter – or, instead, perhaps become a posthumous patron of the Donkey Sanctuary.

Forty-eight hours later the message came through from the French police: the missing person had been found, lying serenely dead in an elongated box inside a caravan, a dozen kilometres from St Nicholas-sur-Somme. Identification was firmly established by the passport found in the caravan: somehow it seemed to have slipped through the lining of a very expensive, albeit rather ancient, cashmere overcoat.

Having received the e-mail herself, it was Sergeant Kate Lucan who personally communicated its import to the DI, the latter reading it through with more than a hint of amusement and gratification.

'Exactly what I told him,' he mumbled to himself.

'Good news…er, Lewis? You did say it would be all right if I called you—'

'Course it is – only if I can call you Kate, though.'

'Course you can.'

'No problem then.'

'No. It's just that – well, a lot of people still think your Christian name is your *surname* – like, you know, that TV Sergeant in *Inspector Morse*.'

Early that same evening, in the station's entrance-lobby, one of the telephonists smiled a farewell to her (now) favourite policeman:

'Goo' night, sir.'

'Goo' night, luv.'

And he smiled back at her.

After all, it hadn't been a bad day at all for Detective Inspector Lewis David Robinson.

With acknowledgement to David Robinson, one of my former pupils.

Acknowledgements

TELL ME WHO TO KILL by Ian Rankin © 2003 by John Rebus Ltd. First appeared in *Mysterious Pleasures*, edited by Martin Edwards. Reprinted by permission of the author and his agent, Curtis Brown Limited.

GEEZERS by Brian Thompson © 2003 by Brian Thompson. First appeared in *Men from Boys*, edited by John Harvey. Reprinted by permission of the author and Random House.

RUMPOLE AND THE SCALES OF JUSTICE by John Mortimer © 2003 by Advanpress Limited. First appeared in *The Strand Magazine*. Reprinted by permission of the author and his agent, Peters Fraser Dunlop Limited.

SCHOOL GATE MUMS by Muriel Gray © 2003 by Muriel Gray. First appeared in *Crime Wave*. Reprinted by permission of the author.

THE CAIRO ROAD by Robert Barnard © 2003 by Robert Barnard. First appeared in *Green for Danger*, edited by Martin Edwards. Reprinted by permission of the author and his agent, Gregory & Co.

ESTHER GORDON FRAMLINGHAM by Antony Mann © 2003 by Antony Mann. First appeared in *Crime Wave*. Reprinted by permission of the author.

NO ONE CAN HEAR YOU SCREAM by Michael Jecks © 2003 by Michael Jecks. First appeared in *Green for Danger*, edited by Martin Edwards. Reprinted by permission of the author.

CHANCE by John Harvey © 2003 by John Harvey. First appeared in *Men from Boys*, edited by John Harvey. Reprinted by permission of the author and Random House.

SOMETHING SPOOKY ON GEOPHYS © 2003 by Lindsey Davis. First appeared in *Mysterious Pleasures*, edited by Martin Edwards. Reprinted by permission of the author.

TAILS by John Grant © 2003 by John Grant. First appeared in *Crime Wave*. Reprinted by permission of the author.

THE ST. VALENTINE'S DAY MASSACRE by Edward Marston © 2003 by Edward Marston. First appeared in *Ellery Queen's Mystery Magazine*. Reprinted by permission of the author.

THE FIELD by Peter Lovesey © 2003 by Peter Lovesey. First appeared in *Green for Danger*, edited by Martin Edwards. Reprinted by permission of the author and his agent, Vanessa Holt.

TURNING IT ROUND by Liza Cody © 2003 by Liza Cody. First appeared in *Ellery Queen's Mystery Magazine*. Reprinted by permission of the author.

CLOSER TO THE FLAME by Jerry Sykes © 2002 by Jerry Sykes. First appeared in *Crime in the City*, edited by Martin Edwards. Reprinted by permission of the author.

BEST EATEN COLD by Laura Wilson © 2003 by Laura Wilson. First broadcast on BBC Radio 4. Reprinted by permission of the author.

THE GAME OF DOG by Reginald Hill © 2003 by Reginald Hill. First appeared in *Mysterious Pleasures*, edited by Martin Edwards. Reprinted by permission of the author and his agent, A.P. Watt Limited.

AMERICAN WAITRESS by Christopher Fowler © 2003 by Christopher Fowler. First appeared in *Crime Wave*. Reprinted by permission of the author.

CAVEAT EMPTOR by Rosemary Rowe © 2003 by Rosemary Rowe. First appeared in *The Mammoth Book of Whodunits*, edited by Mike Ashley. Reprinted by permission of the author and her agent, Dorian Literary Agency.

THE SITTING TENANT by Francis King © 2003 by Francis King. First appeared in *Death Comes Easy, the Gay Times Book of Murder*, edited by Peter Burton. Reprinted by permission of the author.

THE CONSOLATION BLONDE by Val McDermid © 2003 by Val McDermid. First appeared in *Mysterious Pleasures*, edited by Martin Edwards. Reprinted by permission of the author and her agent, Gregory & Co.

DANCING TOWARDS THE BLADE by Mark Billingham © 2003 by Mark Billingham. First appeared in *Men from Boys*, edited by John Harvey. Reprinted by permission of the author and Random House.

INDICATOR by Stephen Volk © 2003 by Stephen Volk. First appeared in *Crime Wave*. Reprinted by permission of the author.

SHADOW ON THE WATER by Peter Robinson © 2003 by Peter Robinson. First appeared in *Men from Boys*, edited by John Harvey. Reprinted by permission of the author and Random House.

MURDER BY GHOST by Amy Myers © 2003 by Amy Myers. First appeared in *Ellery Queen's Mystery Magazine*. Reprinted by permission of the author and her agent, Dorian Literary Agency.

ROOM TO MOVE by Mat Coward © 2003 by Mat Coward. First broadcast on BBC Radio 4. Reprinted by permission of the author.

LIKE AN ARRANGEMENT by Bill James © 2003 by Bill James. First appeared in *Men from Boys*, edited by John Harvey. Reprinted by permission of the author and Random House.

MAJUMDAR UNCLE by H.R.F. Keating © 2003 by H.R.F. Keating. First appeared as a gift booklet published by Crippen & Landru. Reprinted by permission of the author and his agent, Peters Fraser Dunlop Limited.

THE DOUBLE CROSSING by Colin Dexter © 2003 by Colin Dexter. First appeared in the catalogue of the Harrogate Mystery Festival. Reprinted by permission of the author's publishers, Macmillan.